Brighten your world with *Sunday Times* bestseller Libby Page . . .

'A testament to kindness and friendship'
Sarah Winman

'A heart that shines from every page'
AJ Pearce

'Moving and beautifully crafted'
Mike Gayle

'Full of heart'
Lucy Diamond

'Brimming with charm and compassion . . .
a feelgood celebration of community'
Daily Express

'Beautifully written'
Daily Mail

'A joyful celebration of community'
Observer

'Heartwarming'
Good Housekeeping

'Heartwarming and stirring'
Heat

'Feelgood fiction at its best'
Daily Mirror

LIBBY PAGE is the Sunday Times bestselling author of *The Lido* and *The 24-Hour Café*. *The Island Home* is her third novel. Before becoming an author, she worked in journalism and marketing. She is a keen outdoor swimmer and lives in Somerset with her husband.

Follow Libby on social:
🐦 @libbypagewrites
📷 @libbypagewrites
www.libbypage.co.uk

Also by Libby Page

The Lido
The 24-Hour Café

THE
ISLAND
HOME

LIBBY PAGE

ORION

First published in Great Britain in 2021 by Orion Books,
an imprint of The Orion Publishing Group Ltd
Carmelite House, 50 Victoria Embankment
London EC4Y 0DZ

An Hachette UK Company

1 3 5 7 9 10 8 6 4 2

A CIP catalogue record for this book
is available from the British Library.

ISBN (Hardback) 978 1 4091 8826 1
ISBN (Export Trade Paperback) 978 1 4091 8827 8
ISBN (eBook) 978 1 4091 8829 2

Typeset by Deltatype Ltd, Birkenhead, Merseyside

Printed in Great Britain by Clays Ltd,
Elcograf, S.p.A.

MIX
Paper from
responsible sources
FSC® C104740

www.orionbooks.co.uk

FOR BRUNO

CHAPTER 1

LORNA

Euston station, 8.30 p.m. It's midsummer and London sweats and steams, clutched in the middle of a heatwave. The after-work crowds have thinned but the concourse is still busy, figures in damp, crumpled suits staring at the announcement boards where times and destinations flash in orange letters. Families huddle in groups, mothers fanning young children and handing out water bottles as they wait, perched on piles of luggage. A surprising scent of coconut wafts from the glowing doorway of The Body Shop, mingling with the sourer human smells of hundreds of hot passengers leaving and arriving, carrying bags and their own secret burdens. A few discarded evening newspapers litter the floor, trampled underfoot by rushing commuters and holidaymakers. A police officer patrols the perimeter of the station, an Alsatian sniffing the air at the end of a short lead. Occasionally the officer pauses on his route to wipe beads of sweat from his forehead.

We are early. The 9.20 train to Fort William is up there on the board but there's no platform yet. Beside me my daughter Ella pulls her new pink suitcase as though it's empty, her steps light. My own case feels much heavier as it drags behind me. Partly because this whole trip was Ella's idea really, not mine.

I glance across at her, my teenage daughter on the cusp of turning fourteen in just a few weeks' time, as she pauses, staring eagerly up at the clock. Her pale cheeks are flushed with excitement and the warmth of this summer evening and her auburn hair hangs loose, for once in natural curls rather than the poker-straight style she spends nearly an hour achieving each morning. When Ella asked for hair straighteners for Christmas, I refused at first. I've always loved her curls, ever since she was a baby and the soft ringlets first started to grow. I'll always remember the sweet, talcum-powder scent of her head when she was a baby and the feeling of her hair tickling my face when she struggled to sleep as a toddler and shared my bed. Back then I'd often wake with Ella's face pressed against my cheek. Her reddish-brown curls would be the first thing I'd see when I opened my eyes. The thought of her singeing them makes me wince. And yet she was insistent about those straighteners, pleading with me for the first time in her life. So I bought them. When she opened them she nearly knocked over the small Christmas tree in our flat as she leapt over to thank me with an eager hug. That's partly why I agreed to this trip: it's only the second time she's ever truly asked anything of me.

My hair is the same shade as Ella's but even wilder – I long ago gave up trying to control my own curls and today they're pulled off my face in a messy bun, the nape of my neck damp from the heat and the rucksack on my back. How is it so hot? Surely it should be cooler this late in the day, but the heat clings to me.

'Shall we grab some food while we wait?'

Ella glances across at my question. There's wariness in her eyes. We've always been so close: the two of us against the world. But these past few days have tested us like nothing else. I can feel my emotions simmering beneath the surface – anger, fear, grief – but I push them down like clothes stuffed into an overfull suitcase. I may have my reservations about being here but here we are. In the end I agreed to this trip for my daughter's sake. And perhaps for my own too. After all these years, maybe it's finally time to go back to the place I once escaped and to face everything that I left behind.

'Leon?' I suggest, knowing, of course, that it's her favourite. Her lips part into a broad smile and there it is, one of those surging swells of love that so often take me off guard, a love that fills up every cell in my body and makes me feel as though I could levitate. For a second, I forget the reason why we are here and everything that awaits us at the end of our long journey and link my arm through my daughter's.

'Good idea, Mum,' she replies.

Ella waits with the bags while I queue for our food. Ahead of me in the line is a family – two grandparents, a grown-up daughter and three children, one in a buggy, one on the mother's hip and one holding the hand of his grandfather. My stomach twists as I watch them.

'You all have what you like,' the grandfather says, reaching for his wallet.

'Thanks, Dad,' replies his daughter, smiling wearily but gratefully.

I look away, blinking quickly.

'Next please!' calls the server and I return my attention to the menu, choosing two halloumi wraps and the waffle fries Ella loves. A few seconds later I'm holding the steaming foil parcels and returning to our table outside where Ella is wiping a debris of discarded food and litter into a paper napkin. On a neighbouring table a pigeon with one gnarled pink foot hops among a scattering of leftovers. From up here we have a view of the concourse below as well as the platform boards. I can hear the hum of the street outside, the buses pulling up in front of the station and the Friday night traffic crawling down the Euston Road. Even inside, the air feels heavy with fumes and dust: the hot, heavy fug of the city that I have grown used to over the past twenty-two years.

I moved here as a teenager, arriving with a stolen suitcase and a head full of dreams. I quickly learnt how brutal the city can be though, especially when you are alone with nothing but a few hundred pounds in coins and rolled-up notes stuffed in your rucksack. I took whatever jobs I could find. Temp jobs and then years of bar work. It was only when I fell pregnant with Ella at twenty-six that I decided I needed a proper career and trained as a teacher, helped out by a hefty student loan and the council flat I managed to get for us both in a sixties block on the Isle of Dogs, that not-quite island encircled by the muddy River Thames where the shining tower blocks of

4

Canary Wharf glint garishly on the horizon. Over the years I managed to save just enough money to buy our flat from the council, although each month I still feel the same panic that I might not be able to meet my mortgage payment. I always do manage it but the fear is still there, as familiar by now as the sound of my own breath. I've always been anxious about money. Because if something happens – if I get sick or the boiler breaks or I suddenly need something important for Ella, there's no one to bail us out. I know this well because all of those things and plenty more have happened over the years. And each time I've had to find some way to make ends meet by myself.

Ella's phone chirps and she looks down, her hair falling slightly in front of her face. She smiles and types a reply, her thumbs tapping at incredible speed on the screen.

'Ruby and Farah?' I ask. The two girls have been Ella's best friends since primary school. I'm used to seeing them at our flat, preparing snacks for the three of them and hearing their laughter spilling out of Ella's bedroom. I know it makes me a terrible mother to admit it, but many times over the years that noise has caused an involuntary pang of jealousy in my gut. Being envious of your own daughter does not feature on the 'ways to be a good mum' list. But I do envy Ella's closeness with her friends. I lost touch with the ones I used to have and have struggled to make them ever since. Making friends means answering too many questions and revealing too much about yourself and your past. It's simpler to keep to myself, devoting my life to Ella and my job. Mostly I've got used to it but sometimes the loneliness catches me like a splinter.

'No,' Ella replies, not looking up, 'Molly.'

At the mention of the name the reality of the nature of this trip hits me again, throwing me off balance. Is it too late to turn around and head home? We could catch the tube and then the DLR and be back at our flat in less than an hour. Then we could spend the summer how we'd originally planned – visiting galleries and ice-cream shops and reading magazines together in the parks. Just me and Ella, the way it's always been.

My own phone pings and I reach for it in my pocket, the familiar motion distracting me. It's Cheryl.

'**Have a safe journey,**' the message reads. '**Let me know when you get there. xxx**'

The message calms me slightly. If I say that Cheryl is my closest friend it's only really a half-truth. The full truth is that she is my only friend. We first met five years ago when she started as a teaching assistant at the school where I was then a year head and am now deputy head. I remember spotting her on playground duty that first day, playing football with the kids, her large gold hoop earrings swinging as she ran and the children chased her, her smiling mouth painted in bright red. Her laughter rose high and loud above the background din of the playground and I remember feeling an instant need to get to know her – this woman who could make herself heard over a rabble of children. She caught my eye and waved, pausing in the game for a moment and coming over to introduce herself. I'm not sure if we'd ever have become friends if she hadn't been so persistent though, chatting cheerfully to me every day at school and inviting me to go for a drink together after work. At first, she did most of the talking, but over time and as we grew closer she gently coaxed out details of my past. She's the only person who knows at least parts of my story, parts I've always glossed over with other colleagues or with the mums of Ella's friends who've at times made unsuccessful attempts to draw me into their groups.

Cheryl is ten years younger than me and sometimes it shows – when she tries to talk to me about what songs are in the charts and celebrity gossip and I just nod and smile blankly. But mostly the age gap between us doesn't matter. We've grown close over the years and we each know enough about what it means to work at an inner-city primary school run by a chauvinist to understand one another well.

'Thanks,' I type back. '**End of term, hurrah! No more Dave the creep for six weeks! xx**'

Dave, or Mr Phillips to the children, is our head and my boss. He's always made me somewhat uneasy, but ever since he appointed me as his deputy six months ago his inappropriate comments have become worse. If I knew it was going to be like this then perhaps I might have turned down the job. But I needed the extra money. And after ten years of teaching at the same school it felt like the recognition I'd been craving for so long. The recognition I *deserved*. Now I'm not even sure I truly earned the job or whether I was appointed for some other reason entirely. It's a depressing thought.

'**I'm already on to my third glass of wine,**' Cheryl replies. I smile, picturing my friend in the flat I've come to know so well. For my fortieth birthday last year instead of a big party Ella and I spent it at Cheryl's with her husband Mike and their two-year-old Frankie. Cheryl cooked for us while Mike

7

dutifully topped up our wine glasses, pouring a splash for Ella to try too. It was a good evening and I wouldn't have wanted to spend it any differently. But there's still a part of me that imagined something bigger and noisier, if only I lived a bigger and noisier life. It's a thought that has visited regularly over the years – at birthdays, Christmases and New Years when Ella and I have celebrated alone in our flat again. We have our traditions: matching pyjamas at Christmas and watching the fireworks from our window at New Year with mugs of hot chocolate towering with marshmallows. But after we've said our goodnights I always stay awake, wondering if I've let Ella down by not being able to give her more than this – more than me.

Another message arrives from Cheryl and I know that she has seen through my joking tone. Of course she has; she knows me well.

I hope you're doing OK though. It must be so hard. I bet you're feeling nervous. I'm here whenever you need me. Just text or call, any time. xxx

A lump rises in my throat. I picture the black dress folded at the bottom of my suitcase and all the miles and all those years that stand between this station and our final destination.

'Platform one,' says Ella suddenly, her voice high-pitched with excitement. I glance up at the board; is it really that time already? My pulse quickens. This is it. It's too late to turn back now and besides, I made a promise to my daughter. I can't let her down.

We gather our things and move through the station, passing a stand where baguettes sweat behind glass and another where a florist struggles to keep rainbow bouquets from wilting in the heat. Above us dozens of other possible destinations glow in amber, reminding me of all the other places we could be heading. Notices advise us to be alert to anything suspicious and adverts blink and flash in bright lights. And my daughter and I roll our suitcases behind us, weaving in and out of other passengers.

The Caledonian Sleeper waits at the platform, bottle green with an emblem of a stag on the side of each carriage.

'Is it your first time travelling with us?' asks a pink-faced man in a green uniform with a thick Glaswegian accent. He clutches a clipboard and pulls briefly at the collar of his shirt.

'Yes!' Ella says.

'No,' I say at the exact same moment.

This train might look slightly more modern than the one I caught to London when I was eighteen, but I still remember it well. The man in the uniform looks at us both, frowning for a second before regaining his charming customer-service smile.

'Well, here is a brochure about your journey,' he says, handing it to Ella. 'You'll find a card in your room, if you could write down your preferences for breakfast. You're in coach G, right down the other end. Just keep walking.'

'Perhaps we're walking to Scotland,' Ella jokes as we head further and further down the platform. I don't laugh though; suddenly I can't even find a smile.

Finally, we find coach G and another staff member ticks our names off a list and helps us carry our luggage on board.

The train's corridors are so narrow that we have to walk to our berth single file. If we met someone coming the other way we'd have to back up like cars reversing on a country lane. Luckily the carriage is empty for now.

Ella opens the door onto a room not much larger than an airing cupboard.

'This is so cool!'

My daughter has always been an optimist. The room contains a sink, a narrow set of bunkbeds and a small window. Ella dumps her suitcase on the floor and clambers straight up the ladder onto the top bunk. There's just enough space for me to step inside and close the door. As Ella tests out her bed, I stow my suitcase under the bottom bunk and lift Ella's onto the rack above the sink.

The train is mostly as I remember it, with its tiny corridors and long windows. But it's my first time inside one of the cabins. When I took the sleeper train all those years ago I spent the night in the seated carriage. All the saved tips from my job at the local pub hadn't been enough to cover a cabin, especially as I knew I'd need to keep money for when I arrived in London. I didn't sleep all night. Instead I sat wide awake, running my fingers over a pebble stowed in my coat pocket and staring out the window into the darkness.

At 9.25 p.m. I feel a jolt in my stomach as the train pulls away from the station.

'We're moving!' Ella says from her top bunk. She's already changed into her pyjamas and is lying on her bed. Her voice brims with anticipation.

Standing by the window, I watch as the train eases away

from the station and rolls through the city. The sky is a dark lavender washed with peach, city lights starting to glow as evening draws in. Endless office blocks and rows of terraced houses hug the railway line, bricks stained black from pollution. A few lone workers are still visible inside one office while in another I spot a cleaner pushing a hoover steadily between empty desks. I look up at the tower blocks not dissimilar to our own, lives cramped side by side and on top of one another. I wonder if any of the people inside these blocks know their neighbours, or whether it's just me who has lived alongside strangers for most of my life. Some of the blocks we pass are sleek and modern, geometric shapes cut out of steel and glass. But squashed right up close too are buildings with boarded-up windows, supermarkets housed in ugly squat cubes, car parks and junk yards and building sites where cranes make a mess of the skyline. I picture the city stretching beyond the boundaries of what I can see, rolling out in a sprawling mass of buildings and streets, parks and stamp-sized gardens, the backbone of the River Thames arching through its centre. Millions of lives rubbing up alongside one another, crossing over and converging in the sounds of neighbours shouting and the smell of cooking seeping through ceilings and walls.

I can't help but think of our flat, dark and empty now. The collection of stones and smoothed glass on the kitchen windowsill, collected from my daily runs alongside the river. The small living room with photos of Ella on the walls and a few of the two of us, and the growing patch of damp in the corner that I really need to get sorted. And Ella's bedroom, the bed neatly made and a soft-toy puffin named Dora resting on her pillow. Whenever I step inside my daughter's room I dread seeing that Dora has been relegated from the bed. It will happen one day, just like so many things I fear about my daughter getting older. But each time I see that floppy, faded puffin there I thank god it's not today.

Outside the train window the city continues to flash by. This city has been my home for over twenty years but as the train edges towards the suburbs and then out into open countryside it's as though a thread linking me to London strains and then snaps. In its place I feel the tug of a much older connection, one I've tried to ignore for years but that I feel now pulsing under my skin. It's a connection that pulls me north. I picture mountains and black lochs, sheep and sunburnt bracken. Large, sweeping skies and teal sea. Something a bit like terror and something like excitement flutters uncontrolled inside. I gave everything to escape the place where I grew up. And I have resisted making this journey back ever since. I fought against it, ran away from it, hid from it. But despite it all, there is a part of me that longs to see a mountain again.

CHAPTER 2

ALICE

Dust billows in clouds as I give the cushions another firm thump. I don't know why but this house just seems to attract dust. I've spent the whole morning cleaning: hoovering, dusting and washing windows until they gleam and the beach and the sea can be seen crystal clear through the glass. I may have lived here for years but I still can't get over this view. I'm not sure I ever will. Beyond the house the farm stretches around us in rolling green fields and stone walls, Jack's polytunnel (my husband's pride and joy) hunkered in the shelter of the cliffs at the back of the farm. From the living-room window we have a perfect view down the hill that gives this farm its name and onto the beach.

I've always thought of it as our beach. Silly really, because all the islanders use it too, for walking dogs, children's beach parties and barbecues in the summer. But I'll always think of it as ours. It's where Jack and I first got to know each other all those years ago, walking side by side on the sand, him too shy to look me in the eye and me chatting so much, like I always do when I'm nervous, that I worried I bored him. Back then I was just a visitor to the island, a volunteer helping out on the farm on my gap year. Although the farm back then was nothing like it is today; you'd hardly recognise it. It had been neglected for years, the fields barren, the stone walls tumbling down, an air of forgotten-ness everywhere. Jack and the other islanders and volunteers nursed the place back to life. I suppose I played my part too, in a small way. And now it's our home and one of the things I love most about it is having the beach right there on our doorstep. The beach has been my and Molly's playground over the years and even though she's now too old for building sandcastles and making driftwood mermaids I'll always remember the first tottering steps she took there, the way she squealed with joy as a toddler as Jack and I swung her between us, her toes skimming the surface of the cold sea.

As though she knows I'm thinking about her, my daughter bursts into the living room, her short, light brown hair sticking up in all directions on her head and a wide smile on her face. Fourteen years of loving her and it still catches me unprepared sometimes, this fierceness.

'Have you tidied your room?' I ask her. She nods.

'Yes, Mum. And I've made up the camp bed and cleared space in my wardrobe.'

'You star.'

She grins.

'Can I go meet Olive now?'

'Of course, have fun.'

As she turns to leave, her phone beeps and she pulls it quickly from the back pocket of her denim shorts. Looking down, her face spreads into an even wider smile.

'Olive?' I ask. But she shakes her head.

'Ella.'

I can see the excitement on her face, the eagerness and anticipation. It's been there since Jack and I agreed to the plan, so carefully organised between the two girls. I feel a sort of excitement too with a mix of nerves and anxiety thrown in for good measure. How will the next few days go? Will we get through it? How will Jack cope? And what will our visitors think of the house, the farm, and me?

'OK, I'm going now,' Molly says, slipping the phone back into her pocket. I wave from my spot by the sofa and then she is gone in a blur of energy and movement. I watch her half-walking, half-running down the bumpy farm track and spot her best friend Olive in the distance waiting for her. Turning back to the room, I give the pillows another thump.

'I think you have sufficiently plumped those cushions,' comes a voice from the doorway.

Jack leans against the frame, his grey eyes watching me, his face serious. He's dressed in his battered, mud-stained jeans and a grey T-shirt. I picture his muddy boots by the doorstep and the green overalls he wears for the heavier-duty farm work. He must be in for a tea break. As I watch him I picture him when we first met, him nineteen, me just turned eighteen. Back then his hair was longer and free of any specks of grey,

15

his curls messy, his expression serious like it is now. He was so earnest as he worked on the farm but so gentle too, planting seeds with delicacy and care. Just one of the reasons why I fell in love with him.

'You're probably right,' I reply, straightening the throw on the back of the sofa. 'There might be no cushion left if I keep going.'

I expect him to smile, waiting for the skin around his eyes to crinkle and for his irises to sparkle the way they do for me and Molly. His smiles are like an opening, the window into the side of him that wept on our wedding day and when Molly was born and that collects beautiful pebbles and shells from the beach, claiming them like treasure. But he remains stony.

'I don't know why you're bothering.'

I know I shouldn't care, but his words sting. I've been working all day, trying to make the place look as inviting as possible.

'We don't often have visitors.'

As I say it I think of my sisters and a lump swells in my throat. They visit once or twice a year and I try to get over to the mainland to see them too, but it's hard. The journey takes a full day, longer if there's a storm and the ferry is cancelled. It's always been the hardest thing about living on a Hebridean island, harder than the long winters when it feels sometimes as though the sun may never rise. My older sisters have busy lives, Caitlin a GP just outside Edinburgh and Shona teaching mathematics at Aberdeen University. They have their families too, a boy and a girl for Caitlin and three boys for Shona: my gorgeous niece and nephews. It's been a long time since we were all together – last autumn when my sisters came with their families and our parents joined us for a weekend too. I remember how bereft I felt after they all left, wandering through our near-empty house, changing sheets and airing out bedrooms. Shona's youngest, Finlay, left a soft-toy monkey behind and when I found it beneath his bed I hugged it to my chest, breathing in his little-boy smell before calling Shona to let her know the beloved toy was not lost.

Jack's face is hard as he runs a hand along the mantelpiece.

'We don't even know how long they'll stay. It just seems a waste of time to me.'

I give the sofa one final smooth with my hand and turn for the door, squeezing past my husband and trying not to let him hear hurt in my voice.

'I've got to go, I've got my class. I'll see you later.'

I change into my yoga gear and climb into the Land Rover, trying to brush off the conversation with Jack as I drive. I know he's just upset. This is all so hard for him. I focus on the view as I make my way across the island. Kip looks its loveliest today, the sun high in an endless blue sky and the sea stretching out in all directions. The mountain at the centre of the island glows golden in the sunlight, the pine forest deep green at its base as though the branches have been dipped in emerald ink. I still remember arriving here for the first time. It was raining that day, as it so often is up here. I never imagined back then that this island would change my life. I never thought that I would stay.

It doesn't take long to reach the community hall where I run my classes. The women are waiting for me outside, chatting in the sunshine. They are my students but more importantly, my friends. I climb out of the car and greet them with a smile.

'Beautiful day,' says Emma. She is a few years older than me, with pixie-cropped hair and a string of tattoos wrapping round her upper arms. She went to school with Jack and like him stayed on the island, marrying another island native, Duncan McLeod. Together with Duncan's brother George they run the island's tiny brewery.

'No Joy today?' I ask, turning to Tess, a woman in her late twenties in tie-dyed harem pants and a loose-fitting orange shirt.

'No,' she replies. 'She's looking after Harry.'

Tess and Joy own a holiday let on the island and run walking tours and photography workshops for tourists. Their baby Harry is nine months old and sometimes joins my classes, sliding along the hall floor on his belly. No one seems to mind as he crawls beneath their downward dog, giggling as he does. But he's teething at the moment, poor thing, and can be temperamental.

'How about taking the class outside? The hall is so damned stuffy,' suggests Morag, my oldest class member at eighty, but surprisingly flexible for her age. She tells me she used to be a ballet dancer, although I'm not sure whether I believe her because over the years she has claimed to have been a ship's captain, a bomb disposal expert, a stunt double, a horse trainer and the first female firefighter in Scotland. Today she is dressed in a pair of bright yellow leggings and a baggy white T-shirt with 'Choose Love' written on it in bold black letters.

'Good idea. Let's make the most of the weather.'

'While it lasts,' adds Kerstin, the tall woman in her fifties who left a busy job in banking (and her husband) five or so years ago to move here with her cats and has been coming to my classes ever since.

'Is this all of us?' I ask the group.

'Yes,' replies Tess, 'Sarah and Brenda are still on the mainland and Jean wasn't feeling up to it today.'

Brenda is in her sixties and has bright pink hair that always makes me smile and makes her easy to spot when she takes her long walks across the island. She was one of the first friends I made when I moved here. She'd arrived just a couple of years before me so I guess she understood what it felt like to be a newcomer. Now, she's Molly's godmother and is the very best kind: without children of her own she spoils Molly with outlandish but thoughtful gifts and her door is always open for cups of tea and homemade biscuits. Molly and I may be close and she may have her friendships with Olive and the other island children, but it has always been a comfort to know there is another adult besides Jack and me whom she can turn to if she needs to. Not that she just has the one. That's one thing I hadn't quite realised when I became pregnant: when you have a baby here they become the island's child, not just your own. Sarah's another of my closest friends, an island native like Emma, and Molly's best friend Olive's mum. And Jean is the island school's headteacher, but over the years has become my friend too. The same qualities that make her a great teacher – her curiosity and kindness and the interest she takes in everyone from small children to adults – also make her a great friend. A flash of worry sparks in my mind as I think of her. I hope she's doing all right. Despite my concerns, I force a smile.

'OK then, let's get going.'

I may not have my sisters close by, but this somewhat motley group of island women makes up for it. We fetch the yoga mats from the hall and carry them under our arms down to the beach, chatting as we walk. We unroll the mats on the sand and I keep the class gentle and slow-moving, not feeling that energetic after all the cleaning. That is one of the great advantages of being the teacher.

I run classes for tourists too and longer retreats if I get enough interest, but my friends are my most loyal attendees and these are the classes I enjoy teaching the most.

After the session we sit side by side on our mats, facing the sea. Gulls swoop low over the water, the distant ridgeline of the mainland just visible on the horizon. The sun is warm on my bare arms but there's a cool sea breeze. Morag reaches into the waistband of her leggings and pulls out a tiny hip flask, taking a quick swig before stowing it safely out of sight. Tess leans back on her hands, closing her eyes and tilting her face to the sun. I glance at the bags beneath her eyes but also the contented glow that radiates from her and feel a pang as I re-member Molly as a baby.

'So, they arrive tomorrow then?' asks Kerstin.

The other women turn to look at me expectantly. I stretch out my legs, pushing my bare feet into the damp sand.

'Yes, they should be here on tomorrow's ferry.'

My friends nod.

'And tell us again,' asks Emma. 'The girls had been in touch on Facebook? For how long?'

'A year.'

'And you had no idea?'

'None.'

I remember the moment Molly first told us she'd found her cousin online and that they'd been messaging. I couldn't believe she'd kept it so well hidden from us. But part of me was impressed too by her resourcefulness, by the sense of family which has always been so important to me but that I've worried she might not have inherited, what with our smaller, more isolated life. Jack was furious though. I wonder if Lorna felt the same way. It feels strange to think of my sister-in-law, having never met her. Over the years I've thought about her many times. Would she have approved of me as a choice for her brother? What would she make of Molly, my proudest achievement? And why did she leave all those years ago and never come back? I've tried to get Jack to open up about her and about their past so many times but have never made much progress. He just closes up every time I ask him and the harder I try the tighter he seems to curl in on himself.

We gaze out to sea for a moment, all the complexities of the situation sitting heavy in the air around us. I still can't quite believe that tomorrow they will both be here on this island: the sister-in-law and niece I've never met.

'How's Jack doing?' asks Kerstin.

I think back to our earlier conversation and his hard expression.

'Not great. It's all so difficult. I think deep down he wants to see her again, and to meet Ella of course, but I think he's scared too.'

'That's not surprising,' says Emma. 'It's been such a long time. I still remember when she left. She was what, eighteen?'

I nod silently. She was the same age when she left as I was when I arrived. I've tried many times to picture her making that journey to London on her own. How did it feel to ride the train through the night, taking her away from everything she knew, and then to step out into the huge city after a childhood lived among sea and sand?

'And how do you feel?' Tess asks.

I take a long breath.

'I want to make them feel welcome. Whatever else happens I guess I just want to feel like I tried my best to make things work. Made the best of a bad situation, you know?'

Emma leans towards me, draping an arm around my shoulder.

'We'll help you however we can,' she says, giving me a little squeeze. And I smile at her, remembering how kind she was to me when I first moved to the island – how kind everyone was. The other women shuffle slightly closer to me. Morag reaches out her hip flask and I give in and take a brief swig before passing it back with a nod of thanks. However much I may love my husband, would I really have stayed and made my life here if it wasn't for these women?

'I know you will,' I say with a smile. 'Right, I'd better get back and finish getting everything ready.'

We return the mats to the hall and I say goodbye to my friends, hugging them in turn.

*

22

When I arrive back at the farmhouse the kitchen is warm and filled with steam and the smell of garlic and lemon. Jack is leaning over the large Rayburn, one of my aprons tied around his waist and a wooden spoon in his hand. Molly is laying the table, setting out plates and cutlery neatly.

'How was the class?' Jack asks, pulling me gently towards him. I can feel his softness again as though the warmth of the kitchen has thawed his earlier frostiness. I breathe out with relief, placing a hand briefly on his chest. He lifts it to his mouth and kisses my palm and in his eyes I see all the apology I need. I see him.

'It was good,' I say. 'We took the mats to the beach. Morag managed a surprisingly good tree pose despite the whisky I caught her drinking after.'

Jack laughs, the sound bright and sweet.

'That woman certainly knows how to hold her liquor.'

'Aye, that she does. Did you and Olive have a good afternoon, Molly?'

My family and I chat as we eat, sitting around one end of the long wooden table that might have been built for more chairs but has served us three well over the years. After clearing away the plates Molly retreats to her room and Jack and I are left alone, holding hands over the table.

'I'm sorry about earlier,' he says quietly, for a moment looking down at the table. 'I didn't mean to be like that with you. I guess I'm just nervous.'

'I know. I'm sorry too. This must be so hard for you. But we're in this together, OK?'

He meets my eye now and nods slowly. I try to tell him with

my look that he is loved and that whatever happens over the next few days, I will be here beside him. Outside the sun glows above the sea as I take my husband's head gently between my hands and kiss him.

CHAPTER 3

LORNA

It's dark outside now and my feet feel numb. How long have I been standing here by the train window? Glancing up at the top bunk I see that Ella is asleep, her phone discarded on her pillow and one arm dangling off the edge of the bed. Her hair has fallen in front of her face. I very gently brush it back.

Ella may have drifted off, but I know I won't be able to sleep. There are too many thoughts filling my head. The rocking and jolting of the train that seems to have lulled Ella so quickly makes me restless. It reminds me of the fact we are moving, every second bringing us closer and making me more fearful of what will happen when we arrive. I still can't quite believe that after all this time, I'm really going back to the island. That tomorrow, I will see my brother for the first time in twenty-two years. And I will finally meet my niece and my sister-in-law.

Shame and regret rush through me as they always do when I think about my family. I desperately need a drink.

Switching off the cabin light I step outside and pull the door gently behind me.

The bar is situated in the first-class lounge, a carriage filled with cushioned chairs and small tables softly illuminated by lamps. A sign on the door says that standard-class passengers are allowed to purchase drinks to bring back to their cabins, but the carriage is surprisingly empty. A member of staff dressed in a crisp uniform quietly tells me that I can take a seat wherever I like. As I move towards a table I notice a woman who looks my age watching me from the other end of the carriage. She has large grey-green eyes framed by sleek tortoiseshell glasses and faint laughter lines, and her dark hair is pulled back into a low ponytail tied with a colourful scarf. She is dressed in a dark green shirt rolled up to the elbows, jeans and faded, mud-flecked walking boots. On the table in front of her is a glass of red wine and a book held open in one hand. But she isn't looking at the book; instead she stares straight at me, a slight frown on her face. Her expression quickly brightens into a smile and as it does I can immediately tell this is a face more accustomed to smiling than to frowning.

'Lorna Irvine,' the woman says suddenly in a thick Hebridean accent, without the raised tone at the end to indicate it is a question. It isn't a question, it's a statement, and it stops me in my tracks. My mouth drops open and the woman laughs.

'I thought it was you, and that expression tells me I'm right.'

I look more closely at her. And suddenly I see a young girl with pale eyes, dark, frizzy pigtails, huge NHS glasses and an enormous smile. I see this girl beside me at primary school and cycling home with me across the island, our bikes perfectly parallel. My mind flashes forward and I picture this same girl as a teenager, the two of us listening to music together in her bedroom, the glasses replaced with contact lenses and the frizzy pigtails now carefully and self-consciously tended waves. I see my best friend.

'Sarah.'

As the name leaves my mouth, I'm conscious of my lack of accent. I once sounded just like Sarah. But that was a long time ago.

We look at each other, both smiling as though we are children again. But we're not children. And we haven't seen or heard from each other in twenty-two years.

As though just realising the same thing, Sarah's face drops slightly. My cheeks flush. What is there that I can possibly begin to say to my old friend whom I left behind like everything and everyone else? My mind fills with memories of our friendship. How we'd sit together at lunchtime and swap things on our plates – her carrots for my peas, my juice for her extra carton of milk. Her family, who were always so welcoming even when I was too shy to truly thank them for their kindness. The teen magazines Sarah ordered from the mainland with her pocket money and would share with me, the two of us sitting in her bed giggling as we turned the pages together.

The grown-up Sarah indicates the free chair.

'Do you want to sit down?'

I slip into the chair. Now that I've recognised her I look more closely, greedily taking in every tiny detail that might tell me something about Sarah's life now. A simple gold wedding band, nails that are neat but unpolished, a bracelet strung with various charms – a dog, a boat and three gold initials, B, A and O.

I must say something. Anything. It feels so good to see her again. But the silence of decades is stuck in my mouth. Sarah looks at me closely too. What details has she spotted? The lack of a ring on my hand, perhaps. The dark circles of worry under my eyes. My hair that is the same auburn shade as when we were young and still just as curly and unruly.

The silence continues for what feels like a very long time.

'I'm sorry about your parents,' she says. 'You must be feeling all sorts of things.'

I meet Sarah's eyes across the train table and an understanding passes between us. In many ways we are strangers and yet we are so much more than that too. Cheryl has been so kind and supportive since I told her the news. She knows I haven't seen my parents in years but has never judged me for it, doing her best to understand. It's the reason I don't have a bigger circle of friends – this fear of having to try to explain myself and the thought of what people might think. Over the years I've become skilled at avoiding the subject. When colleagues ask me whether I am spending Christmas or the summer holidays with family I say yes, because I am. It's just that my family consists of one: Ella.

But with Sarah I don't have to explain myself. She was there all those years ago, my friend when I felt so alone.

'Thank you,' I manage, the words tight in my throat.

'I wasn't sure if you'd want to come back for the funeral,' she says quietly.

28

The words hit me in my chest and there it is again, the news I still haven't come to terms with. My parents are dead. It washes over me again, this reality that doesn't feel real.

'Honestly, I didn't want to, not at first.'

Because I haven't heard from my parents in nearly fourteen years. I haven't seen them for even longer. And now I never will. Perhaps their deaths shouldn't shake me this much given we've been apart for so many years, by my own choice. What right do I really have to feel upset when I *chose* to cut contact with them? But I still can't believe my parents are really gone. And that it was my daughter who told me.

She'd found out through her cousin Molly; it turns out they'd been in contact for nearly a year and I'd had no idea. Ella admitted everything in a frenzy last week, the secret conversations and then the news that my parents had both been sick and had passed away within two days of one another. Ella said she was sorry she'd kept it all from me but that she wanted to go to the island. She wants to attend the funeral for the grandparents she's never met.

I remember when I first told Ella about Molly. Ella was at primary school and they were doing a project about family trees. The project sparked questions about my family that I'd tried my best to divert over the years, answering with only the briefest of information. This time though, she was insistent.

'I can't do the project if I don't have a family,' she near-sobbed to me one day after school. 'Everyone else has nearly finished theirs and I haven't even started!'

She was close to tears and I felt that old guilt and sadness rip through me – that I haven't been able to give my daughter more. So many times, I've pictured a different kind of life for her. A life full of people: grandparents, cousins, siblings maybe, a father. Instead she's only ever had me. I can't give her everything but I wanted to give her something that day, so I told her.

'I have a brother called Jack, but I haven't seen him in a very long time. And he has a little girl called Molly. She's a bit older than you and she's your cousin. But I've never met her. They live really far away.'

She asked me more questions after that, what Molly was like, what her favourite subject was at school, whether she liked broccoli, what colour her hair was. But I brushed these questions off, partly because I wanted to change the subject and partly because I felt so ashamed at not knowing the answers.

What kind of a person does it make me that I didn't know my parents were so ill? That the last time I saw them I was eighteen years old? When I left it may have felt like the only option for me, but even after all this time the guilt is still there, so easily brought to the surface. Were they alone when they died? Were they in pain? Jack must have been there with them. I'm not sure if that makes me feel better, or worse; worse that when I left the island all those years ago, I left all of that to him and him alone.

'What made you change your mind?' Sarah asks me.

I think about it for a moment.

'My daughter mostly. She's always wanted to know more about her family. I guess I finally realised she had a right to that.'

I think back to when Ella told me everything, last weekend.

30

We were sitting in our favourite café in Greenwich. She'd been quiet all day, so unlike herself. And then she told me. I was so shocked that I had no idea what to say. If I'm honest, I know I didn't react well. I was surprised, and hurt that she'd kept her relationship with her cousin a secret from me. And then there was the grief, catching me off guard. Why grieve for people you chose to cut from your life? I still can't explain it, apart from the simple fact that all the time and distance in the world can't erase. They were my mum and dad.

When Ella first asked if we could go to the island I said no. She grew angry then too, angrier than I've ever seen her.

'They're my family too, Mum, even if I've never met them!' she shouted, turning all the heads in the café in our direction. Eventually, when I'd calmed down, I realised she was right. I've tried all my life to protect her. Everything I've done is because I love her. But that doesn't necessarily mean I've always made the right choices.

'I guess it makes sense that she'd be curious,' says Sarah, drawing me for a moment back to the present. I look at her again, this friend I haven't seen in so long, and seeing her makes me think of my friend back in London.

'It was something my friend Cheryl said too,' I tell Sarah.

Cheryl and I were sitting in the school staff room after the weekend, the other teachers outside enjoying the sunshine. I told her everything that had happened and how desperate Ella was to go to the island.

'Ella has never known her family,' I said. 'All she has is me. So maybe she *should* get a chance to get to know her cousin, to meet her in real life. She deserves that.'

31

'So why don't you go?' Cheryl suggested, simply but with a gentleness too.

'Honestly? I'm terrified.'

Cheryl nodded then.

'That makes sense. All those memories …'

'It's not just the memories, though. What if my brother doesn't want to see me? What if I'm not welcome? I wouldn't blame him after all these years we've been out of touch.'

'Do you want to see him?'

The truthful answer was too complicated to fit into words. So instead I said the only thing I know for certain.

'I've missed him so much. It's been such a long time.'

'It has been a long time,' Cheryl said softly. 'But maybe it's been long enough? Things are different now. You have Ella, you have your life here – a life you've made for yourself, by yourself. You're not a child anymore. You're so much stronger than you think you are, Lorna.'

I didn't feel strong. I still don't. But my friend's belief in me made me want to try to be.

'She helped me see that it might be good for me to come back too,' I tell Sarah now. 'You know, face up to everything I left behind.'

My eyes meet hers and I feel so embarrassed that I look away. Laughter spills from a table on the other side of the carriage where a group of friends share a bottle of prosecco.

'I heard from Alice that you had a daughter,' says Sarah, drawing my eye back to my old friend. 'It's been quite the talk of the island, Ella and Molly finding each other online.'

How strange to hear Ella's name on Sarah's lips. The thought that my daughter and I have been the subject of island gossip makes my stomach flip for a second.

As if reading my mind Sarah quickly adds, 'Sorry, you know what the island's like. Everyone is just really excited to meet her. And to see you again.'

She looks down as she says this.

'So, you still live on the island then?' I ask, not knowing what else to say.

She nods.

'Yes. I've been down in London this week visiting an old university friend who moved there after we graduated.'

'You got the grades after all then. I knew you would.'

I remember how worried Sarah had been that she wouldn't get in to university. She was going to be the first of her family to go and knew how much it meant to her parents, even though they did their best not to let it show.

'Where did you go in the end?' I add.

I left the island before my exam results arrived. I had them forwarded from the exam board to my new address in London. But it meant I never got to find out how Sarah did in her own exams. I remember sitting with her at The Lookout, the island pub where I had a part-time job as a teenager, and going through prospectuses we'd been sent in the post. Sarah liked the idea of a big city but didn't want to be too far away from her family.

'I went to Glasgow and had a great time,' she says with a smile. 'After all that stressing I think I would have had a great time anywhere really. I stayed there after I graduated. But then I met Ben ...'

Her eyes light up and she twists her wedding band on her finger, a smile on her face. But then she looks at me again and the smile slips slightly. I see her closing down, perhaps hesitant about saying too much. I don't blame her, and yet it still hurts to see the friend who once shared everything with me monitoring herself and shifting on her seat in my presence.

'And what do you do now?' I ask.

'Well, being an islander, I do a bit of everything of course, so it's more a question of what *don't* I do. We live on one of the old crofts, so a lot of my time is spent looking after that. We sell jam and chutney in the village shop and to other local islands. I work a few days a week as an assistant at the school. I help out at the village shop sometimes too. And I look after Olive and Alfie, of course. They're twelve and nine and keep me busy.'

Olive and Alfie. Olive and Alfie. I can't quite believe that the Sarah Douglas I grew up with now has her own children. She glows when she says their names, just like she did when she mentioned her husband Ben.

'I bet you're a great mum.'

Her face pales and she fiddles with the bracelet on her wrist, not looking at me. Perhaps it's too much for our first encounter after all this time, but I couldn't help it. It's true.

'How are your parents? Are they still on the island?' I ask instead. I so hope that they are both still alive and well. They were so kind to me when I was young. I owe them so much.

'Yes, Mum and Dad are fine. Getting older, but aren't we all? They still live in the same house.'

I can picture the farmhouse Sarah grew up in so clearly it's as though I'm back there now. Slightly ramshackle and untidy but always warm. Sarah's drawings and later her school reports were always stuck up on the fridge, alongside every single one of her school photographs. Her father was a farmer but had a passion for carpentry and had his own workshop at the bottom of the garden. I remember how he always smelt of wood shavings and furniture polish. Sarah's mother was a cheerful but no-nonsense sort of woman who knew everything there was to know about butchery and gave the kind of hugs that back then always made me want to smile and cry at the same time.

'And what about you?' Sarah asks, lifting her wine glass to her lips. But there's nothing left in it, despite it being nearly full when I sat down. She catches the waiter's eye and orders another glass; I ask for a gin and tonic.

'Are you still an artist?'

A sudden memory of the smell of oil paints and the feeling of charcoal beneath my fingernails. I shiver slightly at the thought.

'I'm a teacher. Deputy head at a primary school in East London.'

Sarah's eyebrows rise.

'I'm sorry if I seem surprised, I just always thought you would make it. You were so passionate. It was your *thing*.'

The waiter arrives with our drinks. I reach for mine immediately, taking a long, deep sip. I feel the effect straight away. If Sarah wasn't watching I'd probably finish the drink in two gulps. Instead, I place the glass back on the table and notice that Sarah has taken a large swig of her wine as well.

She's right of course. Once art *was* my thing. It was the thing that got me up each day, that I loved more than anything. It's how I filled hours alone in my room, how I expressed myself and how I escaped everything else in my life. Back then, I couldn't imagine a life without art. And for a while after leaving the island I would still have described myself as an artist, even when I was working in a bar and hadn't touched a paintbrush in a long time. But now the word seems so alien. It's just not me. Not anymore.

I think back to those afternoons spent with Sarah flicking through university prospectuses. As soon as I saw the brochure for Goldsmiths I knew immediately that it was where I wanted to go. Where I was *meant* to go. But things didn't work out that way. In the end, I didn't even apply.

'When I got to London my plan was to apply to art school,' I hear myself saying. 'It would have meant starting a year later than I'd hoped, but I thought it could still happen. But I guess I hadn't anticipated quite how expensive it would be to live there and how hard I'd find it to support myself.'

I remember that first weekend in the city; I spent it walking into dozens of different bars asking if they needed staff. I felt desperate. Because I *had* to make it work – going back to the island was not an option.

Sarah watches me closely. She takes another sip of her wine and then nods slightly, encouraging me to continue.

'When I got my first bar job so much of my time was taken up with working that the art fell to one side. Each month I'd tell myself that if I just worked more shifts this month, then next month I could focus on painting again. After a while, I

36

gave up pretending that would happen. I missed the deadline for art school again, and even if I hadn't, I had nothing to show for myself in an application. All my attention went on earning money to keep myself afloat.'

And sometimes it was fun. I remember getting drunk with my colleagues in the bar at the end of the shift and feeling for a moment like maybe everything would be OK. I was free, living by my own rules. But then that became my life and the passion I'd once had for painting disappeared.

'With Ella on the way I needed a proper career. That's when I found teaching. And it's been good as she's got older. Having the holidays, being home earlier than I would if I worked in an office … It works for her, for us. And I've enjoyed it too. It's so satisfying seeing the children develop, watching them grow.'

I don't mention Dave Phillips the creep and the increasing challenges of my job. I still enjoy teaching, but in truth over recent months I've come to dread going in to work, not knowing what he might say or do that day and how I will react.

We both take another sip of our drinks. I glance for a second at the long carriage window where the darkness rolls past, glowing lights from house windows flashing by every now and then.

'Why didn't you call me?'

Sarah's voice is quieter now but I can't miss what she's just said. It's the question I've been dreading since we started talking. It would be impossible to continue talking like this – like two old friends catching up – without acknowledging the truth. That as close as we once were, when I left the island I left Sarah too.

Her pale eyes flash as they fill with tears. I see a brief glimpse of nine-year-old Sarah, crying because her favourite lamb on her parents' farm had got caught in a barbed wire fence overnight and died. She saved the tears for the girls' toilet at school, where she dragged me at break time. She rarely cried and knew that her parents and grandparents would disapprove, because despite their kindness they were a family of farmers. Death was a part of life on a farm and on the island. But Sarah was nine and loved animals like they were her friends. I felt honoured that she had saved her tears for me, that she allowed herself to break down in front of me and me alone.

This feels different. I sense the distance stretching between us again.

'I had to leave. You must know that. I had to.'

'I understand,' she says through her tears. 'After everything you went through, of course you wanted to leave. But I just don't understand why you didn't keep in touch. We were best friends. For ages I wondered what I'd done wrong. I thought I didn't matter to you.'

I close my eyes for a moment. When I open them again I look at Sarah's hands, focusing on the charms on her bracelet. I just can't quite look her in the eye.

'I nearly called you so many times,' I say quietly.

When I first arrived in London I was desperate to hear Sarah's voice. I wanted to tell her about the underground and how loud the trains sounded roaring into the tunnels, about the National Gallery that I visited three times in my first week in the city, about the tiny attic bedroom I was renting and my new housemates who came from all over the world and had never heard of the Isle of Kip. But something held me back.

'I so wanted to talk to you. But I was desperate to get away from the island. I didn't want to be reminded of it. And more than anything I didn't want my family to find out where I'd gone.'

'But I would *never* have told them! It was me who helped you leave.'

I will never forget that day. Sarah came with me to the jetty and helped me onto the ferry. That was the last time we saw each other.

'It wasn't that I didn't trust you. I just needed a clean break. I don't know how to explain it exactly, I just knew I couldn't have anything to do with the island. And then as time went on it became more than that too. I felt so embarrassed about the way I'd handled things with you and about how much time had passed. The more time went by, the harder it became to call. I imagined you'd moved on with your life. I wasn't sure if you'd want to hear from me.'

Sarah rubs her eyes.

'I had no idea where you were,' she says, her voice strangled. 'I just missed you so much.'

I take a deep breath.

'I missed you too.'

The train rattles on into the darkness and we sit in silence, two old friends separated by years and miles and all those times I wanted to pick up the phone but didn't.

After a while, she wipes her eyes and stands up.

'I should get some sleep.'

She pulls a cardigan off the back of her chair and picks up her book from the table.

'Can we get a drink together on the island?' I say as she prepares to leave. 'Have a proper catch up? Talk about things?'

There's so much more I need to tell her. Apologies I need to make.

'I don't know, Lorna,' she says, rubbing her arms. 'It's been a really long time. I guess I just need a bit of time to think.'

'Yes of course. Well, I'll be around for a bit anyway.'

'OK.'

And then I watch as she turns and walks away. Last time, it was her who watched me leave on a windswept jetty as the ferry took me on to my new life. Now, I stare into the space where she sat, thinking about our childhood and all the years that have passed since. The time that has gone by feels suddenly irrelevant. I still miss my old friend just as much as when I first left. Could this visit to the island perhaps be a chance for us to reconnect, for me to get my friend back? Or is it just too late for that?

CHAPTER 4

ALICE

The ferry arrives this afternoon. Jack works in the fields, the morning sun bursting through a patchwork of clouds. I watch him from the kitchen window, smiling at the way he moves with such determination and focus, his eyes trained on the soil.

My laptop is on the table beside me, a new email waiting for me from Shona. I make myself a cup of tea, wanting to sit and savour my sister's words. We might not see each other often but we email and message every few days. And once every few weeks the three of us have a Skype catch up, usually each with a glass of red wine in hand.

Shona's email is brief but, as always, funny and interesting. She tells me about students on her course, about some research she is working on with colleagues, and about a theatre production she and her husband Malcolm recently went to see at His Majesty's Theatre in Aberdeen's city centre. There are photos attached too – my nephews Finlay and Cam at a football training camp.

I stare at the screen for a while, wondering, as I so often do, how to reply. I want to share the details of my life with her – these messages are a thread that keep me connected to my sisters. But I just don't want to bore her. I think about the changes in the fields outside, the shoots bursting through soil in the polytunnels. It's delivery day at the village shop in a few days so I will replenish our cupboards. I have plans for a yoga class next week focusing on a particular breathing technique and want to watch some videos online to help me prepare. I need to bake a new loaf of bread too, and have plans to make a roast chicken salad tonight, using lettuce and herbs from the garden. These are the details of my life. But I don't always feel that they're worth mentioning to my busy, intelligent sisters. And then there are my worries about Jean, and about everything that's been happening at the island school ... But I can't bring myself to truly think about those worries, let alone type them into an email.

In the end I write about one of our sheep that escaped a few days ago and how it was found halfway across the island. Brenda was on her way over for a cup of tea and somehow managed to catch the sheep and bundle it into the back of her car. I tell her about Lorna and Ella's visit too, how they're due to arrive later today.

As I press send on the email I hear the front door clicking open and a voice calling inside, 'Good morning, is anyone home?'

'In the kitchen!'

It's Emma, carrying a cardboard box containing a large round tin and six beers bearing the logo of the island brewery. I help her set them down on the table.

'What's all this?'

'Just something from Duncan for you and Jack,' she replies, indicating the beers. 'And something from me for you all.'

I lift the lid off the tin. Inside is a moist-looking cake, the icing a golden brown and currently making a bid for freedom from the top of the cake.

'Ach, it must have shifted in the car,' Emma says, reaching for a knife on the draining board and smoothing the icing. 'Hopefully it still tastes OK though. Coffee and walnut.'

She removes the knife and runs her finger over the icing that clings there and eats it.

'Oh, thank you! It looks delicious. That's so kind of you.'

She shrugs.

'It was no bother.'

'Would you like a cup of tea?'

But she shakes her head.

'I'd love to but I have other errands to run. Jean's feeling rough so I'm popping over there now.'

I nod, and turn quickly to the cupboard by the fridge.

'Take this with you,' I say, handing Emma a jar of home-made jam. 'And send her my love, will you?'

'Of course.'

We hug goodbye and she lets herself out. For a second I pause, worrying about Jean and how she's feeling, but I already have a plan for this morning, a plan I made after yesterday's

43

yoga class. I scribble a note to Jack and Molly (although I'm not quite sure where Molly is, possibly still asleep or otherwise out with Olive), and leave it on the kitchen table. Then I head to the Land Rover.

Tess and Joy's house is on the other side of the island, one of the newer buildings in the village which is not really a village but instead a few houses gathered near the shop, the pub, the school and the community hall. It is painted bright white with large square windows. They have a big garden at the back that overlooks the sea with a modern bothy-style building set back from the house and two large canvas yurts on the grass – all of which they rent out to holidaymakers.

I park up and open their low wooden gate, making my way down the garden path which cuts through flowerbeds planted with thistles, shrubs and bright yellow broom. There's a wooden bench outside the green front door, two pairs of wellies lined up beneath it. A washing line is strung with babygrows, muslins and sheets that flutter back and forth.

There's a brief pause after I knock before Joy opens the door wearing a stained T-shirt and a pair of tracksuit bottoms, her feet bare. She looks extremely flustered and from inside the house I hear the sound of Harry crying and Tess's soothing voice as she tries to comfort him. Poor Joy looks even more exhausted than Tess did when I saw her yesterday.

'Morning, Alice, are you OK? I'd offer you a cup of tea but I think we're out of milk …' she trails off, turning to look inside as Harry lets out a particularly loud shriek.

'Don't worry about that. I just thought I might pop over and offer my babysitting services – I've got a free couple of hours and thought you two might like a break.'

Joy turns back to me, relief and uncertainty on her face. Tess is in the hallway now too, jiggling baby Harry on her hip. His chubby coffee-coloured cheeks are flushed and his brown eyes are damp with tears. But he's quietened slightly, the wee thing, sniffling and chewing his fist.

'That's very kind of you,' Joy says. 'But he's going through quite a fussy stage.'

I wave my hand.

'That's no bother. Molly was just the same.'

Joy glances at Tess.

'I could certainly do with a shower,' she says hesitantly.

'And I would kill for a nap,' adds Tess. 'I didn't sleep at all last night.'

'Well that's decided then. Do you have his carrier? I'll take him out for a walk, it's a nice morning.'

'Thank you, Alice, we appreciate this so much.'

It's the least I can do though, nothing more than what so many of the other islanders did for me when Molly was small. I strap Harry to my chest and his parents lean down to kiss the top of his head.

'You be good for Auntie Alice.'

Harry gurgles in reply. I wave goodbye to Tess and Joy who lean wearily in the doorframe, arms around one another, and set off down the garden path, joining the road that heads through the village and down towards the beach.

'Let's go on a lovely walk,' I say softly to Harry, who has thankfully quietened now. Every now and then he starts to grizzle and I hand him a finger to suck and chew which seems to do the job of holding back his tears. It always did with Molly. I try to distract him too, pointing out things as I walk.

'Look at that big seagull! And can you see that seal out in the bay?'

His chubby legs swing at my sides. Every now and then I reach down for his socked feet, squeezing them gently, or place a hand on his soft, tightly curled hair. I might have been worried about Tess and Joy but I have to admit this wasn't a totally selfless visit. There is nothing quite like the warmth and weight of a baby on your chest. I remember that feeling when I carried Molly, of feeling like she was part of me and that just by holding her I had a huge, important purpose.

I take us along the beach, stepping over strands of seaweed and avoiding the larger rocks and shards of driftwood. We pass a few people out walking their dogs and although everyone here is always friendly I can tell their smiles are wider than normal as they greet me. That's just the effect of babies.

I always imagined I'd have a bigger family. I wanted four children. I imagined the farmhouse filled with noise, mess and laughter, muddy shoes in a towering pile by the door, a washing line constantly strung with pyjamas and socks and school uniforms. But it never happened. I don't think I've ever said it out loud, but the biggest failure in my life has been the failure of my body. I know I'm not supposed to think of it as a failure. That's what all the doctors on the mainland said anyway. *These things happen. It's not your fault.* It's what my sisters and my friends tried to tell me too. But deep down, I still don't truly believe them. The failure sits with me in the pit of my stomach. I guess I've just learnt how to live with it.

I pause for a moment on the beach, lowering myself and Harry down onto a long, wide tree trunk half-buried in the sand.

'Let's just have a little sit down,' I say to him. 'And look at this beautiful view.'

Some of the fishing boats are tied up in the harbour, bobbing up and down on the water. I spot others as tiny black dots out to sea. Harry gurgles, his small hand clasping mine.

At least I have Molly. That's what I've always tried to tell myself. It feels greedy to want more when I have her. She has been the biggest joy in my life. And I guess when I started to realise that the big family I'd imagined might never exist I just tried to love her as much as four children.

Looking out to sea, the worries I've been trying to push away over these past few days sweep in like the waves rolling in against the sand. When I'm at home I try my best to stay busy and focused on keeping the house in order and looking after Jack and Molly. But out here I let my shoulders sink. I run through my list of worries like a checklist in my head. Jack and how he's coping. Molly and what the next few days will be like for her. Jean and how she's feeling and what comes next for my friend. The school and all the problems that have been happening there and what it means for the future of our community. Because the fact is I may have worked hard to build this life here but none of it is certain. It could all be taken away.

47

I tilt my head down and breathe in Harry's perfect baby smell.

'Come on,' I say softly, easing myself to my feet once more. 'Let's carry on our walk.'

CHAPTER 5

LORNA

It's raining on the island again. Water stings my eyes. What's rain and what's the damp breeze whipped in from the sea? Impossible to tell. The wind sighs secrets in my ears. I lick my lips and taste the sharp tang of salt crystals.

I'm standing on the cliff looking out to sea, except I can't make out much at all through the grey fog of rain that hangs over the water. The horizon has been brought right in close today. There's no chance of glimpsing the mainland. Perhaps it's disappeared altogether.

Shivering, I blink through the raindrops that sit heavy on my eyelashes. White-capped waves crash against the rocks below. A gull screeches, wobbling above me like a surfer clinging to a swell. I stretch my neck to watch it and feel a pain between my ribs as it hovers for just a second longer before curving away and out to sea. I have never envied another creature as much as I envy that gull. With wings you're able to fly away.

I turn for a moment away from the sea. The lighthouse towers up into the grey sky and suddenly a beam of light catches me in its glare, dazzling me. Beyond the lighthouse I can just make out the peak of the mountain pushing through a low bank of cloud. Spreading around it is the rest of the island: the one road shiny with puddles, the scattering of houses and the dripping black pine forest.

And then something reaches me on the wind. The smell of smoke rising in the air despite the rain. It seeps its way into my mouth, down my throat, into my lungs. Smoke, and the smell of the sea. Below me, the waves batter the rocks. And I stand alone on the clifftop drenched by rain that feels as though it will never stop falling.

Suddenly the scene before me changes, washed away as though drawn back by the tide. I'm not on the cliff anymore but inland, facing a house that backs onto the pines. I'm aware of the sea behind me down the valley though, even if I can't see it. The waves hitting the sand in the distance sound like a heartbeat.

The house in front of me is a large grey building with peeling green window frames and a black wooden porch. There's a track leading up to the house and a fence with a gate encircling a small garden. But there's nothing much in the garden apart from rocks and a wooden bench. Nothing grows here.

Behind the house is a backdrop of pine trees and above them the dark silhouette of the mountain. The light is fading and the forest casts long, dark shapes like the shadows of giants onto the grass. But just on the edge of the forest there's a light. It's dim at first but grows brighter as I watch it. As I take a step towards the forest I realise there's a fire burning just on the edge where the grass meets the trees. The flames hiss and spurt. There's a smell in the air of petrol and the stomach-twisting stench of burning. Suddenly I'm running past the house and towards the forest. As I get closer I can feel the heat of the flames hitting my face, making my skin tingle and burn. My throat fills with smoke. And yet I keep running, closer and closer towards the fire. Because I know at once what is burning there.

*

I wake suddenly in the narrow cabin bed, gasping for breath, the sheets drenched with sweat. It takes a moment to realise where I am.

It's been a long time since I had this dream. There was a time when a version of it visited me nearly every night. The dreams were so realistic and left me so exhausted that they began to feel more real than my own life. During those days I functioned on autopilot, struggling to stay awake and feeling not fully aware of everything that was happening around me. It was like being drunk but without the warm buzz. At night I collapsed into sleep, unable to prevent the vivid nightmares that would follow me there. Then years and years passed without a single one.

A thin strip of sunlight glows around the edges of the blind. Its brightness tells me I have slept in later than I intended. It's an effort to drag myself out of bed, my body exhausted. I pull on my clothes and check the top bunk. But it's empty. The rational part of my brain tells me that Ella can't have gone far – we are on a moving train after all. But my panic is not rational. Over the years I've found that so little of being a parent is. My emotions seem so often driven by a mix of fear and love that I have no control over whatsoever. Often, I feel like my life is one long drive in a car with no steering wheel.

Thankfully I find Ella quickly. She's standing at the end of the train corridor, dressed in denim shorts and a faded grey T-shirt, leaning against the window, her camera held in front of her. The view outside couldn't be further from the one we left behind in Euston. The train passes along the edge of a large loch, the water silver with liquid sunlight. Behind the loch are hills that arch into mountains in the distance. On the nearside shore is a pebbly stretch of beach where a few sheep pick their way between rocks.

'Morning, Mum!' Ella says brightly, suddenly noticing me standing beside her. She gives me a kiss on the cheek. I smell washing detergent, the fresh scent of recently applied deodorant and something more unique to Ella too – the mix of her hair and skin that means I could pick out my daughter from a line-up of teenagers with my eyes closed and my hands held behind my back.

'Isn't this view amazing, Mum?'

We both look back out the window. The loch has passed by now and instead we're travelling through a wide expanse of moor. Despite being simply a mostly grassy plain, the view is alive with colours. Vivid green and soft yellow where the grass is dry and pale. The dusty mauve of the heather, the grey of rocks rising out from the earth, rich reds and burnt orange bracken. It makes me think of an oil painting and the way the colours mix and blend together. It's not often that I think of painting these days, but the conversation with Sarah last night has nudged open a part of my mind that I've kept shut for a long time.

We pass over a sudden ravine where jagged rocks rise sharply above a Coca-Cola black river. It gathers in tranquil pools before rushing over rocks further downstream and then plummeting into a waterfall. The shutter on Ella's camera clicks as the train rocks its way across the countryside.

Yes, the view is beautiful. I know that. But I can't *feel* it. Because to me, it is tinged with apprehension. As the train moves I sense again that string that binds me to the island tautening. Reeling me in. I thought that by leaving I'd managed to sever that link entirely. But watching the mountains and the moor out the train window I realise these views and the connection to them have been inside me a long time, waiting. I was foolish to think they'd disappeared entirely. And after last night's conversation with Sarah I feel more apprehensive about this visit. It was hard enough talking to her again after all these years – what will it possibly be like with my brother?

I turn away from the window.

'I'm going to see if breakfast has arrived.'

Back in the cabin I find two small boxes and a cardboard drinks carrier waiting, left by the train attendant. I eat one of the lukewarm bacon rolls and drink my coffee sitting on the bottom bunk with the blind still pulled down.

Only when the train begins to near Fort William does Ella bound into the cabin. She eats her now cold roll in two bites

53

while I open the blind and pull down our suitcases. Outside, modern housing estates and the bright light of a Lidl sign roll by, mountains visible on the horizon behind the town.

Stepping off the train together I look around, searching out Sarah's face among the people pulling suitcases and carrying rucksacks on the platform. There are only twenty or so other passengers, the train having stopped at numerous stations overnight and throughout the morning. But I can't see Sarah among them.

'What are you looking for, Mum?'

'Nothing.'

Where has Sarah got to? Did she race ahead of us getting off the train, or did she maybe get off a stop or two earlier? Despite how we left things, I can't help but feel eager to bump into her again. She may have asked for space but Kip is a small island and we are bound to cross paths again before long. Maybe if I find the right words to tell her how sorry I am there's a chance that we can get back what we once had.

But before reaching the island there is still more to our journey: another train and then the ferry. I sleep for most of the second train journey as Ella stands glued by the window, staring outside. As we disembark in the port town the smell of the sea is the first thing I notice. The salty tang catches in the back of my throat, its familiarity even after all these years grabbing me in the stomach and twisting like a knot being tightened. The air is loud with the screeches of seagulls circling the sky, hoping to claim discarded fish in the harbour. A sign points us towards the ferry ticket office. But I don't need the direction. I know this place. It's where I came whenever we visited the mainland. And it's where I would have gone to secondary school, if only I'd been allowed.

There's a small primary school on the island, but no secondary school. So from the age of eleven island children catch the ferry to the mainland school, staying in a youth hostel until the weekend when they return to their families. But my parents didn't want me and Jack to go, so chose to home-school us after primary school instead. I remember the arguments about it well. I wanted to go to the mainland school just like Sarah and the other island children and pleaded with them to change their minds. The thought of the youth hostel, away from my parents and away from the island, seemed like a dream. At the time I never fully understood my parents' decision. But looking back, I think it was one of many attempts at controlling us. The closer we were, the easier we were to hold on to. At least, that's what I think my father believed.

With each step I feel my anxieties rising. Once the tickets are bought we sit in the small waiting room. In the room with us are a young couple with matching rucksacks who look like tourists and a woman in her sixties with pink hair and a husky puppy curled up in a cardboard box on her lap.

Ella immediately walks across and asks the woman if she can see the puppy.

'Of course, pet.' The woman lifts the puppy out of the box and hands it to Ella. Her face lights up, the fluffy bundle of puppy nuzzling into her chest.

'I'm taking him back home. I reckon he's going to cause quite a stir on the island!'

I look closely at the woman. I don't recognise her so assume she must be a local, not a native. The terms for different islanders come back to me in a rush. Natives – those who grew up there, often with families who have been on the island for generations. Next come locals, people who have lived there for five years or more and are an accepted part of the community but will never have quite the status of natives. And below that tourists and 'blow-ins', people who visit with ambitions of settling there but leave after their first winter or two. What category do I fit into now?

'What's his name?' Ella asks the woman, stroking the puppy who is now licking her arm.

'I've called him Puff.'

Ella holds Puff slightly away from her body. Her grey T-shirt is covered in white and black hair. She laughs.

'That's a perfect name.'

'Thanks, hen, I thought so too. So, are you and your mum on a wee holiday?'

The woman looks over at me now, a smile on her face. I attempt a smile back but my heart is racing and I can't quite get my face to respond. Before I can say anything, Ella answers, her voice light.

'Yeah, we're visiting for a couple of weeks.'

I bought a flexible train ticket, not sure how this trip would pan out.

'Here, I guess you want him back,' adds Ella.

She hands Puff to the woman with the pink hair, who gently places him back in the box. I'm relieved that Ella didn't go into the details of our trip with this stranger. But it's embarrassing that it took my teenage daughter to step in and answer with such lightness. I need to get myself together.

'Well if you want to come and visit him at all while you're staying, I live in the blue house in the middle of the island, you can't miss it. I'm Brenda, by the way.'

'I'm Ella, and this is my mum, Lorna.'

I dig deeper for my smile this time.

'Hello. What a sweet puppy.'

'Lorna …'

Is it a frown that crosses briefly over Brenda's face? She looks at me closely and I try not to shrink under her gaze. But then she is smiling again.

'Well, you both have a good trip. It sounds like our ferry is here.'

We drag our suitcases out to the water's edge where a few cars are already driving onto the back of the boat. Only residents are allowed to bring cars onto the island. I spot piles of loo roll and shopping bags in the boot of several of the vehicles. They must belong to islanders stocking up and returning home. There is a van too; it looks just like the one that used to deliver the post and other supplies to the island.

I follow Ella and the other passengers down the path that leads to the pedestrian entrance of the ferry. As we reach the metal ramp I pause, looking back. Behind me lie the car park, the port and the buildings beyond that make up the small fishing town. The mainland and the train that could take me back to Fort William and eventually home to London. Ahead there is nothing but sea and uncertainty. I'm not sure that I can do this. We've come so far already, I know. But once I get on that boat there's really no going back.

'Are you OK, Mum?'

Ella turns to me. Beside her the ferry master looks me up and down, the cars safely parked and the other passengers already on board and up the steps that lead to the café and seating deck.

'Are you boarding, ma'am?'

I glance again at Ella and force a smile.

'Sorry, we're coming,' I say to the ferry master as I loop my arm through Ella's. Her expression is worried for a moment but I give her hand a reassuring squeeze.

'I'm fine,' I tell her, not because I am but because I'm her mother. 'Let's go.'

Ella looks up excitedly towards the waiting boat and together, we step on board.

CHAPTER 6

ALICE

After reluctantly handing Harry back to Tess and Joy, I head to the village shop. Pat Campbell greets me with a smile, a green apron tied around her waist and her half-moon glasses balanced on the end of her nose. She has a clipboard in her hand which she places down on the counter as she sees me, pushing her glasses up into the nest of her grey hair.

'Hello, dear,' she says with a smile.

'Hi, Pat, how are you today?'

She waves a hand.

'*I'm* fine, how are things over at the farm?'

'Busy as ever. Getting ready for the arrival of our visitors later.'

'Of course, it's today, isn't it? I remember Lorna when she was a wee lass. I do hope she pops in while she's here. Will you make sure of it?'

'Of course I will.'

I pause, remembering why I'm here.

'I wanted to talk to you about placing a food order for the wake.'

There's still so much to organise for the funeral. I told Jack I'd take care of it all. I don't want to bother him with all the details, he has so much on his mind as it is and the few times I have brought it up he's looked so dazed, as though he isn't really hearing what I'm saying. I've spoken to the minister – he usually comes to the island once every two weeks for regular Sunday services but makes special trips for other occasions. He's a newer appointment, thank goodness, not the severe, sombre old man who performed our wedding. I would have preferred to get married in the village hall but Jack's parents insisted and as usual, they had their way.

I've sorted the flowers, shared the details with the islanders and been in touch with the funeral home on the mainland. I've decided to hold the wake at our house. I thought it would be easier for Jack than doing it at the village hall – that way if he needs some space he can sneak off upstairs without any fuss.

'Of course,' Pat replies, picking up her clipboard again and the pencil that's tucked in her apron pocket. 'What are you thinking?'

What do you eat at wakes? I think back to the ones I have been to – grandparents, distant relatives and one old school friend who died suddenly a few years ago.

'Sandwiches?'

'Sandwiches, for sure. Any particular kind?'

I try to imagine what my in-laws would prefer. But it feels impossible to decide – whatever I pick I feel like it will probably be wrong. I never did seem to be able to get it right with them.

'How about I get in supplies for a mix?' Pat says, a kind smile on her face. 'You'll need plenty of mayo, I'd think. Some tuna maybe?'

I nod gratefully.

'That sounds perfect. And drink. There should be drink.'

That is the one thing I know my father-in-law would approve of. Would insist on, in fact.

'Of course. It will all be fine, love,' Pat says, reaching out and touching my hand. 'You're doing a great job. That husband's lucky to have you. We were all so happy when he managed to persuade you to stay, you know.'

It's something she's told me many times over the years but it still makes me smile. I feel the lucky one really. When I first came here I was a teenager with no real plans and no real future. I found a new home and a family that might be small at its core, but which includes in its wider circle all one hundred and eleven islanders plus fifty sheep, twenty highland cattle and the gulls on my own stretch of beach.

Pat and I discuss a few more details and then say goodbye. Outside, clouds are starting to roll over the sky, blocking the sun. The weather is so changeable here, just one of the many things I've had to grow used to over time. I've come to enjoy the unpredictability though – it means you never know what kind of day you're going to get. Keeps you on your toes. As I pause outside the shop, watching the grey roll in over the sea like a blanket, I think about my parents-in-law.

The truth is, I feel a bit of a fraud planning all of this for them. If it was one of my own parents, heaven forbid, I'd be grief-stricken, devastated. But I'd be sure of what they'd want. White lilies, Joni Mitchell and a tasteful reception in her favourite hotel in Edinburgh for Mum. Elvis, a ban on wearing black, and a small family gathering to scatter the ashes over his favourite rose bushes in the garden for Dad. Now, I feel lost, guessing at details and feeling guilty for not feeling sadder. They were Jack's parents and Molly's grandparents. But what I feel is not as straightforward as grief. If I feel any grief at all it is for Jack and the complexity of what I know he is going through right now, even if he doesn't tell it to me in words. And for Molly, who has lost her grandparents and is experiencing her first taste of death. I desperately want to get everything right. If I choose the right sandwiches and the right music and flowers, perhaps it will make up for the part of me that is pleased that they are gone. Now, Jack is free. I just wish that he could feel it.

As I head to the car, I decide to pop in on Jean on the way back. I know Emma has already been over today, but I'd like to see her myself. I spot her sitting in a deckchair outside her house, a wide-brimmed sun hat tilted over her face and a cup of tea resting at her feet in the grass.

'Alice!' she says with a smile. 'Do you know how many butterflies I've seen so far this morning?'

There's an empty deckchair beside her, usually occupied by her husband Christopher, but he must be inside or out on his daily walk. She motions for me to sit down and I sink into the chair.

'I don't know, how many?'

'Eleven! Although who knows, I may just have seen the same one eleven times …'

She laughs, the sound as bright as the morning sun.

'How are you feeling?' I ask her.

'So, you're here to ask me boring questions too? I thought you were here to watch the butterflies with me.'

She glances across at me with a grin and I remember when we first became friends. We'd known each other since I arrived on the island, but it was when Molly started at the school that we became closer. Molly loved her. Jean was patient and thoughtful with the children but also didn't hold back from sharing a laugh with the parents. I remember us visiting the school before Molly was due to start and Jean showing us both around, although really the visit was just for my benefit, Jack knowing the school well.

Jean pointed out artwork drying on the tables.

'And this one is particularly interesting. Mushrooms in the forest, you see.' She held up a child's drawing so phallic-looking that Jack and I burst into laughter. Jean joined in.

'God bless them, but it is so hard not to laugh sometimes.'

'How do you manage it?'

'I have a little office at the back of the building. I put classical music on loud and do my laughing in there.'

Jack found it a little strange at first that I was becoming friends with his old teacher. It took him a while to get used to calling her Jean, not Mrs Brown. And I suppose there is an age difference between us, just like there is between me and my friends Brenda and Morag too. But it doesn't seem to matter somehow. That's one of the things that living here has taught me. With so few people here, you learn not to be fussy about the age or background of prospective friends. A friend is a friend.

'Twelve!' I cry, pointing ahead of us at a cabbage white that flutters by the garden fence.

We sit together for a while in the sunshine, counting the butterflies.

'I think I need a little sleep now, do you mind?'

'Not at all,' I reply. 'See you soon.'

We hug goodbye and I try not to think about how thin she has become. Instead, I think about the butterflies.

I head back to the farm, stopping at Brenda's to leave inside her porch a slice of Emma's cake and a note welcoming her and her new addition to her household home. She's due back from the mainland today with her new puppy. Hopefully I'll see them at the harbour later but I can imagine she might be quite popular – although there are plenty of dogs on the island, it's been a while since we had a puppy. I imagine she'll be mobbed. Hopefully it might distract somewhat from our own little reunion. Well, for Jack and Lorna it will be a reunion. For the rest of us it will be hello.

When I pull up back at the farm I spot Molly and Olive on the beach. I scan the fields for Jack but he's nowhere to be seen. To my surprise I find him in the living room, sitting on the sofa, head bowed over something clutched in his hand. He looks up as I step inside but doesn't stir. As I sit down next to him I glance at what he's holding. It's a photograph. Two children stand on a beach – it looks like the one by the school.

They are standing close together and I recognise the little boy as Jack. He has freckles on his nose which have long since disappeared but are visible on our daughter's cheeks, and a broad smile on his face. His head is tilted, looking up at an older girl I've never seen before. Her red hair tangles in the wind and she looks at the camera with a serious expression.

'She looks like you,' I say softly.

'Do you think?' he asks, looking up for a moment. 'I never really saw it.'

I nod, bringing my hand carefully towards the photograph.

'You have the same eyes, and around the mouth too, look.'

He peers again at the photo and I join him, wanting to reach into the past and give that sweet, eager little boy a hug. But despite the pain I know my husband is in now, there's something about the girl in the photo that makes me want to reach out to her too. She looks so very sad.

'How are you feeling about later?' I ask. He sighs and places the photo down on his lap.

'I don't know. Part of me can't wait to see her again. But part of me … God, it's been so long. And even before she left, we'd drifted apart. We weren't close like you and your sisters.'

I think of the email from Shona earlier and the catch-up I will have with both her and Caitlin soon. We might be separated by miles and sea and I may miss them even after all this time but we've never really been apart, not truly. I've always felt connected to them. I can't imagine what both Jack and Lorna must feel, how they've managed all these years being out of touch. So many times, I've suggested to Jack that he call or write to her. I know it hurt him when she left like she did. She has reached out a few times over the years, sending the odd Christmas card and a note to let us know that Ella had been born. But Jack has never replied, or at least not as far as I'm aware. It must be painful for him to have been left like that, but in my mind despite it all she is still family. And having had Jack's parents as my in-laws ... Well, I can't help but think Lorna had her reasons for leaving. I think I may have wanted to get as far away as possible if they'd been my parents.

My mind is drawn back to the plans for the upcoming funeral. Whatever I might have felt about Catherine and Maurice as individuals, they were Jack's parents, which made them part of my family too. For better or for worse. That's why organising the funeral matters so much to me.

Watching my husband now, I wonder how I will greet Lorna later today. He has missed her so much, I know. Perhaps I should be angry. But I can't help but think that she has missed out too. Jack still has this island, the place where he grew up. He has our community, our friends, a network. Did Lorna find that in London? I hope for her and Ella that she did. But it can't have been easy to leave everything and everyone she knew when she was really just still a girl. I look again at the photo of her as a child. She must have been so unhappy, to run away like that and never look back. But maybe if I do my best to open my arms to her on this visit I will finally find the answers I've guessed at over the years, and she will come back to Jack, to us all. And perhaps he will have the chance to have at least something of the relationship I have with my sisters.

'I'm sure she's missed you too, you know.'

He doesn't reply. He tucks the photo inside the pages

of a book beside him. I glance at the title; it's *Finn Family Moomintroll*, the book he used to read to Molly as a younger child. Then he pushes it back into the shelves behind the sofa and the volume disappears among the disordered jumble of all our other books.

CHAPTER 7

LORNA

I'm alone in the ferry café. I can see Ella through the window, chatting to Brenda on the decking and playing with Puff the puppy. She pauses every now and then to take photographs. The young couple who were in the waiting room with us earlier stand at the front of the boat, arms around one another. The wind lifts the woman's blonde hair and throws it back in a tangled mane. She tilts her head back and laughs.

Ella wanted to spend the journey outside so she could watch the island approaching. I told her I needed a coffee and would prefer to sit inside. My Americano sits untouched in front of me.

I still feel bad for how I reacted when I heard Ella speaking to the woman who introduced herself as Brenda. As soon as she said she was from the island something inside me just froze.

Did she know my parents? Does she know my brother? Does she know about *me* and if she does, what does she believe? My parents always had their version of what happened in our family, and it was never the same as mine. I saw a flicker of a pause when Brenda heard my name and I'm sure it's because it was familiar.

If I close my eyes I can picture the mainland retreating behind us, the horizon humped with mountains. I imagine the dark ridgeline of the island in the distance. When I open my eyes, I focus on the mug held between my hands. Carefully, I examine the packets of sauces on the table. Ketchup. Mayonnaise. Brown sauce. There are twenty-four paper napkins stuffed into a holder beside them. I know because I counted. And then there's the emergency procedure sign to read on the wall, familiarising myself with the location of the lifejackets. But however hard I try to distract myself, I can't stop thinking about the island.

I've tried hard to forget the day I left. But I can still remember it as clearly as if I'm watching it on a film. I packed late at night, fitting as much as I could into my parents' suitcase, the suitcase I'd taken from the under-stairs cupboard. We rarely used that cupboard, mostly it was filled with boxes of Christmas decorations. But I was still terrified that my parents would notice the case was missing.

That night I stuffed the filled case under my bed and stared up at the ceiling. After a fitful sleep I got up before Jack and my parents were awake and dragged the suitcase out of the house and down the lane and along the road to Sarah's, just like we'd planned. She met me there, still in her pyjamas, and took my suitcase inside. Then I ran all the way home again arriving just as the sun was rising, my pyjama bottoms damp from the wet grass. I still can't quite believe I managed to make it back without anyone noticing I'd gone. I don't know what would have happened if they had.

That morning, I had breakfast with my family in silence. My hands were shaking but I hid them under the table. I kept glancing at the clock, at Jack, at my parents.

'Is it OK if I go to Sarah's for a bit?'

I tried to sound casual. But this was the moment when my whole plan could have fallen apart. Because they might very easily have said no. They often did. 'You spend too much time with that girl,' my father always used to say. He liked knowing where I was, how long I'd be gone if I did leave the house and who I'd be spending time with. But for once he didn't object.

'Fine,' said my father, 'but be back for lunch.'

My stomach danced with relief and nerves. I washed my breakfast things quickly in the sink. *I'm really doing it*, I remember thinking. *I'm really going to leave.*

Jack was still finishing his breakfast when I left.

'I'll see you later.'

I held his eye for just a second longer than I'd meant to. I couldn't help it. I've always wondered whether that's what made him realise something was wrong. Whether that's why he came to the jetty after I'd collected my suitcase from Sarah's house and we'd walked together to the harbour, sticking to the forest and the path away from the main road so no one would see us. But my brother arrived too late to stop me. Sarah and I had already said a tearful goodbye and I had boarded the boat.

70

The ferry was just pulling away when I spotted Jack running down the jetty, joining Sarah who was waving with one hand and rubbing her eyes with the other. He didn't say anything. Instead he stood next to Sarah and opened his mouth in a wordless cry. I remember staring at him, our eyes meeting. I couldn't look away. I watched him until the boat was far out to sea and I couldn't see him anymore. Until I couldn't see the jetty, or the shapes of the buildings on the island.

The ferry hasn't slowed yet but I can feel it in my stomach. We're nearly there. I leave my undrunk coffee on the table and step outside.

The cool air rushes against my face, filling my ears with the sound of the waves and my mouth with the taste of salt and engine smoke. I walk around the side of the ferry until I'm standing at the front, facing out to sea.

And there it is. The Isle of Kip, rising out from the grey-green water. Or most of it at least. A mist has descended and obscures the top half of the island. As the ferry draws nearer, rocks along the shore emerge out of the haze, making me think of the shipwrecks I read about as a child. I can only make out a vague shape of the island behind. The view is unsettling. It feels as though, having been away from it so long, the island is choosing to hide its face from me. The shadow of the mountain suddenly pierces through the mist. Its familiar shape stirs something deep inside. I realise I'm holding tightly onto the railing, gripping so hard that my knuckles are white. Now I'm actually outside I can't take my eyes away from the view in front of me. Gulls and cormorants fly ahead of the boat as though guiding it in towards the shore. There is a brightening and a sudden parting in the mist like curtains drawing open. And then the harbour becomes visible, the long stone jetty edging out into the sea and protecting the secluded bay where several sailing boats rise and fall on the rippling water. Behind it are the cluster of buildings that make up the village. As we draw closer I can make out the shape of the old pub, The Lookout, the school and the village hall, all built from the same familiar dark-grey stone. To the right of the harbour is a long beach dotted with dark patches of seaweed and rocks.

There is movement in the water ahead by the harbour. The sleek head of a seal breaks the surface, so very dog-like as it pokes its nose out of the water before diving below again.

'There you are, Mum!'

Ella is at my side, her cheeks pink and her hair even curlier from the sea wind. Her face is bright with a wide smile. She links her arm through mine.

'Look, Mum, a seal!' she cries, spotting the silken shape in the water. I can't help but smile at her enthusiasm; seals were such a regular sighting in my childhood that they grew dully familiar, but now I try to look again through Ella's eyes, noting the whiskers and the bright, inquisitive eyes.

'If you're lucky you might see dolphins on this trip too,' I tell her and she lets out an eager squeak.

We stay side by side as the ferry edges nearer and the island grows larger in front of us.

By now the jetty is close. There are cars lined up, some waiting to board the ferry, others waiting to greet passengers. Is my brother's car down there? Will he even be here to meet us or has he stayed at home? I know that Ella passed on the details of our ferry to Molly, but that doesn't mean that he will definitely be here. I feel moisture on my cheeks and brush my face quickly. I don't want Ella to notice that tears have escaped my eyes without my permission. If Jack is here, what shall I say when I see him? I wish suddenly that I had more time. Time to figure out what I'm going to say to him. But also to prepare myself for how I will feel. I haven't seen my brother in twenty-two years. And yet I still don't feel ready.

Water churns below us as the ferry pulls up to the jetty. A crowd has gathered among the cars. We aren't close enough yet for me to make out faces but I can tell immediately that they are islanders. Their clothes give them away. The sun may be breaking through the clouds, but the islanders are wearing wellies in an array of shades from forest green to yellow, all faded and splattered with mud.

Directly below, a man in a navy jumper embroidered with the ferry logo catches a rope thrown down from the boat. He ties it quickly. A shaggy Old English sheepdog leaps at his feet, barking at the boat.

I hear a tiny whimper and turn. Brenda is standing beside Ella, Puff the puppy held tightly in her arms.

'Oh, don't you worry,' she says to the shivering, whining puppy, 'Rex is a big softie, despite what he likes to tell you with that bark of his.'

The words seem to quieten the puppy.

'Time to go down,' says Brenda, turning for the steps that lead into the belly of the boat.

We collect our bags from a crate at the back of the boat and wait as the cars and post van drive off and up the concrete slope. Once the vehicles have disembarked we follow. Water laps up over the ferry ramp. I watch as the young couple jump over the water and onto dry land, their hands linked tightly together. Brenda stomps through the seawater. I hadn't noticed that she was wearing wellies. I suddenly feel foolish for not thinking through this part of the journey. Ella and I are both in lightweight trainers. We watch the water, waiting for it to draw back.

'Now!' shouts Ella. We run forwards, dragging our suitcases off the ramp and onto the shore just as the wave laps behind us, getting the underbellies of our suitcases wet but luckily nothing more. A length of seaweed wraps itself round one of the wheels of my suitcase. I give it a shake.

As we walk up the ramp my eyes move rapidly along the jetty. A crowd has gathered around Brenda and the puppy. Nearby, the young couple meet and shake hands with a young woman who leads them away to her car. The jetty is alive with movement and noise. But among all the movement my eyes are drawn to the man who stands completely still beside an old green hatchback splattered with mud, arms crossed in front of his chest. Two figures stand beside him, a tall, smiling woman in a denim boiler suit and a bright red silk scarf, her dark hair worn in a long plait and a girl who is slim like her mother but with a round face and grey eyes. She is dressed in denim shorts, blue wellies and a T-shirt printed with the slogan 'Save the Sea'. I watch as Ella dashes towards this girl, the pair of them squealing and launching themselves into a hug.

I stand frozen still, looking at the man beside them. He

watches me with his pebble-grey eyes, his eyebrows scrunched in a frown. My heart stretches against the constraint of my rib-cage. His face might be slightly lined, his hair peppered with grey and short, the curls of our childhood gone. But I recognise him straight away. Of course I do. He's my little brother.

CHAPTER 8

ALICE

They look so alike, my niece and my sister-in-law. The same wild auburn hair, milky skin and petite frame. Except Ella has nut-brown eyes. Lorna's are my husband's exactly.

Lorna and Jack stare at each other, neither one moving. I want to nudge my husband forwards but instead I turn first to my niece, unable to hold myself back any longer. She and Molly have just stepped apart from a tight embrace and I reach for Ella's shoulders.

'Let me look at you.'

She blushes as I run my eyes over her, taking her in. I remember when I met my other niece and nephews for the first time. I fell instantly in love with those little babies that my sisters had so magnificently created. Looking at Ella I feel a strange mix of emotions. Jack shares genes with this girl. Other than Molly and her future children, this is likely to be the only child I'll ever meet who does. I hug her tightly.

'Well aren't you gorgeous,' I tell her as we step apart. Her cheeks burn even brighter but she smiles, hiding slightly behind a curl of hair that falls in front of her face.

'Sorry,' I say now, turning towards Lorna instead. 'I'm Alice, it's so nice to finally meet you.'

She looks somewhat stunned as I pull her into a hug too. I just can't help it. This is Jack's sister. At first, she feels stiff against me but then she relaxes and hugs me back.

'It's really nice to meet you too.'

The jetty has cleared now, returning locals and arriving visitors heading to The Lookout or out across the island. It's just the five of us and the two suitcases. I throw a look at Jack, urging him to say something. But he is still leaning against the car, arms folded. Lorna stares at him too, her expression pained. *Come on! Either of you, say something!*

My sister-in law turns back to me.

'Thanks so much for meeting us, it's really kind of you. Is there any chance you'd be able to drop us at the B&B, or shall we try and get a taxi? If there's still a taxi on the island that is.'

There is still a taxi, a beat-up old Volvo driven by Pat Campbell's husband Bob and used mostly in the summer by tourists. But there'll be no need to use his services today. I feel my own cheeks warming now.

'Oh, I hope you don't mind, but when Molly told us you'd booked the B&B we called up and cancelled. You're family. You're staying with us.'

Lorna's expression tells me it might have been a mistake.

77

'Oh,' is all she can manage. Ella, meanwhile, is beaming, her arm linked through my daughter's. At least those two look happy. It makes my heart swell to see them together.

Seeing Lorna's worried expression again though I glance at Jack, suddenly nervous. Perhaps this was all a bad idea.

'That's right isn't it, Jack?'

In silence, he turns towards the car.

'Come on, let's go,' he says quietly. I smile nervously at Lorna.

'Let me help you with your bag.'

Together, we load the cases into the boot. I try to take in more details about my sister-in-law. She wears slim-fitting jeans, trainers and a sporty-looking top. Her face is free from much make-up apart from a light coating of mascara. Her physique makes me think of regular exercise although she doesn't strike me somehow as someone who is particularly interested in her appearance: her look is practical and simple. She is four years older than Jack and there are the beginnings of lines between her eyebrows and around her mouth. Despite her tired, serious expression she is beautiful, her hair and her face striking. I can't stop thinking of Jack as I look at her though – I keep noticing other touches of him. The small but ever so slightly protruding ears which she frequently tucks her hair behind. A very slight dimple in her chin that my husband shares and that I've rested my finger on countless times, feeling the soft dip of his skin.

'Here, you go in the front,' I say, opening the door to her. But she's already climbing in the back after Molly and Ella.

'That's OK, I'll go in the back with the girls.'

As Jack starts the car the girls thankfully fill the air with their excited chatter.

'And the cabins were so small but so cute,' Ella tells Molly.

Lorna and Jack are both quiet as we drive. I glance in the rear-view mirror, listening to my niece and daughter talking and watching Lorna as she stares out the window.

There's a crowd gathered outside The Lookout and they turn in our direction as we drive by. I know that everyone who once knew Lorna is keen to see her again and that my friends are eager to meet Ella and my husband's sister. But I see the flicker in Lorna's eye as she sees the islanders looking this way. It must be nerve-racking to feel so watched, even if I know that everyone (or at least most people anyway) mean nothing by it. I can certainly relate to feeling incredibly visible here on the island. All newcomers are and it was no different for me when I arrived as a volunteer. When Jack and I started getting closer, the interest became more intense. People questioned me about what I planned to do after my gap year, whether I planned on coming back, or staying even. Looking back, I think they just felt protective of Jack as one of their own. I remember Pat Campbell singling me out in the village shop one day not long before I was due to return to the mainland and telling me she didn't think she'd ever seen Jack Irvine looking so happy. It totally threw me. I still hadn't decided what to do. I had a place at university waiting for me. And even though I didn't particularly care about the course I'd chosen, studying was the path both my sisters had taken before me and I thought it would be mine as well. When I finally left and headed home to the mainland I felt the strength of the islanders' disappointment, their disapproval even. But when I realised the mistake I'd made and eventually returned, I experienced the full warmth of their welcome too.

The car winds its way along the road that cuts through the island. I try to see my home through Lorna's eyes, taking it all in for the first time since she was a girl. The wind turbines in the field behind the village are new but otherwise not much about the landscape must have changed since she was here. A few new houses, but the hills and the mountain are the same. The mist has fully cleared now and the sky is blue patched with clouds. The grassy moorland is blanketed here and there in heather, rippling from lilac to mauve to deep pink. Sheep graze among the grass and the heather. Every now and then the road rises in a hump and the sea becomes suddenly visible, flashing brightly beneath the sun. The ferry pulls away from the harbour now and heads out into open water. Does Lorna wish she was on that boat?

We pass by the church, a small white building topped with a cross. In a few days we will all return there for the funeral. As we head alongside the edge of the forest a track veers off the main road and I watch Lorna's eyes following that route towards the house where she grew up. She blinks quickly and our eyes meet in the mirror. I want to say something but Jack is still staring ahead in stony silence so instead I attempt a reassuring smile. We share a look for a moment and then she turns away again.

'Oh, that must be Brenda's house!' Ella says suddenly, pointing towards the blue house on the hill, the walls pale duck egg and the doors and wooden shutters bright cobalt.

'You know Brenda?' I ask my niece, turning around in my seat so I'm facing her.

She nods enthusiastically.

'We met on the ferry. She showed me her new puppy Puff.'

'Oh!' chips in Molly, 'I'm so jealous! Mum said we had to wait to see him because we were picking you up, but that we could maybe go and visit later. Can we, Mum? I'll see if Olive wants to come with us.'

At the mention of Olive I remember suddenly that my friend Sarah and Lorna used to be best friends when they were children. Sarah has told me that much, but otherwise never speaks about Lorna, and however much I've wanted to ask her questions about my sister-in-law I've held back. Now, their daughters will be meeting and perhaps will become friends themselves. I think back to the yoga class a week ago when I told the group that Lorna and Ella would be visiting for the funeral. Sarah stiffened at the news, her expression troubled. After the other women left she lingered behind and sensing that she wanted to talk I walked down to the beach with her, silent until we reached the sand and sat down beside one another. Facing out to sea seemed to make it easier to talk and everything came spilling out in a tumble of words and tears. She told me about the day Lorna left and how she waited every day after that for word of where she had gone or how she was doing but heard nothing.

'I waited for years,' she confessed as I shuffled closer and wrapped an arm around her shoulders. 'Sometimes I thought something terrible might have happened to her. But then other times I thought that maybe she'd found such wonderful new friends wherever she'd gone that she'd just forgotten about me.'

Remembering Sarah's tears, I glance again at my sister-in-law, feeling torn between a sense of loyalty to my friend who spent so long feeling abandoned and has been such a great support to me over the years, and a yearning to establish a connection with this woman who is Jack's last living relative. I picture again the large, bustling family of my imagination, our farmhouse full of voices and footsteps.

'If Ella wants to,' I reply after a moment's pause. 'And if Lorna is OK with it too, of course.'

'I do, I do!' says Ella. 'Can I, Mum?'

She turns to her mother who nods, sending Ella and Molly into another burst of conversation, this time about the new puppy.

'Brenda is a friend of mine,' I explain to Lorna. 'She moved to the island just before I did. We've been friends ever since I arrived. She's Molly's godmother.'

'She's *my* friend too,' Molly adds pointedly. That's one of the things I love about this place. There are only so many children of a similar age so my daughter has grown up counting younger children, older children and adults as her friends. It's given her a confidence that I hope will stand her in good stead when she eventually leaves the island, which I know in my heart she must surely do but which I try my best not to think about.

'How many of the islanders would you say are newcomers these days?' Lorna asks.

So she's talking at last, thank goodness. I launch enthusiastically into my answer.

'Hmm … I guess I'd say about twenty or thirty per cent are indigenous like Jack, folks who grew up here and perhaps have families going back quite a way who did too. Then the rest are newcomers like me. And a good thing too really. We need the young families moving to the island, otherwise the community would struggle to survive. That's what happened on Caora Island, wasn't it, Jack?'

He says nothing in reply. My enthusiasm dips as I think of Caora and what happened there.

'I'm sure you know the story,' I add to Lorna.

'I do, it was something of legend when we were growing up.'

I remember Jack telling me for the first time about the island off the northern coast that was inhabited until a few decades ago. His parents had relatives who used to live there and his mother showed Molly photos once. Over time though, the tiny community declined. Families left for a new life on the mainland or nearby larger islands, growing tired of the relentless wind and rain and the hardships of crofting life on such a small island. When the school closed, all the remaining families were forced to leave. For a while there were just a few of the oldest islanders left, desperately trying to cling on to their homes and survive on the near-empty island. But it became too difficult. The last few residents were evacuated by boat to the mainland in the 1930s.

Over time, the abandoned crofts on Caora fell to ruins and the wildlife took over. Now it's only visited every now and then by a shepherd who travels by boat to manage the sheep, or by visiting ornithologists or wildlife researchers. The island rising out of the sea is a constant reminder to everyone on Kip of the precarious nature of our own life here. A sign of what could happen if the community fell apart. The thought sends a chill through me. It could so easily happen again. And not as some distant concept in the future, but soon. I try my best to shake off the thought but it's still there in the back of my mind, a fear I can't quite bring myself to voice out loud.

The car slows and we turn off the road onto our track, the red and white sign that I painted years ago hanging from the gate and reading 'Hilly Farm' in tall letters.

'Home sweet home!' I say, trying to make my voice cheerful as we bump down the dirt road that runs alongside the beach and then climbs the hill to the farmhouse.

'The Halifaxes' old place,' says Lorna, surprise in her voice. 'I didn't realise that's where you lived. It looks completely different.'

When Lorna has written to Jack over the years, brief Christmas cards and notes I've seen him read then put away in a drawer, the envelopes bore only his name and the name of the island. It was enough to find him. I forget that she mustn't know about the farm.

'Yes, that's it, do you remember it then?'

'We used to play here as children,' she says, her voice soft and a distant look in her eye. 'It was something of a ruin back then though. I think the Halifaxes struggled to manage it just the two of them, despite the best efforts of the other islanders to help out. It looks beautiful now.'

We pull up outside the house, the white walls glowing in the sunshine, the sheep grazing in the front field and the cows lying in the grass in the pasture at the back. Our ancient Land

Rover is parked beside the farmhouse, a quadbike stationed in the mud just behind it. I can't help but wonder how different our home looks to Lorna and Ella's back in London.

'Thank you,' I reply, a sense of pride flushing through me even if really the farm looks how it does now thanks mostly to Jack. I open the car door. 'Jack, do you want to help with the …'

But before I can finish the sentence he is gone, striding away towards the polytunnel. I know this is hard for him, but is he really going to leave me by myself? I feel like a fool left standing alone by the car. I don't want Lorna and Ella to notice though so I force a smile and help them with their bags.

'Let me show you my room!' Molly says excitedly, grabbing Ella's arm. 'You're sharing with me.'

The two girls disappear quickly inside, carrying Ella's suitcase between them. Their footsteps race up the stairs and the sound of their laughter follows them into the house.

I'm left alone beside Lorna, who looks just as awkward as I suddenly feel. My confidence from earlier ebbs away. How are she and Jack ever going to resolve the issues of their past if they won't even speak to one another, and if he is just going to disappear into the fields, turning his back as he so often does on his problems? I grew up in a household where we shouted at one another, opinions voiced at the top of our lungs, but where we confided in one another too. I don't know how to deal with silence. It's been one of the greatest challenges in my marriage, coping with those moments when Jack withdraws from me, disappearing to a place where I can't follow. I look at Lorna, thinking about all the things to do with his past and this woman that my husband has never told me. A pain hits me in the chest.

'Well, I guess it's just us for now then,' I say, trying to sound cheerful. 'Once Jack's with his vegetables he could be out till dinner time. Why don't we have a cup of tea?'

'OK,' she replies hesitantly, her eyes nervous. 'Thank you, Alice.'

And I turn and lead this anxious stranger, my husband's brother and my daughter's aunt, into my home.

CHAPTER 9

LORNA

I'm glad I thought to pack my running trainers. I added them to my suitcase at the last minute, along with a few pairs of leggings and a couple of sports bras. The soft sand is hard going and I pause for a moment, looking back at my footprints marking a trail along the beach. It's early evening but the sun is still high in the sky. I remember the summer days here that stretch endlessly long, longer than down south in London. But in exchange for the summers you have winters where the sun rises only for a few hours, even then often obscured by heavy cloud and driving rain.

The girls have headed out to visit the puppy at Brenda's and Alice is inside preparing dinner. She's been so kind and welcoming, but it makes me feel uncomfortable. Surely, I don't deserve it, and I can tell at once that she is very different from me – open and warm where I can be closed without always meaning to be. I can see exactly what drew my brother to her. She is tall and elegant and brims with cheer even though I can tell she's nervous too despite her smiles.

I haven't seen Jack again since we arrived, except for at a distance coming in and out of the polytunnel or striding across the fields to tend to the animals. I still can't get over the shock of seeing him as a grown man. In my mind he's always been frozen at fourteen, the age he was when I left. When I've thought of him that's how I've remembered him, or sometimes as a younger child. Seeing him for the first time as I stepped off the ferry nearly broke my heart. In his silently staring face I saw everything I've missed and everything that's been lost between us.

I offered to help Alice with the cooking but was secretly relieved when she refused. That's when I suggested I might go for a run. Stretch my legs after a day of travelling. But really, I just needed to get out of the house.

A small flock of elegant wading birds gather on the shore-line. I don't know what kind of bird exactly. I once knew all the names but not anymore. Ahead the sea stretches into the distance, broken only by the shape of a few fishing boats dotted along the horizon.

It felt so surreal to step inside the home of my brother and his family. The house has a slightly dishevelled but homely quality to it, the floors bare except for a few faded rugs thrown over chipped floorboards. At the front of the house is a large living room, the far wall entirely covered with bookshelves. On the other side is a wood-burning stove with somewhat threadbare sofas gathered around it, made cosier by piles of rugs and cushions draped and scattered on top. The walls in the house are busy with pictures and photographs, mostly of Molly at various ages. I know it shouldn't have been a surprise but I wasn't quite prepared for how like my brother my niece is. She has the freckles that he had as a child but which disappeared when he became a teenager, and the same grey eyes. But she has her mother's lightness and openness, welcoming Ella as though they've known each other for years. I suppose they *have* grown to know each other through all those messages they've sent back and forth online.

Upstairs, Alice showed me Molly's room. I paused for longer in that room, trying to absorb every detail I could to build a picture of the girl whose childhood I've missed. A pinboard on one wall is covered in environmental posters displaying messages like 'Say no to plastic', 'Reduce, re-use, recycle' and 'There is no Planet B'. Reading them, I felt a surge of guilt. In London, I've got used to buying a plastic water bottle on the move and although I recycle, I do it only half-heartedly. Among the posters are photographs too. Molly standing on the beach with Jack and Alice on either side, arms wrapped around her, the three of them grinning into the camera. Another image of Molly next to a girl with dark hair and green eyes who I immediately guessed must be Sarah's daughter Olive, the resemblance was so striking. It felt like seeing my friend as a child all over again.

The room I'm staying in faces the sea. It's small but bright, painted a soft lemon, with a comfortable-looking double bed, a wardrobe and a pine desk. On top of the desk I spotted a jug filled with wildflowers.

'From the garden,' Alice said.

My favourite part of the house is the kitchen. Alice and I retreated there after the tour, Ella and Molly already having raced down to the beach. It's the kind of kitchen I'd like if we had more space. In the middle of the room there's a long oak table, a bench along one side and a mismatched assortment of chairs on the other. Behind the table is a large black Rayburn, pots and pans strung from hooks above it. There's a wooden drying rack suspended from a pulley system above too, covered today in an assortment of socks and T-shirts that Alice apologised for while making us tea.

I told her not to worry, of course. In fact, I think the mess made the room even more endearing, giving it a relaxed feeling. But it was exactly this feeling that made me at the same time so uncomfortable. Everywhere I looked, there were signs of my brother and his family's life together. The socks in various sizes drying above the Rayburn. A family photograph stuck to the fridge above a shopping list and a series of scribbled notes. While Alice poured the tea, I sneaked a glance at the notes.

'Helping at the brewery, back this afternoon. Love always, Dad x'

'Happy birthday darling. Another year lovelier. Always, Jack x'

'Headed out for the early ferry, didn't want to wake you both. See you on Saturday. Love you to the moon and back. Dad x'

Who was the person who wrote these notes? Surely not the cold, silent man who met me at the jetty? Suddenly the warmth of the kitchen had felt constricting. I thought I'd be in an impersonal B&B, the choice that felt appropriate when I booked it. Being invited to stay here with them has made me feel such a mix of emotions. I'm greedy to see every detail of my brother's life, and staying here means being closer to my brother, my niece and my sister-in-law. But as Alice asked polite questions about the journey it felt all at once too much and I wished myself outside, able to be alone.

Now, I take a deep breath of salty air, hands on my hips. And I start to run again. After the beach I join the track, side-stepping dips and rocks until I reach the smoother main road. It's good to be moving, my heart pounding and my breath quickening.

But once I'm on the road I feel more conspicuous than I ever do in London. The road is visible from most of the houses on this side of the island. As I head along it in the opposite direction from the harbour and the village, I spot a few people in their gardens. They look up as I pass, but I try to keep running with my head down. Word must have spread that I'm back for the funeral. It's a small island after all and I felt that buzz of curiosity when we arrived at the harbour. What must these islanders be saying about me behind closed doors? *She left and never came back. She hasn't even met her own niece. She's a mainlander now, thinks she's too good for this island. She didn't even come back when her parents were dying.*

I speed up, pumping my arms and focusing on springing forcefully from the ground. The faster I run, the less I'm able to think. When I run fast like this I feel more in my body than in my mind. For the brief moment I'm able to sustain this speed, I am free. When I start struggling to breathe I slow again to a jog.

I can't stop thinking about the house I've just escaped. Alice is doing her best to make me feel welcome, I can tell. But will Jack ever speak to me? Let alone forgive me for my absence throughout the years. I may have sent letters that never received replies, but I could have tried harder. I picture him earlier, standing at the jetty waiting for me, his eyes exactly the same as I remember even if the rest of his face has changed over time. While I was in the kitchen with Alice I couldn't help glancing out the window, trying to catch just a glimpse of Jack. After so long apart even a small sight of him is something. But every time I did see him – his figure stooped slightly as he crossed one of the fields – my heart ached. I wanted to reach out towards him, just like I did when we sat in the car earlier and I thought how easy it would be to lean forwards and place my hand on his shoulder, feeling the warmth of the living breathing him, not just a memory. I knew that coming back here would be hard. But even then, I'm surprised by the extent of this pain. My stomach churns, my eyes sting, a weight presses against my temples. I feel pain in my entire body. I run faster.

The sound of barking makes me turn and look across to a whitewashed crofter's cottage set back slightly from the lane. An Old English sheepdog jumps up and down behind the picket fence that encircles the cottage garden. Rex, I remember Brenda calling him.

'Hi there!' comes a deep voice. A man balances on a ladder propped up against the cottage. There's a toolbox beneath him on the grass and he leans against the roof tiles, seemingly fixing a drainpipe that hangs from the wall. An elderly couple peer out of one of the cottage windows, watching the ladder and the man on it closely.

The man wears jeans and a grey fisherman's jumper and I recognise him suddenly as the man who was working in the harbour when we arrived earlier. At the same time, I realise that my face is damp. I haven't been crying, have I? But as I wipe my cheeks with one hand there they are, droplets streaking my face. Mortified at the thought of this stranger seeing me cry, I turn away from the cottage and keep running, head down.

'I'm Mallachy, nice to meet you too,' comes the same deep voice behind me. But I don't turn back.

I don't stop running until the road becomes another track, sloping up towards the northern edge of the island. The white beacon of the old lighthouse is visible on the edge of the cliff, its tumbling-down old lighthouse-keeper's cottage squatting beside it. The cottage has been abandoned for years, ever since the light became automated decades ago. I head towards it now, up through the field that is thick with grass and wildflowers.

Eventually, I make it to the lighthouse. God, I remember this view. Below, grey cliffs crash downwards into the sea, the water here a completely different beast to the calm, lapping waves at the beach by Hilly Farm. Here the water rages, beating against rocks far below, rising in huge foam-tipped waves and falling again with a vicious slapping sound. Further out to sea looms the mountainous silhouette of Caora Island, now home only to birds and the island's namesake – sheep.

I reach for my phone in the back pocket of my leggings. Thankfully I've got signal for the first time since arriving on the island. I immediately type a message to Cheryl.

Safely arrived on the island. Ella and Molly have clicked straight away. Things harder with my brother. His wife is lovely though. Missing you xx

Cheryl's reply comes a few seconds later.

We miss you too!! (We = me and Frankie, who is making a mess of his tea right now.)

Accompanying the text is a picture of Cheryl crouched next to Frankie's highchair. His face is smeared in sweet potato. Both Frankie and Cheryl are grinning.

I look up from my phone and out to sea. Cheryl and Frankie might be right there on my phone screen, but standing here on the edge of the cliff I find it hard to even picture London. It's just so far removed from the view in front of me – the cliffs and the waves and the abandoned island in the distance. For a terrifying second it feels almost as though London and the life I've made for myself there don't exist at all. I'm a child again, stuck on this island surrounded by sea, unable to leave.

This lighthouse is one of the places I used to come when I was young and needed to get away from home. Sometimes Sarah and I would come together, climbing the hill and breaking in to the lighthouse keeper's cottage. We'd eat sandwiches on the cliff edge or in the dilapidated front room of the cottage if it was raining. But often I'd come here alone. I remember I came here the night of the fire. My hair still smelt of smoke and my eyes stung with ash and tears. That night I stood closer to the cliff edge than I ever had before, even though it was dark and the wind was strong. I think back to the dream I had on the train. The smell of smoke was so strong in my mind, even after all this time.

My phone pings. Another message from Cheryl.

Just give it time. Thinking of you xxx

Can any amount of time really make up for twenty-two years apart? The thought of everything I've missed in my brother's life hits me with the force of the waves beating the cliffs below me. I missed his eighteenth birthday. I missed his twenty-first. When he first met Alice. When he moved from the house we grew up in to Hilly Farm, turning it back into a farm again after all the years it stood derelict. His wedding. The birth of Molly. His first grey hair.

The choice I made all those years ago was rooted in self-preservation. At the time, leaving everything behind felt like the only option. The only way to create my own life. The only way to survive. But as I stand beside the lighthouse, knowing it's nearly time to head back to the farm and dreading seeing my brother again and yet yearning for it in equal measures, I am torn apart by the choice that I once made. Facing the sea, I open my mouth wide and roar. Everything empties out of my

lungs in a wild cry. It's a wail that I have probably been sup-
ressing for years. There's no space for this kind of emotion in
London. In our small flat Ella and I hear each other's slightest
movements. And our home is surrounded on all sides by other
unknown lives.

I howl until my throat hurts. But the wind is stronger and
snatches my voice away. Below, the waves crash relentlessly
against the cliffs.

CHAPTER 10

ALICE

'I was hoping you'd come to the village with me today.'

I'm alone with Lorna again, Jack out in the fields and Molly and Ella heading out earlier this morning on bicycles to meet Olive. Ella seems to have slipped easily into their friendship and I must admit I'm relieved. I knew how excited Molly was to meet her cousin but I also know how close she and Olive are; I didn't want Ella to feel left out. But they've quickly formed a tight group. It's lovely to see them together. Their closeness and contentment highlight the tensions in the rest of the house though. Dinner last night was strained to say the least. I couldn't bear the silence between Jack and Lorna, so filled it with chatter, knowing as I spoke that I must have seemed ridiculous but not able to stop myself. Lorna went to bed not long after the girls. She must have been tired from the journey but I'm sure she also felt overwhelmed.

'You could try a bit harder,' I said to Jack once we were on our own, careful not to let my words carry.

'So could she,' he snapped back.

'Do you realise how childish you sound?'

He shrugged, turning away from me. But he looked so pained that I softened.

'I'm sorry, I know this must be tough. How are you feeling about it all?'

But he only shook his head in reply, his whole body tense, his expression closed off.

'Please, talk to me, Jack.'

But he turned away again, disappearing up to our bedroom. As I lay next to him in bed later it felt as though he wasn't even there with me but was elsewhere. *Come back to me*, I whispered to myself as I faced his back, his body curled up in a tight ball. This morning I feel exhausted, deflated. But also determined to try to make the best of things. What else can I do?

Lorna looks up from the kitchen table, the remnants of breakfast still scattered around us and a mug of coffee held to her lips.

'A group of us promised we'd help change the displays and tidy up at the school,' I tell her. 'I know going to a school is probably the last thing you want having just broken up yourself, but we could use the extra pair of hands. And we'll be going to The Lookout after for lunch, so it's not just work.'

She smiles slightly.

'So, the old pub is still going strong then? I used to work there as a teenager.'

'Very much so,' I reply. I try to picture her behind the bar of the pub as a young woman. Jack told me once that his sister dyed her hair purple when she was a teenager and that their parents were furious. I can't imagine caring in the slightest about the colour of Molly's hair.

'I'd love to come with you,' she says. 'Thanks for asking me.'

'Great!'

I start clearing up but she stands up quickly, reaching for the plates.

'Please, let me help you.'

We clear up together and once we've finished I catch her glancing out the window at the sea.

'It will be good to see my old school again,' she says, not moving her eyes away from the view. 'I was happy there.'

As she says it I so want to tell her that the fate of the school is currently uncertain. I want to unburden myself of my worries about it all. But it wouldn't be fair to put all that on her, especially when she's going through so much already. It's not her problem. She turns back to me.

'I love your style,' she says. 'Those flowers are beautiful.'

I look down briefly in surprise. I'm in denim cut-offs today and one of my favourite shirts that has floral embroidery along the collar and sleeves. I also wove a few fresh flowers into my hair this morning, wanting to cheer myself up.

'Oh, thank you! I know it's probably silly to get dressed up given most of my day is spent feeding animals and helping Jack outside, but it makes me happy. And it makes a change from my yoga gear.'

'When did you become a yoga instructor?' she asks, her grey eyes watching me thoughtfully. It still gives me a jolt to see my

99

husband's eyes staring back at me from her face. We started talking about our jobs last night, one of the few seemingly 'safe' topics of conversation I could think of. When she told me she was a deputy head of a school I struggled to hide the emotions that rushed through me. I so nearly told her everything then about what's been going on, but I forced myself to hold back.

'I started practising it as a teenager,' I tell her, leaning against the kitchen counter and facing her where she stands by the sink with her back now to the window. 'But I became interested in teaching after Molly was born. I guess I wanted something for myself.'

My cheeks suddenly colour, as I realise how it must sound.

'Of course, I adore being a mum.'

But she's smiling, nodding in understanding and I feel a swell of relief.

'No, I totally understand. I remember leaving Ella with a childminder when I was doing my teacher training. It broke my heart to leave her with a stranger but I also loved those hours where I was using my brain and felt like something other than just a mother.'

An image suddenly enters my mind of Lorna alone with a new baby and I can't help but feel a rush of sadness. I've never once had to leave Molly with a stranger. I had Jack, my friends and a whole island to help. Did I take it for granted? Perhaps I still do.

'Exactly,' I say, shaking off the image. 'I help out as much as I can on the farm and I do enjoy it, but it's Jack's passion really. I went and did my training when Molly was old enough for me to leave her, and then I've been teaching classes here ever since.'

I catch sight suddenly of the clock above the fridge.

'We should probably get going.'

I take the Land Rover today; I remember when I first drove it Jack laughed at how many times I stalled it, but now I prefer it to our car. I like its height and the view it gives of the island, and how it doesn't mind being roughly driven up and down our heavily pitted track that leads to the main island road. It still feels strange to have Lorna so close beside me, just inches apart, but also somehow comforting too. I guess I hadn't quite realised how lonely last night's exchange with Jack has made me feel. And with the girls out and about too ... Well, it's nice to have the company. As I drive she asks me about my background.

'I grew up just outside Edinburgh, the youngest of three girls. You can guess what that was like for my old man.'

Lorna laughs and the sound almost makes me jump. I glance across at her. She looks completely different when she laughs. Her grey eyes sparkle, her lips spread into a warm smile. For a moment she seems relaxed, at ease with herself. She reminds me of my eldest sister Caitlin, who has always worn her body with such casual grace that it infuriated me when I was an awkward teenager with too-long limbs and knobbly knees. Lorna looks nothing like the woman who sat at my kitchen table last night, pushing food nervously across her plate and glancing at my husband every time he spoke, a look something like fear on her face.

'I can imagine,' she replies. 'What are your sisters like?'

'Oh, they're brilliant. They're both incredibly clever, they always have been. Caitlin's the eldest and is a doctor. She could have been a surgeon but she chose to be a GP. They desperately needed GPs when she graduated – she's now a partner at a practice outside Edinburgh. Shona teaches a branch of mathematics at Aberdeen University that I've never totally understood.'

When I was young I wanted nothing more than to be like my sisters. But where words and numbers and scientific equations seemed to come naturally to them, often I felt like my brain had a puncture. As hard as I tried at school I was only ever average at most, praised for 'trying my best' but never excelling at any subject. As my sisters won school awards and then gained places at top universities I looked on from behind, admiring and envying them in equal measures.

'I was always more outdoorsy,' I tell Lorna. 'I loved animals, hiking, swimming. I first came to this island on my gap year after my A-levels, as a WWOOFer.'

Lorna laughs again and I find myself grinning too, hearing for myself the absurdity of the word.

'A what?'

The sun slants in through the Land Rover windows, warming my arm that rests on the windowsill, the other on the wheel.

'It means a volunteer. There's an organisation called World Wide Opportunities on Organic Farms – they offer placements. I helped out here at Hilly Farm just after Mr and Mrs Halifax had died.'

'I've been meaning to ask – how did you and Jack come to own the farm?'

'It's an amazing story really.'

And it so easily could have gone a different way, my life and Jack's taking different paths.

'Not having any children or close family they left the house and farm to the islanders as a community, to do with it what they thought was best. It was decided they wanted to make it into an organic farm, so they needed loads of volunteers – I saw an advert about it and decided to come and help. That's when I first met Jack. He was just nineteen then, a year older than me, but was one of the islanders most involved in the project. He'd be down here every day, working the land, rebuilding the fallen-down walls. He didn't know that much about farming back then but there were plenty of older farming families on the island to help him and to show us all what to do.'

'What was he like when you met him?'

Her voice is so eager that it makes my throat tighten. She has missed so much. They both have. Last night's argument melts away for a moment as I picture Jack as he was when I met him and how quickly he got under my skin and into my heart.

'Oh, he was so scruffy! All messy curls and muddy hands. He seemed a little rude at first, but I soon worked out he was just shy. And he was so focused on his work, I think he didn't necessarily want any distractions. But I eventually managed to distract him.'

I don't tell her that as soon as I met him I saw the sadness in him too. Just from looking at him as a teenager you could tell that he carried a pain under the surface, a sense of loss.

'Oh, I bet he didn't mind,' says Lorna, a smile in her voice. 'So that's when you two got together then?'

'Not exactly.' It wasn't as easy as that. 'My placement on the farm ended. By that point I was head over heels in love with

Jack, and with the island too. But I had a place at university lined up. I wanted to do something academic like my sisters, even though I'd only just scraped the grades to get into my third-choice university. I came back home to my parents and got a job at a café until it was time to move and start my course. But I was miserable. I missed Jack and the farm. We wrote letters, we phoned each other, but it wasn't the same as being together. I think my parents could tell how unhappy I was, because one day they sat me down and told me that I didn't have to follow the same path as my sisters, that they loved me for me and they would be proud of me whatever I did.'

Lorna turns quickly away, but before she does I catch a glimpse at her face. She looks as though she is trying not to cry. What really went on behind closed doors when she and Jack were children? I have my own view about what it must have been like to grow up in that house, and it's not a good one. Jack's father was an alcoholic, although no one in the family ever used that word out loud. It was a quietly accepted part of who he was, that lingering smell of spirits as well as the anger that always seemed to simmer beneath his dark grey eyes. I tried my best with his mother, but there was a coldness and a quiet to her that made her difficult to connect with. My in-laws may have lived just minutes away from us but I never really felt comfortable leaving Molly alone with them even if I couldn't have told you in words exactly why – it was more a lingering sense of unease, a feeling of wanting to hold my daughter tightly to me whenever we were around them.

But despite all that I've never managed to get Jack to truly open up about his past. I know that Lorna leaving the island hurt him deeply, but I've always thought she must have been hurting too in order to have left like that. Glancing across at her now I can't help but feel a flash of disloyalty to my husband to admit it so readily, but I like her. There's a quiet strength to her as well as a softness, the two sitting side by side like opposites so often do in us humans.

'That must have been such a relief,' she says, her face and voice composed again.

Thinking back about it now, it was such a strange time. I did feel so grateful to have that support from my parents, but it took me a while to let go of the plans I had made and to decide to return to the island. By choosing not to go to university I was turning my back on the life I thought I'd wanted and the life I'd seen my sisters achieve. In my heart I knew I would never quite be like them. I had to make my own way. But even now I still have moments when I wish I'd got a degree, if only to prove to myself that I could.

'Eventually I made up my mind to go back to the island,' I tell Lorna. 'I rented an old crofter's cottage at first, but saw Jack all the time. And then there was a big meeting at the village hall where Jack was told the islanders had decided to give him Hilly Farm, if he wanted it. Of anyone on the island, he'd put in the most work and seemed to love the place the most. We moved there together, got married and had Molly a couple of years later. And we've been here ever since.'

Looking back, I was so young when Jack and I got married. I may be the youngest in my family but my sisters were still studying when I had Molly. It was nerve-racking, falling pregnant so far away from my family. But in the end, I was overwhelmed with support from islanders I hadn't known for long but who had quickly become firm friends.

'Wow, that's such a wonderful story,' says Lorna.

'I think so. I've been very lucky. But what about you? Is Ella's dad still on the scene? If you don't mind me asking.'

She hesitates for a moment. Perhaps I should have worked harder to dampen my curiosity about her. But after a moment's pause she answers.

'Rob and I were only together a few years. We met in a bar where we both used to work. But he left when he found out I was pregnant.'

'Oh god, I'm sorry.'

She stares out the window again, her gaze distant, her hand rising to tuck her hair behind her ear.

'He didn't want children, it turned out. When he knew I was pregnant he said if we were to stay together it would have to be just the two of us.'

'That must have been so tough.'

She tilts her head a fraction, her eyebrows slightly furrowed.

'It was and it wasn't. For me it wasn't a difficult choice. A baby wasn't part of my plan. I had no money, worked anti-social hours ... But I knew straight away I wanted to find a way to make it work. I guess I felt like I'd been drifting for years, from job to job, from bedsit to bedsit. When I found out about Ella I felt this need to, I don't know, put down roots.'

I try to focus on driving, not knowing what to say. All I can picture is a tiny, dirty bedsit and a young woman pregnant and alone. Whatever pain she may have caused my husband through her estrangement from him, she is first and foremost a woman and a mother. And while she was there, making that awful choice alone, we were here. Jack and I could have helped her.

'So, you raised her on your own?'

'I'll admit, looking after a newborn by myself was harder than I ever imagined when I was pregnant. I was probably quite naïve to begin with. I won't say it was easy.'

I remember those weeks after Molly was born when I felt in total disarray. My body swam with hormones, weeping with joy one moment and sobbing with fear and exhaustion the next. Those long, long nights of desperately snatched moments of sleep. But I had Jack, who woke with me in the night. I had my island friends who dropped round lasagnes and cakes or just popped over to do the washing-up and let me take a shower. My sisters came to stay too, one then the other to spread out the visits. My mum was only ever a phone call away and I remember dialling her number countless times at all hours, questioning her on whether I was doing it right. Poor Caitlin has been on speed dial over the years as well, patiently answering every medical query however small. Who did Lorna have? As I sneak a glance at her I think I know the answer without asking. It's there on her face, in the hard set of her eyebrows, the way she holds herself. This is someone who is used to relying on herself and herself alone.

'Have he and Ella ever met?'

'No. I've thought about trying to make it happen. He's sent me money here and there over the years but he's always been completely disinterested in actually meeting her. I've wondered in the past whether it's been the right choice, not pushing harder for them to have some sort of relationship. Maybe I could have made him change his mind and orchestrated some sort of meeting. But I guess I just feel like no father has to be better than an indifferent one. She deserves so much more than that.'

I catch a glimpse of my wedding ring on my hand that grips the steering wheel, the gold band winking in the light. I suddenly want to hold my husband tightly. Whatever tensions there might be between us right now, he is and always has been a wonderful father. I think back to that day when we first met our daughter, me exhausted in the hospital bed and him exhausted from standing by my side all night. When the nurse helped me hand her to him the tears started to spill down his face. His voice was full of wonder as he looked at her pink scrunched face and said, 'Look what we made.'

'And has there been anyone else?' I ask her, trying to control the shake in my voice. 'Of course, you don't have to tell me that either!'

Again, a brief hesitation before she answers.

'No, not really. I suppose after Rob I decided things would be more straightforward if it were just Ella and me. I've dated, but nothing serious, no one Ella's ever met. It just feels simpler that way.'

Simpler, perhaps, but lonely, I can imagine.

'You and Ella must be so close.'

Her voice brightens now.

'We are. She's a pretty great girl.'

I see the school approaching ahead and slow the car, pulling up on the grass opposite the building. Turning off the engine, I rest both hands on the steering wheel.

'It's so nice to meet her. And you too.'

We pause for a moment, both smiling at one another but clearly a little awkward. She fiddles with her hair again and I shuffle slightly in my seat. It feels so strange – at the start of this car journey she felt like a stranger, but now … I feel like I'm at school again and have just made a new friend. That rush of affection and interest but also the sense of being not quite totally comfortable with one another yet.

'Right, we're here,' I say eventually. 'Shall we go in?'

With a look something like determination on her face, she nods.

CHAPTER 11

LORNA

The school has barely changed. There's new play equipment in the playground but otherwise it's the same old stone building with a gabled roof and tall windows. Beyond the playground walls stretch fields and moor, sheep grazing freely. Just across the road is the beach. Looking at my old school, I can't help but think how drastically different it is to the school I teach at on the Isle of Dogs. Here, it is a mountain that towers above us, not office blocks. Instead of the sound of passing planes and the rumble of traffic there is quiet, except for the hiss of the sea and the occasional bleat of a sheep.

There might be different pictures on the walls but inside the school is exactly how I remembered it too. I am five years old again, sitting next to Sarah in the classroom and nodding along as she declared we were going to be best friends. I can feel the soft fabric of my school jumper and the rough carpet beneath my hands as we sit on the floor for story time. And then I am nine and Jack is joining the school for the first time. I hold his hand and show him where to hang his coat and where to put his satchel. And when he is too shy to put his hand up to answer a question I nudge him in the ribs until he reluctantly lifts it into the air. When he gets it right and his small face fills with a smile I feel as though I could burst with pride.

Inside it smells like pencils, carpet and boiled potatoes.

'Come on, it sounds like they're down here.'

I follow Alice into the one classroom where a small crowd has gathered. I recognise Brenda immediately by her pink hair and by Puff the puppy, who is curled up on a beanbag in the corner. Also in the room are a woman in her late twenties who wears tie-dye harem pants and has a baby held in a carrier at her chest, another young woman in red dungarees with a short afro half-covered by a matching red scarf, a woman a similar age to me with striking cropped hair, a tall woman who looks in her fifties or so, with an ash blonde bob, and an elderly woman wearing a bright green raincoat even though we're inside and it's dry out. There's another woman too but she's facing away from me, busy arranging books on a low shelf.

My eyes follow the sound of the hammering to the corner where a man stands on a ladder, fixing a display board to the wall. My cheeks glow with embarrassment. It's the man I saw at the harbour when we first arrived, the same man I totally ignored on my run yesterday. I look at him more closely this time. He has slightly ruffled greyish brown hair, a broad face, a long straight nose and a dark beard flecked with grey and a hint of red. He is busy working, his sleeves rolled up revealing tanned, muscular arms.

'Let me introduce you to everyone,' says Alice.

Brenda takes me by surprise by pulling me into a rough hug. 'Your daughter is charming.'

I feel myself beaming.

'Thank you, I certainly think so.'

The young woman in the tie-dye is called Tess and her wife, in the red dungarees, is Joy. Their baby is Harry and gives a gurgle as I lean down to stroke his soft cheek.

'He's gorgeous. How old is he?'

'Nine months,' replies Tess, bouncing him slightly in his carrier. 'He's teething at the moment so you might not find him so gorgeous when he's screaming later.' She smiles as she says it though and lifts one of his tiny hands to her face to kiss it.

'I'm Kerstin,' says the tall woman in her fifties, stretching out her hand and shaking mine firmly. 'I hear you live on the Isle of Dogs. I used to work in Canary Wharf.'

'Oh really?' It jars to hear the name of that place here, to even think of all those glass and steel office blocks when standing in this quiet school on this quiet island.

'Gave nearly half my life to the place. Then woke up one day and realised I absolutely despised my job and everyone I worked with. Sold everything and moved up here. Best decision of my life.'

'And her skills have come in handy,' says Alice warmly, smiling at Kerstin. 'She's the island's resident finance whizz. She helps half the island with their accounts.'

The old woman in the green raincoat is introduced as Morag.

'I moved here ten years ago. My children wanted to put me away in one of those awful "homes".' She mimes air quotations. 'So I got as far away as possible! Ha! They didn't like it at first, but they come and visit every now and then.'

I can't help but smile, liking Morag already, just like I do all the other women I've met. Morag lives in a cottage by the harbour, she tells me, where she keeps a list of everyone who comes and goes from the ferry.

'I saw you and your lass arrive yesterday. You were on the same boat as those *tourists*.'

She pulls a face at the word 'tourists'. I'm a little relieved that she doesn't consider Ella and me tourists too. But if we're not tourists, then what are we?

Just then I spot the woman standing beside Morag and before Alice can introduce us too she's stepping towards me.

'It's been so long!' says the woman, who I suddenly realise used to be one of my classmates.

'I didn't recognise you, Emma! Your hair looks amazing.' It's dyed white blonde and is elfin short, very different to the long, mousy hair she had when we were young. It suits her.

'I think the last time I saw you must have been that picnic in the woods, do you remember?' she asks me.

Abruptly the memory comes back to me. It was the spring before my last year on the island and the first sunny day we'd had in weeks. The Easter holidays had just started so my friends were back home from school. I told my parents I had a shift at The Lookout but really, I went straight to Sarah's house; from there a group of us older children walked to the forest carrying blankets and picnic baskets, food made by parents and bottles of beer pilfered from fridges. I came empty-handed but no one seemed to mind. That afternoon we island children ate and drank and listened to music on someone's portable cassette player and played games and celebrated the first day of spring. I got tipsy for the first time in my life, on beer and sunshine. Someone had managed to procure a joint and although I didn't smoke it myself I remember breathing in the sweet smelling air and laughing at how dopey it made my friends. I kept listening out for someone approaching through the woods though – I'd told Jack our plans and invited him to join us.

'You can make something up to tell Mum and Dad,' I said to him. 'Tell them you're studying with a friend, it's what I do.'

Jack was so quiet as a child and spent most of his time at home studying, or at church with our parents. Where I had painting and Sarah and my secret life of reading magazines and watching TV my parents wouldn't approve of at her house, I always worried about what Jack had. When he was very little he joined Sarah and me sometimes, at the beach or at her grandparents' house, but the older he grew the more he seemed to withdraw inside himself and into the role our parents prescribed for us both. I hoped he would decide to come to the picnic that day though. But he never did. Instead, when I arrived home, cheeks flushed from hours spent out-doors, my parents were waiting for me in the kitchen, Jack sitting between them, his face down. As soon as I walked in I knew that my parents knew that I'd lied, and I knew how they'd found out.

'How dare you!' my father shouted. 'Lying to us, running

around the island like a spoilt brat, giving our neighbours every reason to think what they already do – that you're out of control.'

But I was full of beer and confidence so for once I shouted back.

'You're one to talk! You're the one who's out of control. You're always drunk, you're probably drunk right now.'

My mother drew in her breath sharply then, covering her mouth with her hand. Jack looked up, his eyes wide. I could see my father tensing, the rage turning his face bright red. But I didn't stop.

'But I don't care. Soon I'll be leaving for university and when I'm gone I won't have to listen to what you say. I'll do whatever I like. And I'm going to make something of my life, whatever you think of me. I'm going to have a better life than yours. And there's nothing you can do to stop me.'

In that moment it felt good to shout, to watch the shocked faces of my family. I felt, just for a second, invincible. I paid for those words in the end though.

I try to shake off the memory as Emma tells me about how she left the island for some time too but returned ten years ago and ended up marrying Duncan, one of the Macleod brothers who was a few years above us at school. They have two children together, she tells me, Flo and Clover, five and seven.

'Oh, you married a Macleod!' I say with a smile. It was always a running joke about who would end up with Duncan or his brother George, the brothers being two of the only older boys on the island.

'And you already know Jean,' Alice says, turning to the

woman who had been leaning over the bookshelf but is now facing us, looking at me intently. 'Jean Brown.'

Alice places a hand affectionately on the older woman's arm. And I am suddenly looking into the softly wrinkled face of a woman I once knew well. The woman's features broaden into a wide smile.

'Lorna Irvine. I never forget a former student. Especially such a good student!'

When I was a child here Jean Brown must have been in her mid-thirties. She was the school's headteacher, a gentle, curious woman who took us on nature walks around the island, who made paper decorations for the classrooms at Christmas and who always smelt like lavender. Once, she confessed that her cottage was full of moths and so she hung lavender sachets in every room to ward them away, a natural remedy that she preferred to harsher chemicals. I've always remembered that and use lavender in my own flat now for the same reason. Now, her eyes are traced with lines and faint dark circles and her face is thinner. But her smile is the same.

'Mrs Brown! Sorry, I mean Jean. It's so good to see you.'

She pulls me into a hug too, but one that is much gentler than Brenda's. I blink quickly. I never thought that I would see my old teacher again. After we've stepped apart Alice gives Jean a strong hug too. Once they've released one another I glance at Alice and can't help but notice that her smile from earlier has slipped, her eyes slightly red. But then a loud cough comes from the corner of the room and she turns towards the sound, her smile returning.

'And not forgetting, of course, the island's assistant harbour master, our resident handyman extraordinaire, and Jack's good friend, Mr Mallachy Moore.'

'We've actually met already,' I say.

'Well, nearly,' he replies with a wry smile. He reaches a hand down from the ladder. 'I'm Mallachy.'

'Lorna,' I say as I shake his hand.

'And I'm sorry about yesterday,' I add, quietly this time. 'I didn't mean to be rude.'

I can tell the other women are watching us, but they say nothing.

Mallachy shrugs, but there's a hint of a smile at the corners of his mouth. He turns back and resumes hammering.

'Right, let's get to work,' Alice says after a brief pause.

As we work, the women chat. They are cheerful and warm and have an ease with one another that I can't help but envy. Because although they draw me into conversation, asking me about the journey here and my home back in London, I still feel uncomfortable. They're being kind and making an effort to include me, explaining old jokes every now and then or asking my opinion on a certain display. But I know I'm not part of this group. They have the familiarity of people who have known one another a long time. I sometimes forget that this is normal: having a group of friends. I tell myself that I'm fine with just Cheryl and Ella. I've neglected seeking other connections because I've been busy with my job and with raising my daughter and because of all the complications getting close to other people can bring. But in moments like this I see a glimpse of another kind of life.

In spite of my awkwardness I find myself joining in with

their laughter at a particularly terrifying but very sweet child's drawing of a human with a head the size of a planet, very pointed teeth and tiny legs. Smiling with them as Harry is let loose to crawl on the floor and pulls down some books Jean has just organised and she tries but fails to look cross.

I take in a few more details of the classroom around me as we tidy. One of my jobs is to replace an old display, swapping children's posters about the environment with photos taken on a school trip at the end of term – the whole school having a picnic halfway up the mountain. Even the youngest have made it up and beam into the camera, their cheeks pink with the fresh air. This place really couldn't be more different from my school back in London. Here, a photograph of every student is hung in a frame on the wall, making it look like a huge family portrait. The displays are all so creative and colourful. I sense the extra freedom Mrs Brown must have here and remember my own experiences of attending this school. We learnt the core subjects, of course, but a lot of our learning was centred around the island itself. The water cycle taught with the help of the mountain lochs and the rainy weather, art lessons where we would gather materials from the beach to draw, cooking lessons where an islander would come in and teach us a local speciality in the school's small kitchen.

After two hours of tidying and sorting, Jean tells us all we've done enough for the day and that it's time for lunch.

'Are you joining us at the pub, Mallachy?' Alice asks.

He starts packing up his tools.

'No, I'd better get back and give Rex his walk.'

I smile at him, glad the embarrassment of yesterday is

behind us. If I'm to repair my relationship with Jack during this trip it's probably not a good start to ignore and potentially offend one of his friends. And besides, he seems nice and it *was* rude to ignore him like I did.

I join the group of island women as they walk towards the old pub. But as we reach the door I hesitate.

'Scared?' comes Morag's voice beside me.

Very.

'Why would I be scared?'

She flashes me a look that only an old woman missing several teeth can manage.

'OK, maybe I'm a little nervous.'

'Aye, I'm not surprised. There are some awful bloody gossips on this island.'

I'm not sure whether to laugh or shudder. This was once where I worked, where I joined the other islanders in watching people coming and going and exchanging island news. But that was such a long time ago. I manage a tight smile in Morag's direction.

'But they all mean well,' she adds. 'Right, I'm bloody parched, I need a drink.'

Heads turn as we open the door, but thankfully the conversations continue. I scan the room, searching out faces I recognise. Is that Mary, one of the younger children who grew up with me on the island? And I'm sure that older couple look familiar. The woman catches my eye.

'So it is true. Lorna Irvine returns,' she says, stepping away from the bar and towards our group.

'Mrs Anderson,' I say, remembering just in time. She was

little Sophie and David's mother – twins several years below me at school. She and her husband were also my parents' closest friends; I remember seeing them and a group of other equally devout church-goers huddled with my parents near the minster after each service. I try to shake off the memory as I greet her.

'How nice to see you. How are Sophie and David?'

Alice gestures at me, then to a table in the corner where the other women are pulling up chairs. I nod and she joins them, leaving me alone with Mrs Anderson.

'Oh, they are very good, thank you. Sophie still lives here with her family, David is on the mainland but not far away, thank *goodness*. They've both been wonderful like that, I'd have been beside myself if they left the area.'

I look down at my hands.

'And I hear you have a daughter,' Mrs Anderson continues. 'Is she here with you on the island? I hope she's not a tearaway like you were – we don't want her corrupting our little ones!'

She laughs stiffly and I slip my hands into my pockets and dig my nails into my thighs.

'Awful about your parents, by the way,' chips in Mr Anderson, who has been standing by his wife's side. 'They were such good friends and wonderful supporters of the church.'

'Yes, they always did their bit to support the church,' I just about manage. 'Well, I'd better be getting back to my group now. Do pass on my best to Sophie and David.'

I turn and walk away before I have time to say anything else, anything I might regret. I'm shaking slightly, my body stiff.

At the table Morag is already most of the way through a dram of whisky. I sit down beside her.

'That wasn't so bad, was it?' she says. 'Painful but over quickly. Like killing a chicken.'

I've personally never killed a chicken so it's impossible to compare. But I still feel shaky from the conversation. How many other people on the island believe the stories my parents told and the façade of our life they worked so hard to create? And what Mrs Anderson said about Ella – well it was hard not to knock her drink out of her hand. My daughter and I may have our disagreements but she is so good really. I feel immensely proud of her.

Not that I was ever particularly bad. Yes, I dyed my hair purple and there was that one time my father caught me smoking at the bottom of the garden. The Macleod brothers bought a packet when they turned sixteen and shared them among the other kids who were around their age. I took one, curious to see what all the fuss was about. I didn't smoke it there and then, not wanting to embarrass myself in front of my friends if I started coughing and spluttering. Instead I waited for an afternoon when I knew my parents would be out, my father at The Lookout and my mother arranging flowers in the church for an upcoming baptism. I went down to the very bottom of the garden, near the forest, using matches borrowed from the fireplace to light the cigarette. Would smoking it make me feel like a grown-up? Would I suddenly feel cool, sophisticated? As soon as I inhaled I knew it was a mistake. I started coughing immediately. My father must have heard me, back from The Lookout unusually early (I have always suspected he got asked quietly to leave). He was clearly drunk when he reached me and was furious. I've never smoked since.

For years I thought I *was* bad because of the way my parents reacted to things like that one foolish, curious cigarette, and the words they used to describe me. 'Tearaway' 'trouble' 'out of control'. But was I really so bad? I think maybe I was just a teenager.

'Here, take a menu, Lorna,' says Alice, smiling gently and passing me a worn-looking laminated sheet. As I smile back at her I think back to our conversation earlier in the car. It was so unlike me to open up that much about the past, about Rob and what it was like to look after a baby entirely on my own. But there's something about Alice that makes her easy to talk to. She's warm and friendly, but I guess more than that she already knows the thing I try so hard to hide from others – the long estrangement from my family. I don't need to put my usual walls up with her. It surprises me how much of a relief that is.

The other women chat contentedly around me and I focus on the list of options on the menu. When I turn back I notice that Morag has fallen asleep in the chair beside me and is snoring softly.

We place our orders, the barman bringing us several packets of crisps to keep us going, on Alice's instruction.

'So, tell us what you do then, love?' asks Brenda, tearing open a packet of crisps and laying it on the table for everyone to share.

I can't help but glance in the direction of Jean, my old teacher.

'I'm deputy head at a primary school on the Isle of Dogs in East London, where I live.'

A brief silence. Is it just me, or are the other women looking at each other in a slightly strange way?

'A teacher?' Jean asks.

The others watch me carefully. Perhaps Jean told them about my ambitions to be an artist when I was younger. Are they surprised, like Sarah was, to hear that my dream didn't come true? If you'd told me as a child that I would end up as a teacher, not an artist, I would have been surprised too. But I was a child then. And children believe impossible things.

'Yes, I am. Are you still the headteacher here, Jean?'

I have to hold myself back from calling her 'Mrs Brown'.

That look again, passed quickly between the women around the table, and a pause. I'm sure I'm not imagining it.

'Yes, I am. Now, tell me about that daughter of yours.'

Oh, my favourite subject. I could talk for hours. I feel myself puffing up with pride as I tell them about Ella's good grades, her hobbies, her kindness.

When the food arrives everyone tucks in, chatting and joking. Morag is still asleep in the corner. Brenda wolfs down her sandwich and then takes Harry from Tess and Joy so they can eat as well. She bounces him on her knee and blows raspberries on his cheek. Throughout the meal Harry is passed around between the entire group. Is this what it might have been like if I'd had a group of women to chip in and help with Ella when she was a baby? I remember lying alone in the hospital after I'd given birth to her, while around me family members carrying balloons and teddy bears came to visit other new mothers on the ward. I watched them in silence, holding Ella awkwardly to my chest and struggling to get her to feed. In a bed across from mine I saw a grandmother hold her grandson for the first time, one arm scooping him up gently, the other resting on her daughter's shoulder. The daughter reached up from her bed and held her mother's hand.

'I get it now, Mum,' she said.

I'll always remember that. I cried all night when the visitors had left.

Then there was the neighbour in our flat in Whitechapel who also had a new baby and liked to complain to me whenever we bumped into each other in the stairwell about her parents who hadn't bought the exact pram she wanted, but a slightly different (better, I couldn't help but notice) model. And all those visits to the doctor when Ella had a temperature and I worked myself into a frenzy of panic, having no one around to calm me or rationalise my fears. It was all so much harder than I could ever have imagined when I was pregnant. But we did OK in the end. I hope I did OK, anyway.

'You must come to one of Alice's yoga classes while you're here,' says Kerstin. 'She's an excellent teacher.'

Alice blushes, self-consciously patting her braided hair with one hand.

'I'm not sure that's true. But it would be lovely if you wanted to join, Lorna. I teach official classes once a week but we often meet up between them too for unofficial classes.'

'By which she means sitting on our yoga mats and blethering,' says Brenda.

'Yes, we particularly enjoy the seated yoga poses,' chips in Joy, laughing.

'Corpse pose is my personal favourite,' adds Tess.

I join in with their laughter, feeling a warmth spread through my body. With all the thoughts and worries going through my head I didn't expect to switch off even for a moment, but it's nice just to smile with these women and ignore everything else for a while. Especially after Mrs Anderson's comments. It's good to be around kindness.

'That sounds great, thank you.'

I glance along the table and catch Jean's eye. It's so good to see her again. I smile but she returns her attention to Harry, who is now sitting in her lap playing with a set of car keys.

Outside, the harbour is busy with movement and noise. The ferry has pulled in at the jetty, cars disembarking and others waiting to board. The door of the pub opens and a stream of customers pours in. Some glance in our direction but most filter straight through to the bar, ordering drinks and chatting among themselves.

I turn back to the door. Suddenly Sarah is standing in the doorway, a suitcase behind her, her hair tied back with a bright yellow scarf. She smiles in our direction and waves. But as soon as she spots me her smile disappears. She hesitates and for a second, I do too. When we spoke on the train Sarah said she needed space and some time to think. These women are her friends, not mine, however welcome they've tried to make me feel.

'Thanks so much for inviting me to join you all but I think I should be getting back. Check on Ella ...'

I trail off, struggling to think of a proper excuse. As I stand up quickly the table rocks, jolting Morag awake.

'What's going on?' she croaks.

'Alice, I can walk back, you stay here.'

I say a brief goodbye to Alice and her friends, who all look a little surprised at my hasty departure but say goodbye warmly.

'See you at yoga soon.'

'And remember, Ella's welcome any time to come over and see Puff. You too – feel free to pop over for a cup of tea,' adds Brenda.

As I reach the door Sarah steps to one side, not meeting my eye. My throat grows tight as I slip past her. Outside, I lean against the pub wall for a moment. To my surprise, it has been a good day. I've enjoyed getting to know Alice a little and meeting her friends. But there's a comfort in being alone again too, taking deep breaths of cool sea air. Out here by myself I can't say the wrong thing or upset myself by seeing Sarah and remembering how close we once were. I know I should face up to things with her, just like I need to find a way to reach out to my brother and confront what happened in the past. But right now, it all feels too much. I turn away from the pub and begin walking quickly along the road, the sound of over-spilling laughter and conversation from the pub behind me filling my ears. Gradually the sounds grow quieter and then disappear altogether as I continue walking down the road alone.

CHAPTER 12

ALICE

It doesn't take long to find Lorna. She walks along the side of the road, head bent and taking long strides. I pull up beside her.

'Come on, get in!'

She looks up, surprise then worry on her face.

'I'm so sorry, I didn't mean to make you leave, I'm honestly fine walking.'

'It's OK, I needed to get back anyway. Things to do at the farm, as always!'

She hesitates and then opens the door.

'Thank you, Alice.'

The village recedes behind us, my friends left behind in the pub chatting to Sarah about her trip. Lorna and I sit in silence for a while. Outside the sea glitters with early afternoon light and the ferry pulls away from the harbour, churning waves in its wake. Lorna stares out the window, her hands moving rapidly in her lap. Perhaps I should turn the radio on or make some comment about the weather. I can't bear the silence. But she is the first to break it.

'Why are you being so kind to me, Alice?'

The question is blurted out suddenly, Lorna catching my eye and then looking straight ahead again, her cheeks bright red. The question catches me off guard. *Am* I being especially kind? I suppose I am choosing to welcome her more than others might in a similar situation, but it's also no more than the many kindnesses I've received myself from the islanders over the years.

'Sorry, I didn't mean to put you on the spot,' she adds, obviously noting my pause. 'It's just I've been thinking about it since I arrived. I can understand Jack not wanting to talk to me. But you've made me feel so welcome.'

I take another moment to reply, this time wanting to choose my words carefully rather than filling the spaces with my chatter.

'I've always said to Jack that you must have had your reasons for leaving and cutting contact,' I say eventually. 'That's a hard thing to do – no one would choose to do it if they didn't feel they had to.'

I hear her let out a breath and see her shoulders sinking slightly as though some tension has just been released.

'It's true,' she says quietly. 'It was the hardest thing I've ever done. But people don't always see it that way. I suppose it's why I never really tell anyone about my situation.'

Suddenly it starts to make sense to me why she seemed so

torn earlier with my friends, laughing and joining in with us one moment but tensing and withdrawing slightly the next. She appears to me now like someone who is not used to letting people close. I wonder how many people know the truth of what she's been through.

'To so many people the thought of being cut apart from your family seems totally inconceivable,' she adds.

I suppose to me it is too. I can't imagine ever losing touch with my sisters or my parents. I think it would feel like losing a limb. But Lorna isn't me.

'I guess people who think that are people who are lucky enough to have wholly happy families,' I reply. She looks at me closely, a question in her eyes, and I quickly continue. 'Don't get me wrong, I'm one of the lucky ones. I have great sisters, great parents. But I've had friends who haven't been so lucky. I guess that's why I could always understand why you did what you did.'

I focus on driving but can't help but notice her beside me, wiping her palms on her jeans.

'And besides, you're forgetting that your parents were my in-laws. I know what they were like.'

I think back to the comments my father-in-law would make when he watched the news about the people he didn't approve of, people who simply weren't like him. How my in-laws managed to influence all of my husband's major decisions, like where we got married and who came and where we spent our holidays. Since marrying Jack, I have never once spent Christmas away from the island. Whenever I argued for us to take up offers from my sisters to stay with them he always feigned needing to stay and keep up the farm, but I knew that really, he didn't want to deal with the consequences of going against his parents. Because they had stressed to him countless times how heartbroken they would be if he did, how we would ruin their Christmas. They were excellent manipulators. It still breaks my heart that my sisters eventually stopped inviting us.

That's why the preparations for the upcoming service have been so hard for me. How do you plan a funeral for people you never liked?

'Jack couldn't really see it,' I say, gripping the wheel tightly. 'He might not seem like it to you now, but most of the time he's so laid back he could fall over. He never stood up to them, he always did whatever they wanted but managed to convince himself he didn't *mind* following their wishes. But I saw it. I saw how controlling they could be. I could see how if you weren't as ... well as *malleable* as him growing up it would have been hard. Impossible even.'

I think back to those Christmases and the church wedding I don't think Jack really wanted either. What would have happened if he'd pushed back on them? Lorna lets out another sigh.

'When we were growing up, I tried to make him see that our family life wasn't ...' she pauses, clearly choosing her words carefully, '... normal. But I don't think Jack ever really recognised that. He managed to deal with things with a quiet sort of acceptance. I never could. I never blamed him for not wanting to stand up to them though. He was younger and was a shy, quiet child. And our parents encouraged him to stay that way. But it made things ... hard.'

'I can imagine,' I reply. 'His gentleness is one of the things I love the most about him. But honestly, it can be maddening sometimes. Let's just say he isn't a fan of conflict.'

She nods and I realise how refreshing it is to speak to this woman who grew up with my husband. She may not have seen him in years but she *knows* him in a way that perhaps no one else does. That's just the way with siblings. They are with you throughout those pivotal moments that shape you into the person you will eventually become. I don't think that thread can ever really be broken, not completely.

I listen with a greediness, eager to understand her past so that I might better understand my husband.

'There was a distance between us long before I left the island,' she says, 'Each time I dared to push back at our parents or suggested to Jack that he might do the same, he withdrew. And I began to doubt myself. If my brother couldn't see it, were things really as bad as they felt to me? Honestly, it made me feel like I was going crazy.'

I'm grateful for the sunshine as it falls through the windows and for the view of the sea and the mountains ahead. Otherwise I think I might feel as though I was falling into the past, or at least an imagination of the past conjured by Lorna's words. The Land Rover feels hot and stuffy and I roll down a window, enjoying the wind in my hair and on my face.

'They call it gaslighting these days,' I say. 'Jack has never told me that much about his childhood, but from the way his parents always talked to him, the way he behaved around them … Well, I've always wondered.'

I pull onto the verge for a moment to let another car pass.

It's Bob Campbell and I wave, then continue back onto the road. We pass by the church, the forest and the track leading back to the house where Lorna and Jack grew up and where Catherine and Maurice lived until they died.

'What were they like?' Lorna asks quietly. 'I mean, with you, what were they like? I've always wondered if they … I guess I wondered if they ever changed.'

I'm uncertain for a moment what she wants to hear. Would it be harder for her if I told her that they *had* changed? Would she regret the choice she made? And do people ever really change?

'I always found your father unnerving. He'd be so quiet one moment and then would explode the next. And there was the drinking of course. We all noticed it – I think the whole island must have known – but no one ever really said anything about it. It was just one of those quietly accepted things. Mad really.'

I shake my head. Were we wrong to allow him to stew in his drink and his anger? Could anyone have done anything to change things, to help him even?

'He wasn't always like that,' Lorna says. I raise an eyebrow, urging her to go on. 'I mean, he was never warm and fluffy, not at all. He was strict and always had a certain hardness to him. But then he had the accident at work and it was like overnight he became incredibly bitter.'

Jack told me that when he was very young his father worked in construction, helping build new houses on the island and travelling over to the mainland for jobs too. But there was some accident – a falling scaffold – and after that he never worked again. All his life he walked with a cane, but I could always tell that even that was a struggle. But whenever I tried to help, offering my arm or rising to get him something so he didn't have to he'd become so furious that in the end we all learnt to just leave him to it.

'I guess that must have been hard on him,' I suggest.

'I think it was. We lived off his disability allowance but mostly from money our mother inherited from her parents. I think it pained him to be so totally reliant on other people.'

I think back to when my father was made redundant from the accountancy firm where he'd worked for years. I was a teenager and still living at home. For several months my usually sunny father withdrew, spending all his time in the garden or sitting on the sofa watching daytime television. I'd rarely seen him in anything other than his work suit or his gardening overalls, but he started wearing pyjamas in the day, often still in them at dinner time. Then he got a new job and the suit and the smiles came back. But I'll never forget that time when he slipped and when darkness ventured into our home. I guess it was the first time I truly realised that my strong, jolly father was capable of falling.

'Wounded pride,' I say.

'I saw him crying once,' continues Lorna. 'Not long after the accident happened. He was in pain and I caught him weeping in the living room. He was absolutely furious when he spotted me. I don't think he ever forgave me for that – for seeing his weakness. He couldn't stand it.'

I can imagine.

'And what about your mother, what was she like when you were young?'

She tilts her head to one side, her forehead creased with thought.

'I think mostly she was afraid of our father. She never stood up to him, although I can understand why. I always wanted her to be stronger though, for Jack and me. She was our mother at the end of the day. But I understand it.'

I picture Catherine, her shoulders hunched as though she wanted to fold in on herself. But I think of Molly too and how I would do anything in the world to protect her. At least, I hope I would. Who can really know for sure what they'd do if things were different?

'Not much changed, then,' I say.

'I tried to get her to leave him, you know.'

'Really?'

She nods, running her hand through her hair.

'Many times. I even researched places off the island that we could rent, Mum, Jack and I. But she didn't want to go. She told me she loved him and we all just needed to try harder to make him happy.'

We sit in silence for a moment. For once, I don't know what to say.

'I tried to get Jack to leave too,' she says, her voice soft and quiet now. 'I told him I'd get a job and find us a flat and I'd look after him.'

'He didn't want to go?'

'No.'

How would our lives have been different if Jack did leave? We would never have met. Molly wouldn't exist. But would he have had a bigger, bolder kind of life? Would he have felt free?

Or was he always destined to stay on the island? I think of our friends, our community. And then I try to picture him in a tiny apartment in London with Lorna, traffic blaring outside their window, no sea, no sheep, no mountain. I can see why Lorna left. But I can also see why Jack stayed. I just can't picture him in a city; I think he would have hated it.

'I've always been so grateful that Jack is nothing like either of his parents,' I tell her.

Because he might pull back from me sometimes, disappearing into his own thoughts. But he never shouts. At first it was a shock for me after growing up with two very vocal sisters. But eventually his quietness became a relief. He is gentle and I am so grateful for that.

We've reached the farm now and I pull up outside the house and turn off the engine. Lorna's head is slightly bowed, her hair falling in front of her face.

'I know he's been giving you a hard time,' I say, turning to my sister-in-law, 'but he's a good man. He's a good husband, and a good father. I think he's just missed his sister.'

She lets out a small, animal-like sound.

'I've missed so much. Too much, I think.'

She turns and looks at me now, her grey eyes swimming. I can't help but feel sorry for her. I reach out a hand and squeeze her arm.

'You're here now.'

She nods her head, wiping her eyes.

'Thank you for being so kind to me. I'm so pleased to have finally met you. And I so want to make it right with him, Alice. I know there's nothing I can do about what's already happened and all the time that's passed. But I at least want to make things better. I really do.'

I turn my head towards the fields and she follows my gaze.

'Then tell him that,' I say in a soft voice. Slowly, she nods.

CHAPTER 13

LORNA

I find Jack in the polytunnel. His back is to me and he faces a wall of runner beans, their stalks clinging to bamboo stakes in the soil. He reaches carefully among the delicate plants and plucks off the beans, dropping them one by one into a large bowl. It's warm in the tunnel and the air smells sweet and earthy. I step forward in order to watch my brother more closely. But my shoe catches a stack of pots I hadn't noticed and sends them falling to the ground. Jack turns around quickly. For a second his face is open and poised for a smile, but then it shuts down again, his lips pressing tightly together. I suppose he was hoping for Alice or Molly, not me.

'Hello, Jack.'

He ignores me and turns back to the beans. Maybe I should leave. I could head back inside and find Ella and Molly and see what they're up to. I feel like I've barely seen Ella since we've arrived and it feels strange, given how much time we usually spend with one another. I could join Alice for a cup of tea in the warm kitchen. But Jack is in here and I desperately want to be with my brother. Even if it's hard.

I rearrange the fallen pots and step further into the poly-tunnel. With one hand I brush the leafy tops of the carrots in a bed beside me. I can picture them buried beneath the surface, grown from seeds by my brother, checked and watered and nurtured with care.

I never imagined that he would grow up to become a farmer. Jack never really had one particular career ambition when we were growing up. He went through phases of course, like all children. At first, he wanted to be an astronaut.

'You need to be a genius to be an astronaut,' I remember our father saying.

Then it was a football player.

'How many famous Scottish football players do you know?' was our father's response. The names Jack listed made no difference to his opinion. 'What kind of a job is that, kicking a ball for a living?'

I think that maybe he couldn't stand the thought of our dreams when his own career ended so early. Another person might have pushed us harder, wanting us to enjoy and achieve what he never could. But what happened to our father made him jaded, angry at the thought of others' success.

For a while, Jack wanted to be a train driver but like most other job options, that would mean leaving the island. And although we sometimes daydreamed together about sunny holidays or going backpacking together, deep down I felt sure that Jack would never leave it for good. For him, those day-dreams of ours always seemed like just that. But for me, they were so much more. The thought of leaving and getting away was the thing that drove me just as strongly as my need to draw and paint.

I think back to the pride I felt in the car earlier when Alice told me about Jack's dedication to the land here and how he learned about farming from the other islanders and through practice. I feel that pride again now, standing inside what feels like my brother's green kingdom. I watch his back as he continues along the line of runner beans. Just like when I first arrived, I imagine reaching over and placing a hand on his shoulder. It would be so easy. All I have to do is reach out my hand. And yet it also feels like the hardest thing in the world.

'I know you'd rather I weren't here. I know this is hard, on all of us, but I think we should talk.'

He says nothing. Outside, a sheep bleats. I jump slightly, the sound so different from the noises I'm used to hearing back at home. At what point in my life did the sound of sirens and traffic become more familiar and comfortable to me than the sound of sheep and the ocean?

'I'd really love it if we could spend some time together while I'm here.'

Jack lets out a sharp burst of air, something between a grunt and a sigh.

'I don't think there will be time for that. My life hasn't stopped just because you're here.'

Of course he is angry. I didn't expect anything else. But it still hurts. He places the bowl of beans on the floor and reaches for the hose. I hop out of the way just in time to avoid tripping as he pulls it towards the beds.

'I'm busy,' he continues. 'The farm keeps me busy, then there's arrangements for the funeral and I still need to tackle sorting out Mum and Dad's house and all their things and god only knows how long that's going to take me.'

'I can help.' As I say the words my skin grows hot. 'I can come with you and help sort the house.'

What will it be like to step inside the house we grew up in after all these years? To be among our parents' things, to see my old room again …

Jack waters the beds in silence. But then he turns off the hose, drops it onto the floor and turns around. Those grey eyes bore into me. It is almost too much to look at him. And yet I cannot look away.

'Fine,' he says. '*I* cared for them for years, *I* looked after them when they were dying. But fine, come and *help* at the house. I'll be going over there in a couple of days.'

Then he turns and walks away out of the polytunnel. I want to follow him and to apologise, for everything. I might have chosen to cut my parents from my life but I should have tried harder to keep in touch with him, even if it seemed at times impossible. I never meant for things to become such a mess. But for now, all I can do is lean against one of the vegetable beds and catch my breath, my brother's words sitting inside me like a stone lodged in my throat.

I stay in the polytunnel for a long time. Sometimes when Ella is out at the weekends I like to sit in her empty room. I perch carefully on the edge of her bed and look around, taking in the small details of her life and personality that remain behind even when she isn't there. Like how the shedded skin of a snake still holds the shape of the life that once flowed inside it. I'm always careful not to disturb anything or leave a sign that I was there. I don't want her to feel I've been snooping around. Because I don't think of it as snooping. It's just a way to feel close to my daughter. To breathe in the smells and sights of her at thirteen that I know are fleeting, having already lost those that clung to her at two, six, eight, twelve... I already knew loss before becoming a parent. Perhaps it prepared me well. Because among the joy that my daughter brings me are all the daily losses too. Those versions of her that will never exist again, the moments I can never get back.

Now, I pause among the rows of vegetables, taking in the sweet, green smell of hundreds of leaves and the dark dampness of freshly watered soil. These are my brother's smells. I will never get to know what he was like at eighteen, twenty-one, thirty. All I have is now. I might have been reluctant about returning to the island, held back by fear. But now I'm here I want to try to make things right.

As I sit I can't help but think about the conversation with Alice in the car just now. Thoughts of my parents that I've tried so hard to push away come flooding in. My father's rages and his breath that always smelt like alcohol and breath mints. My mother who seemed to pull away from Jack and me the worse things became in our house. By the time I left the island she could barely meet my eye. Suddenly, I remember the last time I spoke to her.

141

I'd just arrived home from the hospital with new-born Ella. She was sleeping soundly in her pram that I'd put in the middle of the living room. The flat felt at once fuller and emptier than it had ever been before. Despite my new baby's tiny size, curled up in her bundle of blankets, her presence seemed to fill the whole flat. But the room was quiet and the small coffee table was bare, no cards or flowers welcoming us home. Not that I'd been expecting anything, of course. But in that moment the realisation of quite how alone Ella and I were hit me with a force that brought me to the floor, slumped against the sofa in front of my new daughter.

I drew my phone from my pocket and dialled my parents' number for the first time in years. I don't know what I was really thinking. I hadn't spoken to them once since I left the island. Perhaps I hoped that the arrival of a granddaughter would change things. It might not be able to fix things between us exactly but perhaps at least some sort of relationship might be possible. I think maybe I was just lonely and frightened and needed my mum to tell me it would all be OK.

'Hello?'

I remember hearing my mother's voice on the other end of the line; it sent an electric jolt through my body. There are some things that no number of years or miles can allow you to forget. Your mother's voice is one of them.

'Hi, it's me.'

'Lorna.'

Her voice shook. I suddenly felt my nerve falter too. What was I doing?

'How are you, Mum?'

'Me?'

She sounded so surprised that I wanted to drop everything, go back to the island and force her to leave with me. Jack too if he wanted. Maybe they could find an apartment nearby in London. It would be the four of us: Mum, Jack, Ella and me. They both refused to leave all those years ago but maybe they would come with me now?

'What do you want?' she said instead of answering, her voice changed now, harder somehow.

Ella was asleep beside me, her skin pink and wrinkled, her tiny head sparsely covered with downy hair. Right then I wanted to pick her up and hold her tightly against my chest, to breathe in that new smell of her. But I didn't want to wake her.

'I know it's been a long time, Mum. But I wanted to tell you that you have a granddaughter. She was born two days ago. Seven pounds two ounces. The doctors say she's healthy, she's perfect. I'm calling her Ella. Ella Irvine.'

There was a slight pause on the other end of the phone, and then my mother spoke again.

'We already have a granddaughter.'

'What?'

I couldn't quite believe what I was hearing.

'Your brother's daughter, Molly. She was born last year.'

My little brother had a daughter. I had a niece. And I'd had no idea. Since I left the island, I'd hoped that my brother might get in touch. I wrote to him several times, including my address, but he never wrote back. I wrote to my mother too, trying to persuade her again to leave my father and the island. But I never heard from her either.

'You're not married then?' my mother added, making my skin prickle. I thought about my parents' devotion to the church and their old-fashioned views. I knew how much they both disapproved of unmarried mothers.

'Can we see her?'

Her voice cracked slightly then and in that crack I felt a sudden possibility of a different future for me and my daughter. Ridiculous really when I think about it now, but back then I suddenly pictured my parents turning up to Ella's school performances with cameras slung proudly around their necks. I pictured my father dressed as Father Christmas and my mother helping me make Ella's birthday cakes. They were things they never did for me, but maybe they could do them for their granddaughter. People change, don't they? Even as I listened hopefully into that silence, I'm not sure I really believed it was true. I just wanted it to be. I wanted to believe my parents could be different and that in being different they could be the grandparents my daughter deserved. And I was exhausted and alone and my mother's voice was in my ear for the first time in years.

'I don't know,' I said, hesitating. I looked again at Ella and then around at the small flat, still in disarray from when I left for the hospital. Could I really do all this on my own? When I was pregnant I'd been determined that I could, but with my living, breathing daughter beside me, things felt different. Is it normal to feel so exhausted, I wanted to ask my mother? Is it normal for feeding to hurt this much? When will I start to feel like a mother?

'I wouldn't mind you seeing her, Mum, but only you. Do you understand?'

A pause.

'That's not fair.'

'Really? After everything that happened?'

'Why can't you forgive him? It's been such a long time, Lorna.'

I steadied myself against the back of the sofa. And in that moment, I realised that no matter how much time had passed, I couldn't forgive my father. And I couldn't forgive my mother either. Over time I'd come to realise that she was a victim too. I wanted her to be happy and safe and free. But I still couldn't forgive her for letting it all happen. Even if I wanted to, even if maybe it would make me a better person, I just couldn't.

I held the hot phone against my ear, waiting for her to say the words I'd waited years to hear. *I'm sorry. I should have protected you. I miss you. I love you.* Instead there was just silence.

'I think perhaps it was a mistake to call,' I said eventually. 'Mum, you know how to reach me if things change. If you want to come and see Ella on your own, you can. But I'm not coming back.'

She drew a breath then as though she was going to say something. I waited.

'Goodbye, Lorna. You take care of yourself.'

And then the line went dead. I never heard from her again. After that call I shuffled close to Ella, reaching my face down so I could feel the soft warmth of her breath.

'I promise to keep you safe,' I told her that day. It's a promise I've spent her whole life trying to keep.

*

145

I could stay here among these plants all day, going back over these memories. But I know I need to get out. I need to move. I head back to the farm and change into my running gear. Alice is in the kitchen kneading bread dough, her arms covered up to her elbows in flour. I feel a sudden yearning to be with Ella but she and Molly are nowhere to be seen.

'They're probably on the beach or at Olive's,' Alice says with a shrug. How is she so calm? Back home in London I can't imagine being that relaxed about my daughter's whereabouts. But here the sea marks the edge of the children's domain; everything else within it is free to be explored.

'Going for another run?' Alice asks, brushing flour across her face as she pushes a strand of hair out of her eyes. 'It might rain.'

I think I'll take my chances. The sky is blue, the sun shining brightly onto the sea. I'm not quite sure what my sister-in-law is talking about.

'I'm sure I'll be fine.'

'OK, enjoy your run.'

'Thanks, see you later. And thanks again for earlier, Alice, it was good to talk.'

I'm still surprised how much I've opened up to Alice. It's so unlike me; I've spent my life trying to keep my past in its neat box, tucked away out of sight. But it feels different with her. I don't have to hide so much. We share a smile and then I head outside, taking a deep breath as I step through the door.

I start at the beach. Today, it's occupied by a herd of Highland cattle. They lie on the sand, seabirds hopping between them. I slow to a walk, careful not to disturb the dozing cows. One among the herd stands close to the water's edge facing out to sea, seemingly admiring the view. I look out too, trying to see the view around me as if afresh and not as the place where I grew up and which holds so many painful memories. The horizon is scattered with patches of cloud but they are too far out to worry me. A light breeze ruffles the surface of the sea. The beach is streaked with patches of dark black sand in intricate, feather-like patterns, scattered with the occasional pale shell or pebble. And yet it is still hard to find it all beautiful. My limbs and chest feel heavy.

I pick a particularly interesting pink shell from the sand and slip it into the pocket of my leggings. I'll leave the cows to contemplate their existence on the beach. This time when I reach the lighthouse and the cottage I don't turn back; instead I continue east, following the cliffs around and down the north-eastern edge of the island. The wind is stronger now and roars in my ears as I run high above the sea. Clouds that not long ago were a distant grey blur are now hurrying closer towards me. Damn it. I'd forgotten quite how changeable the weather can be on the island. Perhaps I should have listened to Alice.

The cliff begins to slope down towards the beach, the jetty and the village visible in the distance. The air chills and goosebumps begin to prick my bare arms. I run faster, but in the end I can't outrun the weather. The sky turns as dark as a ripe plum and fat droplets of summer rain fall on my skin. The wind has picked up now too, tugging at my hair and slapping against my skin. Damn it, damn it.

I'm in the open with nowhere to shelter, the rain pelting down on my skin. Looking around me I spot a house I hadn't noticed before, perched at the far end of the beach. It's a new-build and is set back slightly from the dunes, a boat moored at the end of a wooden jetty in a small cove in front, straining at its anchor as it rocks on the now turbulent waves. I pick up my pace and head towards the building. My exercise clothes are soaked through. This is rain unlike anything we ever experience in London. It's island rain, rain that stings as it pummels against my arms, rain that crashes into the sea and drowns out even the sound of the waves. How had I forgotten this rain that falls so hard even in the summer?

The house is clad in wood with long windows facing the sea and, thankfully, has a large porch at the front. There are no cars parked outside the building which I take to mean no one is home. I race for the porch and watch from beneath the protection of the sloped roof as the rain pours outside.

Should I wait it out here until the rain passes? But that could be a long time, looking at the heavy black clouds in the sky. Maybe I should just make a break for it, but the thought of continuing on my run seems suddenly very unappealing. I've come further than I'd intended – it would take a while to get back now.

Shivering and unsure what to do next, I spot a pick-up truck bumping along the track leading towards the house. There's a dog in the back and the sound of its barking reaches me over the hiss of the rain. As the truck pulls up in front of the house I take a closer look at the dog. It's a sodden Old English sheepdog. Before I have time to move, the truck door opens and Mallachy steps out, dressed in waterproof trousers, wellies and a navy raincoat.

He looks me up and down. My sodden T-shirt clings to my body, tendrils of hair drip around my face and my arms have turned lobster-red with the cold.

'Great weather for a run,' he says, his voice raised in competition with the sound of the rain.

'It was fine when I left,' I shout over the rain and Rex's barking.

Mallachy looks up at the sky. It is slate-grey and the rain pours down as heavily as ever.

'Aye, it's a beautiful day for sure!'

His trousers and coat are shiny with moisture, but he at least looks much warmer than I feel. He lets Rex out the back of the truck and the dog immediately bounds across to me. Before I can step out of the way he jumps up, leaving two muddy paw prints on my T-shirt.

'Leave her alone, Rex!' Mallachy shouts, but I can tell he is trying not to laugh as he glances at my muddy top.

'I'm glad you're finding my distress amusing!'

He follows Rex towards the front door until he is standing right beside me. He's taller than I remember from our brief meeting at the school yesterday, and broader too. With both of us beneath the porch we're forced to stand close together. He gives me another look.

'I suppose you'd better come in then before you drown,' he says, pushing open the unlocked front door.

Inside, Mallachy removes his boots and hangs his jacket on a hook by the door. I take a good look around. We're standing in a modern, open-plan room with a kitchen island in the centre and a living area behind, a grey sofa and a leather armchair facing a large wood-burner. The far side of the room is taken up by floor-to-ceiling windows with a view stretching out to the sea, obscured now by curtains of rain. An engine boat is tied up to a decking that stretches out into the water. Inside, the wooden frame of the building has been left exposed and matches the table in the corner and the two wooden chairs. My eyes are drawn to a set of pictures on the wall – a loose yet expressive ink sketch of a puffin, another of a sea eagle, and finally an oystercatcher. I don't know what I'd been expecting from Mallachy's home, but I don't think it was this.

Rex flops over to a cushion by the sofa as Mallachy hangs up his coat and pulls off his waterproof trousers to reveal jeans beneath. I pause awkwardly by the door.

'Your home is beautiful.'

'You sound surprised,' he says, turning back to me with a flash of a smile.

'I guess I didn't have you down as a trendy minimalist,' I reply, glancing at his muddy jeans, the wellies by the door and his hair which looks in need of a good cut. Is there even a hairdresser on the island?

'Aye, I'll take that,' he replies. 'I'm glad you like it though. It's always nice to have your work appreciated.'

I look around again, taking in the elegant lines of the central room which manages to feel spacious yet cosy at the same time.

'You built this house?'

I must sound as impressed as I feel because he laughs, a brief, joyous burst of noise that makes Rex thump his tail even harder from his cushion. I meet Mallachy's eyes for a moment and we look at one another across the room. Is it just me, or is the room suddenly considerably warmer?

'You look like a drowned rat, come and sit down.'

My cheeks grow even hotter. I fold my arms around my body as Mallachy drapes a towel over the sofa for me. I perch awkwardly on the edge, aware of my hair dripping onto the towel.

He leaves me on the sofa as he pulls down mugs and a teapot from the kitchen cupboards. While the kettle boils he pushes open a door on the right-hand side of the room. I catch a glimpse of an airy space, a desk scattered with papers and in the middle, a large easel. My heart beats quickly at the sight but then the door closes again and Mallachy is handing me a large, rust-red woollen jumper.

'Here,' he says. 'Don't want you catching hypothermia on your second day on the island.'

I mumble a thank you and pull it over my head. It smells of dog and pine needles and something that I immediately recall as the scent of oil paints. I watch Mallachy more closely as he passes me a mug of hot tea and sits down in the armchair. Every now and then I find myself glancing over towards the closed door in the corner.

Rex has fallen asleep, one of his paws twitching slightly. Outside, the rain continues to pelt the sea and the dunes, droplets sliding down the window pane. The room is warm and I feel sensation returning to my toes and fingers. Mallachy flicks on the radio and for a moment we sit and listen, not talking.

'I love this song.'

'Me too,' says Mallachy.

'I'm sorry again that I ignored you the other day. It was rude of me.'

I speak into my mug, unable suddenly to meet his green eyes.

'I know it's probably not an excuse, but I was upset. You've probably heard all about it, but I grew up here and haven't been back in a really long time.'

'I try not to pay too much attention to island gossip,' he says, stretching his legs in front of him and reaching down to absentmindedly stroke Rex's ears. 'I prefer to hear things from the people who are actually involved. Besides, I know what it's like to have your story become the latest form of entertainment.'

'Oh really?'

'I caused quite a stir when I first moved here.'

He talks half to me and seemingly half to Rex.

'How long ago was that?'

'It must be seven years now. I bought this land on something of a whim and lived in a caravan on the plot while I was building it. I was an architect back on the mainland. I thought it would be creative but I ended up mostly designing the same type of office block over and over. But I'd always dreamed of building my own house.'

'And it took you a while to settle in here then?'

'You could say that. I suppose I kept to myself at first. I was so focused on getting the house done. And you don't exactly move to an island because you're looking for company. Rumours quickly spread about me. I heard the things people said about me, that I was wild, a recluse, antisocial …'

I nearly laugh out loud.

'You don't seem antisocial to me! And yesterday at the school – well, Alice and the others clearly think the world of you.'

His ears glow pink and he looks down at Rex again, scratching the top of his head.

'Aye, well they're good folk, most of them anyway. And I guess I *was* a bit antisocial when I first came here. I'd just got divorced and I suppose life hadn't really panned out like I'd thought it would. I wouldn't say I was a bundle of laughs back then.'

I want to ask Mallachy about his divorce. I picture a young wife, perhaps also an architect or a designer. But he moves on quickly.

'Over time the islanders got to know me though.'

'I know I grew up here but being back now ... Even though most people have been kind to me so far, I can't help feeling like an outsider, like a mainlander. I suppose after all this time I am.'

'I don't know about that, although I must say an islander would probably have brought a raincoat with them today.'

He smiles at me and I can tell he is joking.

'How did you settle in here in the end then?' I ask him. 'What changed with the islanders?'

I can't help but think about my conversation with Mrs Anderson and the curious glances when Ella and I arrived at the harbour yesterday. Alice and her friends have been welcoming but I can't help but feel there are others on this island who are not so pleased to see me back here.

Mallachy tilts his head slightly.

'I guess I needed my space at first, but once the house was underway I started turning up more frequently at The Lookout. I realised I'd been sitting in my caravan feeling angry that the islanders weren't being more welcoming, but I hadn't made any effort myself. For all their gossiping, they welcomed me once they actually got to know me. I turned up to island events. I offered my services when I heard the village hall needed some repairs. I even went to church a few times.'

'And it all helped then?'

'Aye, it did. The islanders helped me get the job as assistant harbour master. Some of them still drive me crazy, but I've made friends too. Now I can't imagine living anywhere else.'

I look around the room again, it seeming even more impressive now that I know he designed this space himself.

'What drew you here in the first place? Why this island?'

He looks at me with an amused expression on his face.

'Do you really need to ask that? Just look.'

Together we turn and look outside at the rain-soaked view, the horizon hazy with mist and the long grasses in the dunes bowed over in the wind. I think it looks incredibly bleak. I shiver, even though it's warm inside. But Mallachy smiles, his gaze resting on the beach and the waves crashing against the sand.

'I visited here on holiday years ago, when I was a student,' he continues eventually. 'I suppose it just stuck with me. The different way of life, the complete opposite to the corporate environment I went on to work in. Self-sufficiency, being away from it all … It's the kind of place that stays with you – it gets in your blood. The smells, the sound of the sea, the rain even.

For years after that I would dream about the island. It's the place I thought about whenever I pictured leaving the city and my job behind and building my own house from scratch. And when things got particularly bad with my ex-wife the island just kept coming back into my mind. I guess you could say that just that one visit was enough to plant a seed – for years after I felt the roots pulling me back here.'

I know what it feels like to dream about the island and to be linked to a place by an invisible thread. I felt it pulling me back on the train journey north, I felt it when we drove past the track leading to my childhood home, when I stood by the lighthouse looking out at the familiar view. I'm surprised to find that I feel it now, sitting inside Mallachy's home.

I point at the ink sketches on the walls.

'Are those paintings yours?'

His ears glow again as he nods.

'They're beautiful,' I say, standing up to look closer at each image. 'They're so simple but you've captured the spirit of each bird perfectly.'

He stands too and motions for me to follow him to the door at the end of the room.

'If you like the rest of the house you might like this room too. It's my favourite.'

The walls and roof are made entirely of glass, held up by the same wooden structure that has been left exposed in the living room. As well as the easel I spied earlier, I take in an old dresser stacked with jam jars filled with brushes, pencils, charcoal and paint tubes. There are lined-up bottles of ink, pads of paper and dozens of art and architecture books arranged on the shelves as well as in piles on the floor beneath the dresser. Peering closer, I notice that the papers covering the desk are sketches. I catch a glimpse of them – a fishing boat, the jagged outline of the island's mountain, Rex asleep by the fire. I want to pick them up and leaf through every one. On the opposite side of the room to the desk is a sofa covered in blankets.

I hold a hand up to my face.

'Are you OK?' Mallachy asks, the faint lines on his forehead deepening into a look of concern that only makes the feeling in my stomach worse. I reach a hand out to the desk to steady myself.

'I'm fine.'

Mallachy is still watching me. I want to turn away. But before I even know what I'm doing I find myself speaking again instead.

'I used to want to be an artist. I wanted it more than anything. I had a space a little like this in my bedroom.'

Looking around Mallachy's studio, I think of the easel that Sarah gave me for my twelfth birthday, handmade with the help of her father. It stood proudly by my bedroom window, facing out to sea. Over the next few years I painted in every spare moment I had for myself. My fingernails were constantly dirty with paint. Sometimes when I went to bed at night I found bright clumps of oils in my hair.

I painted with a kind of hunger. When I was at my easel hours could pass by without me noticing, until my mother would call me down for dinner. Painting made me forget those other more present hungers – for food but also for affection, laughter, love – and instead think only of the drive to create.

My parents never commented on my paintings, let alone hung them in the house, so my bedroom walls were filled with my own paintings and drawings, pegged up to string. When things were particularly hard or when I doubted myself those pieces of paper and canvas reminded me of what I held inside me. Colour, light, creativity, strength.

My eyes sting and my throat grows tight. I haven't painted in twenty years. It was once my reason for getting up in the mornings, the one thing that would make me feel optimistic about the day ahead.

'Feel free to look around,' Mallachy says gently.

I start off by running my hand over the dresser, lifting my fingers to stroke the soft bristles of the paintbrushes. Then I crouch and examine Mallachy's collection of books. As I explore the titles we start to talk. About our favourite artists, about the architecture practice Mallachy used to work for, about the benefits of oil paints versus watercolours versus gouache. He tells me how much he loves the Scottish National Gallery in Edinburgh, saying he makes the trip across to the mainland several times a year specifically to visit the gallery. I admit I've never been, a fact that makes Mallachy hold his head and groan. My parents would never have allowed me to make the trip when I was still living at home. And I've avoided returning to Scotland ever since I left. It surprises me how close I come to admitting this to Mallachy, this man I barely know. He seems at ease, his face lighting up at each new topic. I realise I feel relaxed too. I feel calmer than I have done since arriving on the island.

'Sorry if I'm bombarding you,' he says eventually. 'I love

living here, but no one else on the island is particularly artistic. Or at least they don't want to talk about different types of paintbrushes with me for half an hour.'

'No, it's nice. It's been a long time for me too.'

When did I last speak like this about art? I don't think I ever have really. Growing up, Sarah was supportive of my passion but was more interested in music than paintings. I'd hoped that Goldsmiths would be where I'd meet likeminded people, where we'd discuss our shared passion for hours. But when that didn't happen, and when I eventually stopped painting altogether, I stopped using that part of my brain. I shut it off as much as I could. It would have been too painful otherwise. I visit galleries in London if I can persuade Ella to come with me, but unless it's a photography exhibition she usually prefers to browse the gift shop than talk at length with me about each piece. The closest I usually come to art is when I help the children wash paint from their hands at school, or if one of the youngest gets a crayon wedged in a nostril and I have to accompany them to the first-aid room.

'If you ever want to come and use this studio ...' Mallachy says, trailing off and shifting awkwardly on the spot. His eyes are bright and his face feels suddenly familiar, even though I know we'd never met before I set foot on the island again. I'm stepping closer to him and he responds by moving closer too. I feel the heat radiating from his body. The hairs on my arms stand on end. And then I become aware of the quiet. Looking up at the glass roof, I realise the rain has stopped. Sunlight breaks through the dark clouds and shines on my face. The light dazzles my eyes as though jolting me awake from a dream. *What am I doing here?* I take a sudden step backwards.

'I'd better go.'

Mallachy watches with a confused expression as I stumble out of the studio. But I need to get out. Now. I rush through the house towards the door and leave without saying goodbye.

It's only when I'm back at Hilly Farm that I realise I'm still wearing his jumper.

CHAPTER 14

ALICE

'How *are* you?'

My eldest sister's voice reaches me through my laptop, the familiarity of the sound making my chest tighten. I've shut myself away in the bedroom for a video call with my sisters, the one time when I'm insistent with my family about not being disturbed. No helping Molly find a shoe or book that she's lost, no farm chat with Jack. This is my time.

Caitlin's face fills my screen, her dark bob tucked behind her ears, a glass of what looks like gin and tonic beside her on the bedside table. Like me, she's propped up in bed, pillows arranged around her. At the sound of her voice I feel as though the air has been knocked out of me. All my worries rise to the surface again, ready to overspill if I let them.

The screen flickers and Shona's face appears too, slightly blurry. She's holding a very large glass of red wine.

'Sorry I'm late,' she says. 'I just managed to get the boys to finally stop arguing and to watch a film together. I may have bribed them with large amounts of Haribo. Dr Morton, from your professional viewpoint, am I a terrible mother?'

Ever since my eldest sister graduated after all those long years of study, my family have rarely called her by her first name. To us, she's Dr Morton. It sometimes results in confusion from people who don't know us that well. They mistake the title for formality, when really it's an endearment only used by those closest to her. In reality we could call Shona Dr too, as a few years ago she finished her PhD. She's too modest to use her title though. I don't think that I'd be the same if things were reversed. I think I'd wear a badge with the word 'doctor' in huge letters. I'd never take it off.

'Well, I'd be something of a hypocrite if I did,' replies Caitlin. 'Although you should know by now that doctors are the absolute worst at following medical advice. You remember how long it took Doug to go and get that rash properly checked out …'

Caitlin's husband Doug is a doctor too and they work together at the same practice. Although it's always been a point of pride for me that it was my sister who climbed the rungs to become partner of the surgery.

'Oh yes, and how are your husband's genitals now, Doc? I hope you're not having to apply that ointment every hour anymore?'

'I *told* you the rash was on his stomach, his stomach!'

'Yes, and I didn't believe you. Would you really wait that long to get it checked out if it wasn't something awfully embarrassing? I think not.'

'That's because you are incredibly rational, Shona. You know that a fear of doctors in someone who actually *is* a doctor isn't entirely rational. Although perhaps it comes from living with me? God, I hope not ...'

I sip my wine, smiling as my sisters volley back and forth. This is how it always is. When we all lived together mealtimes would be dominated by those two having a long conversation, their stream of words barely unbroken. Sometimes they'd argue and the words would grow snappy and loud; at others they'd discuss in great detail something that had happened at school or that they'd seen on the news. Back then I wished that I could join in too but usually couldn't find the words. Over time it became so normal to sit in silence watching them that it's something of a comfort to listen to them now. It makes me feel nostalgic. And it's a distraction, pulling my mind back from the thoughts I don't want to dwell on.

'But anyway,' Caitlin says, her eyes looking directly into her webcam, making it appear as though she is looking me dead in the eye, 'I was just asking Squirt how she was doing.'

So, no escaping that question after all then. Shona nods, taking a glug of her wine.

'Yes, how are things over there on fish island? Are you holding up OK?'

When I first told Shona that I was moving to the Isle of Kip she misheard me. She thought I said 'kipper'. Although my parents were supportive of the move my sisters were a little perplexed at first. Not about me choosing not to go to university; in fact they both confessed that they thought it was probably for the best, that perhaps my talents lay outside of academia. But they didn't know why I wanted to move some-where so small and remote.

'Won't you miss going to the cinema and out to restaurants?' Caitlin had asked me.

'And won't it be a little, I don't know, *conservative* out there?' was Shona's misgiving.

I'd told her about the island's environmental credentials, how they were striving to be as eco-friendly as possible. Over the years it's been wonderful to watch those aims come true. Thanks to wind turbines and solar panels we're now pretty much energy self-sufficient. And for such a small place we're a more diverse bunch than people might think. Kerstin is origin-ally from Germany and teaches German and French lessons at the school, being fluent in both. Joy's parents are Ghanaian and have since retired back there; Tess and Joy try to get there once a year to visit. Pat does a special order for Joy at the shop so she can cook her favourite foods that her mother taught her how to make and which she used to be able to get readily when she lived in Birmingham, where she and Tess met. Morag has started buying the same products and with Joy's help now lives mostly off rice *jollof, waakye* and rich stews. 'Why did I waste most of my life eating all that bland crap?' she said once. 'I don't think I ever want to eat a bloody potato again, unless it's one of those sweet ones.'

Then there's Kamil, Natalia and their baby Lena who moved here a few months ago. I've been trying to persuade Natalia to come to my classes, although so far she still seems a little shy. I'm determined to work on her though. And Brenda may have long ago lost her accent, but she grew up in Canada and every now and then you can hear her singing 'O Canada' on her walks around the island, usually in autumn when she says even now she misses the trees and the maple syrup waffles her mother made when she was a girl.

My sisters have visited many times now and have become friendly with my group of friends, all of us congregating in The Lookout for a good catch up and wine session whenever they're here. But I know they would never choose to live somewhere like this themselves. I think even after all this time neither of them totally understands my decision to live here, or perhaps even my life as a whole. Despite my encouragement over the years, neither of them has ever done yoga: Caitlin prefers climbing mountains and Shona has an expensive gym membership that I'm not totally sure she uses. And they are both so rigidly practical that I know they don't really get the more spiritual side of the practice. I think they would probably laugh their way through one of my classes.

'We're doing OK,' I say, trying to sound cheerful. 'Jack is struggling of course but thank goodness he's got the farm and his vegetables to distract him. I think we're going to have a bumper crop with how hard he's working.'

I think about all the other things I'm not telling my sisters. The distance between Jack and me and how difficult I find it every time he withdraws from me. How hard I'm trying to hold things together in the house, to encourage Lorna and Jack to talk and reconnect. I know no one's asked me to play the role of go-between, that I've put it on myself, but it's still exhausting. Especially as somehow, I find I care too much to stop. I think about Jean too, and all my worries for my friend.

And there in the back of my mind is a fear for the whole island that I've come to love, and what the future holds for us. Will we still even be here in ten years or so time? But I can't bring myself to say all this to my sisters. They have their own problems and their own lives. And there's something about the screen between us that makes me hold back. Perhaps if I was with them in person … But it's too hard like this.

'I guess that's understandable. I know Doug worked more hours than ever after his father died. Sorry again that I can't get over for the funeral, sis,' says Caitlin.

'Yes, me too,' adds Shona. 'Are you sure you'll be OK?'

Neither of them could get the time off work. I don't mind though. They know that I was never close to Jack's parents and I told them that it wasn't worth making the journey. If I had really needed them I know they would have been there, regardless of work. When Molly was two I fell pregnant again. I was so excited. But I miscarried at four and a half months. I was too upset to speak to anyone or even to leave the bed, but Jack phoned my sisters. They were both there on the island two days later. They stayed for two weeks.

'I'll be fine,' I say now, swallowing tears not at the thought of the funeral, but at the memory of that time. They didn't try to cheer me up, instead they were just there, helping out around the house and taking me out for walks if I felt up to it. Nothing could take away the sadness, but having them there helped.

My mind is still in the past when Caitlin asks me, 'So, what's she like?'

'Who?'

'Jack's sister!'

'Oh ...' I strain my ears, listening out for the sound of the shower. Lorna is just back from a run. As predicted she did get soaked but she didn't seem to mind. In fact, she seemed in a very good mood. Hearing the sound of the water and the hot water tank humming I continue. 'You know, she's nice. We've been getting on well. She's clearly been through a lot and she and Jack are barely talking. But she and I ... I don't know, I guess we're becoming friends. I like her.'

'Well that's good,' says Shona, her wine glass nearly empty now. 'I imagine things with her and Jack will take a while. I mean, you don't just get past something like that straight away. I'm not sure you ever can.'

With a sinking feeling I realise that Shona is probably right. I've been so keen for Jack and Lorna to reconnect and to work through the past because it has always made me sad that Jack doesn't have what I have with my sisters. And perhaps selfishly I want Lorna and Ella in my life. I want my family to grow. But maybe I'm being naïve. Perhaps a reconciliation is just a fantasy.

'It's good that you two are getting on well though,' adds Caitlin. 'Although we'll always be your favourite sisters OK, Squirt?'

I smile, wishing I could reach through the laptop screen and touch my sisters. I wish we were all together in the same room sharing wine rather than connecting like this from our three separate houses, our three separate lives.

'Of course,' I reply.

The conversation veers back to the day-to-day: difficult

patients at the surgery, a new colleague at the university. We talk about our children and I tell them about Ella and how well she and Molly are getting on. We say our goodbyes and agree to talk again soon after the sound of shouting rises in the background at Shona's house.

Once my sisters are gone I stare at the screen for a moment. For a second, it feels like I might fall apart. But I can't let myself do that. I stand up, take a final sip of the dregs in my wine glass and return downstairs.

I prepare a simple dinner for us all: roasted vegetables with buttery couscous and a herb dressing from the garden. As expected Jack and Lorna say very little to one another, although I catch Lorna glancing across at Jack several times throughout the meal. Ella and Molly are windswept from a day spent outside and full of stories of the beach clean-up they started with Olive today and how they are roping in the rest of the island children to help out tomorrow. Throughout the meal I can't help but notice that Ella's replies to Lorna's questions seem somewhat curt. It surprises me; she has seemed so polite so far, but there definitely seems to have been a shift in her mood. It only seems noticeable when she interacts with her mother though: she thanks me effusively after dinner and helps tidy up.

It seems Lorna has noticed something too though because once the table is cleared and Jack is in the living room and the girls have gone upstairs, she turns to me.

'Is it just me or did Ella seem a little distracted tonight?'

I focus on wiping the work surfaces, careful not to say the wrong thing.

'They're teenagers – Molly gets into funny moods some-times. Usually they pass soon enough.'

She sighs and I recognise in her wrinkled forehead the worried expression of a mother.

'You're probably right. I just can't help but feel like some-thing's wrong. Like maybe I've done something wrong.'

'I'm sure everything's fine. She'll come to you if she needs to. That's the way with Molly anyway. I can ask her again and again if something's wrong but it's only when she's ready that she'll open up to me, usually at some totally unexpected moment, like when we're driving somewhere or doing the washing-up.'

Lorna smiles.

'Ah, those car journey conversations. What is it about being in a car that makes kids open up?'

I glance towards the door, careful to keep my voice low.

'Jack's the same. Except our best conversations have prob-ably happened when we were in the tractor together.'

I think back to that time when, bumping together across our fields, he'd shared for the first time how he really felt about the baby we lost.

'He'd be three now, wouldn't he?' he said out of the blue, the tractor rolling over the ruts and dips in the earth. I didn't need to ask him who he meant. 'I often think about what he'd be like, you know. What he'd look like, even what he'd smell like – whether he'd have a different smell to Molly. I think he probably would.'

He's never mentioned our lost baby again. But that one conversation was enough. At least I knew he hadn't forgotten.

168

'She'll come to you when she's ready,' I say and she smiles tentatively again.

Later, when we've said goodnight and Jack and I are undressing in our room, the curtains drawn and the door closed, I can't help but think about that conversation with Lorna. Jack is turned away from me, his back stooped as he steps out of his trousers and pulls off his socks.

My phone glows next to the bed and I reach for it, seeing a stream of new messages in my 'yoga girls' WhatsApp group. There's an update from Jean: she is heading to the mainland tomorrow with her husband for a hospital appointment. That ache I've almost become used to by now returns to my chest. The others have sent messages of luck and love and I type one too. I suggest that we might all meet her at the harbour to wave her off but she replies saying she doesn't want the fuss.

'Whatever you want. Sending a big hug xx' I reply.

'Thank you,' types Jean. 'But let's talk about something else now. Does anyone have any gossip for me?'

I watch as another flurry of messages comes in. Kerstin's son is planning a trip to the island with his fiancée and she's feeling nervous: it will be the first time they've met and her son still isn't thrilled about her choice to leave her job and his father to move here.

'No gossip here,' writes Joy. 'We're just hoping for a decent night's sleep ...' Followed by an emoji of a baby and a devil.

There's an exchange of supportive messages and queries about how Tess, Joy and Harry are getting on, as well as a message from Brenda checking in on me. I write a quick reply, reassuring Kerstin about her son's visit, sending crossed fingers for a good night's sleep for Harry, Tess and Joy and telling them I'm feeling a little frazzled, but otherwise OK. Then I turn my phone over and lean back against the pillows.

Jack reaches for the two glasses of water he brought upstairs with him as he does every night, passing one silently to me and placing the other on his bedside table.

When we got engaged I didn't realise that some of the things I would love most about marriage could be this – the small thoughtful gestures, the mundane togetherness. Two glasses of water on two bedside tables, watching my husband undress for the thousandth time and waiting for that moment that signals the end to every day when his weight and his warmth fill the space beside me in our bed. But I can't help the niggling part of me that wants something more too – that wants him to open up to me the way my friends do with such ease.

'What do you think of Molly's beach clean-up?' I ask him. 'She said they collected five bags of rubbish. It's crazy how much stuff gets washed up.'

Jack nods as he slips in next to me. His body is cool and I nestle closer to him in an attempt to warm him. He slides an arm beneath my neck and I lie against him, hearing his heart beating through his chest.

'Molly and Ella seem to be getting on well,' I try again, attempting to edge us gently closer to what I really want to talk about. 'She's a sweet girl.'

I can feel Jack's body tensing next to mine.

'Yes,' he replies quietly.

'I spoke to Lorna today. She seems to really want to try and make things right with you.'

'Don't you think it's a bit late for that?' His voice catches me off balance with its coldness. But then he sighs again.

'Sorry, darling. She spoke to me today too. Or at least she said she wanted to talk.'

'And?'

'I don't know. I just don't know if I can.'

His body feels so stiff next to me. Sometimes I feel as though his reluctance to talk isn't so much a choice as a physical block. I've tried in the past to encourage him to try therapy but he has always told me he doesn't think it would be worth it. I remember the way he described it once. 'I just don't think I'd have anything to say,' he'd said. 'Or at least I don't think I'd be able to say it out loud. It's like the words can't make it past my throat.'

I want to help him find those words, to let him release whatever it is that lurks inside him. For himself but selfishly for me too. My sisters and their husbands talk about everything. Sometimes I envy that so much it hurts.

'I did say I'd go to the house with her though, to start sorting through their things.'

I reach my hand out through the dark until I find his and grip it tightly.

'I'll come with you.'

'It's OK, I can do it on my own.'

'I'll come with you,' I repeat.

Silence, and then he squeezes my hand.

'Thank you.'

The toilet flushes down the corridor and footsteps pad in the direction of the spare room. A click as the door down there closes.

'It's so strange having her in the house,' Jack says.

'You didn't have to offer to have them stay here, you know, they would have been fine in the B&B. I can still phone up and sort a room out for them if you want, darling?'

I feel him shaking his head beside me.

'No. She probably won't come back again. If this is her last time on the island she should at least be here with us. Even if it's hard.'

He pauses and I wonder whether to say something but to my surprise he continues.

'I do want her here, Alice, even if I know I'm not doing a good job of showing it.'

His voice is strained and I reach up and stroke his forehead.

'I know you do.'

I don't want to push him, but this is more than he's said to me about how he's feeling since she's arrived. Perhaps it's the darkness that loosens his words. I shuffle even closer and then try again, wanting to make the most of this brief moment of openness.

'But you don't know that she's not going to come back. This could be the start of something. Maybe if you two had a proper talk …'

But he shakes his head again.

'There's no point. She left once and I know she's going to leave again.'

I imagine Jack at fourteen, watching his sister leaving the

172

island on the ferry. However much I might have bonded with Lorna since she arrived, and whatever reasons she might have had for leaving, I still think of that boy left behind on the island and I ache for him.

'I always thought she might come back for me,' he says quietly into the dark, 'but she never did.'

I want to tell him what Lorna told me – that she wanted to take him with her – but I sense that's not what he needs right now. Instead, I stroke his cheeks and as I do I feel that they're damp.

If I'm totally honest, sometimes I wonder what my life would have been like if I'd married a different kind of man. Someone more open, who didn't have these silences and these moods. Over the years we've had our downs as well as our ups. We fought countless times about his parents and the demands they put on him, as well as thousands of other forgettable things. And our inability to have another baby challenged us too, at times bringing us closer together but at others feeling as though it might pull us apart. I suppose that's just marriage though. But so too is this: feeling like my heart could break in two with love and pain for him, kissing his tear-soaked cheeks in the darkness of our bedroom, holding him tightly to me and wishing the world was a better, kinder, easier place if only for him.

'It's going to be OK, my darling,' I say softly, not because I know how but because it's the only thing to say.

CHAPTER 15

LORNA

I still feel embarrassed about what happened at Mallachy's studio yesterday, or what *nearly* happened. I barely know him and certainly didn't expect to end up in his house when I headed out on my run. But we had such a good time in his studio. And then there was that current that seemed to pass between us. I could suddenly imagine what it might feel like to step closer, to tilt my face up towards his, to wrap my arms around his waist ...

It's probably just because it's been a long time since I was last with a man. That must explain the feeling of intensity I experienced in his studio. The possibility that it might be anything more than that is too much to contemplate. I'm not here to meet someone. I don't do relationships. My life is all about Ella – the two of us against the world. It's been that way for years and we've managed OK, haven't we?

The sound of Alice stepping inside the kitchen brings me out of my thoughts. It's morning and Ella and Molly have already headed out with rucksacks and bicycles, Ella's camera slung around her neck. I tried to kiss her before she left but she wriggled away. I hope she's OK. I want to ask her what's wrong but remember Alice's advice. Ella will come back to me when she's ready. At least I hope she will.

Alice carries a basket filled with eggs and places it on the table. She's wearing pale jeans rolled up at the ankles and a polka-dot shirt tied loosely at her waist.

'Wow, are those all from your chickens?'

'Yep! We provide most of the eggs for the village shop. Speaking of which, I really need to go down there today and do a food shop.'

'I can go for you if you like,' I volunteer.

'If you don't mind, that would be great,' she replies. 'It's a busy day here. I need to get back out in a minute and help Jack fix one of the walls in the fields before the sheep work out the gap is there and start going for a wander. And if you leave this morning you'll catch the ferry and can pick up our post – if that's OK? It's a long walk though, take my bike.'

Alice's purple bike is splattered with mud, a basket on the front and a plastic milk carton lashed to the rack on the back with a shopping bag folded up inside. She hands me a helmet. The last time I cycled was here on the island when I was a child. Back then, my bike was my freedom. I cycled to and from primary school with Sarah, and often to Sarah's house or her grandparents' house after school. There is a long downhill section leading to the village and on the way to school Sarah and I would freewheel, the wind rushing through our hair, laughter pouring from our mouths and trailing behind us. It meant pedalling uphill to return home but it was always worth it for that brief feeling of lightness and joy I experienced every morning. When we cycled fast like that I felt almost as though I was flying.

I was eleven when my father took my bike away, coming to the end of my last term at primary school. One morning when I woke up and prepared to cycle to school with Sarah I found my bike was missing. My father told me it had broken, but he wouldn't tell me how. In any case it never got replaced despite my pleading. My father drove me to school that day. I spotted Sarah out the car window, cycling alone. After that I always had to ask one of my parents to drive me if I wanted to visit Sarah or anyone else on the island, or instead face the long walk, often in the rain. I remember my father smirking every time I asked for a lift.

'See how much I do for you?' he'd say. It was part of the background rhetoric of my life. That I was a burden, an inconvenience, and should be eternally grateful to my parents. For a long time, I believed it.

And then Sarah left for the secondary school like all the other older children, leaving the island during the week and returning on weekends and during holidays. When that happened, I would have given anything to have just one more day cycling to school with her, feeling as though our wheels could leave the ground.

But despite how much I used to enjoy cycling it's been a long time and as I climb onto the bike I'm giddy with nerves.

I kick off and wobble immediately, veering from left to right. I really hope no one is watching. I don't look behind me to check. Gripping tightly onto the handlebars I rattle down the track. This is harder than I remember. I swerve precariously around dips in the road, trying to avoid the deepest puddles and the largest rocks. At moments I'm convinced I'm going to slip and come tumbling off. But somehow, I manage to maintain my balance. When I reach the main island road the tarmac is a smooth relief.

The rain of yesterday has disappeared and the sky is powder blue. From the road I have a sweeping view across the island. The inky green of the pine forest, the rolling moor dotted with sheep, the scattering of cottages with Scottish flags in the gardens and the long beach that leads down to the jetty and the village. I spot Mallachy's house at the far end of the beach, the boat calm today by the jetty. I think of the smell of his jumper and picture his studio filled with sketches and feel my heartrate climbing, my cheeks warm with embarrassment. I should have brought his jumper with me and dropped it off on the way to the village. I'll return it tomorrow and just hope he's out. I'm not sure I'm ready to see him again just yet.

My thighs burn as I climb the hill that sits beside the mountain. I might be a runner, but being on a bike again fires up different muscles, muscles that I haven't used this way in years. It's a kind of pain that isn't painful though. It makes me feel alive. Nearing the top, I spot Brenda's blue house standing just back from the road and the pink flash of her hair as she leans over in the garden, lifting a ball and throwing it for Puff the puppy. As she stands she spots me and gives a big wave. I wave back.

And then I crest the hill and see the village spread out below me, seagulls circling the harbour and the ferry approaching through the mist out to sea. As I cycle up and over the hump of the hill the bicycle speeds up. I can feel it in my stomach, gravity pulling me down, the wind brushing against my face and grabbing my hair. The air stings my eyes but I keep them wide open. I pedal fast, building up speed, the moor and trees flashing by in bursts of green. And then I stop pedalling and let myself freewheel. I go even faster than I remember as a child. It's terrifying. What would happen if I came off? But I'm also grinning, cold tears of wind and joy sliding down my face. The salty air fills my lungs and I imagine I am eight-years-old and Sarah is by my side. I let out a shriek of happiness, the sound causing a cluster of sparrows in a nearby tree to leap from their branches and disperse into the sky.

As I reach the village I press hard on the brakes, the bike screeching and clattering to a stop. That's when I spot Sarah, not the eight-year-old Sarah of my imagination but the real-life adult her standing outside the village shop, her arms holding a cardboard box piled high with groceries. She's watching me and I feel a thrill as I notice she's smiling. Her smile feels like an invitation and I reply by smiling back.

'Hello,' I say breathlessly, leaning the bike against the shop wall, wondering for a moment if there's a bike lock in the basket and then remembering where I am and that it doesn't matter. I can tell Sarah is trying not to laugh.

'Do you realise how mad you look?' she says eventually, still smiling.

'Oh definitely,' I reply, peeling the helmet off my head, my hair springing free in a damp frizzy mass around my face.

She lets out a laugh and I just want to catch that laugh, hold it tight to my chest and never let go.

'I'm not going to lie, you were pretty wobbly. I kept thinking you were going to fall off. When was the last time you rode a bike?'

'With you.'

Sarah's eyebrows rise and she opens her mouth then closes it again.

'Oh.'

I want to tell her that those moments cycling with her were some of the happiest of my childhood, that I think about them all the time. But despite her smile, I think perhaps we're not there yet.

My eyes suddenly fall on the community noticeboard just behind Sarah. Among outdated posters for an Easter service at the church and an evening with a visiting musician that took place in May, there are signs advertising a choir, a new egg delivery service run by Alice and Molly, and a poster promoting the weekly yoga class Alice runs at the village hall. The class takes place tomorrow night.

'Do you want to come to yoga with me tomorrow?' I blurt suddenly.

I watch as her expression shifts, as though she is choosing which emotion to wear.

'Um, well I do usually go ...'

'Great!' I reply quickly. 'See you there then?'

Sarah pauses, shifting the weight of the box in her arms. Then she nods.

'See you there.'

As she walks away towards her car I step into the village shop with a bounce in my step. The shop is so crowded I have to dodge two dogs and a small child. Outside, the ferry is drawing closer to the jetty. Ferry time means post, deliveries to the shop and generally an opportunity for the whole island to catch up. It certainly feels like most of the island is here as I navigate my way between the shelves, densely stocked with everything from tins and dried pasta to toilet roll and cleaning products. A couple dressed in near-matching yellow raincoats examine the biscuit selection intently; I recognise them as the couple who shared the ferry with us from the mainland. Stepping over an empty crate on the floor I spot Jean Brown by the fruit and veg, dressed today in smart trousers and a shirt, an overnight bag at her feet. She talks quietly with Kerstin. They look deep in conversation. Should I go over? I don't want to seem rude if they look up and notice I've been in here a while. I eventually head over towards them.

'Good to see you both. Going somewhere nice I hope, Jean?' I nod at the overnight bag.

She looks flustered, glancing from Kerstin to me and then back to Kerstin, who raises an eyebrow. Jean smooths her hair.

'Just to visit my sister,' she says quickly, her forehead suddenly pink. 'And I think that must be the ferry here now, I'd better go.'

Kerstin pulls her towards her and hugs her tightly. When the two women part they both blink quickly, before Jean heads to the shop door where a man whom I recognise immediately as her husband (although with less hair and more wrinkles than

180

I remember) greets her, taking her bag from her and wrapping an arm gently around her shoulders. They are just about to leave when a small voice belonging to a child who is trailing around after a parent in the shop cries, 'Mrs Brown!'

The child runs up to Jean and hugs her around the waist. I smile, remembering how well-loved Jean was as a teacher when I was young too. But then the child lets go and Jean is bustling out of the door with her husband. What were Jean and Kerstin talking about before I arrived? And why did they seem so upset and flustered just now?

'Right, I'd better get all this back,' Kerstin says before I have the chance to say anything else, lifting the full bags of shopping at her sides. 'Do pop round for tea at some point.'

I smile, remembering Brenda's invitation too. And then she's heading for the door, greeting a few people briefly as she passes.

I reach for a basket and begin the search for the things Alice has asked me to pick up. It feels strange to be in this shop that was once so familiar. Now, I have to search carefully for every item rather than simply heading to the same shelf as usual without even thinking. Is there anything more disorientating than doing a food shop not in your local supermarket? This island shop may be a fraction of the size of the Tesco I visit back home, but I still feel lost.

As I pause by the cans, I suddenly hear my name.

'Did you hear that Lorna Irvine is back on the island?'

I freeze, my arm reaching out for the shelf.

'I know, I couldn't believe she had the gall to come back!'

The voices sound as though they are coming from just on

181

the other side of the aisle. Am I even breathing? I'm not sure I am.

'Her poor parents. After everything they did for her. Do you know her mother had to home-school her to keep her out of trouble? The mainland school wouldn't take her because they'd heard she was too much to handle.'

As I listen to them, wincing at their version of things, I suddenly spot the shopkeeper behind the counter. Mrs Campbell, that was her name. She isn't moving and I can tell she is listening to the conversation too. Then she looks up and meets my eye. She has aged, but I still recognise her.

'Excuse me, Doris Anderson!' she says suddenly, her voice loud and sharp. 'I won't tolerate gossip and lies in my shop! If you're going to talk like that you'll have to get your food from some other shop.'

'I, I, well I don't know what you ...' stutters the voice I now recognise from our conversation in the pub the other day. 'But, there *isn't* another shop.'

'Quite,' says Mrs Campbell, folding her arms across her chest.

I listen to the sound of shuffling footsteps and turn around just in time to watch Mrs Anderson and a couple of women I recognise as my parents' church friends disappearing out the door.

I let out a sigh.

'Do you think they saw me?' I ask Mrs Campbell.

'And so what if they did! I hope it would make them feel right disgraceful for talking like that. And they call themselves Christians!'

She shakes her head.

'But no, dear, I don't think they saw you,' she adds more softly. 'Anyway, come over here! Let me see you!'

She reaches across the counter and as I stretch out in response she covers my hands with both of hers, tough, weathered hands that are nonetheless warm and strong around mine.

'It's so good to see you again, dear,' she says with a smile.

As I look at Mrs Campbell the memories come flooding back. I remember her handing me sweets as a young girl when I trailed behind my mother on our weekly visits to the shop. And then there was the time when my period first started and I was too embarrassed to tell my mother. I was twelve, and by that point I'd learned not to talk to my mother about anything particularly personal. The conversations I'd tried to have with her about my father and the plans I'd tried to make for her, Jack and me to escape had come to nothing. If anything, they created a gulf between us, both of us uneasy around one another. That day was a weekday so Sarah was away at school. So I walked across the entire island with toilet tissue folded inside my knickers, arriving at the village shop soaked from a sudden downpour that hit while I was walking. I remember feeling cold, frightened and deeply ashamed. But somehow, without having to say anything Mrs Campbell guessed what had happened and brought me the things I needed from the shelves. She let me use the toilet at the back of the shop.

'I don't have any money with me,' I remember saying quietly, my head tilted towards my shoes.

'Oh, don't you worry about that, love,' she'd replied.

Back in the shop now I swallow back tears. Somehow over

the years I'd forgotten this woman and those small but meaningful acts of kindness.

I finish my shopping and lift my basket onto the counter.

'Thank you,' I say as she hands me the bag and my receipt.

I hope she knows I mean for far more than just the shopping.

'Anytime,' she replies gently. 'You are always welcome here, Lorna.'

A smile spreads across my face.

Outside I load the bicycle. As I'm piling things into the basket my phone buzzes. There's a text from Cheryl that was sent yesterday but has only come through now I have signal.

How's it going? Taking Frankie to the zoo today.
He's been a right monkey this week so I might leave
him there!!!! xxx

I try to call her back but the phone cuts out, my one bar of reception clearly not enough to connect me. I wish suddenly to hear the sound of my friend's voice. Instead, I type a message. I nearly tell her about Mallachy and the strange moment we shared in his studio. But what would I even say? I can't quite understand or explain that sudden feeling of connection I experienced. He's a complete stranger. And besides, I ran away.

Instead I type:

Sorry for the slow reply. Dodgy signal here. Hope
you had fun at the zoo and that you changed
your mind about leaving Frankie there! Things still
strange here, but at least the sun is shining. x

On an impulse I take a photo of the view and send it to her, boats bobbing in the harbour, the stretching sea and the mainland just visible on the horizon. On my way back to the farm I pause a few times along the way to take a few more pictures: wildflowers swaying in the breeze, a lone sheep on a hillock facing out to sea, a close up of the vibrant moss that clings to rocky outcrops alongside the road. Maybe I should have brought my proper camera on this trip. But it didn't even enter my head when I was packing. This isn't exactly a holiday, after all.

Arriving back at the house I spot Alice in the field on a quadbike, the sheep scattering around her as she bumps across the grass. I can tell the house is empty as soon as I step inside; the quiet fills every room. Now is my chance to wander more freely. I don't know what I'm looking for exactly. Anything that tells me more about my brother and the life I've missed. I pause by the staircase, looking closely at the pictures of Molly and the family that line the wall. In the living room I scan the bookshelves. There's a shelf of classics, several of paperback crime novels with peeling covers, a collection of science fiction and a few coffee-table books. There are several local history books about Kip but also about the surrounding islands.

And then I pause on a book I hadn't expected to see. It's a very old copy of *Finn Family Moomintroll*, tucked in the middle of one of the lower shelves. I reach out a hand and touch the spine. Suddenly I'm a child all over again.

When Jack was little he had nightmares. Every night he would struggle to sleep, terrified of what would be waiting for him in his dreams. Once I knew our parents were downstairs or in their own room I would sneak into Jack's room and read to him.

Reading seemed to be the only thing that helped Jack to sleep. *Finn Family Moomintroll* was his favourite. When we were very young I couldn't read all of the words so would make up parts of the story for him. But as I got older I was able to read the whole thing to him. I'd sit next to him in his bed and read as much as I needed until he fell asleep. I never told him, because I was trying to be a good big sister, but I had nightmares too. I think I needed that book just as much as Jack did.

I pull the book off the shelf, running my hand over the faded cover. It's been years and years since I read this book. I could never bring myself to buy it for Ella. But if I close my eyes I can still remember the opening line of the story.

I reach to place the book carefully back on the shelf, but as I do so something falls from between the pages. I pick up a photograph that has dropped to the floor.

Jack looks about six years old, his face scattered with freckles. Which must make me ten, standing next to him with an arm around his shoulders. It looks as though we are on the beach by the village, near the school. I can't remember who took the photograph but I remember the feel of the sun on my face, my little brother standing by my side. My expression looks so serious as I face the camera. But Jack isn't looking straight ahead. He is looking at me. His head is tilted up towards mine and he is smiling. Looking at the photograph a thought enters my mind like a moth slipping in through a window. Maybe there is hope for us yet.

CHAPTER 16

ALICE

I can hear Ella and Molly talking in the kitchen as I sort through the washing in the utility room at the back of the house. Their voices blur into one another, a steady stream of chatter. I lean back on my heels, listening. I catch the sound of Lorna entering the room and wishing them good morning, then finish loading the washing machine and join them all in the kitchen. As I step inside, Ella is just asking Lorna a question.

'Mum,' she says, using the same dragged-out voice Molly uses when she wants something. I try my best to suppress a laugh. Lorna catches my eye and we smile at one another knowingly.

'Molly says that Uncle Jack and Aunt Alice's friend Mallachy has a boat and does tours, and that he could take us over to Caora Island.'

Is it just my imagination or does Lorna stiffen slightly? Ella perseveres.

'Olive's dad has a boat too but it's only a really small one and he says he doesn't trust it to go all the way there, that we'd be better off asking Mallachy instead. He might even take us to see the puffins that nest on the cliffs below the lighthouse, isn't that right, Molly?'

'Yeah, his trips are great. Mum, can we ask Mallachy to take us?'

I glance again at Lorna, trying to read her expression.

'Well, I don't mind but Auntie Lorna has to be OK with it too. And you have to check with Auntie Sarah if you want Olive to join you. And then of course you'd have to ask Mallachy.'

'So, what do you think, Mum?' says Ella. 'Can we?'

Her eyebrows furrow and I wonder if I've said the wrong thing. Perhaps I should have given Molly a vaguer answer and checked with Lorna separately. Maybe Ella can't swim? Or perhaps Lorna doesn't trust Mallachy to take the girls out – I suppose she barely knows him after all. I guess living in a big city is different, you grow warier of other people. I forget that it's not totally normal to leave your door permanently unlocked, to let your children flit in and out of neighbours' houses and to not always know exactly where they are but to not worry about that. They can't go far.

'We'll see,' replies Lorna after a moment's pause.

Ella sighs and rises from the table, loudly stacking her breakfast things in the dishwasher before disappearing upstairs. I expect Molly to follow but she lingers for a moment, looking carefully at Lorna. I wonder suddenly what she's making of

188

all this. She's been so busy with Ella and Olive that I haven't had any alone time with her since our visitors arrived. She seems happy, excitedly showing Ella around the island. And there's the beach clean-up initiative too which the girls have now expanded to include pretty much all the island children. They're planning on writing letters to our MP about getting the government to do more to combat the problem of single-use plastics. But despite her cheerfulness and her impressive drive, these past few days have been unsettling. It's all a lot to take in.

'What was Dad like when he was little?' she says suddenly. I see Lorna's eyebrows rise and feel mine lifting too. I watch as Molly leans forward slightly, clearly eager for an answer, and realise that I want to hear too.

'Only, he never really talks about his childhood,' Molly adds quietly, flashing her glance in my direction before looking down at the table. 'And I've seen barely any photos of him when he was little. There are only a couple that Dad's shown me and there were never any at Grandma and Grandad's house. I suppose I could have asked them but …'

Despite the fact Molly only sees them a couple of times a year, she has always been closer to my parents than she ever was to Jack's. Ever since I finally persuaded Mum and Dad to get a laptop I sometimes hear their voices coming from Molly's bedroom and peer inside to find that she's Skyping with them, my dad's face enormous because he doesn't believe the laptop's microphone can pick up his voice so insists on sitting millimetres from the screen.

'Your dad had freckles just like you,' says Lorna and a smile breaks like sunshine across my daughter's face. I can't help but smile too.

'He loved the Moomintrolls,' she continues, 'and his toy train. He was clever, but didn't like putting his hand up in school.'

'That sounds a bit like me,' Molly says eagerly then adds quickly. 'Not that I'm clever, just that I don't always like putting my hand up.'

I watch her wriggling in her seat with embarrassment, poor thing, but Lorna smiles reassuringly.

'I'm sure you are very clever. Your mum tells me you're doing really well at school. And it must have been daunting going from the island primary school to your secondary school on the mainland.'

Molly shrugs slightly but her pink cheeks give her away. My heart gives a painful little squeeze.

I think it was harder for me than it was for Molly when she started secondary school. I always knew the day would come – I'd known ever since she was born that if we were to stay on the island, her leaving for secondary school was just something I'd have to deal with. Jean did her best to help prepare me too.

'Everyone finds it tough at first,' she told me. 'But they all adjust.' Over the years she organised several excursions to the mainland with the children to try to get them used to the idea of what was to come, and I volunteered on every one. I remember a particular two-day trip to Glasgow to take the children to the galleries and museums there. Sarah volunteered too and Jean, Sarah and I spent those two days shepherding children who were not used to a big city during the day, and at night sharing wine Jean had smuggled along with her in her back-pack, in one of the rooms in the cheap hotel we'd booked out for the trip.

The year before Molly was due to finish primary school it all became painfully real though. I even tried to persuade Jack that we should move to the mainland. I couldn't bear the thought of only seeing my daughter at weekends and holidays. I grew angry at Jack. I'd moved my whole life to be here with him, far away from everyone I knew. Having to say goodbye to my daughter – it felt like he was asking too much of me. Olive is a year older than Molly so had already started at the mainland school and I remember turning up on Sarah's doorstep one evening in floods of tears, telling her that I couldn't do it, I couldn't let Molly go.

Sarah took me inside, poured me wine and called Jean to come and join us. Together the three of us talked.

'So, you've got the secondary-school jitters,' said Jean. 'Everyone gets them.'

'I didn't want to let Olive go either,' Sarah added. 'And that first day when I waved her goodbye on the ferry … I'm not going to lie, it was awful. But now she's settled there and she's happy. She's made new friends and she really enjoys the inde-pendence. And when she comes back home she seems even happier to be here. She even lets Alfie play with her.'

We all laughed then.

'I've watched your Molly grow up,' chipped in Jean. 'She's a really resilient little girl – I know it must be hard but these new stages in their lives are opportunities for the children to flourish. And she will, Alice, I truly believe she will.'

191

'It's tough letting go,' said Sarah. 'But I see how happy and confident Olive is now. I don't think I'll ever be pleased about seeing her go off on that boat but she's happy and that's the most important thing. Besides, what choice do we really have? Tell me honestly, do you really want to move to the mainland? To start all over again?'

They both looked at me then and I realised that Sarah was right. I was dreading Molly leaving but I didn't want to move. I didn't want to leave our house, our beach, my friends. This island may not be where I imagined I would end up when I was younger, but it has become my home.

Despite Molly's excitement about the new chapter in her life and the new freedoms it would involve, I knew she had her reservations too. We both cried that first day when she left. But over time I came to see what Sarah and Jean promised I would. My daughter getting used to the new way of things and eventually becoming happy, more independent and somehow surer of herself.

'It was a bit strange at first,' Molly tells Lorna. 'Especially being away from home all week. But it's been nice to meet other people too. Some of my mainland friends are coming to visit the island soon. That'll be really cool.'

Lorna nods, smiling. But there's something else to her expression too, a certain sense of regret. Jack never really explained to me why he and Lorna stayed at home rather than going to the mainland school like everyone else. I never thought he particularly minded it, but when I was having my wobble about Molly I raised home-schooling her as an option. Really, I had no idea how I'd do it. I'm far from academic, how would I possibly teach my own child? But I felt so desperate I was willing to try. But when I mentioned it Jack shook his head.

'No,' he said firmly, 'I won't trap her like that. We have to let her have her freedom, Alice, even if it's hard.'

And like an extra jigsaw piece fitting into place I felt like I suddenly understood my husband and his story a little better.

'Can you remember anything else about Dad?' Molly asks.

Lorna glances outside, her expression distant.

'He loved searching for shells and driftwood. Whenever we walked on the beach we would search for things together. I always gave him my best finds – a particularly beautiful shell, a bit of smooth glass. When I gave them to him you'd think he'd just been given a new bike or something. If I was ever on the beach without him I'd keep my eyes wide open, searching for things he might like.'

Molly's eyes light up.

'He still does that! One second ...'

She disappears but is back a few moments later, clutching the small wooden box that usually lives in our living room, by the TV.

'He calls it his treasure box,' Molly says, handing it over. I watch as Lorna traces her hand over the lid and carefully opens it. Slowly she removes object after object, turning them over in her hands. A circular pebble the colour of a raincloud. A smooth white shell the shape of a baby's ear, the inside perfectly pink. A shard of jade sea-glass. A coin, smoothed so flat by the sea that it is impossible to tell to which currency it once belonged. I've never really understood why Jack keeps all this stuff, but looking at Lorna I notice that her eyes have grown misty.

'Thank you for showing me this, Molly,' she says, placing the items gently back inside and closing the lid. 'I have a similar collection back at home. It used to be our thing, collecting this stuff together. I had no idea he still did it though.'

'Shall we go?' comes a voice at the doorway. Ella is standing there, a backpack over her shoulders. Molly springs up with a smile.

'Yes, let's go. See you later, Mum and Auntie Lorna.'

I want to ask Lorna more about Jack when he was younger but she is standing up too.

'I might go out for a walk if you don't mind?'

'That's fine, I've got some work to do here.'

'I can stay and help if you like?'

'No, you go, it's fine.'

She nods.

'OK. I think I left my shoes upstairs though.'

Once she's gone my eyes fall on a bag on the table that I hadn't noticed before. I spot what looks like a jumper spilling out of it, but it doesn't look like anything Lorna owns. It's a heavy knit, rust-red. It looks vaguely familiar. There's a piece of paper half-sticking out too.

I know it's terrible. I know I'm being nosey. But I just can't help myself. Glancing towards the corridor I reach across and lift the corner of the paper, taking a quick peek.

There's a handwritten note.

Mallachy,

Here is your jumper, I'm sorry I forgot to give it back to you sooner. Sorry also for leaving like I did. Thank you for keeping me from drowning in the rain and for the tea – it was kind of you and I'm sorry if I seemed rude. It seems to be a habit of mine, although not my intention. If the offer still stands to come and visit your studio again, I would very much like that.

Lorna

Immediately I return the note and the bag to their exact position, a flush of guilt but also excitement rushing through me. Lorna and Mallachy... When I introduced them at the school I couldn't help but think they might get on. Their shared interest in art, his warmth but also the way we've all learned by now that he likes time alone too, just like Lorna seems to with her walks and runs. I don't suggest going with her like I might with my friends. I can tell she needs that time to herself, and that's OK. But I can't rush ahead of myself. It's none of my business, it was unfair of me even to look at the note. And it might be nothing anyway.

Lorna steps back inside, reaching for the bag and slinging it over her shoulder.

'Are you sure you don't mind me popping out?'

'No, of course not. Have a nice walk.'

'It's your yoga class tonight, isn't it?' she says, pausing.

'It is! Do you still think you'd like to come?'

'Yes, I'm looking forward to it.'

'Great.'

Then with a slight wave, she turns and is gone.

I reach for my phone, checking for any updates from Jean about how her appointment went. But there's nothing. The worries start to creep in but I do my best to push them back. There's too much to do, what with preparations for the funeral and the wake and all the chores that always need doing around the farm. I don't have time to fall apart.

CHAPTER 17

LORNA

'So, do you do yoga back in London?'

Alice drives the Land Rover up the track, dressed in loose exercise clothes and a floral headband.

'Um, not exactly,' I reply.

I accepted the invitation to join Alice's class because I was pleased to be included. And then when I saw Sarah again at the shop I figured it might be a good way to try to start building bridges with her. At least it will put us in the same room together. That's got to be a start. But I hadn't really thought about the fact that I've never been to a yoga class before in my life.

It's early evening and Jack is still working in the fields. Alice and I left Molly and Ella in the kitchen where they are preparing dinner for when we return. It was a surprise to hear that this is a weekly tradition for Molly, who has been cooking since she was very young. Aside from the occasional cake or tray of flapjacks, Ella rarely helps me out in the kitchen. Not that I'm much of a cook myself. I'm not sure you could call heating up a pre-made pasta sauce cooking. During the weekend I do try to cook from scratch, but always very simple recipes that we've had a hundred times before. The food Alice has cooked for us while we've been here has put my feeble attempts to shame and made me think that perhaps I really should make more of an effort when we get back to London.

The thought of the city slips into my mind in a sudden flash of sirens, crowds, steaming pavements and our small flat on the Isle of Dogs. But then the Land Rover lurches through a particularly deep pothole in the track and I'm brought back to the island. I look out the window and it catches me how relieved I am to see the sea.

'Well, I'll keep it gentle. And just remember, yoga isn't a competitive sport. It's OK if you don't get it straight away, just as long as you give it a go.'

Stepping inside the village hall brings an onslaught of memories. Balloons and birthday cake at children's birthday parties here when I was young, Irn-Bru drunk from sticky plastic cups. Tea and homemade cakes after every big service at the church – Good Friday, Easter Sunday, the Harvest festival. I remember my family standing with their church friends, always somewhat separate from the other islanders.

I also remember the celebration that was held here at the end of my last year at primary school. I was emotional all day, knowing that I'd not be continuing with Sarah and the others on to the secondary school on the mainland. I won an art prize at the ceremony. In reality, every one of the children at our small school won some sort of prize. But when Sarah was awarded hers, her parents and grandparents still stood up and cheered so loudly Sarah's face turned the colour of beetroot. But my parents weren't there. I'm not sure what happened and why they didn't make it. My father had probably got himself into no fit state to leave the house and my mother would never have come on her own. I remember how disappointed I felt that they hadn't been there, if not for me then for my brother, who was still small for his age and who shook when he collected his own prize from Mrs Brown, for science.

'Why don't you mind that they weren't there, that they don't even care that we won?' I hissed at Jack later that evening, my anger spilling out beyond my control.

He had shrugged then, in that way that always infuriated and depressed me in equal measures. It was a shrug that said he accepted things the way they were and that maybe I should too.

'Everyone got a prize,' he said. He was right, of course. But that didn't explain the sense of having been let down and the sadness that my little brother was growing up, like me, never to expect praise.

Standing in the same village hall again another part of my memory of that day comes rushing back, something I'd forgotten before stepping back inside here. When Jack and I stood up to collect our awards there wasn't silence like I'd expected there would be, knowing that our parents weren't there. There was cheering and clapping, coming from every person in the room.

I rub my eyes and breathe deeply, trying to push away the memories that are threatening to overwhelm me. This is not the moment to get upset. I focus instead on the room as it is now. There is a soft scent of eucalyptus in the warm air that rises just above the still familiar 'village hall' smell of old tea and musty carpet. Purple mats are arranged in lines facing a black mat at the front, towards which Alice is now heading. The room is already mostly full.

I spot Sarah, Brenda, Tess, Kerstin and Emma. And to my surprise there's Morag, dressed in a pair of bright pink leggings and an over-sized T-shirt that hangs off her skinny, wrinkled arms. She smiles and waves and then grabs her right ankle and lifts it high into the air, demonstrating her impressive flexibility. Is this the same old woman who fell asleep in the pub just a few days ago? Maybe there's something to this whole yoga thing after all.

I glance at Alice, who is talking intently to a nervous-looking woman I don't recognise. She catches my eye and gestures for me to join them.

'Lorna, this is Natalia's first class too. I've been trying to persuade her to join since she moved here. I'm so glad you made it. I promise to go easy on you both.'

Natalia laughs. In one corner of the room the other women gather in a huddled group.

'So have you heard from Jean?' I just make out Emma asking Brenda, who shakes her head. Alice glances over at the mention of Jean's name and a cloud passes for a second across her face, but then she looks at her watch and places her hands together.

'I guess we'd better get started.' She turns to face the whole room. 'Ladies, if you'd like to take a seat on your mats.'

I pick one just behind Sarah and sit down too.

'Hello, everyone,' says Alice in a soft voice. 'I'd like to say a special welcome today to two people who are attending this class for the first time: Lorna and Natalia. Welcome, both of you.'

A few 'welcomes' come from the women at the other mats and I feel mortified but there's also something nice to it too. I catch Natalia's eye and we exchange a glance that tells me she feels the same way.

'Now, let's begin.'

Soft music and the sound of Alice's voice fill the hall. As she guides us through each movement, starting with a series of deep breaths sitting on the mats and then moving to our hands and knees, her voice sounds encouraging but at the same time has a presence to it that I haven't heard before. She sounds in her element, and it's immediately clear that this is her *thing*.

Accompanying the music and Alice's guiding words come the sounds of each woman in the room breathing, sometimes in unison, sometimes falling out of sync when the pace of the movements quickens. On the whole I manage to follow most of Alice's instructions. Her friends were right – she is a good teacher. Every now and then she comes over and helps to adjust my position or suggests a variation on the pose the others in the class are holding that is easier for a beginner. When she pushes gently on my shoulder blades as I attempt a downward dog I recoil slightly at the touch. I don't mean to. It's just been a long time since anyone touched my bare skin like that. And

I'm sweating and probably looking nothing like I'm supposed to or like the other women in the room. I'm probably doing a terrible job. But she's calm and encouraging, and the next time she gently adjusts me there is something comforting about her touch. How much of a relief it would be to have someone adjust me like this in my everyday life. Someone to soften my voice when I raise it without meaning to, to help me say the right thing to my daughter and my brother.

If I'm honest I've always avoided yoga in the past, thinking it would be too slow. I've never been very good at moments of stillness. It's in stillness that the thoughts creep in.

The other women in the class stand straight as trees with their arms held above their heads. I try to copy them, glancing around for slight sways or wobbles. I fix my attention on Sarah's back in front of me. She seems so firmly grounded. Alice might be telling us to focus on nothing but the sound of our own breath but I find it impossible. Can you ever really switch off your thoughts? I can't anyway.

Another memory works its way in, this time scented with vanilla sponge and jelly and ice cream. It's Sarah's tenth birthday party, celebrated here inside the village hall. After blowing out her candles, Sarah relit them so I could have a chance to make a wish too. Later that day when all the other children had left, I asked Sarah what her wish was. I've never forgotten what she said.

'I wished that you'd be happier.'

As Alice instructs us all to bend and bow, sweeping our arms to the floor, I feel blood rushing to my head. As we rise again, arms held above our heads once more, I remember myself at ten years old. Tangled, unbrushed hair, nails bitten so close to the flesh that they often bled around the edges. Unhappiness always seemed to cling to me, so that even at a birthday party filled with balloons and laughter and so much sugar that our heads ached, Sarah could see my sadness as clearly as if it had been an uninvited guest in the room.

'Now, if you can all make your way to the floor, we are going to end with shavasana, or corpse pose.'

Finally, a pose that I should have no problem in mastering. Alice instructs us to lie flat on our backs, arms slightly apart from our sides with palms facing upwards, eyes closed.

'Focus on the sound of your breathing and the noise of those breathing around you.'

I listen to my breath rising and falling steadily. It is almost calming. But with my eyes closed there is more space for the thoughts and memories to fill my mind. I think of Jack on his first day at school and how Sarah and I sat next to him and introduced him to the other children. I felt so proud to be his big sister, my arm slung around his shoulder. But when I stepped off the jetty earlier this week the man I saw was a long way from that little boy. I recognised him at once and yet he felt like a stranger.

I squeeze my eyes tightly shut. I knew that coming back to the island would be hard. But maybe I hadn't quite acknow-ledged the sense of loss that I'd feel being back here. Because as I lie on the floor, trying to empty my mind but feeling it become close to overflowing instead, I think about how much I have lost over the years. Sarah, my brother, my parents even.

And I cannot shake the lingering feeling that has followed me my whole life. That it's all my fault.

'Feel the ground beneath your back,' says Alice softly. 'Feel it supporting you.'

I sense the mat beneath my shoulders and below it the hard ground pressing against my spine, my calves, the back of my head, holding me up.

'You are supported,' Alice says.

I'm breathing more quickly now. My eyes are damp and stinging. But I'm not crying. I'm not going to cry. I try to focus on the sound of the island women breathing around me. The room is one sleeping creature, taking deep, steady breaths. But even though my breath joins in, I know deep down that this feeling of belonging is just an illusion. Because I am on my own. I have been for most of my life. That's just the way it is. It's just me and Ella. I have no right to feel so alone, because this is what I chose for us. This has been my way of protecting us.

Alice's voice rises above the sound of our breath.

'You are safe.'

Right here, right now, maybe I am safe. But I also know what it means to feel as though my life is a walk alongside a cliff edge in the dark.

'You are here,' says Alice.

And I can't help it – the tears slide freely down my cheeks now, falling onto the mat beneath me. I am here. I am back on the island I never thought I would see again. Back in the place I once called home. Back among the people I left, and many who have arrived after me. And I feel utterly lost.

The sobs come from deep within my body. I try to stop them but it's useless now. My body shakes, my legs and arms tense and trembling. But there is a sudden warmth on my right shoulder. Then my left. Then my elbow, my wrist, my ankle. Warmth flows through my whole body like a current. What's happening?

Opening my eyes, I see the island women crowded around me, each with a palm placed gently on a part of my body. There's Morag, with a hand wrapped around my left ankle, smiling toothily. And Brenda by my left arm. Tess placing a hand gently on my shin. Sarah by my right shoulder. As I see Alice at my left side I think I understand what they are doing. They are holding me. Even Natalia is here beside me, the whole class of women crouched beside me and touching me gently.

Normally I'd pull back from physical contact like this. I hate it when someone bumps up against me on the tube, even if it's accidental. But this feels different. My breathing slows. Looking up, I meet the faces of Sarah on my right and Alice on my left. They look down at me with expressions softened with concern. Looking at Sarah I see the ten-year-old girl who used her birthday wish to ask for my happiness.

Easing myself up slowly, the women step back slightly. All except Sarah, who is still crouching down beside me. Do I reach out first or does she? It doesn't really matter, does it? Because we are hugging each other, arms held tightly.

'I'm sorry,' I say into her hair. 'I'm so sorry.'

I want to tell her more, that I should never have lost touch with her, I should never have let her go. But for now, this is all I can manage.

'It's OK,' Sarah replies, 'It's going to be OK.'

Is it? I don't even know what OK might look like. But I am breathing more calmly now and the tears have stopped at least. Eventually we pull apart and stand up. The other women are up now too, the yoga mats abandoned and the incense burnt out. The hall smells like damp and biscuits again. And I laugh. I don't know why. But the laughter rises inside me like bubbles. And suddenly the other women are laughing too. It's as though the class and the tears have released some of the tension that I'd been carrying tightly like a heavy bag I didn't want to put down, or didn't realise that I could.

Eventually, after warm goodbyes with the other island women, Alice, Sarah and I are left alone in the hall.

'Sarah, you should join us for dinner,' Alice says suddenly. 'Pick up Ben and the kids on the way. An impromptu dinner party! Molly's cooking but I've got a lasagne in the freezer we can get out too, so there'll be plenty of food.'

Sarah glances at me and we smile at one another.

'That would be great,' she says and as she does so she slips her arm through mine like she used to do whenever we walked side by side, so easily, so gently. Having her beside me feels like climbing into your own bed after being away from home for a very long time.

We walk to the cars together and say goodbye. I'll see Sarah again shortly but it stills feels a wrench as she lets go of my arm and climbs into her own car to go home and change and collect her family.

As Alice drives us back to the farm I let out a sigh. She

doesn't comment on my earlier tears and it feels like a sort of kindness.

'Your friends are lovely,' I tell her.

Her face fills with a smile.

'Oh, I know, I'm so lucky. It's one of my favourite things about living on this island. I mean, there are other places we could live but I just couldn't imagine not living close to my friends.'

I think of Cheryl back in London and the comfort it's given me over the past five years to know she is just around the corner. But I think too of Sarah and Emma and the other friends from my childhood that I let slip away when I left the island. When I've thought of this island over the years I've thought mostly of my parents and my unhappy home life. Maybe it made leaving easier to forget the happier memories, those moments in my childhood where the clouds parted and for a moment I felt bathed in the glow of a golden sun. My friends were that for me, once.

CHAPTER 18

ALICE

Molly and Ella are bursting with excitement when they hear that Olive and her family are joining us for dinner. I hope it wasn't meddling to invite them, it's just when I saw Sarah and Lorna together after the class I couldn't help myself. Of course it's always lovely to have Sarah and her family over but it felt like a chance for them to catch up too.

'It smells wonderful in here, girls.'

Ella lays the table while Molly stirs a pan on the Rayburn. I open the freezer, pulling out the frozen lasagne that I keep in there for emergencies.

'I'm sure this won't be anywhere near as nice as what you've cooked, darling,' I say to Molly, kissing her on the forehead. 'But I don't want anyone to go hungry.'

'No, it's fine, it's a good idea, Mum.'

'I'm just going to take a quick shower,' says Lorna from the doorway but before she turns away Ella calls her back.

'Mum,' she says. 'A delivery arrived for you while you were out.'

Ella and Molly meet eyes and stifle giggles as they look quickly away again. Ella points at the table where I suddenly spot a jam jar filled with sprigs of heather, a slightly lopsided twine bow tied around the rim of the jar. There's a note propped up against the jar and Lorna blushes as she reaches for it.

I don't mean to. I really don't. But as I turn back from putting the lasagne in the oven my eyes fall on the piece of paper.

Lorna,

It's true you're making a habit of being rude to me, but it seems I find myself making a habit of forgiving you. Thank you for the buttercups – how did you know that they are Rex's favourites? You are welcome at the studio any time.

Mallachy

I look away quickly, hoping that Lorna didn't catch me being nosey. But her head is tilted down at the note, her cheeks pink as she folds it and slips it in the pocket of her leggings.

'So, does this mean we can go on that trip on Mallachy's boat?' Ella asks, eyebrows raised and a grin on her face.

Lorna's cheeks turn an even brighter shade of pink.

'I said we'll see. Right now, I need to go and have a shower before the others get here. See you all in a minute. Thanks again for the class, Alice.'

She disappears upstairs, clutching the note and the jar of flowers.

'Well that was weird,' says Ella.

'Come on, girls, it's none of our business, let's get on with finishing getting everything ready.' I say it as much for myself as for them. But my mind returns to the thought that entered my head yesterday, that Mallachy and Lorna might get on well. Could this perhaps be the start of her putting roots down on the island again? Could Jack get his sister back after all this time? And could this help solve the problems we're facing – could *Lorna* be the one to help us keep this community together? But no, I can't let myself think like that. And besides, I made a promise that I wouldn't tell Lorna what's going on. I have to stick to that.

Once the table's finished I race upstairs to change. Jack is in the bedroom peeling off his muddy farm layers and dropping them in the wash basket.

'Good class?' he asks me, kissing me on the cheek as he buttons a clean shirt.

I want to tell him about everything that happened – how Lorna broke down and how it felt as though something dropped away tonight, a final barrier that she'd been trying to hold up like a windbreak on a blustery beach. But I don't know how to find the words. As I watch him stepping into clean trousers I think about all the other things that are unsaid between us at the moment.

'It was good, thanks. How was your day?'

'Fine.'

I take a breath but a knocking comes from the front door downstairs.

'You go,' I say, reaching for my own jeans and pulling them on. 'I'll be down in a second.'

He nods, closing the door behind him. I pause on the bed, jeans on but still just in my bra, feeling suddenly exhausted. What's wrong with me? My good friends are downstairs – I can hear Jack greeting Sarah, Ben and the children and the excited chatter of Molly, Olive and Ella. But my head spins. The thought of going downstairs and hosting, even for people I love so much, feels for a moment too much to handle. I'm being ridiculous though. This dinner was my idea. I must just be tired from the class. I pull on a striped shirt, swipe a dash of coral lipstick on my lips and head downstairs, making my steps as light as I can manage.

'Hello! Hello!'

Sarah greets me with a hug, even though we only saw each other moments ago. Jack is already opening a bottle of wine supplied by Ben, who kisses me on the cheek with a smile. I've always liked Ben. Quiet but friendly, with black curly hair that their son Alfie has inherited and a gentle demeanour. He and Jack are well-suited friends and it warms me to see them already chatting away to one another.

The girls pour soft drinks and fuss over the pot on the Rayburn while Alfie surveys the table, making sure the cutlery and napkins are all perfectly parallel. The room is warm with voices and laughter and I relax, returning to myself again.

There's a brief pause as Lorna enters the room, looking down somewhat shyly.

'Lorna, let me introduce you to everyone!'

Ben kisses her on the cheek too and Alfie reaches out a small hand for her to shake, his expression serious. Olive gives a little wave from the other side of the room.

'It's so nice to meet you all,' says Lorna.

'Would you like wine, Lorna?' asks Jack, holding up an empty glass.

She pauses for a second, struggling to hide the surprise on her face. Is this the first question Jack has directly asked her since she arrived? I notice as he meets her eye, not glancing immediately away, and something does a little skip inside me.

'I'd love some, thank you, Jack.'

'Dinner's ready!' cry the girls.

I sit Lorna and Sarah next to one another, with Ella opposite.

'So, you went to school with Mum,' Ella asks immediately. 'Was she naughty? Did she do well in her subjects?'

I spot the hungriness on Ella's face, reminding me of the questions Molly asked Lorna this morning. Sarah smiles and tells a few stories: the two of them riding their bicycles to school and Lorna winning an egg-and-spoon race on sports day.

'My eggs meanwhile were scrambled on the floor,' she laughs.

'Oh, but you were brilliant at so many other things, Sarah,' chips in Lorna. 'Remember how you used to help me with equations? I just couldn't get my head round them but you were so great at explaining it all. How funny that I'm the one who's ended up a teacher!'

Sarah glances at me but I look away, not quite able to meet her eye.

'You enjoy your job though?' asks Sarah.

'I do. I really enjoy teaching the children, but …'

She pauses then, taking a sip of wine and looking across at Ella. Everyone else at the table is watching Lorna now, apart from Alfie who is building a somewhat unstable-looking structure out of spare glasses and cutlery.

'Well,' continues Lorna, 'the truth is I've been getting a bit of grief from my boss recently.'

Ella looks up.

'What? Mum? You didn't tell me that. What's going on?'

'It's OK, darling, it's nothing I can't handle. It's just a hassle, that's all. It's nothing I haven't had to deal with before, I guess it's just the first time it's been in a work environment.'

Ben nods.

'I know what you mean,' he says. 'I work remotely for a web developer and my boss can be a real taskmaster. Setting projects with impossible deadlines, emails on a weekend … He doesn't really seem to have a concept of boundaries.'

I watch as the faces of the women around the table redden slightly. Because I don't think Ben does know what Lorna means. I think back to the instructor who taught my yoga teaching qualification. He seemed nice at first, energetic and enthusiastic about his job. But as the course went on he became more and more hands-on, but only with the female members of the group. He'd always be adjusting someone's stance or getting incredibly close, so close I could feel his breath on my skin. It was a residential course and I remember one evening at the communal dinner table he came up behind me and started rubbing my shoulders, telling me I looked tense. I froze as his

213

hands worked their way along my shoulders and down my back, the others in the group looking in our direction and then glancing quickly away.

I never told Jack about it. I didn't know how to explain the uneasy fear I felt as the instructor rubbed my shoulders with his hot hands. It was just my shoulders, after all, it could have been so much worse. Some people might have seen it as a friendly gesture. But it didn't feel like it. It felt like by putting his hands on me without my consent, and in front of everyone else, he was laying some claim to me and my body. Showing that he was in control and could do what he liked. If I'd told him to stop I'm sure he would have made a big fuss, making it seem as though I was the one being unreasonable. So I just sat there and let him touch me, feeling sick to my stomach. And then there were those instances before I moved to the island too, when I was a teenager at school in Edinburgh. A man pushing too close up against me on the bus, groups shouting things from a construction site that might have been meant as flattery but made me feel gross and ashamed, and the time I thought someone was following me and I ducked into a corner shop and hid in there, phoning my dad to come and collect me.

I look across the table at Molly, Ella and Olive. Do they understand what Lorna is talking about? I hope not. But as I look at my daughter I know deep down that it is something she will inevitably face herself one day, even if I try my best to shelter her for as long as possible. One day she will leave the security of this small island and the safety of our home. And there will be nothing I can do to protect her. The thought terrifies me.

'This food is delicious girls,' says Lorna with a smile.

Conversation resumes, Jack and Ben talking at one end of the table and Sarah, Lorna and I chatting sometimes among ourselves and sometimes with the children too. We eat and drink, opening another bottle when Ben's runs out. It is the most comfortable meal we have had since our guests arrived. Perhaps having the others here helps; it takes the pressure off Jack and Lorna, off us all. Jack certainly seems more relaxed, topping up everyone's wine, including Lorna's, and smiling and laughing with Ben. Eventually I notice the kitchen clock and the empty bottles, and Alfie whose head dips onto his chin. Sarah spots him at the same time.

'Well this has been lovely but we should really get going, get this one to bed.'

Everyone says goodbye, Jack and Ben shaking hands, the girls hugging as fiercely as if they won't see each other in weeks instead of tomorrow. Sarah and Lorna exchange a hug too, somewhat awkwardly but still, it's something.

'I'll see you out.'

I follow them down the corridor, leaving the others behind in the kitchen clearing up. Ben carries Alfie out to the car, Olive following behind, but Sarah lingers in the doorway. She rests a hand on my arm.

'Did you hear what Lorna said?' she says quietly. 'She isn't enjoying her job, maybe we could ...'

But I interrupt her.

'No. We promised, remember? We can't tell her anything.'

Sarah sighs.

'I suppose you're right. It just feels like it could be a sign – like it could maybe be an answer ...'

I shake my head.

'Her life is in London. I know you've missed her, and Jack has too even if he doesn't say it. But we have to solve these problems on our own. It wouldn't be fair to tell her. She'd only feel guilty, and pressurised. And I know you don't want that and neither do I.'

She rubs a hand across her forehead, looking suddenly tired.

'You're right, I know. Have we had any more applications?'

'No, not yet. But there's still time.'

But even as I say it I know it isn't quite true. With each day that passes, we're running out of time. We hug goodbye, holding each other tightly for a moment before letting go.

In the kitchen Jack, Lorna, Molly and Ella are busy tidying up. Lorna passes Jack plates and he stacks them in the dishwasher. The girls collect rubbish and wipe the table. I watch them all for a moment, a glow spreading through me.

'How about we go to the house tomorrow?' Jack says, straightening and looking Lorna in the eye.

'Of course. Whatever you want.'

He nods and returns to loading the dishwasher.

'I think it's time you girls went up to bed, sweethearts.' Ella and Molly say their goodnights and head upstairs.

'I think I might go up too,' says Lorna, yawning. 'I drank more than I realised.'

She's right. My head feels foggy, my lips bitter with the taste of red wine.

'Yes, me too, we can do the last bits in the morning.'

Jack leans against the Rayburn as Lorna crosses towards the door.

'Good night, Lorna,' he says.

She pauses and turns back, a half-smile on her face.

'Good night, Jack.'

We undress on opposite sides of the bed and then slip under the covers next to one another.

'How are you feeling about going to the house tomorrow?'

'I'm OK,' he says, but he looks up at the ceiling, his expression serious. I turn over in bed, curling up on my side. It's been a good evening but the worries are creeping in again. Jack turns his body so he's tucked behind me, an arm around my waist.

'Are *you* OK?' he says softly into my ear.

'I'm fine, just too much to drink.'

The thoughts bubble up inside but I don't want to burden him. He's just lost his parents and he's trying to reconnect with his estranged sister. He's got enough on his mind. But as I squeeze my eyes tightly shut, trying to control my breathing, I realise suddenly what a hypocrite I am. I want him to open up to me about his past and his feelings. And yet the truth is, there's so much I'm not telling him either.

After a few moments of holding me he rolls away and we fall asleep facing away from one another.

CHAPTER 19

LORNA

We are silent, the only sounds the rumble of the engine and the clatter of summer rain on the roof of the Land Rover. Alice is driving Ella and me in the Land Rover and Jack and Molly are following behind in the car, empty boxes piled on the back seats in preparation of our task.

Beside me Ella stares out the window, her arms tightly crossed, her teeth biting her bottom lip.

I can't tell if it's the hangover or the prospect of returning to my childhood home that is making my stomach churn like a washing machine on a spin cycle. I close my eyes. When I open them, I'll be back in my room in London where I've lived for the past decade. The window will be open, the smell of the Thames drifting in on a breeze. The sun will be shining, the tarmac outside hot and steaming. Ella will be in her bedroom next door listening to music and humming to herself.

I blink open my eyes. Raindrops trickle like tears down the car windowpane. Outside, it looks as though a painter has swept a grey wash over the entire canvas of the island. Grey sky seeps into grey mist, into grey moor, into the shiny dark grey of the wet road. So much for it being the height of summer. But this is an island summer after all.

Suddenly, the Land Rover turns off the main road. I feel it first through the bumps that vibrate up through the car seat, telling me that we are on the track leading home. I close my eyes tightly shut. The Land Rover jolts over a particularly large pothole and I remember swerving around it on my bike on the way to school. I can picture the exact spot on the track and the feeling of the bike handlebars rattling under my hands, making my fingers numb. The car slows and only then do I open my eyes again.

We are pulling up in front of a large grey house with a black porch and peeling green window frames. Alice swings the car into a drive at the side of a garden that is empty except for a bench and a scattering of dull rocks. Behind the house is a view I know so well I can feel it in my eyelids, in my skin, in my bones. The dark black of the pine forest and erupting above it the grey hulk of the mountain, today blurred by rain, its edges distorted.

We sit in silence for a moment.

'Well, here we are,' says Alice.

Ella presses her face up against the car window, staring at the house outside, the forest and the mountain beyond. Her eyes are open wide, one palm spread and placed on the glass. When the girls heard we'd be coming here, they wanted to come too.

'I can show you around!' Molly said to Ella. Then her face had dropped. 'I haven't been back since though.'

'I'll come too,' Alice said. 'The more hands the better.'

Her voice had been cheery but she took a step towards Jack and silently wrapped an arm around his waist, kissing him on the cheek.

Now, no one seems to want to be the first to step outside and across to the house in its uninhabited state. Perhaps it's just the rain, but the building looks even darker than I remember, its walls the same shade as the mountain, its porch the colour of the black pine trees. I shiver.

The sound of a car door shutting comes from behind us and I turn to see Jack stepping out of the car into the rain, Molly following behind with a bundle of bin bags in her arms. Alice is opening her door now too, followed by Ella. I take a deep breath, smooth my hair and lift the hood of my raincoat over my head. Then I follow the others into the house, shutting the Land Rover door behind me with a decisive slam.

It's the smell that hits me first. It's amazing how quickly a house can smell forgotten. I breathe in the scent of dust and emptiness. There's something medicinal cutting through too, sharp and artificial in contrast to the mustier smells of an un-aired building. And then it hits me, faint yet unmistakable. The smell of my mother's perfume.

The others disperse into the house as I pause in the hallway. I can hear the footsteps of Ella and Molly upstairs and from the kitchen the sound of the kettle being filled. How is it that this place is entirely the same and entirely different all at once? The tiles are slightly more chipped than I remember and yet I can

220

imagine the feel of them against my bare feet, cold and smooth. Coats and hats hang on hooks by the door and I recognise none of them but they are still unmistakably my parents'.

Stepping along the corridor I'm shocked by the sight I see through the open door of the living room. Two empty twin beds, lying where the sofa used to be. Around the beds are signs of a life lived in one room: folded piles of clothes, empty mugs, bottles of pills lined up on a side table. The sheets on the beds are neatly made. Where are they? Where are my parents' bodies? And how were these beds carried down the narrow staircase and by whom? I know the answer, of course. Jack. Jack carried the beds, Jack made the cups of tea and administered the medication. Jack took them to the mainland for hospital appointments and dealt with the reality of what needed to happen following their deaths. I steady myself against the doorframe, trying not to breathe too deeply the sweet, sickly smell that lingers in this room, and yet tasting that other bitter taste in my mouth – guilt. Will Jack ever forgive me for all the things I left him with when I left the island?

I find him in the kitchen sitting at the table next to Alice, both drinking from steaming mugs. A third is waiting for me on the sideboard.

Despite our brief moment of connection last night, here Jack won't look at me. I reach for the tea in silence, quickly taking in the changes in this room: a calendar of bird photographs left open on February, a new washing machine and a tea-towel hanging from the oven displaying a picture of the Algarve. Did my parents visit or was it a gift from a friend? Either option seems somehow out of the question.

221

'So, how do you want to do this, darling?'

Alice looks carefully at Jack, her hand resting on top of his.

'I want to get rid of it all,' he replies, his voice dry.

Neither of them asks me what I think. I'm not surprised, of course. I drink my tea silently.

'Get rid of it all,' Jack repeats. 'Unless there's anything Molly wants to keep. Otherwise chuck it.'

'OK,' Alice says, placing her hands on either side of her husband's face and kissing his forehead. 'We can use the boxes for the charity shop and the bin bags for rubbish. I'll take the boxes over to the mainland next week. Does that sound all right?'

Jack nods, very slightly.

'Why don't you and I start down here,' Alice says. She is still holding his face in her hands. He looks down at the table but she looks at him. If you asked me on a typical day whether I was happy being single I would say yes. It's what I chose for myself. But today is not a typical day. Today is a day when I would give anything to have someone hold my head in their hands.

'I'll start upstairs,' I say quickly. I grab a pile of boxes and a few bin bags and leave Jack and Alice in the kitchen together. I hear Alice's voice trying to sound cheerful, 'Right, a broken tin opener. Chuck?'

My legs feel soft beneath me as I climb the stairs, running my hands along the familiar smooth wood of the banister. I picture Sarah's house growing up, where the walls either side of the stairs were lined with photos of Sarah on her own and Sarah with her parents and grandparents at various ages. The walls beside the stairs at my brother's house are similar, Molly frozen, smiling, in dozens of frames. Here, the walls are bare except for a few framed prints of boats.

The first room I reach is the room that belonged to my parents. Growing up, I rarely saw inside this room, the door remaining firmly shut most of the time. Today it is slightly ajar and I push on it and step in. The room is almost empty, most of the furniture having been moved downstairs. There are indentations in the carpet where the legs of the two twin beds once stood. A small wooden cross hangs on the far wall but otherwise the walls are bare. Faded blue curtains hang in the windows and I spot the dressing table where I would sometimes spy my mother brushing her hair through a crack in the door. There are a few bottles on the table and a jewellery box, and I run my hand over each object, picking up a thick trail of dust.

On the other side of the room, my father's side, lie a pair of brown lace-up shoes and a pair of glasses, abandoned on the floor. I look closely at the shoes, remembering standing before my father, my body tense, my eyes fixed on his shoes. Back then, his shoes were more than just shoes. They were my father. The sound they made on the stairs or the landing told me what kind of mood he was in, my heart quickening in response. The sight of them in the corridor when I arrived home from school made me step inside and pull the door behind me extra quietly. But now, they are just shoes. It seems inconceivable that my mother and father, once two forces as strong in my life as gravity and the weather, could be reduced to this: a dressing table, a few discarded bottles, a pair of brown lace-up shoes.

Enough. I leave the room and continue along the corridor. Hearing soft voices, I follow them to what used to be the spare room. Instead of the magnolia room I remember, filled with boxes and a rarely used double bed, is a blue room painted with a series of white waves. On the floor in the middle of the room sit Molly and Ella. Molly lifts toys and books out of a wooden chest at the foot of the single bed. The chest is decorated with shells.

'Oh, I remember this one!' Molly exclaims. 'Grandma bought this for me for my tenth birthday. I guess I was too old for teddies by then but still ...'

Molly gives the bear, fluffy with a green bow around its neck, a quick squeeze and places it on the floor among a growing pile of toys. Ella sits next to her cousin, her knees pulled up to her chest, her arms wrapped tightly around herself.

'So, they painted this room specially for you?' she asks quietly. As Molly reaches for a book in the pile of belongings Ella pulls the teddy bear with the green bow against her chest.

'Yeah,' Molly replies. 'They said I could stay here whenever I liked, although I never stayed the night. Mum didn't want me to, I don't think. They didn't get on ...'

Molly trails off, her hand hovering over another bear, this time pink with a white skirt. The floorboard on the landing creaks and the girls look up. Ella immediately drops the bear she had been holding.

'Mum! What are you doing?'

'I ...'

My voice won't work. I look again at the pile of toys on the floor, the carefully painted walls, the curtains which I only notice now are decorated with a print of tiny shells. This was Molly's bedroom? And my parents did this? It is a room for a grandchild who is adored. It is a room that was decorated with attention and care, filled with things to make a child smile. It makes no sense to me that the parents I remember could create a room like this, and yet on another level it does. Looking at this room, I feel once again the fear that has sat in the pit of my stomach since I was a child. That my parents were not incapable of love, I was just unlovable.

Ella looks at me, her face stricken, the bear abandoned beside her. I see the confusion on her face and I understand it, because I feel it too. Why did she not get the family that all her friends take so carelessly for granted? The family that she deserved? Why did she never get books or toys from grandparents, a room outside our flat that she could call her own? I wish I could answer the questions I see flitting back and forth in her eyes. But I can't.

Instead, I wave the boxes and bin bags that I'm still carrying in my hands.

'I'm just looking around before getting to work.'

'Well we've got it covered in here,' Ella snaps, arms folded across her chest.

'I can see that.' There's a cardboard box in the corner of the room but it is currently empty, as is the bin bag next to it. 'I'll leave you girls to it, I'll just be along the corridor.'

Ella turns away from me, examining a pile of Molly's books. I retreat from the room.

'See you later, Auntie Lorna!' Molly calls after me. It still feels strange to hear her call me that.

My feet carry me along the corridor to my old room before I know whether I'm really ready to see it again. My body knows these few paces well and it's my body, not my mind, that brings me to the door at the back of the house. I don't want to. My hand reaches for the handle. I pause. My fingers turn the handle and push the door.

The entire room is filled with boxes stacked on top of one another and reaching nearly to the ceiling. The floorboards creak as I step inside, shuffling around the door and into the small clear area of floor. Just visible over the top of one stack of boxes is the view outside. My life may have changed beyond recognition and this room might look nothing like the room I grew up in, but the view outside is still the same. We might age, but the forest does not, or not in any way we know how to notice.

I feel as though the room is shrinking around me, squashing me into the corner. I need to sort through these boxes. I promised Jack I would help. But where to start? I trace one hand along the wall. If I look closely, I can still make out the faded marks where my paintings and drawings used to hang from strings, the only place in the house where they were on display. If I close my eyes, I can see my easel standing by the window, facing outside.

But before I can open any of the boxes, footsteps are crashing up the stairs and along the corridor. I spin around. Jack stands in the doorway, his shoulders heaving, his face red. He stares at me, his grey eyes meeting mine.

'Why?' he says, his voice loud and trembling, his face flushed with rage. I take a breath. Ever since I stepped foot on the island I have been waiting for this anger. I know I deserve it. And yet I was met instead by silence. But deep down I knew it would come eventually.

I stand opposite him, his anger radiating from his body like a burning heat.

'I've had enough of not talking about it, of pretending like everything's fine and that we can just carry on as though nothing ever happened. I want you to tell me why. All of it. Why you left. Why you didn't tell me. Why you never came back, not even ...'

His voice breaks off now as he gasps for air. His hands are clenched by his sides. My brother, my little brother.

I find my voice deep inside, pulling it up through the tears that catch in my throat.

'I had to leave. They were impossible, Jack. This life was impossible. I couldn't survive it.'

I remember again the night of the fire. How I left the house and walked in the dark to the lighthouse. The wind was howling and yet I stood right on the cliff edge, closer than I'd ever stood before. It's then that I made up my mind to escape. It was many months until I actually managed to leave, but that night I knew I had to go.

Jack shakes his head now and although his hair is short and thinning I see a mop of curly dark-blond hair, a dusting of freckles on his nose.

'It wasn't that bad,' he says.

My stomach clenches. Because this is the hardest part. This is why when I left I had to leave my brother as well as our parents. My brother, whom I felt so proud of on his first day of school, whom I read Moomintroll to in the night, staying up beside him until he fell asleep. We started life as allies, my brother and I, but as we grew older our differences started to show. I asked my parents questions and stopped believing in God, and sneaked out with my friends as much as I could. I confronted our mother, pushing her to leave my father. I dyed my hair and found painting and threw myself into that, finding this well of creativity I didn't know I had but that gave me a feeling of strength and hope for a different kind of life off the island. I tried to take Jack with me, inviting him to join me with Sarah and my other friends, and encouraging him to find his own passion too and to contemplate a life beyond our four walls. But the more I encouraged, the more he seemed to withdraw. I know he was younger than me and was scared. But it's one of my biggest regrets in life that I wasn't able to reach him, that somewhere along the journey of our childhood, we lost each other.

'It was bad, Jack. Don't you remember? The way they were, it wasn't OK.'

I mustn't cry. But my eyes are filling now, because these are the things I've tried my whole life to escape. These are the things I've spent years trying to accept.

'I don't know why they were the way they were. I think Dad's injury didn't help – it made him so bitter, so angry, I guess because he felt useless. And Mum, she was so clearly scared of him but she still let us down. She let him control us. Maybe he needed to because he couldn't bear the thought of us having our own lives after his hadn't gone how he'd wanted. But it wasn't normal. How come we were the only children who weren't allowed to go to the school on the mainland? And the guilt – that way they had of making you feel constantly guilty, even if you didn't know why. The thing is, it was never our fault, Jack. We were just kids.'

It took me years to realise that. Even when I finally did come to that conclusion, I still felt flashes of guilt and doubt every now and then. I still do. Perhaps it was my fault? Each time the doubt comes it rocks me and makes me question my decision. Maybe I did the wrong thing? But then I remind myself of everything my parents did and didn't do. I cling onto these memories, even though they are painful. Because they are the only things that stop me from going completely mad.

Jack shakes his head.

'You overreacted, you always overreacted.'

I bite my lip so hard I can taste the metallic tang of blood. That's what my mother always used to say. I can hear her voice now as clearly as if she is in the room, quiet but still clear as her words hit me.

'It's not as bad as you think, Lorna. I know he's not perfect, your father, but he's been through a lot. We just have to try harder to be good for him. My father was much worse, you know. It could be worse.'

'And besides,' Jack adds, 'you were difficult. That's why we didn't get to go to the secondary school like everyone else – because they wouldn't take you. And Mum worried I'd find it too hard on my own so that's why she kept me at home too.'

'You still believe that?' I say to Jack now, looking at him closely.

I can see a question dart across his face, but when he doesn't say anything, I continue.

'That's what they told everyone, of course. That I was wild, out of control. But I was just a teenager, Jack. Yes, I dyed my hair and got caught out smoking the only cigarette of my life, but so what? At the time I thought maybe I *was* bad. Dad told me it so many times that I thought maybe it must be true. But ever since having Ella … Yes, she misbehaves sometimes or questions my decisions. But that's normal! She's just a kid. Doesn't Molly do the same? I was just a kid, Jack. I didn't deserve it, any of it. Neither did you.'

He says nothing but I can see he is thinking, that my words are shaking him. Am I getting through to him? Might I finally be able to break the hold my parents had over him now they are gone?

'I think really they just hated that I wasn't like them, that I wanted to leave the island, and had dreams of my own.'

'I had dreams too, once,' he replies, louder now, his face flushed red. 'But when you left I had no choice but to stay. I couldn't leave them on their own, with no one.'

He fixes me with those grey eyes, his tensed body filling the doorway in front of me. Shame twists in my stomach.

'I know. I'm sorry. Honestly, Jack, I have never stopped being sorry about that. I would have taken you with me if I thought you'd come. But I knew you wouldn't. And I had to leave.'

He shakes his head. I can tell he still doesn't understand. And I need my brother to understand. So, I pause for a moment and then in a quiet voice I say, 'Do you remember when I showed you that bruise?'

I remember pulling my jumper sleeves down over my hands at school and always refusing to take it off, even on a rare warm day. I remember my teacher asking about a bruise on my leg and telling her I fell off my bike.

'Silly Lorna walked into the dresser again,' my father said one evening at the dinner table as my mother served our food. 'You need to be more careful, Lorna, you broke your mother's favourite mug.' He pointed to the dresser, where a willow-patterned mug lay in shards. For a moment I wondered if my father was right. Perhaps I *did* walk into the dresser. The mug was broken, after all. I looked up at my mother for reassurance but she wouldn't meet my eye. Then, beneath the table, I placed a hand to the spot where the new bruise flowered on my wrist. I pressed down lightly and felt the pain bursting beneath my hand. It was a pain that reminded me of what I knew to be true, that made me feel less like I was losing my mind.

I somehow always knew that my father never treated Jack the same way he treated me. Jack was young and obedient. My father didn't need to try too hard to control him. And I was the one who had seen him crying in the living room after his accident. That's the first time it happened.

It was late, and I'd come downstairs for a glass of water. The living room door was ajar and I could see my father inside, slumped over in a chair weeping. My mother was crouched opposite him.

'It hurts so fucking much,' he said through gritted teeth, one hand on the small of his back, the place I knew never to bump or touch since his injury. The other hand held a bottle of amber liquid. He took a deep swig from it. Even from where I stood in the hallway I could smell that smell I'd recently come to know so well.

'What can I do?' my mother asked quietly. 'We could take you to see another doctor on the mainland? Use some of the money from my parents?'

He laughed but it was unlike any laugh I'd ever heard before, cold and sharp.

'That's right, my wife the saviour. Keeping the family afloat with her death money.'

He lunged forward and my mother flinched backwards, but as though changing his mind he leant back again, taking another swig from the bottle instead.

All the while the tears slid down his red cheeks, his nose streaming too. I couldn't believe it. My father shouted and cursed, but he didn't cry. Never.

Perhaps I shifted slightly on the bottom step, but suddenly my father looked up and spotted me. I've never forgotten his expression. Fury, but something else I didn't recognise at the time but have come to understand now. Shame.

'Come in here,' he said quietly. Somehow his quiet, calm tone frightened me far more than if he'd shouted.

My mother stepped back to the other side of the room, watching us both, her arms wrapped tightly around herself. She was trembling.

I stood in front of my father, my head dipped, knowing that somehow I'd done something very, very wrong by seeing what I'd seen. When he swung his fist towards me I felt almost like I'd deserved it.

The next morning, I watched as my father prepared breakfast for Jack, talking to him gently. But with me he was silent. I knew then that things were somehow going to be different from now on. But I still had to check that Jack was OK. I remember slipping into his bedroom later that day when our parents were out, our mother at the village shop and our father assisting on a new building project, more, I think, because the islanders involved felt sorry for him and less because he was much use on a building site anymore. I took advantage of the rare moment alone to try to have an honest conversation with Jack.

I found him where our mother had left him, reading his school books in silence.

'Hi, buddy, I wanted to talk to you about something.'

He turned away from his books and looked at me.

Not knowing exactly what to say, I rolled up the sleeve of my top and showed him the purple bruise that wrapped its way around my arm.

'Dad has never done that to you, has he?' I said quietly.

I remember the way he looked at my arm and then at me, his eyes wide. He shook his head, his mouth slightly open.

'You tripped over,' he said, his eyes fixed to the bruise. 'That's what Dad said.'

'No, I didn't, Jack.'

But he continued to shake his head.

'You're clumsy, you've always been clumsy. That's what he told me.'

I opened my mouth, about to say something else. But then the front door closed downstairs and we both stiffened at the sound of our father's voice. I rolled down my sleeve and we never spoke about it again. I could deal with the bruises as long as my little brother was OK. I would just plan my escape.

In the doorway now, Jack's eyes widen at my words.

'You were a clumsy child,' he replies quietly. 'You were always tripping over or falling off your bike.'

But his voice is uncertain now. I can almost see the thoughts flitting behind his eyes, the things my parents told him battling with what I'm saying now, and perhaps with the memory of that day when I tried to talk to him about what had been happening.

It's my turn to shake my head now.

'No, I wasn't. Jack, our parents are dead!' I can't help but raise my voice, my sadness and frustration overwhelming me. 'You don't have to believe what they told you anymore. Please, just listen to what I'm trying to tell you. Think about what our childhood was really like. I need you to understand, I need you to believe me.'

He opens his mouth and closes it again, his expression still confused.

'I was still your brother though,' he says eventually, his voice shaking slightly now. 'You could have kept in contact with me.'

'I tried. I wrote to you, but you never wrote back.'

He is silent now, caught out. I never really expected him to reply, but I still looked out in the mail for an envelope with his handwriting.

'You could have tried harder.'

Maybe I could, but would it really have made a difference?

'Even if you had replied, Jack, I honestly just didn't see how it was possible for us to have a relationship,' I admit.

'But why?'

I reach my hands out beside me, tears hot on my face.

'Because of this! Because even now, you don't believe me. You must at least remember the fire?'

My head is full of it again. The glow of light near the forest, the feeling of the grass beneath my bare feet as I ran towards the flames ...

Jack's forehead creases.

'They told me you did that.'

Is there a hint of hesitation in his voice? I shake my head, tears stinging my eyes as I remember it all.

'That's what they told everyone. But think about it, Jack. Why would I do that?'

I can smell petrol and burning and find myself struggling to breathe. Everything changed after that night.

He rubs his face again. I can almost see the conflicting thoughts passing through his head like clouds. Everything I'm trying to tell him weighed up against everything our parents told him for years and years.

'I don't know, Lorna. I haven't seen you in over twenty years. Who do you really expect me to believe?'

The tension in my body is unbearable. I close my eyes slowly then open them again.

'Me. I want you to believe me, Jack. Because I'm your sister. And because I'm telling the truth.'

He stares at me, his face twisted. I want to reach out for him and run away all at once.

There are footsteps in the hallway and suddenly Alice, Molly and Ella are there, drawn to my old room by our raised voices.

'Is everything OK?' Alice asks nervously. Molly and Ella

look between Jack and me, at my tear-stained face and Jack's tense frame, his hands clenched by his sides. He says nothing.

'I should leave,' I say, wiping my face with my hands. 'I never should have come. Come on, Ella.'

'But I ...'

Her eyes flick to her cousin, who looks just as bewildered as Ella does.

'Come *on*,' I repeat, more firmly this time. We have to get out of here. This has all been one big mistake.

Molly squeezes Ella's arm and gives a little nod.

'See you later,' Ella says quietly to Molly, before turning and storming down the stairs. I follow behind, taking the steps two at a time. There is not enough air in this house. In the kitchen I grab my brother's car keys from the table.

Ella is waiting in the corridor, her shoulders slumped, her arms tightly crossed. Her eyes flick to the keys.

'Mum, what's going on? Did something happen? And what are you doing?'

What *am* I doing? I fling open the front door, rain still falling onto the porch roof with a clatter.

'Ella, get in the car.'

I've never seen Ella look at me the way she does now. It's as though she is seeing me for the first time and realising that her mother is at best deeply flawed, at worst mad. After a moment she lifts the hood on her coat and follows me into the car, climbing in the passenger seat and slamming the door.

I turn the key in the ignition, the sound of the engine surprising me. So, I'm really doing this. I lift the clutch and press down on the accelerator.

'Did you and Uncle Jack have an argument? We heard shouting. Is everything OK?'

I know I should answer her but I feel too upset and confused to formulate anything coherent.

The hatchback shakes as I drive down the track, loose stones picked up by the wheels and flung to the edges of the road. When we reach the smooth tarmac of the main road I press even harder on the gas. Puddles of water rest on the surface of the road and as the car drives through them waves spray onto the verge. The rain is so heavy now that I can see only a short distance ahead. The rest of the island is blurred by water and the sea is entirely obscured by mist.

'Mum, you're going too fast!'

Headlights flash out of the gloom and I press hard on the brakes, swerving onto the grass to avoid the car that is travelling the opposite direction. Once the car has passed I pull away again, driving slightly slower this time.

'What's going on, Mum? What just happened in there?'

My daughter wants me to have the answers, to reassure her with some neatly packaged wisdom, something reassuring. That's my job. But how can I possibly do that job when I am falling apart?

'Uncle Jack and I had an argument. Things about the past.'

'What things about the past?'

'I don't want to talk about it, Ella.'

I don't mean to snap at her. I mean to love her, to calm her, to look after her. But what we mean and what we say are not always the same thing.

'You never want to talk about it! You treat me like I'm a

little kid, like I can't handle anything, like none of this affects me. But it does affect me. This is my family too. And I just don't understand it. I've been thinking about it ever since we got here. Molly, and Alice and Uncle Jack ... They all seem so normal. I always thought they'd be like these crazy, awful people from the way you never wanted to talk about them or for me to meet them. But they're not. They're actually pretty amazing.'

I grip the steering wheel hard, focusing on the road ahead. I just need to get us back. I just need to get us home.

'I used to think we never saw your family because of something they did. But coming here and meeting them, it makes me wonder whether it's actually because of something *you* did.'

We've reached Hilly Farm by now. I stop the car. Ella looks at me, waiting for me to say something. But before I do she opens the car door and dashes out through the rain, head down and hugging her coat to her body, disappearing inside the farmhouse. I turn off the engine and sit with my hands gripping the wheel, listening to the rain that falls like shattering glass on the roof. Alone in the car, I place my forehead on the wheel and stay there until my hands have stopped shaking. I stay there for a long time.

CHAPTER 20

ALICE

Jack slumps back against the pile of boxes, his shoulders heaving. The rain pelts against the window.

'Daddy?' asks Molly cautiously, stepping towards him. She hasn't called him that in years. I reach out an arm for her, pulling her back.

'Sweetheart, why don't you go and carry on sorting through your room?'

She looks across at Jack, who hasn't moved and doesn't look up, and then back at me.

'Is he OK?'

'Everything's going to be fine, darling, don't you worry.'

I kiss her on the forehead. Uncertainly she glances across at Jack again and then turns and leaves. I close the door softly behind her and join Jack, leaning myself up against the stack of boxes beside him. His body trembles, but I can't tell whether it's with tears or anger.

We'd been sorting through the kitchen when he stood suddenly and turned away. I thought nothing of it, imagining he needed a moment to himself, that perhaps being here in the house where he grew up surrounded by his parents' things was too much for him. I didn't follow him, instead continued sorting through the cupboards. But then I heard shouting coming from upstairs. Heading up to see what was going on I bumped into Molly and Ella in the corridor, looking anxiously at one another and then down the hall towards the noise. The girls followed behind me. But by the time we arrived in the doorway Jack and Lorna were quiet again, staring at one another as though across a great distance. And then Lorna had left, taking Ella with her. Last night I was sure they'd taken a small step closer to one another, but now this ... Lorna must have taken the keys for our car because I heard the rumble of an engine over the rain and the sound of tyres spinning on the damp track.

I place a hand gently on Jack's knee.

'Darling? What happened?'

He shakes his head, his chin dropped to his chest, hands clenched by his sides. But he says nothing.

'Sweetheart, please. Talk to me.'

I twist my head, trying to meet his eye. But it's like I'm not there.

'Please,' I say again, feeling desperate now. I perch next to him in this room full of boxes thinking about all the things we're both shutting away.

'We should get back home too,' I say eventually, when it becomes clear he's not going to say anything. 'You're clearly not up to doing any more here today. We'll come another time.'

For a moment I wonder if he's not going to move but when I stand and head to the doorway he follows silently. I gather a bewildered Molly, leading her downstairs with my arm around her as Jack follows behind. She doesn't say anything either but her face is washed out. I try to reassure her by pulling her slightly closer to me.

I climb into the driver's side of the Land Rover and Jack steps in silently beside me. The rain has stopped now but there are still dark clouds on the horizon, the threat of more rain in the air. Outside, the island is damp and green. Inside the car the air is stale and silent.

When we reach the farm, our car parked up out front, Jack strides quickly away towards the fields. I slam my door and run a few paces after him.

'Jack, please,' I shout, my voice lifting on the breeze coming in from the sea, the same breeze that tangles my hair and lifts the edges of my jacket like a sail. 'You can't keep running away from your problems.'

He turns back now.

'Running away? I'm not the one who ran away.'

'I know, but ...'

Before I can continue he walks away again.

'Jack! Jack!' But he ignores me, his strides determined as he heads further off into the fields, leaving me behind. Tears sting at my eyes but I brush them away. I don't want to upset Molly. I turn back to her, forcing a smile on my face.

'It's OK, darling, Dad just needs some space. Shall we go and check on Ella and Auntie Lorna?'

I reach my hand out to her. She stopped holding my hand a few years ago and although it brings me joy to see her growing up, it breaks my heart a bit too. I never realised it at the time, but there must have been a day when she held my hand as usual and then never held it again. But she takes it now.

Voices come from upstairs and we follow them up to Molly's room. Ella is sitting on her camp bed, Lorna opposite her by the door.

'What do you mean?' Ella says to her mother as we step inside.

Molly dashes immediately over to Ella, sitting down next to her on the bed.

'Is everything OK in here?'

Lorna turns to me, her face stricken.

'I was just telling Ella that she needs to start packing. I'm really sorry but we have to leave.'

Ella's face drops and my stomach does too.

'I thought you just meant we needed to leave Grandma and Grandad's house! I know you and Uncle Jack fought, and that house was kind of creepy, but ...'

Lorna winces slightly, rubs her hands on her jeans and shakes her head.

'I'm sorry, darling, I didn't mean just here. We need to go back to London.'

She turns to me now.

'Alice, I'm so sorry. You've been so kind to us both and I really appreciate it. But I can't do this. We just have to go home. I've called the B&B and they've said we can stay there tonight, and then we'll catch the ferry tomorrow morning.'

What is there to say? My husband is outside, angry and silent, unwilling or unable to open up to me. Any visions I had of him and Lorna reconnecting and my family gaining two more members are crumbling around me. And there is also that secret hope I've tried my best to ignore, that Lorna might be the answer to this island's problems, that she might be the one to pull us all back from the brink. I can't believe I was so foolish.

Ella stands up suddenly, her hair wild around her face.

'No!' she shouts.

There's a moment of pause, all of us clearly surprised by the strength and volume of Ella's voice.

'I'm so sorry, sweetheart,' replies Lorna, her voice pained. She seems to have shrunk somehow, withdrawn in on herself. She hugs her arms across her chest, her shoulders slumped. She looks nothing like the woman who shared dinner with us and Sarah's family last night, laughing and talking and throwing furtive smiles down the table towards Jack.

'No!' Ella shouts again, even louder this time. 'You just don't get it! I've never had a family! Everyone has a family. *Everyone*. Apart from me. And now I've found mine and you want to take me away.'

I flinch, not sure that Molly and I should be witnessing this, not sure it's our business, but unable to move. And I suppose if I think about it we *are* part of this. Whatever might have happened in the past, we *are* part of Ella's family. Tears overspill her eyes but she wipes them away furiously. Molly looks up at her, her mouth slightly open, as Lorna and I stare on too. Ella's anger takes up the whole room.

'I don't want to go back. I like it here. I'm making friends here. Molly, and Olive... Haven't you noticed that I haven't spoken to Farah or Ruby once since I've got here?'

I glance at Lorna and notice a hesitation, a flash of surprise across her face, that feeling of being caught out.

'I *knew* you hadn't noticed,' Ella continues. 'And it hasn't been just this trip. It happened before. They told me a few weeks ago that they don't ... that they don't want to be friends with me anymore.'

Her voice trembles and breaks now. I want to hug her but I know it's not my place, and besides, she looks so tense and stiff that I'm not sure she would accept an embrace right now. She looks away, not meeting Molly's eye now, embarrassment flushing her face. Lorna swallows, but her voice is measured when she replies.

'I'm so sorry about your friends, honey. I really am. And I'm sorry we have to leave. I'm not doing this to upset you, or you, Molly sweetheart.' Because Molly and Ella are sitting close together now, arms wrapped around one another. They look so much like sisters that I have to look away for a moment.

'I wish things were different,' continues Lorna, 'I really do. But I just have to get off this island.'

It's hard not to feel offended. I didn't grow up here, but this has become my island. I may have thought of leaving when I couldn't bear to say goodbye to Molly, but I love it here with a strength that means I know deep down I will never leave. Except I might have to. We all might have to. It takes me unawares, the reality I've been trying hard to ignore, to solve somehow. I've been trying desperately to find a way to hold this island together, to make sure that we can stay, and here Lorna is, desperate to leave. But I know this has nothing to do with me. I can't change Lorna's past and I can't change the distance and tension between her and Jack, however much I might have hoped I could. It's too late.

'Can't we at least stay for the funeral?' Ella asks, quieter this time. Her tears have won the battle and slide freely down her face.

I watch as Lorna squeezes her eyes tightly shut for a moment, clearly fighting her own tears.

'No, sweetheart. I'm sorry, but no.'

Ella's shoulders slump now, all the energy and anger draining from her, replaced by sadness and a look of defeat. She and Molly still cling to one another, holding so tightly and sitting so close that it is hard to tell where one girl ends and the other begins. Looking at them, Lorna's face softens.

'One more night. We can stay one more night. If that's OK with you, Alice?'

It catches me off guard to see her looking at me now, Molly and Ella turned in my direction too. I haven't had time to arrange my face, and suddenly can't find the energy for the smile I'd usually force. All I can do is nod.

Lorna and I leave the girls in Molly's room, closing the door behind us. In the corridor we stand awkwardly in front of one another, the friendship I felt we'd started to build over the past few days feeling suddenly fragile. She runs her hands through her hair.

'I really am sorry, Alice, I've tried, but I just can't get through to him. I think it's just too late for us.'

Her eyes are red. I don't tell her that I think I know something of how she feels – that despite how strong I thought our marriage was and how much I love him, I feel like I can't get through to my husband either. I don't tell her that I feel like a failure. I'm failing at connecting with my husband, I've failed at building the big family I dreamed of, I've failed at helping Jack reconnect with his sister. And I'm failing the island too.

'I should go out and find him,' I say, and she nods. Gently, she places a hand on my arm and then turns to the spare room, shutting the door behind her. I don't go outside though. Instead I shut myself in my own room and climb into bed with my clothes on.

CHAPTER 21

LORNA

I'm back in the house where I grew up, leaning against the kitchen sink, a kettle held aloft in my hand as I make myself a cup of tea. The sun is setting outside, golden light etched around the pine trees at the bottom of the garden. But there's another glow too and as I look closer I make out orange flames dancing at the point where the garden ends and the forest begins. It's beautiful, in a way, the fire. And then the mug slips from my hand, splashing my bare feet with scalding liquid. But I barely notice as I push the door open and run outside. Because somehow, I just know. I know that something is very wrong.

Damp grass between my toes and the soft give of the earth as I run through the garden towards the glow. My skin grows steadily hotter, the air thick with smoke that scratches at my throat.

The first thing I see is my easel, smouldering on the top of a crackling, hissing bonfire. The bonfire is made from a burning mound of paper, canvas and wood. Oil paints slide like tears down canvases that then catch alight and burst into flame. Paintbrushes burn and drawings crinkle at the edges and disintegrate into nothing. The air smells of ash and paint and petrol. I slide to my knees in the grass, the heat of the bonfire smarting my cheeks. Perhaps I should run for the garden hose? But I know it's already too late. There's no chance of saving anything. And besides, I am pinned to the spot, tears streaming down my ash-flecked face, a heaving sob escaping my lips. Everything I worked towards, everything I dreamed of ... I watch, helpless, as it burns to nothing.

And then I see them, two figures in the shadows by the trees. I spot my father first, arms crossed over his chest. My mother is beside him but lingering slightly behind, her fingers rubbing the gold cross that hangs around her neck. She doesn't meet my eye. As I look at my father again I notice a petrol can resting in the grass at his feet.

'Well,' he says, his voice steady. 'It looks like you won't be going to London after all.'

For a moment I can't find my voice; it's lost beneath tears and the smoke that fills my throat.

'How could you?'

My voice comes out as a croak. My father says nothing, his arms still crossed over his chest. I look at my mother now, willing her to look at me back.

'How could you let him do it, Mum? Mum!' But she won't look at me. I sink to my knees in the grass and sob.

I wake suddenly, hands gripping the sheets. In the darkness I can just make out the shape of my suitcase by the door and a jar of heather on my bedside. I went to bed early, unable to face the heartbroken faces of Ella and Molly. Telling them my decision felt awful; it was nearly impossible to hold it together. I felt like a monster as I watched Ella's tears fall. My darling Ella, my world. But after that conversation with Jack I just knew that coming here was a mistake.

My heart pounds like it always does when I have this dream that is not really a dream. I lie in the darkness, remembering.

The fire happened the week after that picnic in the woods, when my father confronted me and for once I shouted back. *'I'm going to have a better life than yours. And there's nothing you can do to stop me.'* How I came to regret those words I said that day.

After the fire had burnt down to its last embers, I headed silently upstairs to my room to check whether my father had missed anything. Maybe there was something left, just something? But the walls were decorated only with empty strings and pegs where just that morning my drawings had hung. A bare space by the window where my easel should have stood. Standing there in my empty room felt suddenly too much, so despite the darkness sweeping in and the breeze that was becoming a strong wind I ran out of the house and up to the old lighthouse. I ran and ran until my legs ached, until my lungs felt clear of the smell of smoke and in its place was damp salty air. I remember the feeling of the sea wind hitting against me as I stood on the cliff edge in the growing darkness and listened to the sound of the waves crashing below.

I lost everything in the fire. Every painting, every drawing. All my equipment. My father told Jack that I'd started the fire. That I was emotionally unstable and had got into a frenzy, not thinking my work was good enough. I told Sarah the truth of what had happened but made her promise not to tell anyone. I couldn't bear the thought of anyone else knowing what had happened.

That night I stood closer to the edge than I ever had before, imagining how easy it would be to take a step forward. I pictured what it might feel like for my stomach to drop, to experience that sensation of falling.

Of everything that happened when I was young, this is the memory that has haunted me for years. And my brother doesn't believe it happened.

Coming here has surprised me in so many ways. It has been an unexpected joy to meet Molly and Alice. I never thought I'd be given the second chance to reconnect with Sarah again, or to see my old teacher or the shopkeeper who was so kind to me. Alice and her friends have all been so welcoming and have shown me some of what I missed out on when I left and have continued to miss by never trying to build a group of friends in London. Then there's Mallachy, the happy afternoon we spent in his studio, the way my heart thumped when we stood close together and the sweet scent of the heather he gave me that comes through the darkness now at my bedside.

But I don't belong here. Seeing Jack again as an adult has filled me with happiness but also a deep sense of sadness and regret. For a while I thought that perhaps there might be hope for us to repair our relationship. But I was wrong. How can we step closer to one another if we don't believe and understand one another? This is why when Ella suggested this trip I was so hesitant. Because in the end, it is just too painful. Sometimes it is easier to stay away than to try to build bridges and fail. To let silences stretch over years rather than reaching a hand out across the vast and lonely emptiness.

CHAPTER 22

ALICE

When I wake up the first thing I do is reach an arm across the mattress, feeling for Jack's body. He came to bed later than me, slipping in silently beside me when I was just drifting into sleep. To my relief my hand meets the soft warmth of his back. I shuffle closer. The room is dark, the sleeping house quiet around me. It must be the middle of the night. I can just make out the light patter of rain and the back and forth of the sea down on the beach.

Despite being awake now, I can feel the fear from the nightmare I just had lingering in my mind. It all felt so real. I dreamed I was in a hospital, looking down at a ghostly figure I barely recognised as my friend, and Jack and Molly's old teacher. Lying awake in the darkness, the thoughts I've been trying to push away for weeks come rushing in.

The truth is, I still haven't told Jack that Jean is sick. I can't bring myself to say the words aloud. If I hold them inside, perhaps it isn't true. I just can't quite accept that my friend, the friend who taught my husband and my daughter and who has always seemed so cheerful and so strong, is ill. She has been back and forth to the mainland for appointments at the hospital's oncology department, but has only kept us loosely updated. I get the sense she isn't telling us everything. We've all tried to stay positive for her. On good days, I feel hopeful. There is so much more that they can do nowadays and everyone in our group of friends seems to know a story of someone who had cancer but has since made a full recovery. But some days it's hard to stay optimistic.

She kept teaching right up to the end of term but instructed the school governors (of which I'm one, alongside Sarah and some parents of younger children still at the school) to start looking for a replacement for the new term. So far, we haven't had a single application. We've placed adverts online, using photos of the newly tidied classroom as well as a few of the island itself, all shot to make it look as beautiful as possible, and have asked friends on nearby islands to spread the word. But so far, nothing. We have willing parents on the island who could band together to form a temporary solution, but despite their enthusiasm, no one here is qualified to take on the school long term. The reality is, if we don't find a new headteacher the school will eventually have to close. This is not the first time that this cold reality has hit me in the dead of the night, keeping me awake while Jack sleeps silently beside me.

The young families will be the first to leave the island.

There's already a noticeable tension among the parents as families decide whether to try and move to the mainland over the summer or hold out for a suitable applicant for the role. We'd stay as long as we could, but eventually the population would decline, just like it did on Caora. New families would stop arriving and one by one the families already living here would leave. Eventually it would no longer be viable to keep up the pub and the shop. The ferry service would probably reduce too until one day our home would become a ghost island. A school is the heart of an island like ours. Even for people who don't have children, having one here matters. It's the thing that keeps our remote life viable.

I wonder, not for the first time, where my friends would all go if we did eventually have to leave? Surely not to the same town or village. We'd all scatter, the community that has become so important to me breaking up and falling apart.

I've kept these fears about the school to myself too. Jack has enough on his plate without me adding to his worries. I'd hoped that we'd have found someone by now. And then when Lorna arrived and told us all that she's a teacher ... Well, I have to admit a spark of hope ignited inside me. I saw it on the faces of my friends too. Maybe Lorna could be the answer to our problems? But Jean made us all promise not to tell her what was going on.

'But maybe she'd want to help?' suggested Sarah. But Jean had been adamant.

'No. I will not put that kind of pressure on her. These problems are ours, not hers.'

And now Lorna is leaving and any hope I might have felt

dies away. I glance across at my husband, sleeping silently beside me. What is he dreaming of right now? What did he and Lorna say to one another at the house that made her want to leave? I hug my knees to my chest, listening to the sound of the rain and the sea outside in the darkness.

CHAPTER 23

LORNA

Last night I couldn't wait to leave the island. But confronted with my packed suitcase this morning and the prospect of the ferry in a few hours I'm surprised by how sad I feel. I think it's best for everyone if Ella and I go back to our life and let my brother and his family return to theirs. But I'm going to miss the people I've met here, and Sarah with whom I've only just reconnected. I'll even miss the sound of the sea. The island scenery was starting to grow on me too; it will feel strange to return to concrete and brick.

I take a deep breath and cross the corridor to Molly's room. I feel so bad for how things went with Ella last night. I love her with every cell in my body but it doesn't mean I always say or do the right thing. I knock gently on the door. When no reply comes, I knock a little harder and ease open the door.

'Ella sweetheart?'

Molly's bed and the camp-bed where Ella has been sleeping are empty, the duvets neat. Ella's suitcase is at least zipped shut in the corner. Perhaps they are already downstairs having breakfast.

'Ella? Molly?' I call as I step into the kitchen. But the room is empty, the curtains still closed and last night's mugs resting on the counter above the dishwasher. I pull open the curtains. The sky has grown darker, brooding clouds rolling in slowly from the sea. I call the girls' names in the living room too. Maybe they are out in the fields, having a last look around together before Ella leaves. But as I peer out the window all I see are the cows and sheep grazing as usual.

This doesn't feel right. Where *are* they? I climb back up the stairs two at a time, not worrying now about the noise my feet make against the floorboards. Jack and Alice's bedroom door is closed and I hesitate then knock. There's a sound of shuffling followed by footsteps, then Alice is at the door in a dressing gown. I'm surprised to spot Jack still in bed behind her; usually he would be up and out on the farm at this hour.

'I can't find the girls.'

Alice turns back to Jack. He is already stepping hurriedly out of bed. I glance away as he pulls a pair of jeans on over his boxer shorts and reaches for a T-shirt.

'I'm sure they're around somewhere,' begins Alice, but Jack is racing to the door.

'Have you looked through Molly's room?'

'I just saw they weren't there. Ella's suitcase is packed though.'

Jack follows me along the corridor while Alice slips back inside to get dressed. In Molly's room Jack looks around, pulling back the duvets and peering under the beds. He lifts up Ella's suitcase.

'It's empty.'

'What?'

Jack unzips the case. There's nothing inside. I spin around, frantically searching the room. What's happening? And where is my daughter?

'But where's her stuff?'

Molly's room is neat and ordered. There are none of Ella's clothes on the bed or chair or hanging in the wardrobe.

Alice appears, dressed now and rubbing her eyes.

'Maybe they're down on the beach, saying goodbye?' she suggests.

I make my way quickly to the window and fling it open, leaning out so I have a full view of the beach. It's empty apart from a scattering of seabirds resting on the sand and one lone Highland cow. *Where are you, Ella?*

Jack rummages in Molly's wardrobe, pulling things out one by one.

'Her tent has gone, and her rucksack.'

For the first time, Alice's eyes widen in alarm.

'What are you suggesting?' she says nervously.

Jack meets my eye and for the first time since arriving on the island I am sure that I know exactly what my brother is thinking. *They can't have.* But it's the only answer, the only reason why they and their belongings are missing. I hold my brother's gaze, silent thoughts passing between us.

'They've gone, haven't they?'

Jack nods.

'But gone *where*?' Alice says, letting out a high-pitched laugh. 'This is an island!'

I don't care if it's an island. My daughter is missing and I need to find her. I need to find her right now.

'Come on, we'll go out in the Land Rover,' Jack says firmly. 'Someone might have spotted them.'

Jack drives and I sit in the back, looking out the window through binoculars. But all I can see are grey fields; there's no sign of the girls. In the passenger seat Alice makes several phone calls, alerting people that the girls are missing and asking them to join us at The Lookout to form a search group. It seems her panic is sinking in now too – she talks in a strained voice and takes a deep breath between each phone call.

We drive a loop of the island but there's no sign of Molly's tent or either of the girls. This island always felt too small. But as I strain my eyes through the binoculars it seems to stretch and grow in front of me. There are so many places that can only be reached on foot, places the girls might have fled to hide. I shudder at the thought of Molly and Ella huddled inside a tent on the side of the mountain, the clouds pressing down around them. The wind picks up outside. The long grasses on the moor bend and sway and as we pass alongside the beach the waves rear against the sand. I picture tent poles bending and guy ropes flapping. *Oh god. This can't be happening.*

After a second trip up and down the island road we pull up outside The Lookout. Several vehicles are already parked outside and when we step inside the pub it seems as though most of the island is crammed inside the room. The conversations stop as we enter. Alice's friends from the yoga class step immediately towards us and start asking questions about when we last saw the girls. In the corner of the room, with Rex sitting at his feet, is Mallachy. Our eyes meet across the room and an image flashes in my mind: a jar of heather beside a bed, a folded note. I spot Sarah and Ben next. Olive is there too, standing slightly behind them, her head bowed and her eyes red. To my surprise I spot two people next to Sarah too, a man and a woman in their seventies, both dressed in waterproofs and leather hats.

'Oh Lorna!' comes a voice and Sarah's mother Linda is suddenly enveloping me in a strong hug. My mind fills with the smell of hot-buttered crumpets, tea brewing in Sarah's kitchen and the sound of Sarah's mother whooping and clapping for both Sarah, Jack and me at that school awards ceremony. For a second, I forget why we are both here. And then I step back, wiping my face. Sarah's parents still look like Sarah's parents but it jolts me to see how they have aged – the grey hair, the lines on their faces and the way Sarah's father Doug stands with a slight stoop.

'Look at you,' he says, reaching a hand out to cup my chin. It is a gesture so gentle that I feel tears stinging my eyes. I am suddenly not forty, but about ten years old.

'But oh, you poor love,' says Sarah's mother. 'We'll find them both no bother, don't you worry.' And that's when the first tears start to fall.

CHAPTER 24

ALICE

'Thanks for coming, everyone,' Jack says in a strong voice, gesturing for attention. The room falls quiet. 'As my wife sensibly says, this is a small island so the girls can't have gone far.'

Did I really say that? Outside, the black clouds churn above a choppy sea. My friends are all here, along with most of the islanders. Joy gives my arm a gentle squeeze, Harry sleeping against her shoulder. Sarah glances across at me, her smile tight and strained. It's some reassurance to have them all here and to know that my friends, these islanders, care deeply about Molly and her safety too. I look across at them all and just seeing them here grounds me slightly, makes me feel a little less like I might float away.

'But in any case,' continues Jack, 'we're worried about them, especially with the weather closing in, so it's really great to have your help. I think the best thing to do is to split up into groups and take charge of different parts of the island.'

I watch as he gives out instructions and people nod and head off in small groups. I'm glad he's taking control. It's so surreal how quickly this day has changed, how fully fear has consumed me. Up until now this island has always felt so safe to me. I've never minded letting Molly run wild, feeling grateful that we have none of the risks of a big city here. But now all the other dangers flash before my mind. Steep cliffs, slippery rocks, storms, changing tides, raging waves. We've warned her about all of these things, of course, and up until now she's always been so careful, understanding the need to respect the natural world and its power that surrounds us here on the island. But I took it for granted that she would always be that way, that she'd grown up knowing her boundaries. How stupid not to consider that one day she would want to push them.

Most of the search parties have headed out into the rising storm and now it's just us, Lorna and Sarah's family left in the room.

Jack sinks suddenly down into a chair, his face pale, all the energy and focus of just now draining away. I crouch next to him and take his hand. He stares straight ahead, his expression dazed. He looks as though the reality of the situation has just hit him all over again. I know how he feels.

There's silence for a moment, no one seeming to know what to do. And then I notice Lorna straighten slightly beside us, wiping her eyes.

'OK,' she says in a steady voice. 'Sarah, can you and Ben head to the forest with Linda and Doug and search there?'

They nod and head outside, Sarah giving both Lorna and me a quick hug before she goes. Olive follows closely behind, still looking down at the floor.

By now Jack has his head in his hands, his shoulders crumpled. I search for something reassuring to say, but how can I possibly reassure him when I feel so terrified myself?

'Why don't you two stay here to be around in case anyone finds them?' Lorna suggests gently. But Jack quickly pulls himself to his feet.

'No, I'm going to come with you. I'm going to look for my daughter.'

Of course he is. We both are.

Lorna nods.

'Shall we try the lighthouse cottage? It's where I would have gone if I were them.'

'Good idea,' I say, pulling myself heavily to standing. 'At least it's dry there. Hopefully we'll find them there and can give them a telling-off and then this will all be over.'

I picture them huddled inside the old cottage and something suddenly lifts inside me. It makes sense. It's the most sheltered spot on the island but still remote, only reachable by a steep dirt track. But when we eventually reach the lighthouse, soaked by the rain that has now started to pour and whipped by the wind that tears at our clothes up here, they're not there. The cottage is empty apart from a few planks of wood and a scattering of abandoned birds' nests. I'd been so sure they'd be here and my heart sinks. I picture the two of them, my daughter and my niece, out there somewhere alone and cold in this driving rain.

'Perhaps one of the other groups has found them already,' I say tentatively, looking across at Jack who is still pale, his brow furrowed.

'Yes, let's head back to The Lookout,' he says.

We take a last look along the clifftop but it's exposed here so it would be impossible for Molly and Ella to hide. I stop myself from peering over the edge.

When we arrive back at The Lookout Sarah, Olive, Mallachy and Rex are waiting for us.

'What's going on?' Jack asks, looking at the somewhat un-likely group. 'Where are the others?'

'We left Ben searching with my parents in the woods,' Sarah says. 'But Olive mentioned something that I thought you should know.'

Sarah places her hands on Olive's shoulders and pushes her gently forward.

'Come on, sweetie. It's important you tell Jack and Alice what you told me.'

My heart thumps inside my chest.

Olive's head is still bowed but now tears drip from her lashes down onto the toes of her wellies. Sarah tightens her grip slightly on her daughter's shoulder, squeezing reassuringly.

'I thought it was nothing,' Olive says through her tears, but the way she wipes her face and catches a quick, gulping breath makes me freeze, my heart pounding in my throat. Whatever Olive is trying to say, it is clearly not nothing.

'They were both obsessed about going to Caora Island. They'd been talking about it non-stop for days. Molly wanted to show Ella the abandoned crofts and to try to see the puffins …'

264

I glance across at Lorna and our eyes meet. I remember Ella and Molly asking us both if they could go with Mallachy, Lorna's reluctance to say yes to Ella and how I felt I'd put my foot in it by agreeing more readily to Molly. Lorna looks away again, her cheeks colouring.

'Molly always said that she thought she'd be able to survive over there, even though it's been empty for years. And then the boat ...'

Olive dissolves into sobs now. Sarah wraps her arms around her and kisses the top of her head.

'What boat?'

Sarah looks up at me. She swallows, her lips tightly pressed together.

'When Olive told us how much the girls had been talking about the island we decided to head down to the harbour. Ben's boat is missing.'

'Oh my god.' I know Ben's boat. It's small, not something any islander would use to make the crossing to Caora Island, certainly not in this weather. Down at the harbour the waves smack against the jetty, the sky above an angry grey. Rain falls in a sheet. This can't be happening. Lorna holds a hand up to her mouth and Jack stands stiff at my side.

'My little girl,' I cry out, unable to hold it together any longer. 'What are we going to do? Should we call the coastguard?'

Mallachy steps forward. Before he can speak I understand suddenly why he is here. It seems Jack does too because he looks at him and says, 'Your boat. Do you think you can manage the crossing in this weather?'

We all watch as Mallachy pauses for a moment and looks

outside. His eyes narrow slightly and he frowns. Then he looks back at us.

'Yes, I think so. I know these waters well. It will be much quicker than phoning the coastguard on the mainland.'

There's something about the way he pauses before speaking that makes me believe him. Besides, what choice do we really have?

'OK then, let's go,' says Lorna.

I pull the hood of my raincoat up. For a second Jack and I look across at Lorna and the three of us nod grimly in understanding. Despite everything that happened yesterday, right now we are united. The look we share says we each know how it feels – the churning in our stomachs, the fear that races through our blood, the terror of being a parent.

'We'll wait here,' says Sarah. 'Perhaps the boat just came loose somehow in the storm and the girls are still on the island. Mallachy, call the coastguard if it gets too rough.'

'I will.'

We head out into the rain in the direction of Mallachy's boat, Rex following behind us. As we walk, the wind and the sound of the waves seem to dull and all I can hear is one phrase repeating itself over and over in my head. *Please let them be OK. Please let them be OK. Please let them be OK.*

CHAPTER 25

LORNA

My daughter is missing. I still can't fully comprehend it. Ella is missing.

Rain lashes against my face as Mallachy's boat rises on the crest of another wave, the sound of the engine barely rising above the crashing of the water. We lurch then fall, the hull slapping onto the surface of the sea, salty spray ricocheting in all directions. Mallachy grips the wheel, feet firmly planted and eyes narrowed, staring with focus out into the mist where Caora Island is only just visible on the horizon. Rex stands at his side barking into the wind, fur sodden. Jack and Alice sit opposite me, gripping onto each other and the railings. Alice's face is buried into Jack's shoulder, just above the life jacket Mallachy insisted we all wear. With one hand Jack holds Alice's head, smoothing strings of wet hair out of her face.

I feel the surge of another wave in my stomach. Nausea and fear rise inside me, pulsating through my blood and making my limbs stiff and heavy. My skin feels raw, whipped by the wind and the rain. I lick my cracked lips and taste the sharp tang of salt.

I want to close my eyes and bury my neck down inside my sodden coat and the padding of my life jacket. But I must keep them open. I can't let myself look away from the island in the distance. If I keep my focus out there, perhaps my desire alone will reel us in, pulling us into the shore. I must not picture Ella and Molly making this crossing last night or in the early hours of the morning, huddled inside a small boat and buffeted by the waves. But in my head, I hear the sound of my daughter's cries and waves crashing against a tiny hull.

'We must be getting closer!' Alice shouts suddenly, lifting her head, her expression stricken. Looking at her, I realise this is my fault. I think back to the conversation with Ella last night as the cousins clung to each other on Olive's bed. I did this. They fled because of me, because I was tearing them apart. I've never felt so sick at myself in all my life.

Alice looks wildly around her and then lets out a strangled cry.

'Why aren't we getting closer?'

Her sobs are lost for a moment as the boat tilts and rips through another wave. Mallachy nearly stumbles this time, but manages to maintain his grip on the wheel.

'The tide is against us,' he shouts into the wind. 'I'm doing the best I can.'

I squint into the rain. But Caora Island still seems so far

away. Alice is right. We've been on this boat for over half an hour but it really does feel as though we're getting no closer. Maybe the girls are still on Kip after all? Maybe Ben's boat being missing was a coincidence – perhaps it simply became untethered in the bad weather?

I glance across again at Alice and Jack. There are droplets of water rolling down my brother's face. Is it just the rain? But then his body shudders with a silent sob. His eyes are tightly closed but then he opens them and looks across at me, his mouth slightly open but no sound coming out. Alice is buried into his side again, seemingly oblivious to his tears as she cries into his jacket.

Watching Jack, I see him again at fourteen, that same soundless cry caught in his throat as I left the island for good. I see him when he was younger, curled up in his bed, shaking with the fear of the nightmares he knew would be waiting for him when he went to sleep. I see him smiling up at me as I handed him a perfect shell found on the beach. For a moment I think back to the words we exchanged yesterday in the house where we grew up, the house where we fought in our own different ways to make it through the life we'd been given. It still hurts to know that even after all these years he believes my parents' version of the truth over mine. But he is my brother and he is Molly's father. And for once I understand how he feels, because I feel it too. Our daughters are lost and I have never been so afraid. I lean forwards and reach out my hand.

He looks at my hand for a moment. I leave it there, hanging in the space between us. And then for the first time in more than twenty years we are touching one another, our hands

269

intertwined. His fingers are cold and damp. But this is my brother's hand. The rain pours and the boat rocks and tilts and I hold Jack's hand tightly in mine.

And then he shifts away and pulls back his arm and the connection between us is broken. We are two islands again, separated by time and silence. I sit alone, watching the restless sea and listening to the sound of the waves and the beating of my own heart.

'There's something in the water!' Mallachy cries.

Jack and I leap up. Alice is on her feet too, gripping the railing of the boat and peering overboard. She starts to scream.

'Oh my god. Oh my god.'

What has she seen? I stare in the water but can see nothing but the dark waves coiling around the boat.

'Lorna, take the wheel a second,' says Mallachy. Before I can protest he steps away and rushes to the side where Jack leans over, arms outstretched towards the water.

I don't want to see what they are reaching for. I grip the wheel tightly, feeling the weight of the waves against the hull and realising the strength Mallachy has been using all this time just to keep the boat from spinning and veering with the force of the water. He must be exhausted. Rex barks loudly as Jack and Mallachy scramble and reach out for something at the side of the boat. But I look ahead. If I keep looking ahead, whatever they have found in the water does not exist. If I keep looking ahead, everything will be all right.

There's a clatter of wood meeting wood and I can't help but look over now. A single oar is pulled out of the sea and dragged on board. I feel a warmth on my shoulder. Mallachy is there, his hand resting on my arm.

'I can take over now,' he says and I step quickly away, joining Jack and Alice by the lost oar.

'It might not be theirs,' Jack says quickly.

'No,' I reply. But I'm not so sure. Alice covers her mouth with her hand and says nothing.

'Mallachy, what do you think?'

He doesn't look at me. And that terrifies me.

'I think we should get to the island. It's getting closer, look.'

He's right. The island still looks far away, but it's growing gradually larger, the grey shapes of the old crofters' cottages now visible in the fields. I strain my eyes for any sign of the girls. But there's nothing. Ben's boat is nowhere to be seen. Could they really have made it this far in his small boat with just one oar between them? I look down into the black, swirling water and an icy fist clutches my heart.

I have spent my life haunted by nightmares. But I suddenly don't know why I was ever afraid of the visions that visited me at night. Those were nothing compared to this. I stand on the edge of the boat by the railings, wanting to cry my daughter's name into the wind.

Suddenly the boat lunges violently on a wave that rears up from underneath us. I'm thrown forward against the railing, the air winded from my body. Gripping my stomach with my hands, I take a gasping breath.

'Are you OK?' comes Alice's voice over the wind. But now another wave hits, even stronger than the first. I lurch forwards but this time the rail doesn't break my fall, I'm thrown up and over, grabbing out for the side of the boat with my hands. But all they meet is air and then darkness as I plunge into the sea. It's cold. It's so cold. My mouth is still open and I swallow seawater, choking on the salty brine. Darkness and a battering of churning waves. And then my life jacket does its job and I burst up into open air. I take a deep breath but another wave slaps into my face, making me swallow another lungful of water.

'Lorna!'

I flail around me, reaching out for the side of the boat. But I must have been pushed around by the waves because I'm not as close as I should be. My eyes are so filled with salt water that I can't quite make out the boat or who it is calling to me, but I recognise the voice.

'Lorna, I'm throwing you a lifebelt,' shouts my brother, so loud his voice cracks, hoarse and broken.

I hear Mallachy's voice and Alice's too but I can't make out what they are saying. All I can hear is my brother shouting my name.

'Lorna, it's coming now, watch out.'

But just as I hear a splashing sound and catch a flash of orange a little way ahead, another wave rolls over and I'm pushed momentarily back under again, down into the darkness. More salt water in my mouth, my nose, pressing against my ears. For a second, I am pinned under the surface, waves rushing over me, but then I break up to the surface again. I look around wildly, disorientated. My eyes sting so much it hurts to open them.

'Over there Lorna, you're so close!'

There it is. A burst of orange in the grey sea. I kick frantically towards it, using all my strength to push against the waves. The lifebelt is smooth under my hands and I grab on tightly.

'I've got it!' I yell.

'OK, we're pulling you in. Just hold on tight.'

I'm exhausted but don't let myself loosen my grip on the orange plastic as I'm tugged through the waves and towards the boat. As I draw closer I can make out the figures leaning over the side. Jack and Alice, pulling together on the line. Mallachy is behind them, focused on keeping the boat steady.

'Have you got her? Have you got her?' I hear him say. Beside him Rex barks and barks.

I'm by the side of the boat now and Jack and Alice are reaching their arms towards me.

'Yes, we've got her,' says my brother as I hold onto them both and they drag me up, sodden and exhausted, into the boat. I can barely stand but Alice has her arms tightly around me, not seeming to care that I am soaking her.

'Oh, thank god,' she says as she holds me. 'Thank god you're OK.'

I break apart from them both, coughing and wiping my face.

'There are blankets in the compartment under the seats,' says Mallachy. 'I've got to get us through this but help yourself. It's important to keep her warm.'

Rex lunges at me, tongue lolling, and I pull him towards me, holding his warm body against mine as Jack and Alice disappear for a second into the galley.

'God you scared me there. Are you all right?' says Mallachy. His face is fixed on mine, his green eyes shining.

'I'm OK.'

But I'm not, not really. I've swallowed a lot of water and feel battered and bruised by the waves. And I'm shivering from the icy cold of the sea. But that's not it. I can cope with all of that. But being overboard and truly confronted by the rage of the storm, I wonder how anyone could possibly have made this crossing in a rowing boat with one oar. And if one of the girls fell overboard …

'The weather was fine last night and this morning,' I say, voicing my thoughts out loud as much for myself as for the others. 'If they made the crossing last night or in the early hours they should be OK. They are both strong girls. Even with just one oar I think they could have managed it.'

I'm not sure how much of what I say I actually believe, though. Jack and Alice pile blankets over my shoulders and on my lap.

'How are you doing?' Jack asks. All I can do is nod. We look out to sea where the waves continue to rise and fall. I can't stop shivering. And not just because of the cold.

They sit down beside me, their bodies either side of me helping to warm me up a little. No one says anything. I look again at the single oar pulled out from the sea.

After a while the waves die down slightly and the boat continues forward, bobbing and rocking now instead of the violent lurches of earlier. The rain continues to fall above us but it is easing slightly, falling with a constant beat now rather than in a raging shower.

'I see the boat!'

Mallachy points towards the shore, gripping the wheel

with his other hand. I nearly stumble again as another wave rolls beneath us, but Jack and Alice reach out, steadying me. Together, we head towards the railings, staying close to one another. Somehow, we are now just a hundred metres or so from the island. There is the tumbling-down silhouette of the old church in the distance, there the grey stone walls of what used to be homes, there the white backs of sheep that graze in spite of the storm. Directly ahead I spot a small cove that had been hidden before. Unlike the beach to the right that is being pummelled by waves, this cove is protected by a small headland and the water is much calmer. And there on the pebbly shore is a small boat. Or at least, most of it. As we pull in closer I see a gash in the side of the boat's hull, splinters of wood scattered on the beach.

I lift a hand to my face. I've been trying so hard to stay positive and not to let the worst-case scenario play out in my mind. But looking at that small, broken boat it truly hits me. Today I might lose my daughter. I might have already lost her.

The others are silent too. Jack and Alice hold hands and stare at the beach, their faces pale.

'I think we might have to wade,' says Mallachy, the boat slowing and the engine growing still. 'I don't think I can get us in any closer.'

In silence he drops the anchor. I'm the first over the side, climbing down into the sea. I'm drenched already so the cold doesn't even register as I wade without pause towards the beach. Next is Jack, splashing down and helping Alice behind him. As I reach the shore I turn back and am surprised to see

275

Mallachy following us into the water too, Rex leaping after him and swimming to shore.

We gather around the little boat. The hull is half-filled with water and splinters of wood. I don't need to ask if it's definitely Ben's boat. Because there is one word written in cursive letters on the front, next to the crack. 'Sarah'.

No one moves.

'Hey, there's the other oar,' says Mallachy suddenly, pointing to a piece of wood a little further up the beach. It matches the one that was pulled earlier out of the water and onto Mallachy's boat. Is finding this second oar a good sign or not? I have no idea.

'Molly! Molly!' Alice strides up the beach, shouting with all her strength. Jack follows her, calling his daughter's name too.

'Go on, Rex,' Mallachy says, ruffling his ears. The dog runs away, sniffing the ground and scattering darting rabbits in all directions.

Together, Jack, Alice, Mallachy and I set off across the island. I call my daughter's name and Molly's too. We search the cottages by the sea front. Could the girls be hiding in here? But they are all empty. Grass grows up between dilapidated floorboards, ivy wraps around glassless window frames and birds' nests cling to bare beams, but there's no sign of the girls. The island has grown wild in the years it's been uninhabited; birds disperse skittishly from trees as we walk and the sheep look up at us curiously before returning to grazing. Ahead is a low, long building, the roof missing and the window frames bare like most of the other buildings on the island. We head towards it, calling the girls' names. Jack steps through the open doorway and we follow behind.

Inside is a large room. My eyes fall with surprise onto a scattering of decrepit wooden desks. Twigs and leaves line the floor. There's a broken, rusted clock buried in a pile of moss.

'This must have been the school,' says Alice quietly.

There's something about this place. It's so sad, so empty. I glance at the broken desks, trying to picture the children that once sat here.

'It's sad, isn't it?' Alice says quietly, and I notice that her eyes are red from crying. 'This once would have been the heart of the island. All those people who used to call this place home … And now everything's gone.'

Her voice shakes. I shiver, thinking suddenly about the possibility of returning to my flat in London without Ella.

'Let's try the church,' says Jack, turning away from the school. Alice lingers for a second longer and then follows us, wiping her eyes. The church is near the middle of the island. It's one of the few buildings that still has a roof, or most of it anyway.

Jack and Alice are first to the doorway and I follow behind with Mallachy. As we step inside a clutch of birds shriek and flap away up through a gap in the roof. But other than the birds and a set of dusty pews, the church is empty.

The reality of the situation hits me like one of the waves in the sea and I sink down, sitting on the end of a pew. We were supposed to be going home. And I was supposed to look after my daughter. It's my job, it's the only thing, when it comes down to it, that really matters. I bow my head, my body cold and numb.

'What are you doing?' comes Jack's voice.

'Praying.'

'I thought you didn't believe in God?'

'I don't.'

I rest my forehead against the chipped wood of the pew in front. It is slightly damp, rough against my skin and smells like rot and childhood church services. The cold has seeped its way into my blood, my bones, the tips of my fingers and toes. I'm stiff with it, exhausted by it. I'm all out of energy and I'm all out of hope. It's as though the last remnants of optimism I clung to have simply blown away like cobwebs caught in the wind.

'We need to keep looking,' says Jack. I know he's right. But I can't bring myself to move. I can't face what we might find or the fact that we may find nothing at all. I want to lie down on this damp, dusty pew, birds shuffling in the rafters above. And then I want to stay here forever. I can't go back without my daughter. If she is really lost, then so am I.

I'm aware of the others hovering around me, perhaps unsure whether to wait or leave me here and continue the search. Alice and Jack exchange some words but I can't make out what they're saying; they use hushed voices reserved for husband and wife.

'Come on,' says Alice by my ear, wrapping her arm around me. 'You can't give up.'

I can't tell her that I already have. Because it's her daughter who is missing too.

'What are we going to do?' says Alice to the others, more urgently this time. My head spins. I can't think clearly. Cold, and damp and a memory of Ella as a baby, her downy soft head cradled against my chest. I sink into thoughts of her. Her first day at primary school in that uniform that was slightly too big and that made tears catch in my throat. She couldn't understand exactly why I was crying but she twirled for me, showing off the new clothes and kicking up the shiny shoes on her feet. A trip to 'our' café in Greenwich where we shared a strawberry milkshake and a piece of chocolate fudge cake and she talked about a history project that I can't remember now but which she spoke about with such eagerness at the time. How have I forgotten what it was she said to me that day? I didn't think at the time that I needed to remember, or that one day I'd sit in an abandoned church on an abandoned island and wish I'd remembered exactly what my daughter told me about that specific piece of homework. That I'd wish I could remember every single thing she'd ever said. I guess I thought I'd have a whole lifetime of her words.

'What's that?' says Mallachy suddenly.

I lift my head slightly. The church is quiet as the others pause too, ears straining. And then I hear it. Rex's sharp bark, carried on the wind.

'Maybe he's found something,' says Jack.

I thought I had no strength left. But with the help of Alice at my side, I pull myself up from the pew. I follow the others out of the church and into the open air again, where the rain is finally dying down and a fragment of light forces its way between the clouds, shining suddenly on the damp grass, the dripping heather, the stone walls of the empty cottages. Rex barks again.

Mallachy points to the far side of the island.

'Over that way.'

The four of us head off quickly, following the sound of Rex's barks. We stumble along an overgrown track in the direction of another cluster of cottages in the distance. Jack has an arm loosely around Alice's waist and together they help each other over the rocks and dips in the track and through the particularly dense patches of heather and grass. I try to keep up, forcing my numb, frozen limbs to work. The barks get louder as we near the cottages.

But there is something else now too, I'm sure of it. Another sound. I pause to listen and catch the sound of a voice. It's a sound that hits me firmly in my heart, because I know that voice.

'Mum!'

Suddenly, I'm running. I'm trembling and exhausted, but I'm running. I catch up with the others, who are breaking into a run now too, Jack and Alice shouting 'Molly!' as they run towards the cottages. And then I overtake them, leaping over rocks, tearing through bracken. I run faster than I've ever run before, on legs that feel made of concrete. I spot a cottage without a roof, a tree growing in its centre, the branches reaching out where the roof once was. And then I see Rex, darting out of the building, barking and barking.

I push past him to an open doorway, which reveals a tree in the centre of what once was someone's home. Beneath the branches is a tent. And standing just outside the tent are two girls, holding onto one another.

'Mum!'

Her voice wobbles, but it's her voice. It's my daughter's voice. Molly stands beside her, eyes red. I run forward and wrap my arms around them both. They're here. They're alive. They're OK. Jack and Alice are here now too and Molly breaks free from me and runs towards them.

'Molly!'

They reach their arms out for her, Molly disappearing beneath their embrace, both Jack and Alice rocking their daughter against them. I'm left alone with Ella who grips me tightly, her body cold and shaking.

'Mum, Mum,' she says into my hair, tears streaming down her face, her arms trembling around me. I hold her with all the strength I possess.

'I've got you, darling. I've got you.'

CHAPTER 26

ALICE

'What were you *thinking*?'

As I clutch Molly tightly against me, Jack's voice rings out loudly in the air, sharp and hard with anger. She flinches against me and I hold her closer. I can't help it. There will be time for anger but right now all I can feel is relief.

'Seriously? How can you have been so stupid?'

Jack's arms move at his side as he talks, his face scowling.

'I'm sorry,' Molly says in a slight whimper.

'Oh great, you're sorry, so that makes everything fine then. You nearly got yourself killed, and your cousin too. Because I know this was your idea, Molly, so don't try to tell me otherwise.'

'It was both of our idea,' says Ella now, lifting her head from the cocoon of her mother's arms. Like me, Lorna is holding

Ella as though she may never let go. Lorna's face is pale, her clothes still damp from the sea, but there's a faint, faraway sort of smile on her face as she holds onto Ella. Mallachy and Rex are nowhere to be seen; they sneaked away once they saw the girls had been safely found, giving us some space. Molly separates herself slightly from me and even the tiny gap that forms between us sends a jolt to my gut. Come back. I want to wrap my arms around her entire body and feel the warmth of her, just to reassure myself that she is really here and is really OK.

'You're right, Dad,' she says. 'It was my idea. Ella's just being kind.'

'But ...' starts Ella, but Jack interrupts.

'Not only have you been stupid but you've been selfish. You've totally destroyed Ben's boat. The entire island is out looking for you back at home. And you put us all in danger too.'

'I know. I *know*.' Molly is crying now, wiping her face with the back of her grubby hand. Her hair is matted with salt water and she looks younger than fourteen. Later, I'll find time for the two of us to talk alone and I'll tell her how her father cried with fear today at the thought of losing her.

'What *happened*?' I ask now, placing my hands either side of my daughter's face and looking her in the eyes. She bows her head.

'We didn't want to say goodbye. Then I thought of the island. How we could hide here, how that way Ella wouldn't have to go home. We set off at first light. I knew where Ben moors his boat, I knew we'd find it there. It was surprisingly easy to untether the boat and get it out of the harbour. I thought it would be OK. There were clouds and a breeze but that was all. We'd nearly made it across by the time the weather turned.'

She takes a deep breath, half air, half sob.

'It was so scary. I don't know what happened. We were so close but suddenly there were these huge waves. We let go of an oar.'

I picture the two girls on that tiny boat at dawn, lost out at sea.

'We only had to get a little further and then we'd make it. We managed as best we could with the one oar, getting gradually closer. But as we approached the beach the boat hit a rock. It started letting in water. It was so scary. But we got gradually closer and closer and then we jumped into the shallows and dragged the boat up the beach. We were so relieved but with the boat ruined I had no idea how we'd get back. We came here to shelter and decide what to do next. But then we heard Rex ...'

I close my eyes for a second, reliving that moment as we heard Rex's bark and ran across the island. But Ella's panicked voice brings me quickly back to the present.

'Mum? Are you OK?'

As I look over I see that Lorna's eyes have closed, her body slumped against Ella.

'Mum?'

Ella shakes her slightly but Lorna doesn't move. Her lips are blue, her skin so white it looks translucent.

'Oh shit,' says Jack, stepping forwards quickly and taking the weight of her against him as Ella steps back, a horrified expression on her face. I open my arm and she rushes towards me; I pull her and Molly both close against me.

'Mallachy!' shouts Jack and in a second, he is there – he must have been nearby. When he spots Lorna slumped against Jack alarm springs to his face. He rushes over and supports the other side of her.

'What's happened?'

'It must have been the fall in the water. She's freezing. We need to get her back to the island. Now.'

Together Jack and Mallachy lift Lorna's limp body, her eyes fluttering for a second then closing again as they carry her between them out of the cottage.

'What's the matter? Is she going to be OK?' asks Ella frantically, looking up at me with panic in her large brown eyes.

'Come on, girls, we have to get moving. Leave the tent, someone can come back for it. Ella, don't worry, everything's going to be OK.'

Molly grabs her rucksack and I usher them both outside, keeping them close to me as we half-walk, half-run back to the boat, Jack and Mallachy ahead of us with Lorna carried between them, Rex following at Mallachy's heels.

When we reach the beach, we work together to carry Lorna through the shallows and lift her on board, and I help the girls up as Mallachy and Jack take Lorna under the shelter of the wheelhouse. Once on board we join them and I grab all the blankets and towels I can find and drape them over Lorna's sodden clothes. Her head lolls against the window of the wheelhouse, her body slumped in the seat. Ella kneels at one side of her, holding her mother's hand. At the other side is Jack.

There's silence as Mallachy sails us back to the island. The weather has turned around, so much so that it's as if there never was a storm. The sea is still and quiet, the sky becoming bluer and bluer as the clouds part. Rays of sun shine down on our island home, making it look beautiful as it rises out of the sea in the distance. But I barely feel the warmth of the sun as I stand on deck with Molly, watching the island grow closer. Molly may be at my side but one fear has quickly been replaced with another.

'She's going to be all right, isn't she?' Mallachy asks, turning to me from where he stands at the wheel. I'm aware of Molly's eyes tilted towards mine too, red from seawater and tears. And I think how often I'm in a position like this, reassuring people around me that everything will be OK when inside I have no idea what is happening, fear racing through me like a swollen river.

'She's going to be OK,' I reply, trying to keep my voice steady. 'We just need to get her home.'

The boat edges closer to the shore and I wrap my arms around my daughter, wondering if she knows that this hug is as much for my own comfort as it is for hers.

CHAPTER 27

LORNA

I am back on Kip, searching the island for my daughter. Rain falls on my bare arms, making me shiver. How long has it been raining? Perhaps forever. I'm on my own; the others have given up but I can't stop. Brambles scratch at my skin as I drag myself across the moor, calling Ella's name.

'Mum!'

I stop, searching wildly around me. Where is she? I can hear her but I can't see her, the rain blurs my vision and the island stretches out around me, a wild expanse of hills and mountain, trees and heather.

'Mum!'

She must be nearby, she must be. I call her name again and again. And then I see her, lying beneath a tree, her body slumped against the trunk. Her skin is milky white, her lips a pale blue, her eyes closed. I rush for her and suddenly my brother is at her side too.

'Hypothermia, I think,' he says in a hushed voice. There's another voice that sounds like Alice's, although I can't see her anywhere.

'What should we do?'

'Keep her warm,' replies my brother. 'And we'll phone for the air ambulance if she doesn't improve.'

I reach for my daughter's limp body and pull it towards me, holding her tightly. I can feel her heart fluttering against mine, just like it did when she was a toddler and shared my bed at night.

'She needs rest,' says Jack. And then he reaches out and holds my hand.

*

Sunlight streams through yellow curtains. They are half open and move slightly back and forth. I can smell the sea on the breeze and something sweeter too. A flash of colour to my left: a jug filled with poppies, buttercups and sprigs of heather. I take a deep breath of the fragrance, feeling it swirl through my body like wind filling a sail.

There's a weight on my chest and as I open my eyes fully I see a pile of blankets and duvets covering my body. It's an effort to move beneath them but I shift slightly, adjusting my heavy limbs. I'm in the yellow room at Hilly Farm. How did I get here? And why am I not at home in London? I was supposed to be going home, wasn't I? And then I remember. The storm. The boat trip across to Caora Island. And my daughter, shivering in my arms.

'Ella!'

My voice escapes me as a hoarse croak. It feels as though sandpaper is being rubbed against my throat. A shuffling comes from the other side of the room. I look across and spot a new armchair I hadn't noticed before and in it, my brother. He opens his eyes and tilts his neck from side to side. From his position it looks as though he'd been slumped asleep, arms crossed over his chest. A book has fallen open at his feet.

'You're awake.'

I open my mouth, trying to force words through my dry throat. But the bedroom door opens and Ella rushes inside, followed by Molly and Alice, who carries a tray of tea things.

'I thought I heard voices,' says Alice as Ella leaps onto the bed. I wince slightly as she jogs my aching body but I don't care. She lies next to me and wraps her arms around my neck.

'Are you OK, darling?' I ask her.

She pulls away from me slightly and looks at me carefully. Her cheeks are rosy and her eyes bright.

'*I'm* fine!'

I reach for her again, feeling her forehead with the back of my hand. She feels a normal temperature. But could that be a trick of her body? Should I still be worried anyway?

'But I thought you had hypothermia.'

She looks at me in a strange way again and I notice that the others are staring at me the same way too.

'Mum, *you've* had hypothermia. You've been in bed since yesterday.'

Really? How is that possible? The events of yesterday feel like a blur.

'Molly and I are fine – as soon as we got back and had hot showers we were totally OK. But you … You started shaking like crazy. And then you just went sort of all sleepy and floppy. It was really scary.'

Can that really be true? Flashes of memories come back to me. Someone carrying me upstairs, my feet bumping on the wall. Who was it, Mallachy? My brother? I look over at Jack again in the armchair in the corner. How long has he been sitting there? I suddenly remember waking in the night and seeing a shape in the corner, a body curled up in this chair.

Alice steps forwards and places her tray down on the bedside table. 'It's so good to see you awake. It's been a while since you had anything to eat or drink. The pot's nice and hot.'

She pours from the teapot, adds two sugars and hands me the steaming mug. Wrapping my hands around it I feel sensation returning to my fingertips, warmth spreading through my body.

'We don't have a doctor on the island, of course,' says Alice. 'But Ben is the island's first-responder and has extensive first-aid training. He came to check on you yesterday and again earlier this morning. Your temperature is doing much better so he doesn't think you need to go to hospital, you just need to rest and stay warm.'

'I hope you're feeling OK, Auntie Lorna,' says Molly, looking up somewhat nervously from the end of the bed. Like Ella, she looks surprisingly OK despite the events of yesterday.

Jack throws her a severe look.

290

'Now that you've seen her you can go back to your room.'

Molly lowers her head and tiptoes away without making a fuss.

'She's grounded,' says Jack, turning back to me. 'And probably will be until she's eighteen. I still can't believe how stupid they were.'

I feel Ella flinch beside me.

'Thank you for the tea, Alice. And thank you both for taking care of me. But is it OK if I have a moment alone with Ella?'

Alice adjusts the cushions behind me and places a hand on my forehead. Then she nods and disappears out the door.

'Fine,' says Jack. 'But I'll be back in a bit to check on you.'

His tone is gruff, but the deep indentation in the armchair as he stands up to leave tells me all I really need to know. I remember for a second the argument we had at our childhood home. His words still ring inside my head but the argument also feels a long time ago now. So much has happened since.

Once the others are gone Ella sits up next to me in the bed, hugging her knees into her chest. Before I can say anything, she lets out a sob.

'I'm so sorry, Mum. I know what we did was really stupid. And it's my fault that you're unwell. I'm so sorry.'

I look across at her and her dark eyes throw me off balance. It's hard to believe after that terrible boat ride through the storm that Ella is really here in front of me and that she is well and safe. A cough rattles inside my chest and I pause for a moment, unable to speak. Once the coughing has subsided, my body aching from the effort, I turn to my daughter again. She watches me anxiously.

'I was so frightened,' I tell her, my throat sore as I speak. 'I've never been so terrified in all my life.'

'I know.'

'You have to promise me never to do anything like that again. I don't know what I would do if something happened to you, Ella. You're everything to me, I hope you know that.'

Ella nods her head, biting her bottom lip.

'I know.'

I sink back into the pillows, suddenly exhausted.

'Can I get you anything?' she asks.

I shake my head. Enough talking for now. I need to sleep. Ella rearranges the blankets on the bed and smooths my hair back with her hand, just like I've always done for her when she's been unwell.

The door opens and Jack peers inside.

'Your mum needs to sleep,' he says to Ella, his voice softer than when he spoke to Molly earlier. 'But you can come and check on her again soon, OK?'

She nods, kisses me on the cheek again and heads for the door.

'But we'll talk properly soon,' I say to her. I need to talk to her about Ruby and Farah, and the argument we had before she ran away. We need to talk again about going home. But for now, I'm not going anywhere.

Ella disappears and Jack steps inside and resumes his position in the armchair.

'You don't have to stay,' I say.

'I know.'

He shuffles in the seat, getting comfortable. He picks up his book again and as he does I notice the cover this time. *Finn Family Moomintrolls*. I feel myself sinking towards sleep, darkness filling my body.

'Lorna, I'm sorry about ...'

But I shake my head gently.

'I'm sorry too. But not now. Later.'

Jack nods and reaches for his book. And I let myself give in to sleep as it rolls over me like an extra blanket.

CHAPTER 28

ALICE

'Are you coming to bed?'

I keep my voice quiet, careful not to disturb Lorna who sleeps silently in the bed. Jack looks up from the armchair, his expression distant. We've barely spoken since we got home; he's spent every moment here, sitting in the armchair by Lorna's bed. Each day a circle of mugs and books has grown around the base of his chair and each evening I clear them away.

'The girls are already asleep. Molly hadn't quite finished her chores but I could tell they were both exhausted, so I told them to call it a night.'

The chores are part of Molly's punishment from her father. I would have been softer on her, I can't help it, but I can't deny that this grounding of hers will do wonders for the house. Jack glances back to Lorna, watching her as he replies. Her face is tilted away, her hair slightly obscuring her face and the blankets pulled up close to her chin. A rush of affection warms me as I look at my sister-in-law. How strange to think that just a week ago we'd never met. Now we've been through so much together.

'She'd better finish them tomorrow,' says Jack.

'Of course.'

I'll let him keep up Molly's grounding for a few more days, but I'm sure his anger will ease over time. And I can tell that both Molly and Ella feel bad enough as it is; I've never seen Molly put as much energy into housework as she has over the past couple of days. She has already apologised to Ben too, offering to use her pocket money to help fix the boat. He refused of course, because he's a kind man. But she's going to go down to the boatyard and help him with the repairs.

I reach out my hand, resting it on Jack's shoulder.

'Sweetheart?'

But he doesn't move.

'She could have died,' he says, so quietly I almost don't hear him.

The memory of that boat ride from hell flashes into my mind. The waves, the rain and the terror at what might have happened to my daughter.

'But it's OK,' I say gently. 'We have our daughter back and she's OK.'

But he shakes his head.

'Not just Molly.'

I follow his gaze to his sister, covered in blankets and asleep in our spare room. Ben says she is going to be all right, thank god, but it felt like touch and go for a while. We nearly phoned the air ambulance when we arrived back on the island, but Ben was over within minutes of us getting back and did an amazing job of checking on her and telling us what to do.

'Is she going to be OK?' Jack asked over and over again. 'Should we phone the ambulance?'

Now, the colour has returned to her face, her cheeks pink as she sleeps quietly.

'I lost her once and I could have lost her again.'

Jack reaches out and places a hand on the bed covers, just next to Lorna's face. She shifts slightly but doesn't stir.

'I don't think I was a very good brother. I think that's maybe partly why she left.'

He looks up at me and for the first time in days I feel like I'm fully seeing him. His face is soft. Gently I move the chair from in front of the small desk and sit down beside him.

'What do you mean?' I say quietly, glancing at the bed again, but Lorna continues to sleep soundly.

'All these years I've blamed her for losing touch. But she wrote to me. I just never wrote back. I could have done, but I didn't. I think maybe because I was still angry with her or maybe because it felt too hard. But I guess it must have been hard for her too.'

I consider this for a moment.

'I suppose it's hard on everyone when there are things unsaid,' I say, 'when there's any stretch of time when you're not communicating. It becomes harder and harder to say the words aloud.'

I swallow hard, and he nods.

'There was a party in the woods once, with all the island teenagers. She invited me. And I so wanted to go. But instead I told our parents about it. I didn't mean to, but it was like I didn't even know how to be the kind of child who would sneak out and have fun with the others. I desperately wanted to but I couldn't. I couldn't be like her and I hated it.'

I reach across and place a hand on his knee and he places his palm on top.

'You were young. It wasn't your fault.'

'But maybe it wasn't hers either. I've spent years thinking it was. But she was just a child. When I was young I always thought of her as an adult in a way, because she was older than me and was confident in ways I wasn't. But she was just a kid. When Lorna was fourteen I thought she knew everything there was to know, but I look at Molly ...'

His voice cracks now and I know without him having to say anything that like me he's thinking about that awful journey across the sea in the storm, discovering the oar and the broken hull and finally finding our daughter huddled under a tree.

'Molly needs us to protect her,' he continues. 'Lorna needed that too.'

We both watch her for a moment, the blankets rising and falling with her breaths.

'Let's go to bed,' I say gently.

He nods and we turn out the lights and walk hand in hand to our room, stopping via Molly's bedroom to open the door a crack and peer inside at the two girls sleeping. Ever since arriving back on Kip I've found myself checking on Molly each night, just to make sure she is there and she is OK. Despite being back on dry land I still have a lingering sense of being on that boat in the storm, as though my stomach is still out at sea even if the rest of me is back here at home.

'They're so alike, aren't they?' says Jack. 'Not just in the way they look but in their personalities. They could be sisters, not cousins.'

I lean my head on his shoulder and he kisses my hair.

Alone in our room we undress and slip in next to each other like we have thousands of times before. He passes me my glass of water which I set on my bedside table as he places his down on his.

And then I say the words I should have said months ago.

'Jack, there's something I need to tell you.'

We sit side by side in our bed, our hands held across the covers, as I tell him about Jean and about what it means for the school and the island too. I tell him about the hospital appointments Jean did her best to cover up, the way she's steadily grown too unwell to attend my classes and how much we miss seeing her there every week, and about the job advert for the headteacher position that has gone unanswered, despite myself and the other governors sharing it with the local islands and anyone else who we think might be interested. By the time all the words are out my cheeks are streaked with tears, my body exhausted from all the emotion. But there's a sort of lightness too, a feeling of having shared my load, of not having to carry it alone anymore.

'Why didn't you tell me?' he says, wiping my tears with his thumb.

I shuffle slightly, uncomfortable now.

'I didn't want to worry you, you have enough going on.'

He shakes his head, his grey eyes glinting in the lamplight.

'But that's not the way it works. Alice, it's not your job to take on everything, to be the one telling everyone that things will be OK. I love you for it, and Molly does too, but we can help you too. I want to know when you're worried, when you're upset.'

He looks at me with such concern, the hardness and distance of the past few days gone. But I can't forget that it was there, and that so often it is, pulling us apart from one another.

'But, Jack, so often I get the feeling that you're holding things back from me too. I guess it makes it harder to open up when there are things you don't tell me.'

He sighs deeply, reaching a hand up to rub his jaw.

'I know. I know, and I'm sorry.' He reaches an arm around me again, pulling me close to his warm, familiar body, this place that has always felt so safe.

'It makes me feel lonely sometimes,' I say quietly.

'It makes me feel lonely too,' he replies.

Then he takes a deep breath. He tells me everything Lorna said to him at the house yesterday. I place my hand gently against his chest as I listen, as he tells me about the bruises that came and went when Lorna was younger and the fire that destroyed her artwork.

'And what do *you* remember?' I ask him softly.

He frowns now, his expression troubled.

'It's so hard, it's like my brain feels foggy. I don't know which memories are real, or which have been painted to look a certain way. But I think I believe her.'

I nod, thinking back to the conversations I've had with Lorna myself and also the way she has of opening up then holding back slightly, as though used to protecting herself. I think of Molly and Ella asleep in the room down the hall, their faces sweetly innocent as they dream dreams their parents will never get to see. I think of the way Jack, Lorna and I ran for them when we saw them huddled there in that cottage on the abandoned island, how we held them against us with all our strength. And I think of my in-laws, and how uneasy I always felt around them even if I couldn't pinpoint exactly why. Now, it makes sense that I never felt comfortable leaving Molly alone with them. Thank god I didn't.

'I think I believe her too.'

We're silent now, looking across the room we both know so well, decorated with photos of our life together, our clothes hanging on the back of the chair, our books stacked in the shelf. I wonder if for Jack, learning what he has learned might be like stepping inside a room like this only to find someone has moved all the furniture and repainted all the walls. The room you thought was so familiar is actually a totally different place.

Not knowing what else to say, I turn to him and ask him the question that has been on my mind since Lorna arrived.

'Do you think we should tell her about the job at the school? Maybe it might make her want to stay? You could get to know each other properly again and make up for all those years you spent apart. Molly and Ella could really become like sisters. And honestly, I'd like her to stay too. I've liked having her here.'

But Jack shakes his head, a sadness etched on his face.

'No. If she stays, it has to be her choice. Because she wants to, not because she feels she has to.'

'You're right,' I reply, knowing immediately that he is, however much I might want otherwise. After everything she's been through, she deserves that much: her freedom.

'And what about the island?' I add. 'What about our home, Jack?'

He sighs again. He has put his whole life into this place, these fields, this house, this life we share together.

'We'll stay as long as we can. And whatever happens, we'll face it together, won't we?'

I reach up and kiss him on the mouth, feeling his rough stubble against my chin and the warmth of his body against mine.

'We will.'

CHAPTER 29

LORNA

Has hot water ever felt quite so pleasurable? I'm taking my first shower in days and as the droplets fall against my skin I press my palms against the tiles and tilt my face up towards the stream of warm water. It feels good to be out of bed and to be doing something as normal as taking a shower.

For the past few days I've been confined to the yellow room, drifting in and out of sleep and getting up only to go to the bathroom and to eat and drink, propped up against pillows. Whenever I woke up there was always someone sitting in the armchair in the corner of the room. Sometimes Ella, sometimes Alice, usually my brother. During the nights I dreamt of the storm and Caora Island.

Now that I'm awake and feeling back to normal I need to make some decisions. But first I must talk to my daughter.

Molly is hunched over the kitchen floor, carefully mopping. Ella works beside her, wiping the kitchen surfaces with vigour. Alice sits at the end of the table drinking tea. My brother isn't there, though.

'Oh, you're up!' says Alice, jumping up from the table and pulling me into a warm hug. I'm used to Alice's hugs by now and I hug her back, enjoying the strength with which she squeezes me.

'How are you feeling?' she asks when we step apart.

'Much better, thank you. What's all this?'

I gesture towards the girls, who are both pink-cheeked with the exertion of cleaning.

'It's part of Molly's grounding,' replies Alice. 'And Ella offered to help.'

Ella looks up from the hob which she has now moved on to scrubbing.

'Is it OK if I borrow my daughter for a while?'

'Of course!'

'Come on, Ella, let's go for a walk.'

The sun is warm on our shoulders as Ella follows me silently onto the beach. The sea is calm and full of sunshine, the storm of a few days ago a memory. I find a gathering of large rocks and sit down, gesturing for Ella to join me. We face out to sea together.

'Are you going to shout at me now?' Ella says quietly, pulling her legs up to her chest.

I sigh, looking at a dark shape wheeling above us. I recognise that elegant, powerful silhouette. An eagle. It lets out a sudden cry and I feel the sound reach deep into my chest and

303

grip it as though the bird itself has wrapped talons around my heart. The sea stretches ahead of us, a shining mirror of gold in the morning light.

'I don't want to shout at you, darling. I'm just so relieved you're OK. One day if you choose to become a mum too, you'll understand what it's like to worry that much about your child. You'll also learn that just because you're a mum, it doesn't mean you always say or do the right thing. I'm sorry I upset you so much that you felt running away was the only option.'

'I'm sorry we did it, Mum. I know it was stupid. I'm so sorry.'

She watches me carefully, fixing me with those brown eyes and I reach out and squeeze her shoulder.

'I know you are, darling.'

I saw yesterday how terrified she looked when she curled up next to me in my bed, anxious to see me unwell. I hated seeing her so worried about me.

'Not just for what we did though,' she adds. 'For what I said too. You know, the day before.'

She looks down now.

'When I said that I didn't have a family, I didn't mean it, Mum.'

I swallow hard. All those photos of Ella growing up with just me for company, just me for support.

'I do have a family,' she says. 'You're my family. You're an amazing family.'

I squeeze my eyes tightly shut, digging my nails into my palms to stop myself from crying. It's all I've ever wanted to be for her. But I think maybe it's not enough. I look at my daughter closely and see how much she has changed over the past few years. Her face tells the story of her childhood but also reveals so much about the woman she is going to become. As each day passes there is more woman on her face and less child. She will always be my baby, but she is not a baby anymore. It's been hard to accept, but I can finally see that now.

'Thank you, darling. But maybe you weren't entirely wrong. I know I should have realised this sooner, but it must be very lonely for you sometimes.'

I tried my best to give Ella all of my attention when she was little but sometimes she would still end up playing solitary games, reading alone or, more recently, listening to music in her bedroom by herself. I've always wished I could have given her a different kind of life – a bigger, fuller kind of life.

She nods at me.

'Sometimes, I guess.'

'Of course you wanted to find your cousin and wanted to stay here as long as possible. Of course you wanted to know your family. I've always told myself that I kept us apart to protect you, but I think maybe it was to protect myself too. I've found it harder than I expected coming back here, and I'm sorry that's affected you.'

'Why did you leave the island, Mum?' she says now, a breeze lifting her curls around her shoulders. 'And why didn't you ever come back?'

It's the question I've been avoiding answering for years and years. It's the thing I've fled from and tried to protect my daughter from. But maybe she doesn't need quite as much protecting as I always thought. Maybe what she needs instead is honesty. And maybe now, she's old enough to hear it.

'I didn't have a very happy childhood here. My parents were very strict …'

I watch her face, working out how much to reveal, how much she can handle.

'My father drank too much and he sometimes got angry. Really angry. It wasn't a good environment to be in. I didn't always feel safe.'

My daughter's face clouds but she nods at me, urging me to continue.

'Luckily, I had my friend Sarah and her family, they were always lovely to me. But I knew quite early on that I would one day have to get off the island and away from my parents. I tried to persuade your Uncle Jack to do the same, but we didn't deal with the situation in the same way. We were very different.'

'So that's why you left, to get away from your parents?'

I nod.

'Yes, honey. And I wanted my own life and that couldn't be here.'

'But Uncle Jack stayed.'

'Yes, Uncle Jack stayed. I thought maybe I'd be able to persuade him to come with me. But in the end, I knew he wouldn't leave. I don't think he could. So I went alone. But it was so hard to leave him behind.'

She nods, brushing a strand of hair away from her face. She looks suddenly so serious, so grown up.

'I guess that's why he's been so weird with you since we arrived then, Mum? No one likes being left behind.'

I swallow hard and she talks quickly again.

'Sorry, I didn't mean to make you feel bad. I'm just thinking this all through. I understand now why you left. That must have been so hard for you. But I guess I can also understand why Uncle Jack might feel sad too.'

I reach my arm around her.

'You're right, sweetie.'

'Do you think you two will be able to make up?'

I look out to sea, at the sun glowing on the horizon and the silhouettes of birds flying in the sky.

'I don't know, darling. I hope so. But maybe too much has happened and too much time has passed.'

'Maybe if you just talk to each other you'll find a way?'

Her suggestion is so simple and yet I know at once she's right. It's time Jack and I talked – really, properly talked. About all the things we didn't have words for as children, all the things we've spent years avoiding, the silence growing heavier every year that went by. It might not change anything, but I think speaking the truth is something we both need to do for ourselves as much as for each other.

Ella and I sit for a while in silence, facing out across the beach. Pebbles and shells dot the sand, a flock of wading birds paddle in the shallows and ahead the sea stretches endlessly into the distance. God, this island. I never thought I'd see it again. I certainly never thought I'd bring my daughter here. And yet here we are. Somehow, I find that I'm glad we're here. I'm glad I'm sitting here on this beach with my daughter, both looking at the same view I know so well but have been apart from for years.

'There's something else I've been thinking, Mum,' Ella says.

I turn to her again. 'What you said earlier, when you said I must be lonely sometimes. Well, aren't you too? It sometimes makes me sad that I'm all you have. And Cheryl too, but apart from that …'

She trails off, the sentence hanging in the air between us. I am used to spending every day worrying in some way about my daughter – whether she's warm, happy, whether I'm doing an OK job. But how much of her life has she spent worrying about *me*? And *am* I lonely? I think, maybe, I've been lonely for so long that I'd forgotten what it was like to feel any other way. Until I came here. Since arriving on the island there have been a few brief moments where that loneliness has cracked like ice on a lake. In the yoga class with all the island women, discussing art with Mallachy in his studio, with my brother's family and Sarah and hers as we shared dinner together around the kitchen table.

I pull Ella towards me.

'How could I ever need more than you?'

She leans into me for a moment and then pulls away slightly.

'I don't know if it's totally normal though, Mum. I've been thinking about it a lot and I wonder whether we're designed to just have one person who's our person. Even if they love us enough for a hundred people.'

Her words hit me in the chest. Sometimes I feel over-whelmed by all the things I have left to teach Ella before she becomes a fully-fledged adult and eventually leaves me to set off on her own in the world. But every now and then it strikes me that my daughter might know more about this world than I ever will.

'You're getting so wise. And so tall!' I nudge her playfully and she laughs.

'I'll be taller than you soon.'

'I'll just have to get into wearing really high heels.'

She nestles in next to me.

'So, tell me about Ruby and Farah,' I say, pulling her a little closer. 'What happened there, darling? You three were so close.'

The sun shines down on us both as Ella tells me about how things first started changing with her friends a few months ago. How Jasmine Matthews joined their group and the dynamic was disturbed. How they started teasing Ella for the fact she hasn't started shaving her legs yet and prefers sporty crop tops to 'proper' bras.

'I know it might be hard to think of it like this, honey,' I say after a moment's thought, 'but it doesn't sound like Ruby and Farah are very happy in themselves. Happy people don't need to put other people down. It sounds like they're going through some stuff – that maybe they don't feel all that confident at the moment and are taking it out on you. Which isn't fair of course, but what I mean is that the way they're acting says everything about *them* and nothing about *you*.'

Ella frowns, considering this.

'I guess ...' She trails off, looking again across the beach.

'I mean, I do like clothes,' she continues, her face softening again. 'And if there were any actually cool guys at our school I wouldn't mind having a boyfriend. But I'm interested in so many other things too, you know? But they think it's not cool to like hiking or sailing or going on adventures anymore.

That's why I so loved it when Molly and I started chatting on Facebook. She just got me and made me feel it was OK to be different.'

From the moment we've set foot on the island the girls have been inseparable. They've been apart their entire lives. They deserve at least a few more days.

I stand up, brushing the sand from my jeans and hands.

'Come on, I think it's time to get back – and for you to give your cousin a hand with all that cleaning!'

Ella stands up quickly.

'So we're not leaving?'

'Not today, no. And tomorrow is the funeral. We might as well stay for that and for a bit after too if you like.' Ella wraps her arms around me, just like she did when she was younger. We walk back to the house side-by-side, her arm through mine, my arm through hers. 'We've come all this way, after all.'

Because we have. It's felt like such a long journey. But I'm realising that maybe it's not over just yet.

CHAPTER 30

ALICE

I watch Lorna and Ella walk along the beach, from a distance
their silhouettes barely distinguishable from one another. It's
turning into a beautiful island morning, the sun crisp as a coin
in the sky. It makes me smile to look at them and I turn to
Molly, who is currently standing on a stool dusting the top of
the kitchen cupboards, and smile up at her too.

'Time for a break I think, shall we have a piece of cake?
Don't tell Dad.'

She hops down from the stool and hugs me.

'I love you, Mum.'

I kiss the top of her head.

'I love you too, sweetheart. And your dad does too, so much.
He was just worried about you, we both were.'

'I know,' nods Molly. 'And I'm really, really sorry.'

'I know you are.'

'Do you think Dad will ever forgive me?'

'Of course he will, darling. I think he already has. Now, how about that cake?'

It still feels such a happy relief to have my daughter here, safe and well after that awful, terrifying search for her. And with Lorna feeling better now too it feels like at least some sort of calm has returned to the house. When Lorna and Ella return inside from the walk I'll make a pot of tea and ask them to join us for cake. Perhaps I can persuade Jack in from the fields for a break too.

Molly fetches plates as I carry the cake tin and a knife to the table. My phone suddenly buzzes in my pocket and I place the tin down, the knife still held in one hand as I reach into my pocket with the other.

It's a message from Sarah.

Are you busy? Jean's husband just called in a state. I'm about to head over there – the others are already on their way.

The knife drops to the table with a clatter. Oh god. What's happened? Is Jean OK? My heart races, my skin growing hot.

'Mum? Are you OK?'

I grab the car keys from the end of the table.

'I've got to go out, darling, I'm sorry. Can you let the others know when they're back?'

She nods, her face anxious.

'I'm sorry. See you later, sweetheart.'

I drive quickly across the island, my palms sweating. The island flashes past but I barely notice; all I can think about is Sarah's message and what might have happened. As I pull up outside Jean and her husband Christopher's house, a stone cottage not far from the school, I spot Sarah's car just in front of me. She opens her door and steps out and we greet each other with a hug.

'What's happened?' I ask her, my voice filled with panic.

'He didn't say exactly, just that we should come over.'

I follow her through the small garden and we knock on the door, standing close beside one another. It's at least some small comfort to have Sarah here next to me, but I still can't stop the thoughts and questions that are whirring inside my mind. Christopher answers the door, his eyes red and an apron tied around his waist. These past few months have aged him and there are deep lines etched between his eyebrows.

'Oh, thank you for coming,' he says shakily, opening the door wide. 'Hopefully you might be able to talk some sense into her. The others are inside. Would you like some tea?'

He leads us into the hallway, where framed school photographs line the walls, Jean pictured in each one at various ages, surrounded by grinning school children. On another day I might pause to find Jack, Lorna and Sarah in one of these photographs and Molly and Olive in another, but not today.

'What's happened, Christopher, is everything OK?'

He sniffs slightly, wiping his hands on his apron.

'I'll let her tell you. Come on through.'

He leads us into the small living room where Jean sits on the sofa, surrounded by our friends. Brenda sits next to Jean,

Tess, Joy and Harry share an armchair in one corner, Morag perches in another and Kerstin and Emma are on the floor. In the middle of the room is a coffee table piled with tea things, books stacked on a glass shelf below. Christopher weaves his way between the women and pours from a large teapot, handing Sarah and me a mug each.

'Thank you, Christopher,' I say, not telling him that the tea is cold. Sarah and I take it in turns to lean over and kiss Jean on her cheek. Then Kerstin and Emma shuffle to make room for us on the floor.

I look across at Jean, trying to meet her eye, but she looks away.

'I'm sorry about all this fuss,' she says somewhat stiffly. Her face is pale but she's still wearing her usual light covering of make-up, the pale pink lipstick that normally suits her feeling unnaturally bright against her now.

Christopher collects a handful of empty mugs and retreats to the kitchen.

'I told him it's my choice,' says Jean gruffly, 'but he won't listen.'

Jean runs her hand along the arm of the sofa. There's a small table at her side with a lamp resting on a stack of books. The whole room is filled with books. It always has been but each year more seem to appear, new shelves built by Christopher in different spots around the cottage to accommodate Jean's ever-growing collection. I remember her lending Molly books about the environment earlier this year, and when she was younger an old edition of classic fairy tales. This island has no library, but we do have Jean.

'What choice, Jean?' I ask her, trying my best not to sound too frantic, but failing.

Jean sighs, looking across at me now and glancing around at the others too. My friends look up at her, each poised and waiting to hear what she has to say.

'The hospital called today,' she said. 'They want me to go back and start chemotherapy. But I've decided I'm not going to.'

It feels as though the floor has suddenly fallen away. There's a brief silence.

'Why the bloody hell not?' says Morag.

Jean sighs again, shifting stiffly on the sofa.

'That was Christopher's reaction too.'

Beside her, Brenda takes her hand.

'But really, Jean, why not?'

Jean runs a hand through her grey hair, glancing briefly towards the window. The two deckchairs are still propped out in the sun and I think about sitting there with Jean just days ago, watching the butterflies.

'I saw what it did to my mother. It was awful, just awful. And in the end, it didn't seem to make any difference.'

'But is your case the same as hers?' asks Kerstin. 'I mean, what do the doctors say?'

'The doctors are strongly advising chemotherapy. They seem to think it would have a good chance of being successful. But I just can't bear it. And we'd have to move to the mainland, at least for a while anyway. This is my home. I don't want to leave.'

'Aye, that I can understand,' says Morag. Her children still try every few months to persuade Morag to move back to the mainland, ideally into a residential care facility. But every time she refuses.

'You know we'd help you however we could,' says Sarah. 'We'd come with you to appointments. You and Christopher wouldn't have to do it all alone.'

'Yes,' chips in Emma. 'We could take it in turns to come over to the mainland and stay with you.'

'And we'd water your plants while you were away,' says Joy, Tess nodding beside her. 'Make sure everything was nice for you here when you came back.'

'Alice,' Jean says, looking at me now. 'What are you going to say to try to make me change my mind?'

I realise I'm the only one who hasn't said anything. I look at my old friend, noticing how drawn her face has become, how tired she looks. I think back over our friendship – the yoga classes she's attended alongside my other friends and all the other times when we haven't done much yoga but instead have chatted together in the community hall or on the beach, our yoga mats abandoned. I think of how kind she was to me when I was nervous about Molly leaving for secondary school. The bottle of wine she, Sarah and I shared on that school trip to Glasgow. I can't imagine life without her. She's as much a part of this island as the mountain, the hills, the sea. She's helped raise generations of island children and she's one of my closest friends. The thought of losing her is unbearable.

'Nothing,' I say eventually.

The others stare at me.

'What?' says Brenda.

I close my eyes for a second, not wanting to say the next words but knowing I have to. Eventually I force myself to open my eyes and continue.

'Jean, we all love you, and I'll admit, it's hard to see you make this choice. But as you said, it's your choice. If this is what you really want, then we have to respect that.'

Her shoulders sink slightly, her body relaxing into the sofa.

'Thank you, Alice,' she says, relief softening her face now. 'This *is* what I want.'

Beside me, Sarah sighs.

'You're right. I'm sorry, Jean, of course whatever you want to do, we'll support you.'

'Of course we will,' say Tess and Joy in unison.

'Always,' adds Brenda, wiping her eyes with the back of her sleeve. Before we know it we're all sniffing and wiping at our eyes too.

'Oh don't, you'll start me off too,' says Jean, rubbing her face. I reach across and take her hand, squeezing it in mine, trying my best to control the tears that roll down my cheeks. I glance around the room at my friends, these women who have helped to make this island my home. It feels so unfair, so unjust, so desperately sad. If we lose Jean, there will always be a hole in our group, an emptiness that nothing will ever be able to fill.

'How about we see if that husband of yours can rustle up something a little stronger than tea?' suggests Morag after a while. And perhaps to everyone's surprise, Jean laughs.

'An excellent idea,' she says, wiping her eyes and smiling. And we all smile back too, not because our hearts aren't breaking but because she's our friend, and right now, that's what she needs.

CHAPTER 31

LORNA

By the time Ella and I have walked slowly across the beach and nearly made it back to the farmhouse, it seems that something has shifted between us. We walk up the dusty farm track side by side. I sneak a glance across at her. For once, I see not a little girl but my daughter who is becoming a young woman.

As we near the house I spot my brother in the sheep field. He looks up and to my surprise he catches my eye and starts walking towards us. Ella spots him too and gently removes her arm from mine.

'Good luck, Mum. I'll be inside if you need me.'

She turns away and into the house. I take a deep breath and set off across the field towards Jack, watching his determined strides as he draws closer. Ella was right, Jack and I need to talk. I think again of our argument at our parents' house. I don't know how this conversation will go, but I need to try.

We meet in the middle at the drystone wall that cuts through the fields. For a second, we pause in front of one another, his hands in his pockets, mine hanging at my sides. The sun feels warm against my shoulders. Jack turns and leans back against the wall and after a moment I sit beside him, both of us facing out across the farm. I can hear his steady breathing beside me, as well as the bleat of a sheep a little further away in the field. There's something about all this air around us that feels right for this moment. When he confronted me in the house I felt trapped, hemmed in by boxes and memories. Here I feel freer, the sea breeze on my cheeks and the smell of salt water, heather and the musk of sheep's wool in the air. I wonder if Jack feels the same; he certainly seems less stiff as he sits beside me, his body still.

From here we can see the back of the house, bright white in the morning sunshine, curtains flapping at the open windows. I can make out the figures of Molly and Ella in the kitchen and notice that the Land Rover is gone and wonder for a moment where Alice is. I think she might like to see Jack and me sitting here side by side in the field.

Ahead of us is the hill that slopes down to the beach. There's a figure walking across the sand, a dog leaping ahead of them. Gulls rest at the waterline and bob like buoys on the surface of the sea. I run my hands along the wall where we sit, lichen and moss clinging to the stone and wildflowers growing between the cracks at the bottom where stone meets grass. Suddenly I feel wracked with nerves. I'd been so certain about the need to talk to my brother, but now it feels impossible to know where to start.

'So how do you even build a drystone wall?'

Jack glances at me, his grey eyes flashing in the sunlight. I hold his gaze. He tilts his head slightly, examining the stones at his side. He coughs.

'Well, you have to start by sorting your stones.'

'Yes?'

He glances at me again.

'You need a mix of sizes and shapes. Then you mark out where the wall is going to be and build some sort of frame – you can use wood, metal or string to mark it out.'

'And then?'

He takes a breath.

'And then you get building.'

'It must take a long time. It's so intricate.' I run my fingers over the mismatched stones that make up the wall beneath me. They are all sorts of shapes: smooth and round, sharp and jagged, some almost perfectly spherical, others flat and thin.

'The trick is not to rush,' says Jack. 'You need to keep the wall level, so it can take a few goes to select the perfect stone. It isn't the quickest way to build a wall but once it's built it can last for years.'

'Really? I never understood how they managed to stay up like that. I mean, this feels so strong but I can't get my head around the fact there's no cement or anything holding it to-gether.'

'You don't need cement – the wall holds itself together. It's strong, if you take the time to make it right. Aye, a section might fall down in a storm but you just build it back up again using the same stones. A wall is never totally broken as long as you still have those stones. You can always build it again.'

I blink quickly, imagining my brother building this wall with the help of the islanders.

'It's beautiful.'

A faint smile spreads across his face.

'I think so. I've always thought it's not just a wall, it's part of the landscape. These are local stones, they've been on this farm for generations. They belong to this land.'

I look at my brother leaning against this wall he built himself, dressed in his mud-stained farming clothes, his arms tanned by the sun and his eyes the same shade as the stones that form this wall. He belongs to this land too, I can see it now. I might have dreamt of him leaving with me for London when we were young, but seeing him here I understand why he didn't want to leave. It wasn't just because of our parents and a sense of duty, although I'm sure that had its part to play. He is part of this place. He fits here like the stones that lock together to form this wall.

'This section here is actually the first I worked on,' he continues. 'Most of the walls on the farm had fallen down when we started doing the place up. Sarah's father Doug showed me how to do it. We rebuilt this whole bit together.'

I picture the two of them kneeling in the grass, arranging the stones by size. I imagine Jack would have looked incredibly serious as Doug passed on his wisdom, his face scrunched as he tried to remember it all.

'Well you were clearly a good student.'

He shrugs.

'I guess the stuff I learned at school and in books never really meant all that much to me. Aye, I learnt the facts but I never felt a connection to them. But working here … It made sense, that knowledge passed on from person to person. There were no books, just listening, watching, making mistakes and learning from them.'

We all make mistakes. I've certainly had my fair share of them. Have I always learnt from them though? I don't know. But I'm trying.

'You've done an amazing job here, Jack,' I say, shifting so I'm half-looking at him, half-looking ahead at the fields that surround us. 'With the farm, with Molly …'

He laughs quietly, the sound warming me like the flames of a log fire.

'Aye, she's a good lass when she's not coming up with crazy schemes.'

'How long do you think you'll ground her for?'

'I don't know, the house is looking pretty clean, there's only so many jobs left that I can think of for her to do.'

We smile at one another and my heart races with the simplicity of it.

'She'll be all right,' he says with a small nod.

There's a moment's pause as we continue to sit next to one another, looking out to sea. I've thought about a moment like this for years and years. Just sitting next to my brother, not saying anything even, just there beside one another. How has it taken me this long to get here? I place my hand on the top of the wall, just centimetres from his.

'Jack, I want to tell you how sorry I am. For everything. For leaving, for not saying goodbye, for everything I missed. I'm truly sorry, for all of it.'

The words feel tight in my throat, but once they are out I can't help but experience a rush of relief. I think I've been waiting years to say them.

I watch Jack closely, searching his face for a reaction. He frowns, shaking his head slightly.

'I'm sorry too. You know, I spent years and years being angry with you.'

'I'm not surprised.'

'I was so angry at you for leaving and for not staying in touch. But you wrote to me. I could have written back.'

I think again of those unanswered letters, the jolt I felt whenever a hand-written envelope landed on my mat and the disappointment that followed when the letter was never from him. I never blamed him, but I clung onto hope that he might one day reply.

'This separation ...' he pauses. 'Well it wasn't just you, Lorna.'

I've carried my guilt for most of my life. I don't think it will ever totally go away, but it feels as though my brother has just given me permission to put it down for a moment, to let it go.

'And I've been thinking about what you said the other day at the house,' he continues, rubbing his cheek. 'I've been trying to remember. It's hard though, I feel like everything is foggy, like I'm struggling to see things clearly. It's like I can't trust my own memories.'

I nod slowly.

'I understand. I've felt like that at times too.'

When you're a child, the people around you control your narrative. *Lorna's clumsy, she's a tearaway, she needs to learn how to behave.* It's only after I left the island and grew older that I managed to truly see what had really happened, to put my own words to it. Jack never had that separation. And the thing is, the more that other people tell your story for you, the more it comes to feel real.

'Last night I couldn't sleep and these things kept coming back to me,' he says. 'I remembered the smell of smoke and petrol coming through my bedroom window from outside.'

My chest tightens as I remember the same smell, the smell that has stayed with me after all these years and still visits me at night, filling my sleeping mind with its memory. Flames flickering at the bottom of the garden. My paintings and my hopes for the future burning on a smoking pile of fire. Jack turns to me, fixing me with his grey eyes.

'I remembered it, Lorna. Last night I remembered the fire. And it suddenly made no sense to me the thing they'd always told me, that you started it. Why would you do something like that? Of course you didn't start the fire. They did.'

My throat feels choked and tears spring hotly to my eyes. I let out a sob, my heart racing with the joy and grief and relief of being believed. Jack's hand reaches across the wall for mine. He holds it as I cry and the fields and the sea stretch ahead of us in green and blue.

'I'm sorry, Lorna,' he says quietly, squeezing my hand.

'Oh Jack, I'm sorry too.'

I shuffle closer and lean my head against his shoulder. He

lifts a hand to my hair. I don't know how long we stay there. It could be seconds, it could be years. All I can focus on is the feel of my brother beside me, the way we once were, the way we should always have been.

Eventually, my tears slow and I move away slightly, wiping my face on my sleeve.

'Is it OK if we stay on the island a little longer?' I ask him.

'Stay as long as you like,' he says quietly.

My brother and I haven't been part of each other's lives in over twenty years. There are still so many things we need to discuss, so many questions that need answering. But we are here.

I think again about the advice Jack shared about creating stone walls. Sometimes there are storms, and sometimes things that once felt strong tumble and fall. But they can be built again, one stone at a time. As I sit next to my brother watching the waves lap against the beach in the distance I feel like that's what we are finally doing. We are rebuilding our wall, one stone at a time.

CHAPTER 32

ALICE

'What now?' says Sarah. We're standing outside Jean's house, my friends gathered together, everyone seemingly reluctant to go our separate ways. Tess jogs Harry up and down on her hip, Joy wrapping an arm around the two of them and staring ahead, a dazed expression on her face.

It was hard to leave the cottage. After the tears and a couple of drams of whisky Jean seemed calmer, the stiffness gone from her body and in its place a sense of ease. But it was difficult to say goodbye to her.

'You'll see me tomorrow at the funeral,' she'd said, and I watched as my friends flinched.

'I'm not going anywhere just yet,' she continued. 'I'll see you all tomorrow. Now get on home, all of you.'

I could barely meet Christopher's eye as he showed us out,

his shoulders sagging and the apron around his waist limp and stained with splashes of milk. Before reaching the front door he paused, stretching a hand out to one of the school photographs on the wall and finding Jean among the children, stroking her face with his thumb.

'I take it you didn't change her mind,' he said quietly. Guilt rushed through me. We'd let him down. I shook my head.

'This is what she wants,' I replied, placing a hand gently on his arm. He sighed.

'You're right. I'm just not ready to let her go.'

'I know.'

'Anything we can do to help, you let us know,' said Brenda. 'You aren't alone, OK?'

Now, the door shut behind us and the group of us gathered in the road, the desire to be together pulls us close to one another.

'Shall we go down to the beach?' suggests Emma. But Kerstin shakes her head.

'It's too exposed down there. I don't think I could deal with making small-talk with dog walkers right now.'

I understand what she means. We need to be together, just us, to absorb what just happened, what is happening to our friend.

'I've got an idea.'

I lead them quietly towards the village hall. As usual the door is unlocked and they follow me inside, into this place where we gather every week for my classes. The room is warm, sun slanting in through the windows and creating squares of white light on the lino. On autopilot my friends reach for the mats in the corner of the room and spread them out on the floor, congregating close together around the patches of sunlight. One by one they sit and lie down next to one another. Tess and Joy push two mats up against each other and sit down with their legs spread wide, creating a square of space between them where they place Harry, who pulls himself back and forth between them. Sarah sits cross-legged, staring straight ahead. Emma lies on her back, knees up and feet planted on the floor. Beside her Brenda stretches out next to Kerstin, who slumps on her side. Morag takes a moment to get down onto the ground and I reach out an arm to help her. For once she doesn't wave it away. I sink down to my knees alongside my friends.

We sit in silence for a moment.

'It's just so unfair,' says Brenda, her voice loud and hard with anger.

'Aye,' adds Morag. 'Why Jean? I'm bloody ancient, if the man upstairs wants somebody he should take me.'

'Why does anyone have to be taken anywhere?' says Emma. 'I can't bear the thought of losing any of you, you're like my family.'

Her voice cracks and Sarah reaches across and hugs her.

'You're right,' says Joy. 'I don't know, but I guess with my parents living so far away ... Jean's been so helpful with Harry, you all have.'

Tess nods sadly.

'She was our teacher,' says Emma. 'I just always thought she was invincible, you know?'

'I know,' agrees Sarah. 'Me too. God, it's strange isn't it – if you'd told me as a child that Mrs Brown would end up one of my closest friends I would have laughed.'

Emma wipes her eyes and smiles.

'Me too. But that's the thing about friendship, isn't it? In the end that stuff doesn't matter, does it?'

I look around the room at my friends, at Tess and Joy who are in their late twenties, Sarah and Emma who are several years older than me, Kerstin who is in her fifties, Brenda who turned sixty last year, then Morag, who might have the body of an eighty-year-old but still makes me laugh as hard as any other of my friends can, perhaps even harder. We've all had such different lives, different careers, different experiences of family. Sarah and Emma might have grown up here but the rest of us come from all over, our disparate lives converging here on this small island. But Emma's right. The differences between us aren't what matters. What matters are the moments we've shared together, doing yoga in this hall and on the beach, drinking together at The Lookout, celebrating each other's birthdays and good news, commiserating each other's losses and low moments, laughing together in the sunshine and in the rain. Now, we're facing one of the hardest journeys together as we do our best to support Jean and accept what is to come. I still can't quite comprehend what Jean told us today. But at least I know I'm not alone in the way I feel. And we won't let Jean feel alone either. We'll be there beside her every step of the way, even when it feels impossibly hard.

'Alice,' says Tess, 'do you think you could teach us? I don't know about everyone else but I could do with the distraction.'

'Good idea, if I don't move my body I may just stay here all day,' says Kerstin from where she's stretched out on the floor.

'I don't know …' I'm not sure if I can manage teaching right now.

'Please,' says Sarah. 'I think it will help.'

The others nod. I take a deep breath. I want to help my friends. And maybe it will help me a little too.

'OK then.'

We adjust the mats. I'm not really dressed for yoga and neither are most of my friends but it doesn't really matter. We'll manage.

I choose a sun salutation. The movements are fluid and constant. When you're saluting the sun you get caught up and absorbed by the movements, which is why I chose this. My friends copy my moves, reaching to the ground and lifting arms to the sky, moving from one pose to another with a sense of energy and purpose. As I lead them I think about sun and fire, their power to bring warmth and life but also to destroy. I suppose you can't have one without the other: love without loss, life without death. It's inevitable. But that inevitability doesn't make it any easier. When faced with loss you still want to cling on as tightly as you can. I think about Jean, and Christopher's reluctance to let her refuse treatment.

'Take a deep breath,' I tell my friends, 'and then breathe out and let it all go.'

Should we have pushed harder to change Jean's mind? Perhaps we should go back and try to argue with her, putting forward the case for chemotherapy and its success rates. Despite what I said earlier, I can't help but feel like I've made a big mistake in not fighting harder. I might have said those words, I might have been the one to encourage the others to back down, but deep down I'm not sure if I really feel it. I suppose in the end, letting go can be the hardest thing in the world.

CHAPTER 33

LORNA

Jack and I are still side by side on the stone wall when a sound brings my attention towards the track. The Land Rover trundles towards us and pulls up outside the house. Alice steps out, the breeze dancing in her hair. Her expression looks haunted for a moment, her gaze distant and lost. But then she spots us and a smile brightens her face. She lifts a hand in a wave. Jack and I wave back.

'I'd better get back to work,' says Jack, standing up and brushing his overalls with his hands.

'OK, well I'll see you later.'

'See you later, Lorna,' he says, half-smiling.

When I reach the farmhouse, I greet Alice with a warm hug.

'We did it, Alice, we talked, we properly talked.'

I'm grinning, my whole body glowing with relief and happiness.

'I'm so pleased,' she replies. As we step apart she rubs her eyes quickly and I notice that they are red.

'Are you OK?'

But she takes a deep breath and waves a hand in front of her.

'I'm fine. I'm so glad you two talked, I know he's wanted to, he just struggles opening up.'

'Thank you, Alice. Talking with you has helped so much too.'

She smiles but it's somewhat weak and I notice her eyes glancing away for a second before darting back again. I wonder what's wrong, because something is clearly wrong. But it's also obvious that she doesn't want to talk about it. I don't want to push her.

'It's good to see you up and about,' she says, a somewhat forced brightness in her voice. 'Are you feeling better?'

'Much better, thank you. And thank you for looking after me, both of you.'

As I say it I think suddenly of the other person who was there with us on the island, the person who steered us through a storm and helped us find our daughters. My cheeks grow warm. If today is a day of talking, of stepping closer, then there's one other person I want to see. I picture Mallachy's studio and how we discussed art together there. I remember him jumping overboard on the shore of Caora Island and wading through the water behind us as we set off in search of Ella and Molly. And I think of the smell of his jumper – pine and dog and oil paints.

'Alice, do you mind if I head out for a bit? There's someone I need to thank.'

Her smile grows more genuine now as she looks back at me.

'It's Mallachy's day off – he should be at his house.' My eyebrows rise and she laughs, holding her hands up. 'Sorry, I didn't mean to interfere. I forgot to tell you, but the flowers by your bed were from him.'

Is my face as red as it feels?

'Oh really? That was kind of him.' I picture the posy of wildflowers resting on my bedside table, their smell filling my room.

'So,' she says. 'Do you mind if I ask what's happening there? Just tell me if I'm being too nosy.'

I sigh lightly.

'No, it's fine. But honestly, I have no idea. I'm not exactly practised at this.'

'He clearly likes you, though.'

My cheeks flush even warmer.

'Would it sound mad if I said I'm scared?' I admit. 'I mean, I'm forty years old for god's sake. But I don't really date, I never have, not since Ella's dad. I don't ever want it to get complicated for her.'

'That's very admirable, but she's a teenager now. I'm sure she understands that you deserve to have your own life.'

'I guess.' I think about my earlier conversation with Ella. She is growing up. Perhaps Alice is right.

'And anyway,' she adds, 'dating *is* terrifying. But some of the best things in life are, aren't they? Opening yourself up to other people isn't always easy, because there's always a chance it might not work out or you might lose them. But closing yourself off forever … Is that really living?'

Her words hit me hard. All these years that I've lived mostly alone, shutting myself off from others … Have I really been living?

'What are you waiting for?' says Alice. 'Life is short, shorter than we ever realise. Go see him. Take the car.'

She hands me the keys and a smile spreads across my face. But I pause.

'Are you sure you're OK though?'

I look at her closely, trying to see any traces of that haunted expression I saw just moments ago.

'I'm fine,' she replies. 'Go on.'

'OK. Thank you. I'll see you later, Alice.'

'Good luck.'

With a skipping in my stomach I climb into the car and set out across the island. Everything looks golden in the sunlight. For a moment I feel like singing. And I never sing.

The front door is open when I arrive at Mallachy's, a pair of boots resting beneath the porch. I knock on the open door.

'Lorna!' I hear him calling from inside. 'I'm in the studio, come in!'

I follow his voice to the light-filled room at the back of the house. He's sitting at an easel facing the sea. As I step inside he stands up and turns to me, his green eyes sparkling in the sunshine.

'How did you know it was me?' I ask, glancing briefly across at the easel. It's a nearly blank canvas, just a few sketches drawn on the white expanse. I feel my hands twitching at my side, thinking about filling a canvas like that myself. But then he smiles at me and the easel fades into the background again. It's just one of those smiles that makes everything else disappear for a moment.

'Any of the other islanders would have just walked straight in. Only mainlanders knock.'

The way he says 'mainlanders' makes me know he's teasing me. I rise to it.

'Excuse me, I think you'll find I grew up here. You're the newcomer!'

'Aye, you're right. So, you're better then? I'm so glad.'

'Yes, I'm fine now. Thank you for the flowers. And for helping us find the girls. Honestly, I don't know how I can ever thank you for everything you did.'

He shrugs lightly.

'Anyone would have done the same. I'm just so glad they're OK.'

'They're both writing you very long apology letters.'

He laughs.

'I shall look forward to reading them.'

I pause for a moment, suddenly unsure what to say. Today has been a day of talking, of trying to find the right words to bridge the gaps between people. But maybe sometimes there aren't any words. Instead, I take a step forward and he does too. And something in the air suddenly changes. As I look at him I feel it again, that electricity that rushed between us that first time in his studio. But this time it's different. This time I'm not going to run away. Instead, I tilt my head up towards his and kiss him. And, thank god, he kisses me back.

His mouth is warm, his beard rough against my face. He weaves his fingers through the tangled mess of my hair. We part for a moment and he rests his forehead against mine.

'God, I've wanted this since I first saw you,' he says quietly.

I can't help but laugh.

'What, when I was out running, with mascara all over my face?'

He holds his hand up to my cheek.

'Don't. You're beautiful.'

I don't know what to say to that. Usually when I look in the mirror all I see are the bags under my eyes and each new line that appears on my face. But the way he looks at me makes me feel as though there could be something else I'm not seeing. I kiss him again.

'Seriously though,' he says, pulling away for a second, 'you have no idea. This island is great and all but there's no one here like you.'

'Shh,' I say gently, pressing my lips to his once more.

His grin makes my heart beat even faster. As we stumble into his room and pull each other down onto the bed I feel as though weights are being released, each one dropped lifting me higher. Today it's like I've put down so many things I didn't realise I didn't have to carry forever. Worries about Ella and the guilt about my brother that has been there with me ever since I left this island. It's as though I've been given permission to let go, and perhaps, to be happy too. I haven't felt this light in years. I'm giddy with it, floating on it. Maybe this is what it feels like to really live. I abandon myself to it, to the way Mallachy's touch feels on my skin, letting myself relish every sensation. As we find each other among a tangle of sheets, I feel for a blissful moment totally and utterly free.

*

A whisper in my ear.

'Lorna.'

The sound pulls me awake; I must have fallen asleep. I stretch and open my eyes. Mallachy is propped up on his elbow watching me, the sheet draped over his waist. His eyes are bright and smiling and his hair sticks up messily from his head. I can't help but run my eyes over his bare torso, muscular yet not intimidatingly so, padded round the edges with middle-age. My eyes flick to those hands that held me so gently yet firmly at the same time.

'Don't worry, you weren't snoring,' he says with a smile.

'Oh, I never snore,' I lie. He laughs.

The bedroom is bathed in light and for a second I flinch as I glance out the window; in our haste we forgot to close the curtains. But then I relax. We're secluded on this side of the island: the only creatures who might spot us are the gulls that hop along the sand on Mallachy's small stretch of beach. Slowly we dress again, Mallachy handing me items of clothing from the floor. Once we're dressed, without really discussing it we drift out of his room and into the studio. It's filled with sunlight, the view of the island and the sea stretching out around us.

Mallachy sweeps a pile of papers aside on his desk.

'What are you doing?'

339

'Clearing you a space,' he replies, smiling.

He lays out a few blank sheets of paper, some pencils, a few brushes and a palette of watercolours.

'I don't know if I could. I haven't drawn or painted in years.'

'You don't have to. But everything is here for you to use if you want to.'

I avoid the desk and walk instead around the studio, looking at the spines of books and gently picking up things here and there and placing them down again. A stick of charcoal, a palette knife, a paintbrush. Once, these things felt like extensions of my own body. Once, nothing made me happier than throwing myself into my painting and drawing. Where did that passion go? Did it disappear altogether, or has it simply been hiding?

Mallachy flicks on the radio, music filling the studio.

'Why don't you at least sit down?' he says gently. And this time I do, perching on a stool at the end of the desk. On the table the white paper stares up at me. I pick up a pencil and hold it lightly in my hand.

Beside me, Mallachy sits too and I listen to the light scratching sound as he starts to draw, his head lowered, his hand moving swiftly. I hold my own pencil just a few millimetres away from the paper. Suddenly I want to experience it again – that feeling I once so craved of losing myself to pencil and paper. To show myself that while my life might have completely changed since I was a child, there are still parts of me that are the same. With a slight intake of breath, I make the first mark.

As we work side by side, we talk.

'I don't do this often, you know,' I say quietly, my eyes down on the paper. 'You know, forcing myself on strangers ...'

'Lorna, believe me, you did not force anything,' he replies. 'But I know what you mean, and me neither.' His face flushes and he runs a hand through his beard. 'Actually, I haven't been with anyone since my ex-wife.'

'Wow.'

'Sorry, does that make it weird for you? Maybe I shouldn't have told you.'

To my surprise he sounds flustered.

'Sorry, I didn't mean to sound so surprised, it's just you seem so ...'

He grins now.

'So ... what?' he asks, raising an eyebrow. 'Handsome, charming?'

It's my turn to blush now as I meet his playfully glinting eyes.

'Well, so sure of yourself, I guess.'

'I guess I'm finally over it all. But god, for a long time there I was a total mess.'

I struggle to picture him as anything other than calm. But of course, everyone has something they're dealing with or have been through, you just can't always see it.

'I'm sorry.'

He shrugs, a smile returning to his face.

'Aye, it was hard, but life goes on, doesn't it?'

And I find myself smiling back at him. Life goes on.

It's late afternoon by the time I leave. When I return to the farmhouse I find the whole family gathered in the kitchen, the entire table covered in hundreds of sandwiches. Ella and Molly are busily spreading fillings, Jack cuts neat slices from a loaf and Alice flits between them.

'What's all this?' I ask.

Alice meets my eye, raising an eyebrow questioningly. I want to tell her what happened but everyone else is here so instead I just smile and she smiles back.

'We're just getting things ready for tomorrow,' she replies.

Of course. Reality suddenly hits, jolting me. Tomorrow is the funeral. With everything that's happened today, I'd almost forgotten. Tomorrow, Jack and I will bury our parents. I glance over at him and he meets my eye and for once, he doesn't look away.

'How can I help?' I ask, reaching for a spare apron hanging on the back of a chair. Jack hands me another loaf of bread and a knife.

My phone beeps in my pocket and I pause for a moment to read it. It's a message from Cheryl.

Good luck for tomorrow honey. I'll be thinking of you. Sending a big hug and lots of love xxx

I smile, moved that she remembered the date of the funeral. 'Thank you for remembering,' I reply. 'And for the hug, I needed it. Hope you and your boys are well. Can't wait to see you when I'm back. Xx' Then I slip my phone into my pocket and get started on the loaf.

The five of us work quietly alongside one another, the silence broken every now and then by an instruction from Alice or a burst of chatter between Ella and Molly. When it's quiet it feels different to the silences that have sat between us throughout this trip, though. It feels a contented kind of quiet, the kind of quiet I always imagined other families taking for granted. As I look around the room at the others working and at the growing pile of sandwiches, a thought enters my mind as quick as a blink. This is my family.

CHAPTER 34

ALICE

Jack and I stayed up late last night, talking. I told him about Jean and let him hold me as I cried. It was hard to keep the news from the others, but I didn't want to upset Molly, who loves her old teacher, and my promise to Jean held me back from telling Lorna. Now, it's early, the house silent. I slip out of bed, careful not to disturb Jack, and pull back the corner of the curtains. It's grey outside as though the sky knows that today there will be a funeral. There seems to be a strong wind too, the grassy dunes by the beach bowed over as though exhausted. I glance at the clock by the bed: 5.45 a.m. I know there's no chance of falling back to sleep though. My stomach churns as though hungover, although I didn't drink last night. It must be all the emotion instead. I steady myself against the windowsill for a moment before dressing quickly and quietly.

When I step outside the front door I'm hit by a cool, damp breeze. It dulls my nausea somewhat and I take a deep, clear breath. The clouds hunch low on the horizon. I set off for the beach. Later, I will have to host a wake and hold it together to support Jack and Molly. I will have to smile and serve sandwiches and sit in respectful silence in the church when I really want to scream at the unfairness of it all – at the awful ways Jack and Lorna were let down by their parents and the unjustness of my friend being so unwell.

I reach the dark line on the beach where the dry sand grows grey and damp. Ahead, the sea is gunmetal grey flecked with the white foam of choppy waves. A salty wind blows in my face and through my hair. I face the sea, placing the large tote bag I brought with me on the ground. Slowly, I unzip my raincoat, letting it fall. Then I take off my shoes and socks, feeling the cool sand between my toes, and unbuckle the belt on my jeans and pull those off too. Goosebumps immediately prick my skin as the cold air whips around me.

'What are you doing?'

I turn around quickly at the voice. Lorna stands a few paces away, watching me questioningly, her jacket pulled tightly around her. Her hair is pulled back in a scruffy ponytail and her eyes are shadowed with fatigue. Somehow, it isn't much of a surprise to see her here. Of course she couldn't sleep either.

'I saw you out the window,' she adds. 'I was awake.'

'I couldn't get back to sleep,' I reply. 'I need a swim.'

She looks from me out to the grey rolling waves.

'You're not really going swimming now? It looks freezing.'

Perhaps it does, but I'm used to the cold. And I know in

every cell of my body that this is what I need right now. I want to wash everything away, to feel nothing but the water. It's what I've done in moments of crisis over the years: when my parents called to say my grandparents had died, when Molly was unwell with bronchitis and I stayed up every night with her, terrified as I listened to her wheezing breaths, after my miscarriage. Each time I came here and swam.

'Come in with me,' I say to Lorna now. 'Trust me, it's what you need this morning. It'll make you feel alive.'

Before she can answer I'm tugging my T-shirt off and dropping it on the floor alongside my pile of other clothes. I stride towards the sea in my underwear.

'You're mad!' Lorna calls after me with a slight laugh.

Personally, I think the only madness would be to live with this ocean so close to my doorstep and never swim in it. The wind tugs at my hair and my feet sink into the sand, leaving deep footprints.

'It's fine, I do this in the winter too. The sea will be positively balmy today.'

My feet reach the water's edge. OK, perhaps I might be exaggerating. The water makes my toes curl with cold. I look down; they've turned a ghostly white. But I keep walking, letting the cold water reach my shins. I take a deep breath. And I run. Water splashes around me, droplets sprayed then dropped down in fountains. I tear my way through the waves, the cold gripping me like a vice. I am waist-deep. I am shoulder-deep. I am launching myself forwards, diving into the Atlantic.

Everything is quiet. I squeeze my eyes tightly shut against the salt water. There's a sudden rushing in my ears like the sound of an oncoming train. A pressure builds in my chest, a weight like a person placing a foot on my chest. My skin tingles, water rushing over every inch of my body, enveloping me completely. Then my feet connect with firm sand and I push myself up.

Droplets cling to my lashes and my eyes stream with salt water. The skin around my nose and mouth is raw and stinging, burnt by the wind and the salt. I'm aware of my entire body and every tiny sensation that ripples through me. Cold water slipping between my toes, tugging at my hair, trickling down the backs of my ears. A prickling sensation on my collarbones, the back of my neck, the base of my spine. The cold shifts from a sudden burn to a lingering glow that makes me feel almost warm. I float on my back, my body rising and falling on the humps of the waves. I turn to look back at the shore where Lorna lingers, watching me.

'It's wonderful!' I cry. 'Come on, you won't regret it!'

She hesitates, and then a grin flashes across her face.

'OK, I'm coming!'

'Hurrah!' I splash the water around me as she quickly un-dresses and dashes towards the sea, yelping as she reaches the waterline.

'Bloody hell, it's freezing!'

'You get used to it.'

I lean back, floating and letting my ears fill with seawater. Another yelp draws my attention to the shore and I watch as Lorna takes a few steps forward, the water lapping around her shins, her knees.

'You can do it!'

She takes short, sharp breaths, her arms clutched tightly around her chest, her whole body shivering.

'Shall I count you down?'

She nods.

'OK. One, two, three ...'

And with a shriek and a splash she launches herself forwards and into the water. She swims frantically, her head bobbing above the waves. But after a few moments she slows.

'Oh, you're right,' she says. 'It does get better.'

We're side by side now, both floating and facing back towards the island. It stretches out in front of us, the mountain rising like the fin of a sea creature in the middle. There's light glowing behind it, hinting that this might just be a passing gust and nicer weather is on its way. I can see the whole farm from here, our house and the fields stretching around it, dotted with sheep and cows. My throat grows suddenly tight.

'It's beautiful, isn't it?' says Lorna quietly. I turn to her in surprise.

'I think I never really thought it before,' she continues. 'I guess I was so caught up in my memories of the place that I couldn't see it properly. But it *is* beautiful. It's magnificent.'

I turn away for a second, trying to hold back my tears. Jean's announcement had distracted me from the other pressing worry faced by the island – the fate of the school – but it comes back to me now in a fresh wave of anxiety. We've still had no applications for the job. We're running out of time.

'It is,' I say in reply, following Lorna's gaze back to the island that I call home.

We swim for a little longer, side by side and parallel to the shore. Eventually we head for the land and stumble out of the water. I reach for my bag, pulling out a large striped beach towel and handing it to Lorna.

'Here, you go first.'

But she shakes her head.

'No, I've gatecrashed your swim, you use it.'

'It wasn't gatecrashing,' I reply. 'It's nice to have you here.'

She smiles at me.

'It's good to be here.'

I try to hand her the towel again but she refuses so I quickly dry myself down then pass it to her as I pull on my clothes, my jeans sticking to my still slightly damp, sandy legs. My hair is knotted and tangled and drips down my back but I don't care. When we're both dressed I lay the towel out on the ground and we sit beside one another. I reach into the tote bag for the Thermos I filled with tea before leaving. We pass it back and forth between us, curls of steam drifting into the air from the cup. The warm liquid brings sensation back to my lips and gradually the warmth spreads through my whole body.

'How are you feeling about today?' I ask her.

She sighs, hugging her knees up to her chest.

'I just want it to be over really.'

I nod, feeling the same way.

'I hope you don't mind, but Jack told me what you told him when we were at the house. I just wanted to say how sorry I am for everything you went through. It's just awful.'

'Thank you,' she says quietly.

'You've been through so much. And you've faced so much of it on your own. I honestly don't know how you managed it.'

She passes me the Thermos.

'Here, you finish it.' She glances out to sea then back at me. 'And I'm not alone anymore,' she adds.

We smile at one another and then stand up, shaking the sand out of the towel and heading back towards the house. As we walk she tells me about the afternoon with Mallachy and I do my best to hide my excitement and appear as relaxed as possible.

'Do you think you'll see each other again while you're here?' I ask her.

'I hope so,' she replies quietly.

When we reach the house we both pause. Our clothes smell faintly of seaweed and salt water and our cheeks are flushed from the cold. Her hair is just as tangled and sodden as mine. Part of me wants to run back to the beach rather than facing what is to come today. But at least I don't have to face this day alone. I will have my family by my side. And now, that family includes Lorna too. We nod at one another in understanding and step inside.

CHAPTER 35

LORNA

The churchyard is quiet except for the sound of a crow crying from the church roof. Dark yew trees guard the path through the graves, their trunks gnarled like elephant skin. The church tower rises into the now blue sky and beyond it stands the mountain, dark and impassive. Despite having showered I can still smell the faint trace of salt water on my skin and it calms me slightly, reminding me of this morning.

Ella tugs self-consciously at the hem of her black dress. Beside her, Molly does the same with her black skirt. Alice and Jack are just behind them, holding hands. The five of us stay close together as we walk up the path. We pause for a moment in the churchyard as black-clad figures follow behind us and into the church. I catch Alice's eye and she smiles reassuringly at me.

'How are you all holding up?' asks Sarah's mother Linda as she reaches us, giving both Molly and Ella a hug. Doug shakes Jack's hand and pats him roughly but warmly on the shoulder. As they exchange a few words Linda pulls me into a firm embrace. Before releasing me, she says something quietly into my ear.

'We always thought of you as ours, you know.'

I blink back tears as she lets me go and then disappears with Doug inside the church. Sarah and her family are just behind them and hug us all in turn too. As Ella and Olive embrace each other it's like watching Sarah and me as children. She catches me watching them and smiles at me softly.

'It's like stepping back in time seeing them together, isn't it?' she says.

I've spent most of my life trying to escape my past. And yet for just a second, I would go back if I could, just for a moment of that friendship Sarah and I shared as girls. But perhaps it's not too late for us after all. We can never get back exactly what we had, but we can build something new. She hugs me again and then disappears inside the church.

Next up the path comes Morag, leaning on a stick wrapped with black ribbons and accompanied by Mrs Campbell from the village shop, who gives me a gentle smile. Tess, Joy and Harry arrive alongside Kerstin and Emma, her husband Duncan and their children. Next arrives Brenda, walking beside Jean Brown and her husband. It's the first time I've seen Jean since she left the island a few days ago. I want to catch her to ask her how her visit to her sister was, but am suddenly distracted by the figures approaching just behind

352

her. Mr and Mrs Anderson walk solemnly up the path with a group of elderly couples whom I recognise as my parents' church friends. My skin turns cold. With them is a woman a little younger than me whom I don't recognise immediately. But she seems to know me and introduces herself warmly as Sophie Anderson. Her parents look on stiffly as she greets me.

'I'm surprised she had the gall to come here today,' comes a voice, just loud enough to hear. I can't work out who said it and yet I feel my face burning with shame. Mr and Mrs Anderson and their friends turn and walk primly inside the church door, but Sophie pauses for a moment.

'I'm so sorry about them,' she says once her parents have gone. 'I came here with my mother because she asked me to, but I was hoping to see you too. I wanted to apologise for her, I heard the gist of what happened at the village shop as well.'

I wish I could disappear.

'You don't have to apologise.'

'But I want to. It makes me feel awful that she and her friends acted that way. They're the old islanders and I guess they're set in their ways and their views.'

'So, you don't believe it all yourself then? That I was a terrible tearaway who brought shame on my family?' I try to say it lightly, jokingly. But I can't let go of the feeling that she actually *might*, and so might so many others on the island even if they don't say it to my face.

'Of course not! You're forgetting we went to school together. I actually knew you, unlike my mother. OK, my parents might have a certain view of things, but there are also people here who see it differently. You'll see. Anyway, I'd better go inside. It would be nice to catch up before you head back to London.'

I can't help but feel shaken by the conversation. I reach for Ella's hand and squeeze it. She doesn't let go.

'Is it OK to still be sad?' she asks me quietly. 'Even after everything you told me about what they were like?'

Her cheeks and nose are pink, her eyes red. She brushes a loose strand of hair out of her face and tugs again on the bottom of her dress.

'Of course it is, sweetie. I'm sad too.'

Because no amount of time, distance or pain changes the fact that they were my parents.

Ella turns away slightly, her gaze stretching beyond the churchyard and out to sea.

'I just wish ...' she says quietly, her voice trailing off. The breeze picks up slightly and lifts strands of her curls, tossing them across her neck and over her shoulders. I take a long breath.

'I know, honey. Me too.'

I hug her tightly against me, glancing over her shoulder at my brother. His face is freshly shaven but there's a flash of red beneath his right ear where he must have caught himself with the razor. There's a similar dot of red on the collar of his shirt, a bright speck on the white fabric. His black tie and jacket look awkward; I've become used to seeing him in his farming gear, out in the fields that he's made his own.

'I think we'd better go in too,' Alice says, leading Jack and Molly inside. Ella and I follow closely behind.

It's been over twenty years since I last stepped inside the

church. But the familiarity is immediate and all-consuming. The smell of wood, stone and musty paper. The smooth flag-stones beneath my shoes, the long, arched windows that let in pale streams of light. I remember it all as clearly as if I never left. At the front stand two coffins covered in white and yellow flowers. My parents are in there. My throat tightens. Between the coffins stands a young minister I don't recognise and be-hind him, a large wooden cross. I'm glad that Ella is holding my hand tightly.

The pews are full; it looks as though the entire island is packed inside the tiny church. I walk through the centre and my eyes land on familiar faces. I spot Mallachy in a pew near the back. His beard is neat and he wears a navy suit and tie. Our eyes meet briefly and I feel a warmth in my chest.

Jack, Alice and Molly take a seat on the pew at the very front of the church. But I suddenly waver. For a moment I feel like we don't belong in here, Ella and I. What am I doing here? But then Alice turns and beckons us over, Jack and Molly moving down to make more room. Ella slips in first, next to her aunt, and I perch on the end. I glance along the row: Molly's hands are clasped in her lap, her face slightly dipped. Beyond her sits Jack, staring straight ahead but with eyes that seem not to see a thing.

I turn back to the front where the minister stands between the two coffins, the wooden cross silhouetted behind him. I grip the pew with one hand, the other still held in Ella's. The minister is talking now but I can't really take in what he is saying. He motions us to stand for the first hymn.

Nothing comes out of my mouth, even though I recognise

the hymn immediately. Despite the time that's passed I know its lilting rhythm and can mouth the words without needing to look at my hymn book. But there's no sound. The only thing that comes now are the tears that spill silently down my cheeks. As the music swells around me I cry for the little girl who felt unlovable and who learnt how to cover bruises beneath the sleeves of a school jumper. I cry for Jack, and all the years we've spent apart. I cry for the young woman I was when I sat on the floor in front of my newborn baby and felt entirely alone. I cry for my parents. Today might be their funeral but I know now that I have been living my whole life carrying the grief of who they might have been, of the loss of a mother and father I desperately yearned for but who didn't exist. Among the sadness is something else though, and as I glance across at my brother and his family, Jack silent like me, Alice and Molly singing quietly, I feel it unfurling inside me. A blossoming of hope.

As the hymn ends and we all sit again, the minister speaks.

'And now, Maurice and Catherine's son Jack would like to say a few words.'

Slowly, Jack makes his way to the front of the church, between the two coffins.

Someone near the back coughs. Harry snuffles against Tess's chest and she makes a quiet 'shhh' noise and he falls silent again. From the pocket of his suit Jack pulls out a sheet of paper, folded several times. He unfolds it, the crease lines criss-crossing the paper. He looks down then folds his sheet of paper again and slips it back in his pocket.

'I had a whole speech prepared,' he says, his voice echoing

slightly around the walls of the church. He gestures at his suit pocket, where the sheet of paper sits against his chest.

'You know, the standard eulogy stuff.'

Jack shakes his head slightly.

'But last week my sister Lorna came back to the island. Because, Reverend Stewart, you're right, I am Maurice and Catherine's son. But they also have a daughter. Lorna Irvine. My older sister.'

Around the church, people shuffle in their seats. Ella, Alice and Molly look from Jack to me and back again. But all my focus is on my brother. He looks out at the whole congregation. But I know he is talking to me.

'Since Lorna came back, I've been challenged to look back at my past. I've gone over old memories, questioning what I thought I knew. And the more I try to remember, the more those memories reveal themselves as what they were: lies.'

A quiet mutter of voices spreads throughout the church but is hushed again as Jack continues.

'Lies my parents told about my sister and about our life in general. Things that went on behind closed doors that they worked hard to cover up. Over time, lies can become almost like the truth if they're told often enough.'

My mind fills with all the lies that really did feel like the truth to me at certain points in my life. Maybe I *did* fall. Maybe I *was* trouble. Maybe I *did* deserve everything that happened. It's taken my whole life to believe my own memories.

'The people in there,' Jack gestures at the coffins behind him, 'were my parents, and Molly and Ella's grandparents. But they were not good parents. Maybe they wanted to be once, maybe life just didn't turn out the way they'd hoped it would. Maybe there was a point at which they could have turned things around and become better, kinder, stronger people. I guess we'll never really know. But I can't stand here and pretend they were perfect and say some generic, glowing words. It just wouldn't be right. But I can say what I'm thankful to them for. My parents gave me this island. It's because of them that I'm here and that I have my Molly, and my wife. I'll always be thankful to them for that. And they gave me my sister too.'

He looks directly at me now, although it's hard to see him clearly through my tears. Behind me, I hear someone drawing in a sharp breath and am sure it must be Mrs Anderson. But as murmured conversation spreads through the church, I catch snippets of other muffled exchanges from those sitting around us too.

'I always thought there was something not quite right in that family.'

'You just never know what's going on behind closed doors, do you?'

'I never liked them myself.'

I turn to Alice.

'But the church is packed,' I whisper to her through my tears. An expression of surprise flits across her face.

'They're not here for them. They're here for him,' she says.

And I suddenly see what she means. Jack is no longer on his own. Ben and Mallachy have joined him, each hugging him in turn, patting him on the back as Jack wipes roughly at his eyes. Brenda is on her feet too, and Sarah and Sarah's parents ...

'And they're here for you too.' As Alice says it, I feel arms wrapping around me and Ella from all directions. My daughter is pressed against me as the islanders surround us. Opposite, a similar huddle has formed around Alice and Molly. We're crowded by people I grew up with and people I've met since, people who have welcomed me back in a way I never imagined was possible. I close my eyes, my whole body suddenly glowing. Because I have my daughter in my arms and the strength and warmth of a whole island surrounding me.

CHAPTER 36

ALICE

The house buzzes as more and more islanders arrive from the church, some congregating in the living room, others spilling out into the garden. Out the window I can see Ella, Molly and Olive sitting on the grass facing out to sea. Young children in smart clothes run between the adults, oblivious to the supposedly sombre occasion. As I carry another tray of drinks into the living room I spot Tess and Joy chatting with Natalia and Kamil, babies Harry and Lena staring wide-eyed at one another on the floor. Natalia might not have known Jack's parents but I invited her to the wake anyway. Natalia seemed a little surprised when I made the invitation, but as I watch her talking animatedly with Joy I smile, glad to see them getting on. I didn't want to leave her out, knowing that the whole island would be here. Well, the whole island apart from Mr and Mrs Anderson and their friends who left promptly after the funeral. No one seems to miss them, though, even their daughter Sophie who is currently talking with Emma on the other side of the room.

'Where shall I put these?' asks Lorna behind me, balancing two plates of sandwiches in her hands.

'Just over there thanks, Lorna,' I reply, pointing to the table I've set up in the corner, pushing the sofas back against the walls to make more room. As well as the sandwiches the table is covered in homemade cakes supplied by various islanders. I'm not sure if it's totally appropriate to have quite so much cake at a wake, but people seem to be helping themselves and besides, who cares really what is normal. The funeral was certainly not normal, what with Jack's unorthodox eulogy, but I for one was proud and more than a little tearful to hear him say those words aloud. Finally, it felt like the hold his parents had on him his whole life had been lifted. It was sad too, of course, thinking about what Jack and Lorna went through as children and how his parents ended up driving them apart, but I also thought about Maurice and Catherine and whether they really had wished to be better people. If Maurice hadn't had his injury, would things have been different? I couldn't help but feel a particular pang of sadness for his mother, who was clearly a victim in their family too, even if I'm not sure I'll ever be able to forgive her for not better protecting Jack and Lorna. The minister had seemed startled when nearly the whole congregation rose to their feet to comfort Jack and Lorna, but he judged the mood of the room and finished up shortly after Jack's speech. We all congregated outside to watch the coffins lowered into the earth, and Jack and Lorna stood beside each of their parents' graves and threw a handful of soil down too. But we didn't linger long in the graveyard, the five of us soon walking back to the car side by side, the other island families doing the same. Jack and Lorna shared a quiet embrace then, each holding the other firmly, and as I watched them I struggled again to hold back my tears.

Now, I anxiously search out Jack and am relieved to find him talking with Ben, Mallachy and Duncan. He looks at ease, perhaps more relaxed than he's appeared in weeks. I know it isn't that he's not hurting – this morning he took a long time getting dressed, staring vacantly into space for stretches at a time – but perhaps now that the funeral is over there's a sense of relief too, of letting go.

I glance from Jack to Jean, sitting on one of the sofas beside Christopher, Brenda leaning against one of the arms of the sofa and Kerstin sitting on a cushion on the floor opposite them. Poor Christopher looks exhausted, his suit slightly crumpled and his back stooped. I watch as Jean reaches across for his hand, continuing chatting with the others as she does so. I turn away and retreat into the kitchen.

It's a mess of glasses, beer bottles and plates of food in here and I set to work tidying up a little, preparing another tray to carry through to the other room.

'It seems to be going OK, doesn't it?'

I turn to find Lorna placing a handful of empty glasses down on the end of the table. I wonder whether, like me, she needed to get away from the noise and the bustle of the living room.

'I think so,' I reply. 'I hope everyone has enough to eat.'

She laughs lightly.

'I don't think anyone's going to go hungry, Alice. And thank you for organising all of this, I'm sorry I wasn't more help. But I really appreciate it, and I know Jack does too.'

Her expression drops slightly then and she turns and glances outside, staring ahead in a way that reminds me of Jack this morning.

'I've been wanting to ask you something,' I say now, drawing her attention back to the room. 'Molly told us it's Ella's birthday next week. Now, I know you might have plans back in London and probably want to get home, but if not, I wondered if we might throw a party for her here?'

I came up with the idea last night. We need something to look forward to, a reason to celebrate. The whole island does. And after having missed all my niece's other birthdays, well, it would be special to mark this one now that she's finally here on the island. I know it would mean a lot to Molly too, and Jack.

Lorna looked thoughtful.

'When I asked Ella what she wanted to do this year she said she wanted to do something just with the two of us,' she says. 'But of course it was because she'd fallen out with her best friends Ruby and Farah. I should have known it wasn't like her to not want to do something.'

I recall the shouted words Ella shared that horrible night before the girls ran away. It can be so painful being a teenager and dealing with the heartbreak of friendships gone wrong. I remember from my own childhood that those lost friends are mourned just as hard as any first love. I suppose when it comes down to it, the fiercely close friendships we make when we're young *are* our first loves.

'Well we could certainly do our best to take her mind off all that. It's a bit of a tradition here to throw beach parties for the children.'

Lorna looks at me and this time she's smiling.

'You know what, I think she'd love that.'

'Oh, brilliant! We can have a barbecue. Oh, and there'll need to be a cake ...'

We'll invite everyone, just like today, except it will be a purely joyful occasion. Just for one day, I want to forget everything else. And I'm sure I'm not alone. This party will be first and foremost for Ella, but it will be for Jean and Christopher too. A chance to eat and drink surrounded by their friends, a chance for us to make them know they're not alone. And it will be for Jack and Lorna as well, perhaps an opportunity to create some new, happier memories together.

'Thank you, Alice,' says Lorna. 'It will be a wonderful way to end our trip.'

My heart drops slightly. Because of course, this is inevitable. I may have gained a friend and Jack may have started to rebuild his relationship with his sister, but soon Lorna and Ella will leave and it will be the three of us again. I knew this moment would come eventually, but it's still hard to accept it after everything that's happened. Well, if they're going to leave I want at least to give them the best send-off we can.

'That's settled then,' I say with a smile.

Lorna heads out with a fresh tray of drinks while I do some more tidying up in the kitchen. Remembering the guests who have drifted outdoors, I load another tray and carry it outside, walking round the side of the house towards the back where I can hear the guests talking and laughing. But nearing the corner of the house I nearly bump straight into them: Lorna and Mallachy tucked away out of sight of the other guests, Lorna with her arms wrapped around Mallachy's neck, his head bent down as he kisses her, holding her tightly around her waist. There's an abandoned tray in the grass at their feet. As they see me they jump apart, faces flushed.

'Oh good, it's only you,' Lorna says, relief written across her face. 'I was worried it might be Ella ...'

Mallachy runs a hand through his beard and glances at Lorna.

'Don't mind me!' I say with a smile, sidestepping around them and continuing to the back garden where the other guests are gathered, trying to stop my tray from shaking. As I serve drinks and chat with the islanders, I do my best to smile and nod and say the right thing. But my mind is elsewhere. All I can think about is the strength with which Mallachy held Lorna. If we can't persuade Lorna to stay on the island for good, perhaps Mallachy can?

CHAPTER 37

LORNA

One by one the guests leave and finally the five of us are alone in the house again. With everyone gone we all disappear upstairs to change out of our funeral clothes. When each of us reappears, Ella and Molly in pyjamas, Jack in tracksuit bottoms and a grey T-shirt and Alice in a pair of loose dungarees, the relief at being able to be like this and not forcing smiles and conversation is so great that for a moment we all sink onto the sofas in the living room. No one says anything, but it's OK. It doesn't feel like we have to.

Jack and Alice share one sofa, Alice dipping her head to rest on Jack's shoulder, and I sit with the girls, the three of us squashed close together. I relish the warmth of the two of them next to me and the feeling of closeness it brings. I want to wrap my arms around both of them and pull them close, just like I did on Caora Island when I felt so overwhelmed with joy to see not just my daughter but the niece I've come to care for deeply in just a short space of time. I always thought of her over the years of course, imagining what she might be like and how she was getting on. But to meet her in person and to get to know her even a little … Well it's been more than I could have hoped for.

This whole trip has turned out to be more than I ever imagined it could be. Yes, there have been rocky moments, moments of pain so raw it felt as though I might buckle from it. But it's brought me so much too. A reconnection with Sarah, a new friendship with Alice and an acceptance into her eclectic but lovely group of friends. A sense of finally starting to build bridges with my brother. A step forwards in my relationship with Ella as well, finally accepting that she is getting older and I have to treat her differently as a result. And the surprising sweetness of whatever it is that exists between Mallachy and me. After the emotion of the funeral it was such a comfort to step into the warmth of his arms and give in to the simple pleasure of being kissed by him. It was a wonderful kiss, even if we were interrupted by Alice. I feel my cheeks glow as I remember it.

The silence is broken by the sound of a phone ringing. It takes me a moment to realise the noise is coming from the pocket of my jeans. I'm reluctant to leave the comfort of this spot on the sofa, but when I see Cheryl's name flashing on my screen I say a quick 'sorry' to the others and leave the room, answering the phone as I head upstairs to my room.

'Lorna?'

'Cheryl! God, it's really good to hear your voice.'

'How was the funeral? We were thinking of you today.'

I've reached my room now and close the door softly, sitting on the edge of the bed facing the window.

'You know what, in the end it was OK. It was hard and strange but not as bad as I thought it would be. And do you know what Cheryl? I think things with my brother are actually going to be OK.'

My heart races as I say it, only now letting myself voice my hopes aloud. Nothing will change the time we've spent apart and perhaps Jack and I will never have the kind of relationship that some siblings have. But finally, I can start to imagine us being a part of each other's lives again. Perhaps he, Alice and Molly can come down and see us in London. Maybe visiting the island could become a regular summer thing. With a fluttering of trepidation an image enters my mind: the big table in the kitchen here piled high with the trimmings of a Christmas dinner and Jack, Alice, Molly, Ella and me sitting around it together.

'Oh, that's great news. Did you two talk then?'

'We did. I mean, there's still a lot left to say and of course it's never going to be easy, but it's a start. Cheryl, I've got so much to tell you …'

And I sit in the yellow room that has quickly come to feel like mine, facing down the hill to the beach and the sea that glimmers in the evening sun, and tell my friend about everything that's happened since we last spoke. I describe Alice to her, thinking how well the two of them would get on. I catch her up on Ella's trouble with her friends, and she offers to march round to their houses and give them an earful. And finally, I tell her about Mallachy.

'I mean, I know it's just a holiday fling,' I add, feeling a surprising jolt of pain as I say it, 'but it's been nice. Lovely, actually.'

'I'm so pleased, Lorna! It's about time you had some fun with a nice bloke. So, it wasn't a total mistake of mine to persuade you to make this trip then?'

I can hear the smile in her voice and picture the red lipstick she always wears and how it was her cheerfulness and energy that first drew me to her when she joined the school.

'I wanted to thank you, actually, Cheryl. I'm not sure I would have had the courage to come here if we hadn't had that talk in the staff room that day. You're a great friend.'

There's a pause.

'I'm so glad things are going well for you there, Lorna, because there's something I need to tell you. I've been meaning to tell you for days but then with the funeral and everything … God, I hate to do this on the phone but …'

Hearing the change of tone in her voice I panic. How has she let me rattle on about my news when it's clear whatever it is she's trying to tell me isn't coming out easily?

'Is everything OK? Is Frankie OK? And Mike?'

'No, it's not that. Everyone's fine.'

I let out a sigh of relief.

'It's just that I have news. I don't really know how to say it so I'm just going to say it, OK?'

'OK.'

I grip the edge of the bed with my free hand, steadying myself.

'Mike's been offered a new job. A promotion.'

I let out a happy sigh.

'But that's great, Cheryl! Congratulations to him! I know he's been looking for something for a while now.'

'Thank you. It *is* great news. But the job's in Manchester.'

My relief quickly disappears, replaced by alarm. I can't seem to find any words but luckily Cheryl continues, barely pausing between words.

'I've already called Dave the creep. I thought he'd be mad about me giving such little notice but apparently there are cuts coming in for the teaching assistant budget so it saves him having to make me redundant. He's let me leave straight away. Mike's new boss wants him to start as soon as he can. So we're moving in less than two weeks' time.'

Since arriving on the island it's felt as though life beyond the shores has paused. It's just so hard to even picture London when confronted with all that sea and moorland. But the times that I have pictured it, I've imagined it being exactly the same as when Ella and I stepped onto the train at Euston. The pavements steaming, the parks full of frisbees and dogs and shirtless men burning under the beam of a hot, swollen sun. I picture our flat: bills stacked on the table, my towel hanging on the back of my door from the shower I had before catching the train. I imagine everything as it was, waiting for Ella and me to return. If I'm honest, I expected the same of Cheryl. It didn't occur to me that her life might move on without me.

'So soon, wow.'

It hits me that when I return to school in September, I'll be returning alone, without my friend. How will I possibly get through the days without her there to laugh and commiserate with in the staffroom, without her smiling face spotted across the playground? The thought feels unbearable.

'I know, it's all been so sudden.'

'But it's good though, isn't it?' I force myself to say. 'You'll be closer to your parents and it's a great step for Mike. I'm really happy for you all.'

I can hear a faint tapping sound and wonder if Cheryl is twiddling her hoop earrings like she does when she's nervous or deep in thought. Suddenly I wish more than anything that I was there with her and that we were having this conversation in person. With everything that's happened on this trip I've only exchanged brief messages with my friend but I miss her now with a strength that takes the breath out of me.

'It is good, yeah. We're happy. I've got a few interviews lined up for when I get there and we've found a flat already! It's crazy how much more you can get there, it's even got a garden. I can finally get Frankie that slide I've wanted to get him. But I've been so worried about how to tell you. I'm going to miss you and Ella so much! Promise me you'll come and visit?'

I swallow hard.

'Of course we will. I'm going to miss you too, we both will. But this is going to be good for you and your family.'

'You think so?'

I can hear the mix of hesitation and excitement in her voice.

'I know so. It will be great.'

Muffled noises come in the background and I make out the sound of crying.

'Oh, sorry, honey, that's Frankie, I've got to go. But I'll see you before we leave, yeah?'

'Yes, of course. Speak soon.'

We say goodbye and I hang up the phone, feeling shell-shocked as I sit in the quiet. I try with all my strength simply to be happy for my friend. And I am really; with Frankie getting older it will be brilliant for them to have more space and I know she misses her parents and that it will be a big help to have them closer. But I just can't begin to imagine my life back in London without Cheryl in it. Without my friend to laugh with at work and to celebrate with on birthdays and at Christmas, what really is there waiting for me and Ella back at home? Our small flat where we don't know our neighbours. The job I've had for a decade and which increasingly brings me far more frustration than enjoyment. I can't help but wonder when it all happened, and how. How did I end up living this kind of life, lived within walls, loving and being loved by only my daughter and one close friend? At what point did the large life I'd always imagined for myself become so very small?

I sit for a while longer on the bed, staring out the window. Eventually I pull myself up and return downstairs. The others have risen from the sofas and are tidying, collecting empty glasses that are scattered around the living room and rearranging the furniture. I join in, helping Jack and Alice move the sofa back to its original position.

'Have you told Ella?' Alice whispers to me once the sofa is in place.

'Not yet,' I reply. 'I wanted to do it when we were all together.'

The girls are collecting paper plates in a bin bag, holding the bag between them.

'Ella, Molly, put that down for a minute, there's something I want to tell you.'

Ella's eyebrows dip questioningly. Jack and Alice pause too, the five of us gathered in the middle of the room.

'Ella, how do you feel about staying here for your birthday?'

She squeals.

'Really?'

I nod.

'Alice and I have spoken about it, and I thought you might like to.'

'Of course I would!' she cries. 'I'd love that, Mum!'

Molly grins too, and behind her I catch Jack smiling as well.

'Great. We'll stay until your birthday and then head home after that, OK?'

Ella's smile fades slightly now but she nods. The party will be a perfect way to say goodbye to the island and everyone we've met here. Because we have to leave eventually. The longer we stay, the harder it will be to get Ella settled again before the new school term. However small our life might be back in London, it is our life. Perhaps when we're back I will make the effort to finally introduce ourselves to our neighbours, and with Cheryl leaving the school maybe there are other members of staff I can try to make friends with. It will mean letting my guard down and risking them finding out about my past, but perhaps it will be worth it if it means a chance of creating new connections and a bigger kind of life. But as I look across the room at Molly, Ella, Jack and Alice, I can't help the feeling that grips me. That really, I don't want to leave at all.

CHAPTER 38

ALICE

Over the next few days, things settle into a quiet sort of rhythm at Hilly Farm. Lorna starts helping Jack out in the mornings, the two of them watering the plants together in the polytunnel. I'm not sure whether they talk as they work, or if just being together is enough for them. Either way, Jack seems calmer and more open. We hold each other tight at night, sometimes talking, sometimes just being together, experiencing a closeness that makes my heart feel full with happiness.

The sun shines unbroken for days. Ella, Molly and Olive spend nearly all their time at the beach with the other children, reading on the sand or thinking up new plans for their beach cleaning mission. Lorna joins me for another swim, this time in our costumes and with our daughters at our sides. Ella and Lorna are less accustomed to the cold so shriek as the waves hit their stomachs. But all four of us emerge from the sea with tingling pink skin and broad smiles.

While the girls are on the beach, Lorna and I work on preparations for Ella's birthday party. I've invited the whole island and want the day to be perfect. We place an order for food with Pat at the village shop, rope Brenda in to sort flowers and organise with my other friends to have tables and chairs brought down to the beach from the village hall and people's homes.

Lorna and I make bunting together on my old sewing machine, chatting as we work. So many times, I nearly let slip everything that's on my mind – Jean and the fate of the school and the island – but I remember the insistence of both Jean and Jack to remain quiet so force the words to stay inside. We have assembled a motley crew to help run the school in the short term when it opens again in September, along with the help of a supply teacher who is due to start but who we all know to be only a short-term solution. Just this week we received a message from our local council. They're coming to visit in a little over a week to discuss next steps, but in their email, they made it clear that if a replacement for Jean isn't found soon, they will have no choice but to begin the process of closing down the school. After reading the email I rushed to the bathroom, a sudden wave of nausea rocking me like it has done regularly over the past week. I guess I understand the phrase 'sick with worry' now. Sarah and the other parents with primary-school age children are starting to panic too, and last night Jack told me there'd been interest in his parents' house, which he put on the market just after their deaths, but that the young family from the mainland are reluctant to move things forward. They found out about the vacancy at the school and understandably don't want to complete on the house until they know what's happening.

I channel all my worries into preparing for the party. I know that perhaps I'm burying my head in the sand, but it feels hard to know what else to do. I want to throw Ella, and the whole island, a party they'll never forget. Whatever lies ahead, I want us to have one joyful day of food, laughter and sunshine.

In the afternoons, Lorna heads out alone. Only I know that she goes to Mallachy's house. She tells me they've been spending time in his studio – that he's persuaded her to draw and paint again for the first time in years. When she returns home in the evenings she seems like a different person to the anxious, hesitant woman who first arrived on the island only two weeks ago. While Lorna visits Mallachy, I visit Jean. Some days we take gentle walks together on the beach, others we sit outside her cottage and watch the butterflies. For now, she seems OK, if a little weak, but I'm painfully aware as we sit together that these moments might be numbered. I try my best to shut the thought out though and instead just enjoy the time we spend together, drinking lemonade and counting the cabbage whites.

And somehow, it's now the day before Ella's party. I'm in the kitchen with Lorna, going over the long list on my clipboard.

'I don't want to jinx it, but I *think* we might have everything ready. But maybe I've forgotten something ...'

A light-headedness comes over me and I start to worry again. Maybe I've missed something? Maybe tomorrow won't live up to the image I've created of it all in my mind? But Lorna takes the clipboard gently from my hand.

'It's going to be amazing. You've done so much, you've thought of everything. Ella is a very lucky girl. Now it's time to stop. I called Sarah earlier and she's meeting us in The Lookout for a drink. Come on, let's go.'

I glance at the clipboard on the table.

'I don't know, maybe I should go over it all one more time ...'

But she grabs me by the shoulders and marches me towards the door.

'No, come on, we're going out!'

At the front door we meet Jack, just coming in from outside.

'Jack, I'm kidnapping your wife and taking her to the pub,' says Lorna playfully. He smiles, his eyes sparkling.

'An excellent plan. Have fun.'

When we reach the pub it's busy, and I wave at Morag who's perched on a stool by the bar, chatting to the landlord, and greet several other islanders. Sarah has got us a table in the corner and waves at us enthusiastically. I spot Mallachy and Ben at the bar and notice Lorna and Mallachy locking eyes and smiling.

As we sit down Sarah gestures towards the bar.

'Sorry, when I told Ben I was going to the pub he was jealous! But don't worry, he won't bother us.'

'He could never bother us!' I say, but I know what she means. It's nice to be just the three of us.

Sarah turns and blows a kiss at Ben, and both he and Mallachy raise their glasses at us.

'Right, what can I get you both?' says Lorna, standing up.

'I can get this,' I reply.

'No please, it's on me. What would you like?'

'I'll have a gin and tonic thanks,' says Sarah.

At the thought of gin my stomach gives a lurch. I picture a nice big glass of wine but have the same reaction. Maybe I'm overtired and should just stick to soft drinks for now. I ask for a sparkling water and Lorna raises an eyebrow but then nods and heads to the bar. As she orders, Sarah and I watch her chatting with Ben and Mallachy. She laughs suddenly, her head thrown back. When she arrives with our drinks her face is flushed.

'So, how are things going there?' Sarah asks, nodding towards the bar. Lorna bites her lip.

'Sorry,' adds Sarah. 'But Ben says Mallachy hasn't stopped talking about you. He says it's actually getting a bit annoying.'

The three of us laugh and Lorna glances at me before speaking.

'It's good. It's been fun, I mean. But I'm leaving in a couple of days. It was only ever going to be a fling.'

She shrugs, but her face tells me there's more to it than that. Sarah and I exchange a look. I know that she's been just as hopeful as me that Lorna might stay. It must be hard to think about saying goodbye to her old friend again, but at least this time I feel sure they will keep in touch. I hope we do too. I'm certainly going to do my best to make sure of it.

The pub door opens and the young couple who arrived with Lorna and Ella on the ferry and have been staying at Tess and Joy's bothy come stumbling in, arms around one another, their faces flushed with smiles. They make their way to the bar.

'Well they look happy!' says Sarah.

The young man leans forward and says something to Ted, the pub's landlord. Ted's face spreads into a smile and he reaches across the bar and shakes the young man's hand. His girlfriend stands next to him, grinning too and looking down every few seconds at her hands.

Ted rings the bell at the end of the bar.

'Hey, everyone,' he shouts. 'These two just got engaged, let's give them a good island toast!'

So that's why the young woman keeps looking at her hands. Suddenly I spot it – a glint and wink on her left ring finger. We join the rest of the pub in cheering and clapping, while Ted pours two drams of whisky for the young couple. Morag slaps them both firmly on the back.

'Well, isn't that lovely,' I say. 'And Tess and Joy will be so pleased. I bet they'll use this in their advertising for their bothy now, "most romantic destination in Scotland" or something like that.'

'Oh, they will for sure,' agrees Sarah. At the bar the tourists beam, knock back their whiskies and then kiss one another, gaining another cheer from the room. As I watch them I realise that there's only one person in the pub who isn't looking in their direction. While Ben has his body turned towards the couple, seeming to be asking the young man a question, Mallachy is looking in our direction, straight at Lorna. I don't know if Lorna has even noticed but as I watch him it's suddenly clear from Mallachy's expression that while their romance may have been a fling for Lorna, it's more than that for him. I have to look away; it's just too much to watch the affection and hope in his eyes, knowing that Lorna will be leaving in just two days. Mallachy was a mess when he first moved to the island. It's taken him years to get over his ex-wife. And in a couple of days he and Rex will be alone again.

The cheers and claps eventually die down and the babble of conversation returns to the pub. Sarah, Lorna and I pull our attention away from the bar and return to our drinks. We chat together for a long time, Sarah and Lorna sharing funny stories from their childhood days together, the three of us talking about motherhood and in particular the challenges and joys of raising teenage girls. Lorna asks about my niece and nephews and I show her photos on my phone, photos Sarah has seen countless times but which she joins Lorna in smiling at nonetheless. I tell them a few of the funniest stories from both Shona and Caitlin's jobs.

'They're both amazing,' I say, missing them with a sudden fierceness. 'They're so much cleverer than I am, both of them.'

'Hey, that's not true,' says Sarah.

'But they are,' I reply. 'They always have been.'

I can't help but feel suddenly gloomy. Maybe if I was as smart as my sisters I'd have come up with a plan to save the school and the island. Maybe I'd have been able to change Jean's mind about refusing treatment, but in a subtle way that didn't make her feel like she was being forced into anything.

'I've always known it,' I continue. 'And I think they know it too. Or at least, they know that I'm different to the two of them. When I moved here they thought I was mad. And then I had Ella so much younger than they had their children; they were both still studying when she was born, even though I'm the youngest. And I've never had a proper career, not like them anyway ... I mean, it's been my choice and I love what I do, but I don't think they really take it seriously.'

I adore my sisters. I have always been so proud of them and miss them even now. And I always so look forward to our video calls, even if most of the time I do more listening than speaking. But there are times when I wish they were proud of me too, that I wasn't just their little sister. That I was just Alice, not 'Squirt'.

'Alice,' says Lorna, reaching out and placing a hand on my arm, 'I know I haven't known you long, but I have to say, I think you're amazing. You've done such a brilliant job with Molly, she's so confident and cares about the world. It's impressive. And you are an excellent teacher – I honestly never thought I'd enjoy yoga but you made it easy. And look at everything you've done for Ella's party. You're so organised – I can see it at the farm too. Jack may do most of the work out in the fields but I can tell the whole place would fall apart without you.'

Sarah nods.

'Lorna's right. Alice, have you ever told your sisters you feel this way?'

'I don't want to bother them. It seems so silly, really. I mean, we're all adults. This stuff shouldn't matter.'

'It isn't silly,' continues Sarah. 'They need to know how you feel.'

'Maybe you could invite them on one of your yoga retreats?' suggests Lorna. 'That way they could see you in action and see for themselves how good you are at your job? And it might be a chance for the three of you to talk, too?'

'Oh, I don't think they'd want to do that.'

But I can't help but imagine what it would be like, having my sisters to stay here on the island and having them finally attend my classes. If they saw me teaching would anything change? And could I ever really find the words to tell them how I feel?

'Let's change the subject. Sarah, how's Ben's boat coming on?'

The conversation meanders, until eventually Ted is standing by our table.

'Sorry, ladies, but I need to close up,' he says. Looking up, I realise we're the only people left in the pub. 'I left you at it for a while, you looked so deep in conversation, but I need to get back to the wife or else she'll turn up in her pyjamas and her wellies and drag me home herself. It wouldn't be the first time…'

We thank Ted and head outside into the now cool air, the sun starting to dip in the sky.

'This was so nice,' says Lorna. 'Thank you, both of you.'

She hugs us both warmly. We say goodbye to Sarah; Ben is waiting for her in the car with the radio playing. It turns out he'd been keeping to lime sodas all night so that Sarah could have a drink. In the end I stuck to sparkling water too so I drive us back to the farm, the sky just starting to darken around us.

Lorna sighs happily.

'I can't believe I'm getting a second chance with Sarah,' she says. 'And with Jack too. I honestly never thought it would happen.'

We smile at one another.

As I drive back to the farmhouse I run through everything in my head again, trying to make sure there's nothing I've forgotten. I know it's just a birthday party, but so much seems riding on it somehow. I might not be able to fix everyone's problems or make Lorna stay or solve the issues at the school and the looming threat to the island. But I want to at least throw a party to remember.

Later, when Jack and I are alone in our room, he pulls me towards him.

'Did you have a good time at the pub?' he asks, kissing my neck. Since our heart to heart after the Caora Island incident he's been more affectionate than usual, I think both of us craving physical closeness as well as the intimacy that came from finally telling each other how we were feeling. My skin tingles as he kisses me.

'It was nice,' I reply, struggling suddenly to concentrate as his kisses reach my collarbone.

'Wine clearly agrees with you, Mrs Irvine,' he teases. 'You're glowing.'

I don't tell him that I stuck to sparkling water all night; instead I let him continue kissing my shoulders, his hand in my hair.

'You're gorgeous, Alice,' Jack whispers into my ear. My heart leaps and dives as I tilt my head and kiss him on the mouth. As he kisses me back it's suddenly hard to think about anything except the feel of my husband's arms around me, the warmth of his mouth on mine and the firm and hopeful beating of our hearts as he guides me towards the bed we've shared for nearly fifteen years, the place that feels the most like home.

CHAPTER 39

LORNA

And suddenly, it is Ella's birthday. Fourteen. I can't quite believe it. The sun is shining today; it's a perfect day for a birthday. The kitchen is strung with homemade bunting and a huddle of balloons are tied to the back of one of the chairs. Alice and I prepared it together last night.

Alice turns around from the Rayburn as she hears me enter the room, bacon and eggs sizzling in a pan. It must be the smell that draws the others down too, because first appear Ella and Molly, shortly followed by Jack.

'Happy birthday, my darling,' I tell Ella, kissing her on the forehead.

Her cheeks turn bright red when she spots the decorations and she sits somewhat nervously at the chair, the balloons bobbing above her head. But before long she is digging in to her breakfast, chatting with Molly about the party. Once Jack has finished his food he heads out to get some work done in the fields before the afternoon's party, but not before giving Ella a quick but firm hug.

'Happy birthday. I wish I didn't have to work but at least this way I'll work up an appetite for cake.'

He winks at her and she smiles widely.

Soon after Jack has left, a knocking comes on the front door.

'Can you get that please, Lorna?' says Alice, the dishwasher open in front of her and a pile of plates in her arms.

I'm surprised to see Mallachy standing at the door, a scruffy but beautiful posy of wildflowers in one hand.

Ella appears in the corridor beside me and Mallachy hands the flowers to her.

'For the birthday girl,' he says, his ears glowing pink.

Ella holds the flowers very gently, raising them to her face and taking a deep breath of the sweet smell.

'Oh, thank you! No one's ever given me flowers before.'

I resist the urge to put both hands on Mallachy's face and kiss him firmly on the mouth. This week we've spent every afternoon together. I've become used to sitting beside him at his desk in the studio, the sensation of a pencil or a brush in my hand starting to feel familiar again too. I've been working feverishly, in fact, piles of sketches and watercolours forming beside me, most of which I'm too nervous to really look at once I've finished them in case after all this time I've lost the knack. It's easier not to scrutinise them too closely but it feels so good to be working again, almost as though decades' worth of drawings and paintings are forcing themselves out of me onto the page. Yesterday we took a break from the studio to carry a picnic down to Mallachy's secluded stretch of beach. We ate fresh mackerel salad among the dunes then undressed one another slowly, the sun adding its own kisses to our bare skin. As I look at him now my face grows warm at the memory.

'Hi, Mallachy,' comes Alice's voice behind us. 'Are you all set for today?'

Mallachy nods.

'What's going on?' I ask them.

'A slight change of plans,' replies Alice. 'Molly and I are going to stay here and get the final things ready for the party, but Mallachy's got a birthday treat sorted for you and Ella.'

That's when my eyes look beyond Mallachy and outside, following the track down to the beach. There moored in the water is Mallachy's boat. Ella seems to spot it at the same time too and lets out a squeal of delight.

'Are we really going out on the boat?'

'If you'd like,' Mallachy says quietly, but he is smiling broadly, as though Ella's excitement is contagious.

'Are you sure that's OK, Alice?' I ask. 'I feel bad leaving you with the last bits of prep ...'

But she shakes her head with a smile.

'We've got it all under control, haven't we, Molly?'

So we fetch our things and head down to the beach. It's strange to watch Ella and Mallachy chatting as we make our way to the tiny rowing boat that is pulled up on the sand. She asks him countless questions about the boat. I walk behind them, watching. They seem to be getting on well, and I smile, fighting off the anxiety that lurks beneath. My holiday fling, my daughter and I together in a boat? It should make me nervous. But the sun is shining and Ella is so very happy. I decide to be happy too.

Mallachy rows us out to his boat which is anchored a little way out from the beach, and helps us on board. His hand is warm in mine as he reaches for me.

'Right, let me show you around!'

Ella follows eagerly but I linger behind. It feels like my first time on board – last time was so frantic and traumatic it feels like it doesn't count. Today, I'm thankful that the sky is blue and the breeze gentle. Ella continues to chatter away as Mallachy starts the engine, showing her what he's doing. I feel a swell of movement in my stomach as the boat sets off, out towards open sea.

As Mallachy and Ella busy themselves with the actual steering and running of the boat, I sit at the back and watch the beach and the farm receding behind us. I look up at the farmhouse, picking out the window of my yellow room. I spot the silhouette of my brother in the sheep field.

The boat rolls over gentle waves, salty spray occasionally whipped up over its sides and dampening my arms and hair. The sun is warm against my face and I let myself close my eyes for a moment, listening as Mallachy and Ella continue to chat behind me. I can't believe that my daughter is fourteen. Is she happy with her life so far? Have I done a good job? I know I could have done better. And I'm not sure that I will ever stop worrying about her and her happiness. Even when she is forty, not fourteen. But right now, her voice sounds cheerful and light. When I open my eyes, I glance at Mallachy and he holds my gaze. I try to send him a silent thank you for putting on this day for my daughter. He smiles back and I hope he has understood.

Once we are a little way out to sea Mallachy guides the boat leisurely around the circumference of the island. We drift out to face the lighthouse and peer up at the cliffs.

Mallachy hands Ella a pair of binoculars.

'Take a look up at the cliffs. Look closely, now.'

There's a pause as Ella fixes her gaze up and ahead. And then she lets out a cry.

'Mum, look!'

She hands me the binoculars.

'I never thought I'd see them in real life!'

Her camera clicks as she lifts it from around her neck and trains it on the clifftop. I watch her for a second, her face scrunched in concentration as she takes the photographs. She holds the camera away from her for a moment and her eyes are lit up with pure joy.

I take the binoculars and train them on the cliffs. Patches of grass and flowers cling to the rocks. And suddenly I spot them. A flash of black and white, the distinctive orange and grey of curved beaks.

'Puffins!' says Ella, and I hand her back the binoculars with a smile.

'I heard they were your favourite,' says Mallachy. Before he can do anything about it, Ella is leaping forwards and wrapping her arms around him. He holds her awkwardly to his side for a moment before relaxing slightly and hugging her back. I grin at him and he grins back. Oh, he's done good.

'Thank you,' Ella says as she steps back from him and picks up the binoculars again. 'Thank you so, so much.'

As Ella watches the puffins for a little longer I look up at the lighthouse. I spent so much time exploring the white tower and the flaking, slightly decrepit cottage as a child. It was my place to escape to. In a way, the lighthouse always felt like my lighthouse. Seeing it from this angle I can't help but feel a possessive pull towards it, a sense that I don't want to drift too far from the sight of that white tower.

Eventually, once Ella has taken hundreds of photographs, Mallachy brings the boat closer into the shore and we hug the coastline for a while, following it along to the caves. Every now and then Mallachy brushes alongside me and I feel that now familiar burst of heat rippling through my body.

It's so hard to be so close to him and yet unable to touch him. I almost reach for his hand but stop myself just in time.

All week, Mallachy and I have avoided the topic of what will happen when I leave tomorrow after Ella's party. It's a thought that's sat beside us in the studio and is here on board this boat too, but I do my best to push it away. I don't want to ruin things by pulling a cloud over our sunshine.

As we approach the entrance to the first cave Ella is so focused on looking upwards to take in the dripping, cavernous roof that I dare a quick brush of my lips against Mallachy's cheek.

'Isn't this amazing?' Ella says, her voice echoing.

'It is.'

A seal pokes its whiskered nose out between the gentle waves before diving beneath the surface. In the next cave, the water is dotted with the pale mounds of jellyfish. Mallachy and Ella bring the boat out further to sea, away from the jellyfish, and drop anchor.

'Fancy a swim?' I ask Ella.

'Definitely!'

Mallachy turns his back as we change quickly into our swimsuits. Ella climbs carefully down the ladder but I make a quick decision. I stand on the side of the boat, my toes curling over the edge. And then I dive. My arms pierce the water then the rest of my body follows, my ears suddenly full of sea, a strange underwater sound surrounding me, my chest tightening, my hair spreading in front of my face. And then I burst up like a cork and take a delicious, deep breath of air.

'Great dive, Mum!'

Mallachy watches me too, smiling. I bob in the water next to my daughter who grins across at me, treading water. We swim a few laps of the boat and then clamber, dripping and shivering back on board. Mallachy is waiting with two towels. He hands Ella hers and she moves to the front of the boat to dry off. While Ella's back is turned Mallachy wraps the towel and his arms around me, holding me tightly. And I can't help it. I close my eyes for a second, sinking into his body. When I open them, I spot Ella over Mallachy's shoulder, looking at us both. I step away quickly and Mallachy coughs and busies himself with something on the boat. But to my surprise, Ella just laughs.

'You guys are so not subtle.'

I anxiously push my hair back and watch as Mallachy focuses on doing something clearly 'very important' with a rope (it looks really like he's just fiddling with it). But Ella is smiling. She seems, actually, fine. For all these years I've tried so hard to protect her by keeping my personal life separate from our life together. But right now, she seems more interested in watching a seal out to sea than in what she just saw. I'm reminded again that she is fourteen. My girl is growing up, and perhaps she is more resilient than I give her credit for.

As I get dressed Ella asks Mallachy more questions about the boat. Together, they draw up the anchor. I sink once more into my seat, feeling the sunshine on my face and trying hard to relax and just enjoy the moment.

'Time to head back, I think,' says Mallachy. 'Don't want to miss your party.'

Today has already been so full that I'd almost forgotten about the party. The whole island has been preparing for it all week. I want it to be special for Ella, a birthday to remember. Especially as we'll be leaving tomorrow.

'Look, Mum!'

We are suddenly not far from the shore and Ella is pointing at a crowd of figures on the beach. It looks as though the whole island is there, spread out along the sand. There's a long row of tables pushed together, an assortment of kitchen chairs, stools and deckchairs spread out along its length. The tables are covered in several different coloured cloths and jars of wildflowers, bunting strung along the sides and flapping in the breeze. I can smell charcoal on the air and spot a barbecue, attended by Jack, Ben and a few of the other island men who clutch beers and watch on closely as though Jack and Ben are surgeons performing an important operation. Children run around in the dunes, their laughter reaching us on the air. As we draw closer, familiar faces come into view on the beach. Sarah and her family, waving and smiling. Alice and Molly. Kerstin, Brenda and Puff the puppy who leaps around in the sand. Jean and her husband, sitting in deckchairs facing the sea. Tess, Joy and Harry sitting in the sand alongside Natalia and her family. Morag and Mrs Campbell. Emma and Duncan. Even Sophie Anderson and her children. People from my past and people who have quickly become friends, all gathered on the beach for my daughter. I brush my eyes, blinking hard. As Mallachy drops the anchor a little way out from the shore a cheer erupts on the beach.

'She's here!' comes a voice on the breeze. And as we clamber into the rowing boat and Mallachy rows us to the beach the entire island begins to sing.

'Happy birthday to you, happy birthday to you …'

I turn to Ella and reach my arm around her shoulders. Her eyes are shiny as she stares ahead. I squeeze her tightly.

'Mum,' she whispers. 'Is all of this for me?'

Oh Ella. My darling girl. You deserve all of this and more.

'Yes, sweetheart. Happy birthday.'

It's like a vision from a dream. I can't quite believe I am really here on this island again, that my daughter is fourteen years old and that all these islanders are singing for her. Fourteen years ago, I lay in a hospital bed alone, my new daughter clutched to my chest. I remember those other women in the maternity ward whose bedsides were crowded with visitors. I watched them with fear and loneliness knotted tightly inside my chest. Back then, I didn't think I could really do it. I didn't believe I could look after my daughter on my own. But I did. And look at her now. She grins as she watches the scene ahead of us and I could grow wings and soar.

The final line of the song swells in a roaring crescendo of voices.

'Happy birthday, dear Ella, happy birthday to you!'

The rowing boat grinds against the sand and Mallachy helps us off, the islanders clapping and gathering to hug Ella. I look on, dazed, my eyes damp. There's a presence at my side and Mallachy is there, slipping his hand into mine. He squeezes it and I squeeze back. We let go again but I can still feel the warmth of his fingers in my palm.

Ella soon darts off with Molly, Olive and the other children. I find Alice and Sarah, giving each of them a big hug.

'Thank you, Alice, for all this, it's just wonderful.'

'I didn't do it on my own.'

I look around again; nearly the whole island is gathered here on the beach.

'Lorna, do you want to help with the barbecue?' calls Jack, smoke curling around him. I share a smile with Alice and then join my brother. Since the funeral, we've spent time together in the polytunnel, sometimes talking, but often in silence. It's a silence that feels completely different to the silence that met me when I first arrived here, though. The heat from the coals warms my whole body as I stand beside my brother, turning things occasionally. There's still so much we need to talk about and come to terms with about our past, but for now this is enough. Just being together is enough.

After a while Jack shouts that the food is ready and everyone takes their seats. I help him carry dishes of food across the sand, placing them at intervals along the tables. Charred sausages, kebabs, burgers and corn dripping with butter and dusted with paprika and salt crystals. Herb-crusted salmon that falls into soft flakes, wrapped in tin foil parcels; crispy slices of halloumi and grilled mushrooms dripping with butter and garlic. Alice asked various friends to bring salads and they set them down on the table too in a cheerfully mismatched mix of Tupperware and bowls.

'Wait! Let me take a photo!' shouts Alice. I'm glad she thought to capture the moment; I've been too overwhelmed to take a single picture.

'OK, let's eat!' she says once the photo is taken.

There's a scrabble of movement as people pass dishes to one another, lemonade is poured for the children and beers are handed around for the adults from cool boxes nestled in the sand.

Once the barbecue food has been demolished Alice and Molly lift something onto the table and place it in front of Ella. It's a homemade cake decorated with messy buttercream, scattered flowers and fourteen brightly flickering candles.

'Make a wish, sweetheart,' I say quietly into her ear as Ella leans forward, takes a deep breath and blows. Alice takes a few more photos but I focus instead on trying to capture this scene in my mind. Ella at fourteen, hair wild and curly with salt water, face scattered in freckles, a wide smile on her face, her family and a whole island celebrating with her. I think back to all the birthdays where it's just been the two of us, maybe with a few of her friends coming over in the afternoon. All those times I've cleared up alone at the end of her birthday, wishing I could have given her more. I'm doing my best not to cry.

'Time for presents,' says Alice, and I notice for the first time a huge pile of gifts on a small table behind Ella's chair. I spot my own near the bottom of the pile; I gave it to Alice before we left this morning. I so hope Ella likes it.

Ella begins at the top of the pile, unwrapping each present carefully, her face brightening each and every time a gift tumbles out of the paper onto her lap. 'Oh *thank* you,' she says to everyone. Her sincerity makes my heart feel as though it might burst with pride and love. The gifts themselves bring tears to my eyes again too. A book of landscape photography from Jack and Alice and a 'Save the Sea' T-shirt from Molly, which Ella immediately pulls on over the top she is already wearing. An assortment of homemade jams and chutneys from Sarah and her family and a box of cupcakes from Sarah's mother Linda. From Tess and Joy, a hand-woven leather bracelet; from Brenda, a frame of pressed flowers from her garden. And from Morag: a single dram of whisky in a tiny glass bottle tied with ribbon. Everyone brings something. I'm not sure I've ever known such kindness in my life.

Eventually Ella reaches my present, a flatish parcel wrapped up in bright yellow paper, a sprig of buttercups tucked into the bow of an orange ribbon.

'Happy birthday, darling. Your main present is back in London but I wanted you to have a little something to open today.'

My heart thumps inside my chest as Ella peels back the paper. 'Oh, Mum,' she says quietly.

'Do you like it?'

'I love it. Did you … Did you do this yourself?'

I nod as Ella lifts out of the paper a watercolour painting of Hilly Farm and the beach and sea beyond. On the beach are the silhouetted figures of two teenage girls walking along the sand.

The painting was Mallachy's idea. One afternoon earlier this week he paused at my side and picked up the pile of my discarded pictures.

'This is wonderful, Lorna', he said, and as he turned the painting around I almost looked away, too scared to see my own inadequacies staring back at me. But as I took in the watercolour painting of Hilly Farm and the beach I felt an unexpected sense of pride and relief welling inside my chest. It seems that despite my worst fears, I haven't forgotten after all. It has been there inside me all this time, just waiting for the moment when I would finally lift up a paintbrush again. A bloom of hope unfurled itself inside me. I started work on a few more paintings, then, this time focusing on what I was doing, daring to actually look at what I was creating.

Mallachy helped me make a frame for Ella's painting out of driftwood found on his stretch of beach. Alice provided the paper and ribbon.

'Look, everyone, isn't this amazing? My mum painted it!'

Ella passes the painting along the table. I catch Sarah's eye across the table and we smile at each other. I think of the easel she gave me for my twelfth birthday and she gives me a little nod that says more than anyone else at this table could possibly understand.

Once 'thank you's and 'you're welcome's have been

396

exchanged, Ella and the other children scatter away from the table again. Eventually the adults do the same. Some of the children and their families swim and splash in the sea, their cries rising over the sound of the waves. People lounge on deckchairs and on the sand, chatting in small and ever-shifting groups. I spot the island children gathered around Jean Brown and her husband, who are sitting in their deckchairs talking with Morag and Brenda. Some of the younger children give Jean hugs. I can't help but smile. It seems Mrs Brown is just as well-loved now as she was when I was one of her pupils.

I drift between people, thanking everyone for their kind gifts to Ella. I sit for a while with Mallachy, close but not quite touching, very aware nonetheless of his presence and his warmth beside me.

The afternoon stretches in the way that only perfect summer afternoons do. There's a brief shower (this is still Scotland, after all) but the sun soon comes out again and dries clothes and tablecloths. Later, someone lights a series of bonfires along the beach that glow in the orange light of the setting sun.

I find myself reclining in a deckchair next to Sarah and Alice, a somewhat depleted cool box of beers resting in the sand beside us, as the sun turns the water and the sky a water-colour wash of amber and peach. We've been chatting for a while, but right now we sit in comfortable silence, watching Molly, Olive and Ella practising cartwheels on the sand. Some of the younger children watch on, a few valiantly attempting to copy the older girls.

'I think because of what happened with my parents I forgot the good bits about this island.'

They both turn to me as I speak. Their cheeks are flushed after a day in the sun. I wonder if mine are the same.

'That's understandable,' says Alice, Sarah nodding beside her.

'I forgot about the community here,' I add.

Nearly everyone on the island had some part to play in orchestrating today's party. And all for a girl they barely know.

'And I forgot how beautiful it can be.'

Looking around now as the sun sets into an endless sea, the sand dotted with glowing bonfires and the rest of the island stretching behind us, an island of grass, wildflowers, pine trees and a towering mountain, I feel the beauty of the place as an ache in my bones. It's a beauty that surprises me, that grabs at my heart and squeezes, that makes me feel almost giddy.

'I never thought I'd end up living somewhere like this,' says Alice. 'But I fell in love. Not just with Jack but with the whole place. It just gets under your skin, somehow.'

Sarah nods.

'When I left for uni I used to have dreams about this island,' she says. 'It's a place that never leaves you.'

'I always hoped that it *would* leave me,' I say quietly.

All those years of nightmares. All those years avoiding any mention of the place where I grew up.

'But perhaps it's not the *island* you wanted to escape,' suggests Sarah, her eyes reminding me so much of the child who was once my best friend. 'It makes sense that you felt that way about the island and didn't want to come back. For a long time the island *was* your parents. I imagine it was impossible to think about one without the other. But now they're gone. And this island is just an island again. A rainy, far-from-anything, sometimes boring, but sometimes wonderful island. And it's your island.'

But I shake my head.

'I don't think so.'

Today has been wonderful. But I still remember arriving on the island just over two weeks ago and how much of a stranger I felt. Throughout our time here I've felt pushed and pulled between familiarity and strangeness. The road I know so well I could drive it with my eyes closed. My brother's house which is decorated with photos from years I missed, and where I haven't always felt welcome. The people I recognised immediately when I saw them again after decades apart, faces that have been stored in my mind like books in a library for all these years. The newcomers who seem more like locals than I do. The school and pub that remain largely unchanged and where I spent so much of my youth, the sound and the smell of the sea that I have never forgotten. Is there more that makes me feel at home here or more that makes me feel an interloper, a fraud? I'm still not sure.

'You'll always have a place here, Lorna,' Sarah says firmly as though reading my mind. 'Even if you went away, even if you still live hundreds of miles away, even if things aren't always easy. The places we come from stay with us. You'll always be an islander.'

CHAPTER 40

ALICE

The beach is alive with laughter, conversation and the lingering smells of the barbecue. Looking around, I take in the sight of Ella, Molly and Olive lying side by side in the sand, their legs kicked up behind them as they chat happily with one another. Tess, Joy, Natalia and Kamil sit in a group, helping Harry and Lena build sandcastles that the babies promptly demolish by crawling straight into them. Jean and Christopher sit side by side in deckchairs, Brenda and Morag opposite them. Sarah has risen from her spot beside Lorna and me to help Alfie build a driftwood tower a little further down the beach, and Ben is currently being chased by some of the younger island children. All around me my friends and neighbours smile and laugh, drinking and coming back for second slices of birthday cake.

It's been a good day, but exhaustion washes over me. I thought I'd be relieved that all the planning has paid off and that Ella has had a good birthday. But I can't avoid thinking about the future of the island as I watch my friends. For how much longer will we be able to stay here, enjoying each other's company on this beach that I've grown to love? Right now, the small island buzzes with life but I can't help but picture Caora Island just across the sea, the school abandoned, the buildings crumbling and empty. That island was once full of life too, home to families like ours. A lump lodges itself in my throat.

Music starts up from a portable speaker. Some of the children start to dance, kicking up sand as they shake and wiggle like wild things. Emma and Duncan join in, as do Tess and Joy, Harry carried on Joy's chest. Natalia and Kamil are next on their feet, Kamil holding Lena and swinging her in his arms.

'Dance with me?' asks Jack, suddenly standing in front of me and reaching out a hand. I glance at Lorna.

'Go!' she says with a smile. I rise to my feet, joining my husband. He wraps his arms around my waist and we sway together in time with the music. I look into his grey eyes, thinking about everything we've been through together over these past few weeks. He lost his parents but gained a sister. Our marriage has been tested, both of us struggling to open up to one another but finally ending up closer. There's still so much uncertainty ahead, but at least I know that whatever is to come, we have each other.

Over Jack's shoulder, I watch as Christopher helps Jean up from her deckchair and the two of them start to dance slowly and gracefully. I meet Jean's eye and she smiles. It takes all my strength to smile back at her instead of weeping. She looks tired, but Christopher holds her tightly, as though he may never let go. I wonder if he will ever be able to, or if he will hold on with all his strength right until the end. Perhaps that's just what loving a person that much means. He will never stop holding her or wishing for more time.

The group of dancers gradually grows. As Jack twirls me flamboyantly I catch sight of Sarah and Ben, then Lorna and Mallachy. Eventually the girls join us too, Olive dancing with her parents and Ella and Molly coming over to dance beside me and Jack, the two of them holding hands and spinning one another round and round. The group shifts and changes, Lorna stepping apart from Mallachy to dance with Sarah and me, Molly and Jack dancing together for a moment, then Lorna and Ella holding hands and laughing as they twirl. Growing giddy, I eventually retreat to one of the deckchairs and watch the others continue to dance in the sand. I focus first on Lorna and Ella, trying to hold this moment in my mind for when they are no longer here and it's just the three of us again. Then my eyes drift to Tess and Joy, Harry giggling against Joy's chest. He swings his chubby legs in time with the music.

Another waft of barbecue smell reaches me, making my stomach lurch. I barely managed any of the food today, even though it looked delicious. It must be the stress. But as I glance again at Joy and Harry my heart starts suddenly to race. In a flash, I remember that word Jack used last night. 'You're glowing.' My heart thuds faster and faster. The light-headedness, the nausea, the tiredness … What if it's not just stress? I glance at Jack as he dances with Molly, oblivious to the thoughts whirling in my mind. Surely not, after all this time, after all those years of wishing and waiting? *It can't be.*

I close my eyes, feeling the sea breeze against my face and trying to control the beating of my heart and the emotions that course through me. I breathe in the smell of the sea and charcoal smoke, listening to the sound of voices and the waves lapping against the shore. Slowly, I reach a hand and rest it gently on my stomach. I take slow, deep breaths, feeling my hand rise and fall.

CHAPTER 41

LORNA

Some of the youngest children have been taken home but otherwise the celebrations are still in full swing, groups gathered around the bonfires now as the children (and some of the adults) toast marshmallows on the flames. But after the emotion of the day I need to be alone for a moment. I walk up the sand and back towards Hilly Farm. When I reach the track I pause, sitting down on the grassy bank above the beach. It's nearly dark now, stars beginning to glimmer in the sky.

My head aches slightly, a dull pain from too much beer and so much smiling. It's been a perfect birthday party – the best that Ella has ever had, I'm sure of it. But I can feel myself dipping slightly now, like the inevitable low that comes after gorging on sweets. I want to savour the last moments of the day like the last dregs in a glass of good wine, but instead I find my thoughts running ahead of me. I told Ella that we would head back to London the day after the party. So, as well as a celebration, today is a goodbye. So why don't I feel ready to leave?

'Can I join you?'

Jean Brown is standing beside me, slightly out of breath, her hands on her thighs. I didn't even notice her approaching from the beach. Am I imagining it, or does she look somewhat anxious? It's an expression I feel as though I've seen on her face several times recently.

'Yes of course.' I gesture to the ground beside me.

She sits down very slowly. It's something of a shock to realise that my old teacher has become frail. I remember her taking the class on walks across the island, pointing out particular wildflowers and insects. Sometimes I'd be allowed to hold her hand and I'd try my best not to let the grin I felt inside show on my mouth.

We sit side by side, looking down at the beach. I thought I wanted to be alone, but it's actually comforting to have her beside me. It also pushes aside my thoughts about leaving, if just for a moment.

'It's been a great party, hasn't it?'

But Jean ignores my question and turns to face me, her expression stricken.

'Lorna, I've been wanting to speak to you since the funeral. There's something I need to tell you.'

Her voice is shaking. Worry flutters in my stomach.

'What it is it?'

She gasps, suppressing a sob.

'I need to tell you how sorry I am,' she says in a shaking voice. 'What your brother said at the funeral, it brought it all back and I haven't been able to stop thinking about it since.'

As Jean speaks, I can feel my body tensing. I sit very still, listening.

'It made me think of the unhappiest little girl I ever taught, a girl I've thought about every day since. Of course, it was hard for Jack too. But I saw how he managed to get through it somehow. But you ...'

Jean turns away now and glances down at the beach, her eyes misting over. I can hear laughter and conversation drifting up through the dunes but my eyes are fixed on Jean, the woman who taught me to read and write, who told me about the moths in the cottage where she lived and who let me ring the school fire bell myself during drills because sudden loud noises always used to frighten me.

'I remember the first time you told me you fell off your bike. I decided to believe you. I *wanted* to believe you. The next time it happened, I told myself it must have been another accident. But there was part of me that knew that something wasn't right.'

She takes a faltering breath, a sob escaping her. She turns back to face me now and her eyes fill with tears. I don't want to hear what will come next.

'Lorna, I *knew*. I pretended that I didn't but I knew what was going on. I knew that they weren't accidents.'

I feel as though I'm falling, the ground no longer there beneath me, my body dropping into empty space.

Jean rubs agitatedly at her face. She shakes her head slightly.

'I thought about saying something, about doing something, but this is such a small island. The people who live here are people I have to see every single day. To accuse someone of something like that ... It is a devastating accusation to make anywhere, but in a place like this ... I told myself that I had to be absolutely *certain* if I was going to say anything. And was I certain enough to not only put a whole family through something like that, but a whole community? Because I knew it would have affected everyone. People taking sides, a division that might tear the island apart. I told myself that I was just imagining things.'

She takes another gulping breath. I remember myself so clearly as a frightened, anxious child and then as an angry un-happy teenager – it's almost as though my younger selves are sitting beside me in the grass, watching on as this conversation unfolds. What would they say? How would they feel to hear that the teacher they loved and trusted knew? She *knew*.

'When you left the island as a teenager, that's when I thought maybe I'd been right about what had been going on. Why else would you choose to leave and not come back? I thought that perhaps I should have said something then, but you were al-ready gone. I hoped that it might be the best thing for you, that you'd be happier wherever you ended up. Saying something then couldn't have helped you. I kept a careful eye on Jack though and was in touch with the teachers at the secondary school on the mainland to keep a watch on him too. But other than being quiet and withdrawn, they never saw anything to worry about. There were no "falls", no bruises. For a while it made me feel like maybe I'd been wrong about you too, that

I'd overreacted. But the longer you stayed away the more the feeling grew that somehow things had been different for you than they were for Jack. A sense that I'd been right to worry about you.'

She takes a deep breath.

'I have thought about you and the mistake that I made every single day since you left. You deserved better, Lorna, and you were let down. Your parents let you down, but I let you down too. And I have regretted it every single day of my life.'

My body is shaking again. I wish I could stop it but I can't. I look into the face of the woman I once trusted, a woman who has become an old woman without being particularly old. I know it shouldn't matter. So much time has passed now and nothing can be changed. So why do I feel so upset and angry?

'I felt so safe at that school.'

Jean nods, tears dripping down her face. Maybe I should feel sorry for her, but right now I can't. Instead I feel hot, pulsing anger. For years I've felt immeasurably sad about what happened to me as a child, and at times confused, guilty, embarrassed. But hardly ever angry. Now it takes hold of me, gripping like a fist. I didn't deserve the things that happened to me. I deserved to be protected by the people around me. I was a child. I was a child and I was let down.

'They told everyone I was clumsy. I even believed it myself sometimes too. I felt like I was going crazy.'

All those times I doubted myself and whether I was making things up inside my head. And all that time there was someone who *saw*, who suspected the truth of what was going on.

'I'm so sorry,' whispers Jean. 'I was weak.'

I stand up suddenly, making her jump slightly.

'I need to go.'

I turn away from my old teacher, leaving her among the grass and the wildflowers. I just can't be here anymore. The thought of returning to the beach and the party feels impossible now too. I don't want to ruin the last moments of Ella's birthday. So I quickly make my way to the farm. Once I'm back in the stillness and the quiet of the empty house I sit in the kitchen, my body tense and shaking. It takes a long time to calm down. By the time I hear the front door of the farmhouse open then close, I know what I need to do.

CHAPTER 42

ALICE

Suddenly yearning for a moment to myself, I gather dirty dishes in a washing-up bowl and walk slowly back up to the house, leaving the noise and the bonfires behind me. I need to be away from everyone, to give myself a chance to think. On the way I spot Jean walking quickly down the track away from the house and the beach.

'Jean!' I call after her, but she doesn't turn around. I watch for a moment as she continues along the track. Perhaps I'm not the only one who needs to be alone right now.

My hands full, I walk through the kitchen in the dark, putting down the washing-up bowl and resting my hands for a moment on the lip of the sink. But a noise jolts me, making me spin around.

'Lorna! You scared me!'

She's sitting in the dark at the kitchen table, staring straight ahead. As if waking from a dream she turns to me.

'Sorry. I didn't mean to startle you.'

I flick on the light, the room illuminated in a warm glow, the windows dark squares dotted with the stars that are beginning to flicker outside.

'Thank you again for a lovely party. It was perfect. Ella had a wonderful time.'

'She's still having a good time by the looks of things when I left. I think they're going to sleep well tonight.'

She turns away from me again, staring out the window.

'Are you OK, Lorna?'

'Just a headache. I think I've had too much to drink.'

'You and every other adult on the island! I think there are going to be a lot of hangovers tomorrow. Shall I make us some tea?'

I turn to the Rayburn but she reaches across the table and places a hand on my arm, making me stop and turn to face her.

'Alice, I don't think Jean should teach at the school anymore.'

'What do you mean?'

Did Jean finally talk to Lorna? Perhaps she didn't make it clear that she has already left, but told her about the opening for a new headteacher? Does that mean Lorna has decided to stay? But her reply crushes my spark of hope.

'She told me tonight that she knew about the abuse when I was a child but never told anyone. She knew I wasn't just clumsy, but she didn't *do* anything. I know it was a really long time ago, but if I was a parent with children at the school I'd want to know that.'

It takes a moment for me to really register what she's said. So that's why Jean was walking away so swiftly just now. But how could she? All my thoughts and memories about my friend feel suddenly confused. I don't know how to reconcile what Lorna has just told me with the woman I thought I knew, the woman who taught my daughter and who is one of my closest friends. My head spins, my thoughts suddenly blurry. I sit down next to Lorna, abandoning the kettle and the thought of tea.

'Jean *isn't* teaching at the school anymore,' I eventually manage.

'What?' she asks.

'She's dying.'

As I say the words out loud a pain wrenches my gut. My friend is dying, and she is not the woman I thought she was.

I watch as Lorna's expression changes, the anger softening somewhat, confusion and worry darting across her eyes. When she says nothing, I force myself to tell her the rest.

'She has breast cancer. When she was on the mainland last week she was there for another hospital appointment. The doctors tell her she has to have chemotherapy. But she's refusing. She doesn't want to leave the island.'

I rub my hand across my forehead.

'I'm not defending her. I mean, what you just said … It's hard to hear. I'm so sorry, Lorna.'

I try to picture Lorna as a child and grow hot with anger at the Jean who so badly let her down. Would things have been different for Jack and Lorna if she'd intervened? Maybe they would have been spared years of pain and decades of separation. But I can't help but think too of the Jean who was always so patient and kind with Molly and whom I sat with just this week outside her house watching the butterflies. The Jean who danced with her husband on the beach this afternoon and who was hugged by the class of children who miss her already. They seem like different people, the Jean of the past who made such an awful mistake with Lorna, and the Jean that I know now. Maybe it would be simpler to think that they are different, that over the years Jean has used her guilt at the way she handled things with Lorna to become a better person. Or maybe the truth is that we are all made up of the best and worst things we've ever done.

'She should have told someone. And I'm so sorry for you that she didn't. But I guess none of it matters now, is what I mean to say.'

Beside me, Lorna shakes her head, a deep frown etched into her face.

'I don't know what to say. I shouted at her ...'

'And you had every right to.'

'What about the school? Have you found a new teacher?'

I let out a sigh, my body heavy in the chair.

'No. We've been looking for someone for months. But it's a hard role to fill.'

'What will happen if you don't find someone?'

I close my eyes for a second, picturing the party that we left behind on the beach and how carefree and happy everyone seemed.

'The school will close.'

I don't need to tell her what that would mean for the island. She grew up here. She saw the abandoned classroom on Caora Island, weeds growing up between the floorboards and the desks rotting and forgotten.

'Why did no one tell me?'

'As soon as Jean found out that you were a teacher, she asked us not to,' I tell her.

'But I don't understand.'

I glance warily across at her, not sure what to say. I suppose it's out now, there's no point keeping the truth from her any longer.

'I think she thought that if you knew, you might feel a sense of responsibility. You might feel it was your duty to come back. So she was adamant that we weren't to mention a thing, not about her illness or about the school.'

'But now I know.'

'Now you know.'

She lets out a long sigh, brushing her hair back from her face. We sit in silence for a moment, the air heavy with it.

'I'm sorry you're having to deal with all this,' she says eventually, her voice quiet. 'But you know I still have to leave tomorrow, don't you?'

I nod slowly, because deep down, of course I do. I might have hoped that things would be different, but ultimately, I knew this was the way things were going to end.

'I fought so hard to escape this island,' she continues, rubbing her arm. 'I'm so glad we came back and that I got to see Jack again and to meet you and Molly. But my life is back in London. It's time Ella and I got back to it. It's where we belong.'

'I understand. But you're welcome here whenever you like, you know that?'

'Thank you, that means a lot.'

The quiet is suddenly replaced with the sound of the front door opening and closing and the voices of Ella and Molly in the hallway. The girls tumble inside, Ella hugging her mother tightly. I watch as Lorna leans into her, her face in Ella's hair. I imagine that she's smelling it like I so often do with Molly, hoping she doesn't notice but loving her so much I could inhale her, eat her, hold her like she's small again if only she'd let me. Molly would think me mad if I told her these thoughts, but I'm sure that Lorna understands. She's a mother too. At the thought my hand darts instinctively to my stomach again, a fluttering in my heart.

'Mum, I've just had the best day,' gushes Ella. 'Thank you. And thank you, Auntie Alice.'

She hugs me too and I breathe deeply the smell of barbecue smoke and sea air.

Jack follows behind the girls, carrying a wooden crate filled with Ella's presents.

'The others have cleared most of the other bits, and we can collect the final things tomorrow,' he says, setting the crate down on the table.

'Thank you, Uncle Jack,' Ella says, reaching and hugging him too. For a second, he looks slightly alarmed and stands awkwardly as she wraps her arms around him. But then he softens, leaning down to better hug her back. I glance at Lorna. She watches them closely, her eyes shining.

Once Ella and Jack have parted, Ella turns to Lorna.

'I guess I should go and pack now then?'

She sounds hesitant, perhaps hoping her mother will have changed her mind. I look across at Jack and notice he's turned away, busying himself with some dishes in the sink.

'Good idea, darling,' Lorna replies. Ella's face falls but she nods. Unlike the last time, it seems that Ella has accepted that it's time to leave. She and Molly disappear upstairs.

'You should get started too,' I say to Lorna. 'It's already late. We can finish up down here.'

'Are you sure?'

'Yes, there's not too much to do anyway.'

'OK, thanks.'

Lorna throws a look across at Jack but he's still turned away and doesn't move as she leaves the room. It's only when she's gone that his shoulders sink, his head lowered. He turns slowly around, slumping back against the kitchen units. I want to ask him how he feels about Lorna leaving and to tell him about Jean and the terrible secret I learned today. I want to reminisce about the almost perfect day of sunshine and laughter and weep against his chest with fears for the future. But more than anything, I want to tell him about the thought that I can't shake from my mind, the one thing I daren't quite believe might be true but can't hold in any longer.

'Jack, I think I might be pregnant.'

He looks up now, his eyes meeting mine. And as his tears start to fall, mine do too.

CHAPTER 43

LORNA

The island is dark and silent but I can't sleep. I lie in bed, the covers hot and heavy against my prickling skin, my packed suitcase just visible as a dark silhouette by the door. I can't stop thinking about everything that's happened today. Our trip on Mallachy's boat and Ella catching us mid-embrace, but her happiness too as she watched the puffins and we swam in the sea. The party, with a whole island gathered on the sand for my daughter. And that argument with Jean as the stars started to blossom in the sky and the celebrations continued below us. I think about Alice's revelation too. My old school is clear in my mind, its one classroom covered in displays, the smell of hot lunches and pencils hanging in the air. If they don't find a new teacher soon, the school will close down. And so too, will the island. It's all too familiar, too like the story of Caora which was island legend when I was growing up, a warning to us all about the need to cling on to our community. Alice might have hidden this from me but when she told me the truth I could see the fear and stress on her face and wondered how I'd missed it before. I might have been here visiting what was once my home, but all this time she's been desperately trying to cling onto the place that has become hers.

The island needs a teacher. Could I? For a moment I feel as though maybe I could. It would be a change of pace, a chance to rediscover my love of teaching and to have control over a whole school instead of being someone's deputy. The thought gives me a brief thrill. But then I remember how much I gave up to escape this island. I fought so hard for my freedom and it cost me so much. Could I really come back here after all this time and with all the memories this place holds? This trip has been strange and painful and full of surprising bursts of sweetness. It's been nothing like I expected when I arrived on the mist-veiled shores. Part of me aches to think about leaving my brother, Alice, Sarah, Mallachy and the other friends I've made here. But my life is back in London, not here. Surely, it's a fantasy to imagine otherwise? It's time to get back to reality. However hard it may feel, it's time to say goodbye.

I slip out of bed and dress quietly, taking the car keys from the hook by the door. I know where my brother keeps his keys now and where the wine glasses live in the kitchen. I know which floorboard creaks on the stairs and who in the family snores (Molly, just like Ella).

When I reach Mallachy's house his windows glow like lanterns, the cottage a flickering light against the backdrop of black sea and dark sky. When I let myself in he is sitting on the sofa. He looks up from his book as though he has been waiting for me and as though he knows why I am here. We don't speak this time, or laugh or whisper in each other's ears. Instead we are silent, moving together to his room where the curtains are still open and the stars watch us, blinking, from thousands of years in the future.

It's only later, when we are lying side by side with the sheets tangled around us like a cocoon and my hand resting on his chest, that he speaks.

'So, you're leaving.'

I nod slowly, looking up at the ceiling.

'Yes. My life is back in London. It's time to get back to it.'

'Is there anything I can say to make you change your mind?'

Unsaid words hover above us in the air. If I reached out and grabbed at them, could any of them change things?

'Because I would say it, you know,' he says quietly.

Part of me wishes that he would say those words, but perhaps it is better that he doesn't.

'I'm sorry,' I say. 'Do you wish I'd never come here?'

He pauses.

'Maybe it would make it easier. But no, I'm still glad I met you.'

'I'm glad I met you too.'

I squeeze my eyes tightly shut. When I open them he is there, his face close to mine. He kisses me gently.

'I should get back.' But he reaches out and touches my wrist.

'Stay. Just this once.'

I sink back into the sheets, resting my head against his chest and listening to the dull thud of his heartbeat. I stay there until the sun starts to rise over the sea, when I slip out without saying goodbye. We've said our goodbye; what else is there left to say? Before I leave I take one last glance inside his studio, taking in the desk where we sat side by side and where I found my way back to the thing that once made me so happy. I run my hand across the smooth wood of Mallachy's easel, brushing my palm over the soft tips of paintbrushes. Sometimes things are lost forever, but sometimes we find them again. When I'm back in London I will buy new paints and brushes. I will sharpen a new set of pencils and open a blank sketchbook. And I will spend my spare moments around school work and Ella doing the thing I once loved so much, but needed someone to remind me of. Mallachy has given me so many unexpected wonderful moments over the past few weeks, moments when I've forgotten everything else and just let myself sink into happiness. But perhaps most of all, he gave me this.

I make it back to Hilly Farm before the others wake and return to the yellow room that looks out over the sea, the room where the bed is now neatly made, the borrowed raincoats folded on the chair, the suitcase ready by the door.

*

No one seems to know what to say as Jack drives us to the harbour, Alice in the front and me in the back next to Molly and Ella. Our suitcases are in the boot, plus the extra bag given by Alice to hold all of Ella's birthday presents. For once, the girls are quiet.

I left a few things behind in my room: three parcels addressed to Jack, Alice and Molly. I wonder when they will find them. I couldn't bear the thought of being there myself when they opened them. I would have been far too embarrassed. Instead, I imagine Alice opening hers first, tearing the paper and pulling out the medium-sized canvas. Will she recognise herself in the figure standing waist-deep in the sea, arms outstretched, clouds swirling on the horizon? I hope so. I tried hard to capture her spirit, her defiance that day when we swam together in the freezing sea. Then Molly's, a similar-sized canvas but this time painted in bold, vibrant colours that spell out the words 'Save the sea'. And finally Jack's, the heaviest of the three packages. I imagine he will take more time over his, holding the weight in his hands before carefully peeling back the paper. Beneath the paper he will find a box. A simple thing made from smoothed fragments of wood collected from the beach. Mallachy helped me with its construction, letting me use the materials in his studio. But the design is mine, the wooden shards picked by me from the sand. The box is filled entirely with shells and pebbles. The zebra-striped dome of a limpet shell. A fragment of china with a blue and white pattern. The sharp knife of a razor clam. Nestled among the treasure is a note. I still remember every word that I wrote for him this morning.

Jack,

Every time I'm on a beach I find myself collecting things. I remember how much you used to love searching for shells and rocks when we were young, and how happy you'd look whenever I gave you a new 'treasure' I'd found. It was the best feeling, being able to make you smile. Molly told me the collecting is something you still do. I'm not sure why, but it made me so happy to know that. I suppose it makes me feel closer to you – as though when I've stopped and picked something off a beach on the Isle of Dogs you might have been doing the same thing here on the Isle of Kip. I know that's foolish really, though, and that nothing changes the reality of what happened and all those years we spent apart. But I still like to think of it.

Every time I picked up a shell or a rock or a bit of glass from a beach over the years, I thought of you. I wondered what you were doing and I hoped that you were OK, that you were happy. Coming here, I couldn't shake the habit. This box is the result of two weeks of treasure-hunting here on Kip. It's all the times I thought of you but didn't know quite what to say. I suppose each collected thing is like a word. I would give you the whole beach if I could. There's still so much I don't know how to say, Jack. But I do know that I'm glad you are my brother. You will always be my brother. And I'm glad that I came. I'm glad I got to meet Alice, and Molly, and to see you as an adult. I'm sorry it took so long.

My name is signed in a rush as I struggled to hold the pen steady in my hand. Maybe he'll think it's a strange gift. Maybe he won't understand. But perhaps he will. In the end, it felt like the only thing to give, the only way to tell him how much I've thought about him over the years. I've thought about him every time I've reached for a shard of sea-glass on the shore back home on the Isle of Dogs, every time I've slipped a perfect pebble into my coat pocket. I've thought about my brother every day.

Outside, the island flashes past the window. The mountain, the forest, the sea. They are images I've tried hard to forget. But now ... Now, I think I'd quite like to remember.

As we approach the village I spot the cars. They are lined up along the street, and as we pull into the harbour there are more parked here too.

'What's all this?'

Alice turns around in her seat.

'What, you didn't think they'd want to say goodbye?'

As we pull up in a space opposite The Lookout, the pub door opens and a stream of people comes pouring out. Everyone is here.

Jack, Ben and Duncan carry our suitcases down to the jetty where the ferry is just coming to a halt, waves churning beneath the hull. We make a slow procession towards the boat.

'Safe journey, pets,' says Brenda, giving Ella and me a hug. Puff whines at Ella's feet and she nestles her face into his soft fur as she says goodbye to him too. Ella's eyes are damp with tears as she steps away from the puppy. She sniffs and wipes her face with her sleeve. Tess, Joy and the other women from yoga pass me a sheet with all their phone numbers and ask me to promise to keep in touch.

Everyone hugs us in turn and wishes us a safe journey.

Most of these people I've known for only a couple of weeks. But it feels as though we've known each other for so much longer. These are people who have seen me cry, who attended my parents' funeral, who threw a birthday party for my daughter that we will both remember forever. And we are linked by more than that too. We are held together by our shared knowledge of this place. By the familiar smell and sound of the sea, by an understanding of what it means to live on a small island adrift from the mainland.

I spot Jean and her husband in the crowd. He holds her hand and keeps glancing at her as though she might disappear any moment. With one thumb he strokes the side of her hand. It is hard to look at him too closely, his pain written so legibly on his face. Jean looks up now and meets my eye. I could turn away. But I don't; I step towards her until we are standing opposite one another.

'I'm so sorry you're sick, Jean.'

Her shoulders sink slightly. Next to her, her husband kisses her on the cheek and steps tactfully away.

'Who told you?'

'Alice. I didn't know.'

Would I have stormed off like that last night if I did? Would I have felt so angry?

'I didn't want you to know. And you have nothing to be sorry for.'

She attempts a weak smile but her voice is trembling.

'Sometimes our time runs out. But I'm so glad I got to see you again, Lorna, and to meet your daughter. You have done a wonderful job. And I really am so sorry,' she adds, reaching out and taking my hand. 'I wish I'd been a better, braver person for you back then.'

I hold her hand in mine, thinking about everything she told me last night and how she failed to protect me as a child. But I also think of the island children who greeted her so warmly on the beach at Ella's party, and my own memories of her as a teacher. Yes, she was weak when I needed her to be strong. And yes, she did a bad thing. But sometimes good people do. I don't say 'it's OK' because it isn't. But I squeeze her hand tightly.

'Thank you for saying that. And I was glad to see you again too.'

Jean lets out a breath and her body relaxes slightly. As she steps away I wonder if I will see her again. Her husband sweeps back to her side, scooping his arm around her waist as though the strength of his grip on her is enough to keep her alive. Whatever might have happened in the past, right now I wish that it could be.

Sarah's mother hands me a tinfoil parcel of cake for the journey and kisses me on the cheek. When Doug hugs me goodbye his eyes are shiny and damp.

'Allergies,' he says with a big sniff. 'You have a safe journey and come back soon, love.'

I think back to what Linda told me in the church: 'we always thought of you as ours'. I may have been unlucky with the parents I was given, but that doesn't mean I had nothing. Coming back here has shown me that, reminding me of all the good I forgot too in my attempt to shut out my more painful childhood memories.

'Thank you,' I say, pulling them both towards me for one final hug. 'For everything.'

Sarah is one of the last to say goodbye.

'Keep in touch?' she says as we hold each other.

'I promise. And again, I'm so sorry I didn't keep in touch before. I was so lucky to have a friend like you.'

We step back from one another and she bites her lip and pushes her glasses a little higher up her nose.

'It's OK.' And I think that maybe it will be for us. This time I will keep my promise. I'm not going to let my friend go a second time.

Eventually all the other islanders step back, giving us some space. There is only one person missing, but it's better this way. We had our goodbye last night. By now a couple of cars and passengers have disembarked and others have been loaded onto the boat. The ferry is ready to leave, the harbour master on duty today standing by the ramp, waiting for Ella and me. This is it. For a second time in two and a half weeks I'm about to step onto this ferry, except this time it's taking me away, back to the mainland where I tell myself I belong. This was always the plan: come here for a couple of weeks at most and then leave again. This is the way things were always meant to go.

'Well, have a good journey,' says Alice, squeezing us both tightly, her eyes glistening. 'It was so lovely to get to know you.' After she hugs Ella she steps back for a second and places her hands on her cheeks. 'You are a very wonderful young lady.'

Ella blushes a deep shade of red but she is smiling too.

'Thank you, Auntie Alice.'

'I'm so glad we got to meet,' I tell Alice as I hug her in turn. 'Thank you for everything.' During this visit I've gained not just a sister-in-law but a friend.

426

Ella and Molly hug each other so fiercely that I have to look away. When I turn back they are both rubbing their eyes.

'I'll message you,' says Molly.

'Every day,' replies Ella, sniffing.

'Bye, Uncle Jack,' says Ella, wrapping her arms around his waist. He hugs her back, tightly this time.

Ella drags her suitcase slowly towards the ferry. She doesn't look back and I can tell that she is crying but is trying not to.

'Well, goodbye then,' says Jack.

'Goodbye, Jack.'

I look up at my little brother from whom I was apart for two decades. And I want to tell him the one thing I've wanted to say ever since arriving on the island. That I love him, of course. That I always have, ever since he was small and even when we grew apart as older children and then for all the years that followed when our lives played out in separate worlds. Because despite it all, I never stopped loving my brother.

His arms are strong when they reach for me, as he wraps them around my shoulders. Just for a moment the years and space fall away and we are a family again, held together. We are a shared history, a forever-linked pair, two sides to the same coin. I can't find the words to tell him. But I hold him tightly.

And then it's time to leave. Ella is already on the top deck, her eyes red but her tears brushed away as she waves vigorously back to the island. I stow my suitcase, trying to shut out the sound of the ramp lifting and the ferry starting to chug away from the shore, and the shouts of 'goodbye', reaching me across the water. I chose this. I chose to go home. I want to go home. The stinging in my eyes is just the sea breeze. The shivering in my body is just the cold air.

'Lorna!'

As I hear the voice I climb the stairs to the top deck two at a time. I run to the back of the boat where Ella is standing and waving with both arms. A figure pushes through the crowd gathered on the jetty. There's a bark and Rex bursts through, breaking out from the huddle of people and leaping up and down. And then there is Mallachy, running towards the end of the jetty so fast that it looks as though he might not stop, that perhaps he might continue running straight into the sea. But at the very edge he slows to a halt.

'Lorna!'

His voice is a cry and it hits me deep in the chest. I grip the rail, my knuckles turning white.

'Lorna!'

I open my mouth but nothing comes out. I don't look away though, not until I can no longer see him and the harbour and the village have disappeared, the island just a dark black ridgeline on the horizon. Ella and I are going home, back to the life I have put so much into building for us both. It's the right thing to do. So why do I feel like I've just made a huge mistake?

CHAPTER 44

ALICE

It feels strange to step into the guest bedroom and find it empty. I know they were only here for a few weeks, but it still feels like Lorna's room, somehow. I perch on the end of the bed for a moment looking out the window at the sea, today a dark turquoise. The ferry should have long since reached the mainland by now. They are probably on the train, heading back to Fort William to catch the sleeper. I wonder when we'll see them again. Next summer feels a long way away, especially when I picture my daughter's stricken face as she waved good-bye to her cousin on the jetty and if I think of all the ways our lives may have changed by this time next year.

On the way home from the harbour I stopped in at the village shop, leaving Molly and Jack waiting in the car. There was a single pregnancy test semi-hidden among the shelves of pharmacy products in the shop. As I handed it over to Pat her eyebrows rose, her lips parting in surprise.

'Please don't tell anyone,' I said quickly, looking around to see if anyone was watching us.

'Of course not, love,' she replied, but she reached across the counter for my hand and squeezed it.

I still can't believe those two red lines that appeared once I was home and shut in the bathroom with Jack, Molly outside in the garden. They're so small and so simple but mean so much. We both cried again then, holding each other. Jack quickly took charge, calling the hospital on the mainland to make an appointment for me and organising for Sarah to look after Molly for the night when we go. With the ferry only running once a day we'll have to stay overnight and come back the following morning. He's sorted it all. I don't feel ready for action yet though. Given everything that's happened in the past, I won't feel calm until I see a doctor, and perhaps not even then. I think maybe this pregnancy is just bound to be filled with anxiety. Will everything go smoothly? And if it does, will I even remember how to care for a newborn after such a long time? How will Molly react to an unexpected and much younger sibling? And is now the best time to have another child, when the future of our home is so uncertain? But despite my worries I can't seem to press down the joy that bubbles inside me, making me feel as though I may lift off the ground any moment. The worries are real but I choose to be hopeful, too. Because without hope, what do we really have?

I glance around the room, imagining it as a nursery instead of a spare room. I think I'd keep it yellow, but picture a mobile hanging above a wooden cot, a rocking chair in the corner. Tears spring to my eyes again, picturing this thing I have dreamed of for years.

As my eyes fall on the bed I realise that the room is not entirely empty after all. There are some packages resting on the pillow. As I reach for them I notice our names written on the brown paper: Alice, Molly, Jack.

I lift mine towards me and peel back the paper. Inside is one of the most beautiful paintings I've ever seen. I recognise the view instantly because it's the same view I see every day and have come to love. It's the beach below the farm, our beach. There are two figures running into the water and my mouth spreads into a smile as I recognise them. It's me and Lorna. The version of me she's captured looks different to the person I see in the mirror, though. This woman looks defiant, purposeful and strong. As I look at the painting version of me, my confidence grows. Whatever lies ahead for my family and for this island, I will cope with it. For years I've felt a failure for not leading the kind of lives my sisters have, for being a yoga teacher and a farmer's wife instead of a doctor or a lecturer. But looking at this picture, I feel suddenly sure that I made the right choice. I may not have had a big life full of travel, adventure and a high-flying career. But that doesn't mean that my life is small. I have had my family, my community, my home and a job that I love. Later, I will phone my sisters and invite them to visit and join me for one of my retreats like Lorna suggested. I will tell them my news in person. And maybe I will tell them how I feel about our relationship, but maybe I won't. Perhaps when it comes down to it, it doesn't really matter that they will always think of me as Squirt, their little sister. Because looking at the strong, confident woman in Lorna's painting, I know that I am more than that.

I prop the painting next to the bed and carefully lift the two other parcels.

'Molly, honey?' I say, pushing open her bedroom door. She is busily typing away on her phone, to Ella I assume. The spare bed in here looks strange in its emptiness too. Looking at my daughter, it's hard not to tell her the secret I'm carrying inside. But I want to be certain that everything is OK before I turn her life upside down. I can't help but think she'll take being an older sister in her stride though.

'Your aunt left this for you.'

I hand her the parcel and we sit together on her bed as she opens it.

'Oh, I love it,' she exclaims, holding up a canvas with 'Save the sea' written in bold, colourful letters. 'I think I want to put it here.'

'I'll help you hang it later, sweetie,' I say, kissing her on the forehead. 'I just need to give this to your dad.'

His parcel is the heaviest of the three and rattles slightly as I carry it downstairs. He is in the living room, sitting on the sofa reading a book. It's the same Moomintroll book I caught him reading two weeks ago, the photo of him and Lorna slipped inside its pages.

He looks up, his face tired-looking but stretching into a smile as he spots me.

'I can't wait to read this to the little one,' he says softly. 'I miss reading to Molly, don't you?'

I sit down beside him, resting my head on his shoulder. He wraps his arm around me. I say nothing, but turn my head to kiss him on the cheek. We smile at one another. After a moment's contented silence, I remember the package on my lap.

'Lorna left us some gifts. Molly and I have already opened ours; this one is for you.'

For a moment he just stares at it, the rectangular-shaped parcel on his lap.

'Go on,' I say gently, and he withdraws his arm from around me and starts peeling back the paper. Inside is a wooden box. It looks like it's made from driftwood. He opens the lid and it's filled with pebbles. No wonder it felt so much heavier than ours. There's a note too and he reads it quietly. I turn my head away slightly, resisting the urge to read over his shoulder. When he has finished reading he folds the note and then reaches his hand into the box, running his fingers over each stone. There are shells in there too and fragments of sea glass.

'Some people might find a box of pebbles a strange gift,' I say, laughing lightly.

'But it's perfect,' he replies. His eyes grow misty and I reach out for his hand.

'You miss her, don't you?'

He nods silently.

'By the time we'd managed to find each other again it felt like she was already leaving. But at least I feel like this time it wasn't goodbye forever. And besides, we have so much to be happy about, don't we?'

I still have so many fears for the baby, for myself, for this island and its islanders. Things are still so uncertain, but Jack is right too. Right now, I don't want to let worries or sadness encroach on our happiness. It might not be a cheering, shouting, dancing kind of happiness, instead it drapes itself over us like a blanket or a purring cat. For a moment we sit quietly side by side, letting it warm us. The worries and fears will still be there tomorrow. For now, let us have this.

CHAPTER 45

LORNA

We may have been gone for three weeks but the flat smells stale and empty when we finally arrive home, abandoning our suitcases in the hallway. I'm dazed from the long trip and the journey on the underground that felt like an assault on the senses after the quiet of the island. Was the underground always so hot and crowded? Did the DLR always rattle like a runaway carriage?

It's late morning but all I want to do is sleep. Last night on the sleeper train I lay awake in the narrow bed. At the start of our trip I counted down the days until I could get back to London, but last night I just couldn't stop thinking about everything I'd left behind on the island. I'd thought that Ella had been sleeping but at one point I heard a noise from the top bunk that could have been either a cough or a sob. I spoke her name quietly into the darkness but received no reply.

'I'm going to bed,' Ella says now, carrying her suitcase along the tight corridor towards her bedroom.

Fatigue tugs at my limbs but instead of heading straight to my room I wander into the kitchen. The plates from the dinner we ate before heading to Euston to catch the sleeper train are still neatly stacked on the drying rack. That dinner feels much longer than three weeks ago and I find I can't remember what we ate that night. I do remember how I felt though, anxiety and apprehension buzzing through my veins like too much caffeine. How strange to think that just three weeks ago I'd never met Alice or Molly, and hadn't seen my brother in twenty-two years. I hadn't seen Sarah since I was a child and I'd never met the other islanders. I'd never met Tess or Joy, Brenda, Morag or Kerstin. I'd never met Mallachy.

In one of the flats above a dog barks and a muffled yell reaches me through the floorboards. Outside, I can hear the rattle of cars and buses on the main road that loops around the edge of the Isle of Dogs. I scoop the post from the doormat (takeaway leaflets and more bills) and head to my room where I lie down heavily on the bed. Usually this room feels so familiar that I don't really *see* it. It just is. But now it's as though I am seeing my surroundings for what they are, devoid of the usual familiarity that blurs them into the background. For a second, this is just a house, not a home. A flat in a block filled with other flats, lives I know nothing about, strangers living on top of one another. My room is just a room, filled with the debris of a life. And then I fall asleep. I dream of the ocean. This time though, I am not looking out at it, wishing myself on the mainland. Instead I am swimming in it, the cold water surrounding me and making my skin tingle.

Our second evening back in the flat, Cheryl comes over for dinner. I hug her tightly in the doorway. I've never been so happy to see my friend. Or so sad either. As I step away I rub my eyes. I give her the box of shortbread I bought for her at Fort William and we sit down at the kitchen table, the same table we've sat at together countless times. But this time's different. Now, everything has changed.

'I still can't believe you're leaving.'

'Me neither. It'll be so strange.'

But I think maybe she's just being kind. There's an even greater bounce to her than usual, an ease and lightness as though she is protected by a waterproof layer and any stress is now just rolling off her like droplets of rain. She seems excited and I wonder for how long she and Mike have needed this change.

Over dinner (a cobbled-together meal that makes me miss the fresh vegetables and perfectly cooked meat we ate at Hilly Farm), Ella tells Cheryl animatedly about our time on the island. She tells her about Molly and Olive, about the puffins and the boat trip with Mallachy, and about her birthday party. Hers might be an edited description of our trip away, missing out the arguments, the running away and all the tension, but I still smile to hear her tell it.

'It sounds like you had a wonderful time.'

'I did,' Ella replies.

Once Ella has gone to bed Cheryl and I open a bottle of wine and retreat to the living room, sitting with our legs up beneath us on the sofa.

'So how was it really?'

How to possibly condense everything that's happened over the past couple of weeks into a few phrases? In some ways, it feels as though the past three weeks never happened. Returning to our flat, nothing has changed. And yet somehow everything has too.

'It *was* wonderful. But also awful. And painful. And confusing. And hard, really hard. But yes, at times it was wonderful.'

And so I tell her some of it, as much of it as I can manage to form into words. My brother's coldness, our big argument at our childhood home, our parents' funeral and the day Ella and Molly escaped to Caora Island and I feared I'd lost my daughter for good.

'God, that must have been so bloody frightening.'

'It was.'

I also tell her about Alice, about her optimism and vibrant energy.

'You'd like her, Cheryl, I think.'

And then I tell her more about Mallachy, my cheeks growing warm as I share a little of our afternoons, of our hours spent in his studio.

'You really liked him, didn't you?' she says.

I run a hand through my hair.

'Does it really matter? He's there, I'm here.'

'Of course it matters! Falling in love always matters.'

The words jolt me and I take a deep sip of wine. Love? It seems an absurd thought. And yet … I still remember how familiar he seemed the first time I turned up at his house and found myself looking into his bright green eyes. How, in a short space of time he managed to encourage me to pick up a paintbrush once more, something I wasn't sure I'd ever do again. And I remember the sound of his voice reaching me across the water as the ferry pulled away and how it broke something inside of me.

But I also think about Alice, her surprising kindness towards me and the connection that I felt between us after just a few days. Sarah, with whom I managed to reconnect after all these years. Her parents, who made me feel loved as a child and have that same power still. Molly, a teenager I now feel proud to call my niece. Morag, the old woman who drinks whisky and does yoga and who made me laugh. Brenda, Kerstin, Emma and Duncan, Tess, Joy, baby Harry … Even the island itself felt different eventually. By the end of the stay I was looking at it in a new way, seeing the wildflowers and the beach and the towering majesty of the mountain for what they really are. Beautiful.

'I don't think it's just Mallachy I fell for.'

We look at each other and I know that right now, she can tell exactly how I'm feeling. Because she's my closest friend.

'So, what are you going to do?' she asks.

I let out a deep breath, looking around the small living room in the flat I've called home for more than ten years.

'I have absolutely no idea.'

CHAPTER 46

ONE WEEK LATER

ALICE

'So, what are we going to do?'

Brenda is the first to ask the question that's been in my mind all throughout the meeting with the councillors from the mainland. The meeting is now over and we've shown them to the B&B where they're staying tonight before catching tomorrow's ferry. Now the governors and all the island parents are back in the community hall, sitting on a cluster of chairs, abandoned tea things scattered on a table in the middle. Everyone slumps dejectedly in their chairs, looking down or out the window, seemingly reluctant to meet one another's eyes. There's silence, apart from the sound of Harry letting out a gurgle on Tess's lap. I glance around, waiting for someone to say something. Well, if no one else is going to say it, then I will.

'You heard what they said, there's nothing we can do. Without a headteacher, the school is finished.'

I don't know how I expected the meeting to go. I suppose I thought they'd have a solution. Maybe they'd managed to recruit someone themselves, a teacher from one of the nearer mainland towns who wants a slower pace of life and the chance to have more freedom in a smaller school. I think I was hoping for a miracle. Before the meeting, the prospect of the school closing was a looming threat, but it felt like a distant one. Now, it has become unquestionably real. The councillors seemed understanding, but made it clear that there was little they could do.

'This is always the challenge of this kind of life,' said one of them. 'We can't force people to live and work here. An island community is a fragile one, it's just the way it goes. Either you have not enough young people moving in and an ageing population, or you hit a problem like this where you just can't recruit people for the key roles an island needs filled in order to survive.'

'So, we're just giving up?' says Brenda.

I look around the room again. The faces are sombre. Sarah looks up now, glancing at me and then around the room in turn.

'I feel I should say something,' she says, her voice strained. 'Ben and I have decided to try to sell our croft. We're looking for somewhere near his parents on the mainland. It's just too much having all this uncertainty for Alfie. It would be different if he was at secondary school already like Olive, but I just wouldn't feel like I was doing my job as a parent if I stayed not knowing if there's going to be a school for him in a few months' time.'

'But you were supposed to help with admin at the school in the new term!' I hear the words leaving my mouth, high with panic. Sarah looks down, not meeting my eye.

'I know. I'm so sorry. But as parents, I hope you all understand.'

Ben reaches for her hand. I know that she's only doing what's best for her family, and I'm sure it wasn't an easy choice, but it's suddenly hard to look at her. Everything is falling rapidly apart. I'm not sure how I can possibly get through the coming months and all the uncertainty they hold without my friend by my side.

I notice a shuffling on the other side of the room.

'I didn't know when to tell you all, but I guess now's the time,' says Emma. 'Duncan and I have actually been thinking the same thing. It's just too much of a risk staying here with no prospects for the school.'

'But what about the brewery?' asks Pat Campbell. 'You've run that place for years, and that stuff's the pride of the island.'

Duncan shakes his head sadly.

'George says he'd like to continue running the place, but if I'm completely honest I don't think he can do it on his own.'

Silence settles again as we contemplate another part of the island closing down. I look at Sarah and Emma, trying to imagine island life without them. Now, we see one another several times a week, sometimes more. Without them there will be two more empty mats in my yoga class. It suddenly hits me that with Sarah moving to be closer to Ben's parents, poor

Molly will be losing her best friend. Olive will have to move schools, so Molly won't even see her during the week. In one week, Molly has lost both Ella and Olive.

Glancing around the room, there's one person who's missing. I haven't seen Jean since the party and since Lorna's revelation about the past. I tried to visit her this morning but Christopher said she was sleeping. I wondered whether she was too embarrassed to see me, assuming that Lorna must have told me the whole story. I still don't know how I feel about it. It's uncomfortable to think about my friend making such a huge mistake, especially when I think about Molly and how I entrusted Jean with my daughter when I sent her to school every day. I feel angry for Lorna, and for Jack too, wondering how their history might have been different if an adult had stepped in or at least asked harder, more persistent questions about their home life. I don't think I'll ever be able to forgive her for that. But she's still my friend. Whatever mistakes she made in the past, we still have so many years of friendship behind us. And I'm worried about her. She needs her friends now more than ever, and I can't help but fear that this is the start of her withdrawing from us and trying to face this thing alone.

'Is there really nothing we can do?' asks Tess. Everyone in the room turns to me expectantly. I suppose usually I am the optimistic one, the one with a plan or a solution or at least hope. But as I look at Sarah, then Emma, then out the window where I can glimpse the school down the road, I feel my hope slipping away. I cross my hands over my stomach. This child will not attend the same school as their sister and father.

443

Perhaps they will grow up not remembering this island at all. I may have been so much younger when I had Molly, but I think I took for granted the amount of support I received from the island women who quickly became my firm friends. But now it feels like our community is falling apart. Things will be different this time.

I think about those two red lines on the pregnancy test and the appointment next week that no one but Jack knows about. How strange that just at the moment where we found an unexpected beginning, we're faced with this sense of an ending too. Right now, we might all still be here, but I know that Sarah and Emma leaving will just be the start. With the closure of the school now an inevitability, our island is about to change forever. Some people might say that it's just a place and that there are endless other places to live. But the thing is, this island isn't just a place. It's where I found love and friendship and raised my daughter, watching her take her first steps on the beach and waving to her from the gate on her first day of school. It's yoga classes with a motley group of women I love as fiercely as sisters, birthday parties on the beach, friends popping in and out of one another's homes and keeping an eye on one another. It's the constant smell and sound of the sea, the weather that changes as quickly as the moods of a hormonal teenager, a landscape that seeps into your very bones. Alongside my husband and daughter, this windy, remote, tiny island is the love of my life.

My friends and neighbours turn to me now, their faces downcast. I know I should give them some kind of reassurance. Instead, I shake my head sadly.

'You heard what the councillor said. We can't force anyone to come and work here. I think it's over.'

Right now, I can't manage optimism. I'm heartbroken.

CHAPTER 47

LORNA

In the week since we've been back, Ella has been quiet, staying mostly in her room. In the evenings she talks on the phone to her cousin, the long conversations a stark contrast to her near silence during the day. I keep hoping that Ruby and Farah might turn up at the flat to visit. But they never do. My daughter is lonely, I know. And my heart aches for her. If I'm honest with myself, it's not just her who feels alone.

I manage to persuade Ella out one afternoon; we head to the V&A together and on to a bakery Ella has been wanting to visit all year. But I find that I'm irritated by the crowds in the museum, by the dust that coats my eyes on the tube, by the heat of the city after our time away on the windswept island. I try not to let it show though. How is Ella ever going to adjust to being back if I don't seem to want to be here either?

I buy us both an overpriced cupcake at the bakery.

'Thanks, Mum.'

She's smiling and I know she's trying to look enthusiastic. But I can also tell that her heart isn't in it. On the way home, we sit side by side on the rattling tube. Sweat drips down my back and my legs stick to the synthetic seat. I close my eyes and picture leaping into a cold sea. I send a message to Alice, telling her I'm thinking about our swims together. We haven't spoken in person since I've been back but have been messaging frequently, as I have with Sarah too. But I sense that Alice is pulling back from me somehow; some days she takes a long time to reply and her responses are often short.

Suddenly, it is time to say goodbye again, this time to Cheryl, Mike and Frankie. Ella and I walk to their flat to wave them off in their rented van, the rest of their belongings already having headed north in a bigger lorry.

'I'm going to miss you so much,' I say to Cheryl as we hug, her gold hoop earrings catching in my hair. She smells of bubblegum and coffee and familiarity. 'But I'll call you, OK? And hope the journey goes well.'

She kisses me firmly on the cheek and I picture the bright red mark that she must have left there.

'And come and visit soon?' she calls as she climbs into the van, Frankie waving from his booster seat beside her.

Ella and I watch the van disappear around the corner and then we are left alone in front of my friend's former home. It's a home I know well, but looking up at it now it looks strangely unfamiliar. Without my friend in it, it is just a flat like any other on this street. My friend has gone and I sense the city around me shifting too, altered by her absence. It feels instantly less familiar, instantly duller. With Cheryl gone, what do I honestly have left here? A job I dislike and a tiny flat where I can hear the neighbours every day and every night through the thin partitions that slice through our lives. But what else? What else is there to fill my life in, to colour it between the stark black edges?

Eventually I turn away from the flat, linking my arm through Ella's.

'Come on. Let's go home.'

But even as I say it, it feels all wrong. I say it, and my heart sinks.

The week passes, like time does even when you don't particularly care if it races or crawls. I'm woken on Friday by a knock. Bleary-eyed, I open the door to the flat to see the postman with two parcels, one large and one small. I sign my name in a daze. As the postman turns away I notice his jacket is slick with rain. The heat has finally broken in the city, thank god. I take a deep breath of cool air, the first deep breath I feel I've taken since returning home, and shut the door, carrying the parcels back to my room.

I open the curtains and welcome the view of the rain. Droplets slide down the panes and the tarmac below is black with water. I push the window open a crack to breathe in the smell of the summer rain. Propping myself up against my pillows, I pull the parcels onto my lap. I'll open the smallest one first. Inside is a folded letter and another bulky envelope.

Dear Lorna,

It was so nice to get to know you when you came to visit. I'm sorry that parts of your visit were far from happy. I know it can't have been easy to come back at all and I admire your bravery, even though I know that you beat yourself up for not coming sooner. You were always welcome, just like you are still always welcome. But I understand that it had to be in your own time, on your own terms.

Thank you also for our paintings – Molly's is hanging on her bedroom wall and I've chosen a spot in the kitchen for mine. It's beautiful, thank you. Jack was very pleased with his gift too (it made him cry, although don't tell him I told you that!).

I hope your journey back was OK and that the sun is shining down there in London. I hope these will remind you of some of the happier times during your stay – it was certainly a day we islanders will always remember.

With love from your friend,

Alice xx

I tear open the envelope and a glossy stack of photographs slips out into my hands. On the top of the pile is an image of Ella, blowing out the candles on her birthday cake on the beach. Her cheeks are puffed out, her eyes bright with the glow of the candles. I'm sitting next to her, watching Ella with a wide smile, my eyes trained on my daughter's face. My darling daughter. With my thumb, I stroke the cheeks of the photograph her.

The rest of the photos show different moments from that day. Molly and Ella doing perfect cartwheels side by side on the beach, their feet bare, sand kicked up at their ankles, Ella's curls wild as she spins upside down. Another taken a moment later as the two girls return to the ground and explode into laughter. I look closely at my daughter's face captured in the photograph: its open, unselfconscious expression, a look of pure joy on her face. Another image shows all the tables set up on the beach, the mismatched chairs arranged beside them and the bunting that Alice and I made together flapping in the wind. There's an image of Sarah, Alice and me chatting together around a bonfire, and another of a crowd dancing. I spot Ben and Sarah, Jean and Christopher, Molly, Ella and Olive, and there in the corner of the frame, me and Mallachy. I'm smiling, my hair falling slightly in front of my face, his hands around my waist. There's another of Molly, Olive and Ella that Alice must have asked them to pose for at some point during the day. And finally, there's the image that I do remember Alice taking, of everyone gathered around the tables, ready to tuck into their food. Some raise glasses, others are captured with forks aloft or hands paused in mid-air. Most people are smiling, but baby Harry is captured as he begins to cry, Tess holding him and pulling a silly face in an attempt to make him laugh. Rex is sitting on the sand looking up at the food with envy, as are several other of the island dogs. I spot a bottle of whisky next to Morag, whose mouth is open as though she is mid-conversation. And right in the middle of the photograph are me and Ella: two mainlanders welcomed into the island community. It's a picture of an island and its islanders, of a summer afternoon, of happiness, of busy, noisy, messy life. I'm not sure I've ever seen such a nice photograph.

And then I look up. I'm alone in my bedroom, rain falling on the city outside the window, a city that may hold millions of people but that feels right now as though it is completely empty. It's a city I've lived in for years, but a place where I've never made a network of friends or found a sense of really belonging. I can see now that it's my own fault – I built walls around myself in an attempt to protect myself and my daughter. Maybe those walls kept some pain out but they also shut out joy. This is the place and the life I *chose*, but this summer has shown me how small my life here has been. How small my entire life has become.

I put the pictures and Alice's letters aside. The next parcel is bigger.

'Oh!'

The contents tumble onto my lap. They're drawings. *My* drawings. A rough sketch of a recently sheared sheep standing in a field of buttercups. A watercolour painting of the lighthouse, white against a bright blue sky. A detailed sketch of the mountain. Another of the forest in the rain, pine needles and raindrops rendered in fine, detailed pencil strokes. Rex, asleep on the sofa in Mallachy's studio. My heart jumps as I lift out a drawing of my brother as seen from afar, his silhouette in the sheep field. Another of a jam jar filled with heather and tied with string. A boat moored in the harbour. The old school house, the church, the pub. Drawing after drawing, mostly drawn from memory, all without me really acknowledging

451

what I was doing at the time. But I know now what I was doing. I was capturing the entire island on paper.

Among them is a note. And my hands shake as I read this second letter.

Lorna,

I know you told me you didn't want these and that I should throw them away, but I couldn't bring myself to. I kept a couple of Rex for myself (I hope you don't mind) but thought you might like the rest. Perhaps now that you are back in London you might feel ready to look at them and see how beautiful they are. You have a real talent, Lorna. It would be such a shame not to continue using it.

Thank you for the time we spent together. I felt happier over the past couple of weeks than I've felt in a long time. The studio isn't the same without you. Rex misses you terribly.

So do I. God, do I miss you.

Mallachy x

I take deep, gulping breaths, the note clasped between my hands. And I'm crying, tears sliding down my cheeks and dripping onto the paper, smudging Mallachy's words. Because I miss him too. But even more than that I miss Alice, and Molly and my brother. I miss Sarah, Brenda, Emma and the others. I miss the smell of the sea and the sound of the waves with a strength that makes my whole body ache. I miss it all so much that I feel entirely in the wrong place, like a foreigner in the city and the flat I've lived in for years.

I look again at the pile of photographs that Alice sent and the drawings of the island that came out of my hand after decades of shutting off parts of myself I'd almost forgotten existed. As I cry, I think about all the things I've lost throughout my life. My childhood, my family, and at times myself. But perhaps it's never too late to find these things once more. Perhaps it's never too late to start again. For the chance of a different kind of life.

A knock comes at the door.

'Mum?'

Ella steps inside, still wearing her pyjamas, her face so soft and pink with sleep that I think, as I so often do, of her as a baby. How I fell so fiercely in love with my new daughter and vowed to always keep her safe. I did my best. But somewhere along the line I think I forgot something too. That being safe isn't the same as living.

Ella frowns, spotting my tears and taking a step towards me. Before she can reach me though, the words escape my lips, rising up from somewhere deep inside.

'I want to go home.'

And suddenly home isn't here on this not-quite-island surrounded by the River Thames, in this isolated life that contains only two.

As I say the words Ella's face spreads into a wide, hopeful smile that makes me sure that right now I am making the right choice, a choice that will divide our lives into a 'before' and an 'after'. Because my daughter understands too. Home isn't here anymore. Home is hundreds of miles north, floating out to sea on a tiny, windswept island known as Kip. A place that smells of salt water and pine, where it often rains, where the ferry arrives only once a day and where a mountain and a lighthouse guard the island like watchmen. But more than that, home is the people who live there, islanders who have made me feel, at last, as though Ella and I are not alone in this world.

I remember what my daughter said to me as we walked on the beach that day, an eagle circling above us. *'I wonder whether we're designed to just have one person who's our person. Even if they love us enough for a hundred people.'* My daughter is right. Ella will always be my number one person, my heart living outside of my body in the shape of a girl with wild curls and conker-brown eyes. But in order to really thrive we need more than just each other. She deserves more than that. We *both* deserve more than that. We deserve a bigger life than the life we've been living. Enough. We have been alone for long enough.

Ella takes another step towards me and this time I stretch out my arms as wide as I can. And I know that my daughter and I are no longer islands, adrift from the shore. We are islanders.

CHAPTER 48

ALICE

I've been in a daze ever since the meeting with the councillors. At this week's yoga class my friends were subdued too and we all went our separate ways straight after it finished. I think it's too painful to talk about it all yet, but the fate of the school and the future of the island hangs heavily in the air wherever I go. It was there when I met Sarah for a cup of tea at her house and tried my best to be supportive of her decision to leave, while all the time aching at the thought of losing my friend; it was there when I did my weekly shop, catching murmurings of conversation about it all and spotting Pat's anxious expression, and it's been there at our dinner table every night.

Molly doesn't know yet that Olive and her family will be leaving soon. And Jack and I haven't told her about the baby. I still can't get my head around the fact that there is going to be a baby. I had my hospital appointment earlier this week and to my surprise and relief, the doctor told us that so far, everything seems fine. I still feel nervous though and want to wait a little longer before telling Molly, or anyone else. But among all my other worries, I'm trying to hold on tightly to this joyful secret carried inside my body. Sometimes I wake up in the middle of the night and remember, hopeful, happy tears springing to my eyes.

Today I'm catching up on chores at home, cleaning the house while Jack works outside and Molly is over at Olive's. But I'm pulled away from scrubbing the bathroom by a knock at the door. The sound surprises me: usually an islander would just open the door and shout inside to see if we were home. It takes a while to pull off my rubber gloves and get downstairs. When I open the door, I let out an 'oh' of surprise at who is waiting on the doorstep. I haven't seen Jean since Ella's party. My friends and I have tried visiting but each time we've been met by Christopher who apologetically tells us she's busy or sleeping or not up to visitors. She looks tired, her face make-up free. But there's a flush to her cheeks too.

'Jean.'

'Can I come in?'

'Of course.'

I open the door and she shuffles awkwardly past me and into the hallway. In the kitchen I busy myself with the kettle and mugs, not knowing what to say. For the first time in our friendship, I feel uncomfortable in her presence. I set the tea things down on the table between us, thankful for the focus of this ritual as I stir the teapot, waiting for it to brew.

456

'It's good to see you up and about,' I say. 'We tried to visit.'

'I know, Christopher told me.' Jean stares down at her hands before continuing, 'I'm sorry I wouldn't see you. I've just been so embarrassed. Well, embarrassed isn't the word really. Frankly, I feel ashamed.'

She looks up and meets my eye. As I look at her it's hard to know who I'm seeing exactly. She's my old friend and Jack and Molly's teacher. But now I see her mistakes as I look at her too.

'I'm sure Lorna told you what happened?' she asks. I nod in reply.

'I thought so. That's why I couldn't face seeing anyone. I had to tell Lorna the truth though, I had to apologise to her. It's been on my mind for years. I've felt ashamed for years.'

As I look at her I see it clearly now, this weight that she's carried throughout so much of her life. I'd never thought of it before, but perhaps mistakes are sometimes as heavy a burden for those who make them as for those they hurt. Just looking at Jean now it's clear how much this secret shame has impacted her over the years. She looks exhausted with it and despite it all I feel sorry for her.

'I can't go back and change the foolish mistake I made, although I've wished countless times that I could. But I want you to know that I really did try to learn from what happened. I tried my best to be a better person and teacher. To look with my eyes wide open and to do my best to care for those children. I don't want you to think that I didn't care about them – Molly, Olive, and all the others. I cared about them so much. I still do.'

'I know.' I picture the walls of Jean's home that are covered in school photos, Jean beaming proudly among a huddle of students in each one, and the children who rushed to throw their arms around her on the beach at Ella's party, missing their teacher.

'Would you like a piece of cake?' I add.

'Oh, yes please. Thank you, Alice.' There's relief in her voice as I fetch two plates and forks. She starts to eat but then sets her fork down on the table.

'There's something else I wanted to tell you. I've changed my mind.'

'What do you mean?'

My heart thumps.

'I've decided to have the chemotherapy. Christopher and I are heading to the mainland next week. We've found a cottage to rent near the hospital and are going to stay there for a while.'

Hot tears prick my eyes and I reach a hand up to my mouth.

'Really? Oh, Jean, that is wonderful news.'

'You think so?' she says hesitantly.

'Of course I do!' And then I stand up, push my chair back and step quickly to her side, leaning down to hug her. With a sob, she wraps her arms around me and hugs me back. Whatever mistakes Jean may have made, she is still my friend. Loving a person means seeing their worst and loving them anyway. And I love my friends, every single one of them. I love them fiercely.

After a moment we part, both of us sniffing and wiping our faces.

'I wanted to thank you though,' she says shakily. 'For not

pressuring me into doing anything I didn't want to. It meant a lot to have your support.'

'It's just what friends do,' I reply. We smile at one another, two old friends, neither perfect. As we settle at the table again the landline phone rings, startling me.

'Sorry, Jean, I'll just be a sec.'

I lift the receiver off the wall in the hallway, holding it against my ear.

'Hello?'

'Alice, it's me, Lorna.'

'Lorna, how nice to hear from you. How are—'

But before I can finish she interrupts me.

'Alice, I just realised that there's nothing here for us in London anymore. I miss the island, I miss Jack, I miss Molly, I miss you.'

'Oh, Lorna, we miss you too.'

The front door opens. It's Jack, in his muddy overalls, his face glowing from the fresh air. As he looks at me, raising a questioning eyebrow, Lorna speaks again.

'I never should have left. But I've decided now. We're coming back. And I hope it's not too late, but I'd love to apply for the job at the school.'

For the second time in just a few minutes tears spring hotly to my eyes.

'Wait a second, Lorna, there's someone here who I'm sure would love to hear you say that again.'

I pass the phone to Jack and watch as his expression switches from confusion, to surprise, to a happiness as golden as sunshine. And I let myself properly cry now, for Jack and

Lorna, separated for decades but finally reunited, for Jean and Christopher, for Molly, Ella and Olive and the strength of their friendship, for the school that in an instant has been saved, and for the island I so love. Somehow, it's all going to be OK. The stress washes away, relief filling its place. As Jack and Lorna continue to talk, discussing the logistics of what is to happen next, I glance down, thinking about the tiny person growing unexpectedly and beautifully inside me. Suddenly, I feel more hopeful about their future. I rest a hand on the spot which will soon start to grow like it did when I had Molly all those years ago.

Grow safe and grow strong, little one. You have a whole island waiting to meet you.

CHAPTER 49

THREE WEEKS LATER

LORNA

The lighthouse gleams in the afternoon sunlight, the tower freshly painted and the windows washed. From where I stand on the cliff's edge I can make out an army of clouds trudging slowly across the no man's land of the sea. But for now, the sky directly above the island is clear and blue, the late summer sun warm on my shoulders. Later, it will rain. But that's OK. I have a raincoat tied around my waist and wellies on my feet. And the rain can be beautiful too, I've found, as it shoots arrows of water onto the surface of the sea, decorating it with a pattern of ripples.

Behind me a dog barks and I turn, just as I hear Mallachy's voice from inside the cottage.

'Can you pass me the drill?'

'There you go,' comes Jack's reply.

I rub my hands on the front of my overalls and prepare to head back inside. I glance once more over my shoulder at the sea and smile. Right, to work. I step through the open front door of the old lighthouse keeper's cottage. The door is newly hung and freshly painted a bright shade of buttercup yellow.

'Look, Mum, we've nearly finished this wall,' comes Ella's voice. She's dressed in dungarees, her curls loose around her face and decorated with several specks of blue paint. Molly is beside her, a paintbrush in her hand and a smile on her face. Alice is here too, hair pulled back in a polka-dot headscarf and managing to somehow look elegant in an oversized pair of painter's overalls. In a corner of the nearly painted room Mallachy stands on a ladder fixing a set of shelves to the wall, Jack steadying the ladder and passing him tools from a box on the floor. Rex sits beside the two men, his tail thudding heavily on the recently scrubbed floorboards.

Later today some of the other islanders will be visiting to lend a hand. Sarah has promised to bring cake and a Thermos of tea for the workers, and I wonder if Morag might bring her own supply of something a little stronger. But for now, it's just us.

In a short space of time the once dilapidated cottage has been transformed. Sunlight streams in through the now clean windows and the front room smells of paint and polish. The cottage will be ready for Ella and me to move into in a couple of weeks. The lighthouse itself has been renovated too: once the tower room is finished it will become my new studio. I've already started ordering art supplies from the mainland in preparation. The thought makes me giddy with excitement.

In the meantime, we've been staying with Jack and Alice again. I'm back in what has quickly come to feel like *my* yellow room, and Ella is sharing with her cousin. I glance across at Jack, who is currently passing Mallachy a spirit-level and a screwdriver. Despite the leaps forward we've made, there's still a certain distance between us. I'm having to get to know my brother all over again, catching up on all those lost years. I imagine he feels the same way about me. But at least now, I have plenty of time. We both do. Our relationship will always be scarred by those years we spent apart, and all the misunderstandings and mistruths that came between us. But I'm starting to think that maybe that's OK. Maybe it's possible for something not to be perfect, to even be messy and complicated, but also worth having in its own imperfect form. Seeing him helping out with the renovation of the cottage gives me a rush of hope that we are going to be all right.

Alice tells me he has started therapy. It takes place on the phone, the island not having its own therapist, but perhaps that's better for my quiet brother, the not having to see the other person's face as he talks to them helping him to open up. Finally, he's facing to what happened when we were young. This summer, I feel like I have done the same.

Ella laughs and my eyes are drawn back to my daughter who is now engaged in a paint battle with her cousin, each of them flicking their paintbrushes at one another until both their faces are covered in dots of blue. I feel that familiar tug at my heart at the sound of my daughter's laughter. Next week

Ella will be starting a new school, joining Molly and Olive at the secondary school on the mainland. I'm still not quite sure how I will manage to wave her goodbye on the ferry that first week, knowing I won't see her again until the weekend. It's something Alice, Sarah and I have discussed many times over the past weeks. They both shared how hard it was to see their own daughters leave for the mainland school and the hostel they stay in during the week, but also how they've each seen their children grow as a result, becoming more independent and confident.

Leaving London has required a huge upheaval, and there have been moments when I've wondered whether I've made the right choice for my daughter. But watching her now, I think I can already see the positive changes that have taken place in Ella just over the summer. She stands with her shoulders back. She has stopped bothering with straightening her hair, and rarely wears make-up either, as neither Molly nor Olive do. She has developed a passionate interest in the environment. And she laughs more. In fact, it feels as though she is laughing nearly all the time now. It suits her. I watch her joking with her cousin and my worries melt away for a moment. I don't think I'll ever know if I'm making the right choices by my daughter. But maybe it's just not possible to be a perfect mother. Ella is happy. Maybe, just maybe, I'm doing OK.

If anything, it will be much harder on me than on Ella to see her leave for her new school. She is incredibly excited, just like she was about the move in general. It will be hard to say goodbye to her. But I'm just trying to hold on to the fact that it won't be forever. Letting go is hard, but it is also part of the promise I made to her when she was born – to let her have a freedom that I never experienced as a child. Loving Ella the way I do means sometimes loosening my grip and letting my daughter fly.

Next week will mark a new chapter for me too. It marks the start of my new job as headteacher of the island primary school. I'm already full of ideas of small changes I want to make and art projects I want to do with the children, feeling truly excited about my job for the first time in years. In the end, it wasn't a sense of duty that brought me back to the island and to the school. I came back because I wanted to. At times I've even wondered if it would have been easier if we'd simply never left at all after our holiday here. But I think I needed to leave the island that second time. I needed to know that I could, that nothing and no one was trapping me there. I was entirely free. I still am.

I thought there might be problems leaving my old role in London, but when I mentioned to Dave Phillips that I was considering making a formal sexual harassment complaint about his inappropriate comments and conduct he let me go quietly without asking me to work out my notice period. Our old flat in London is on the market and the estate agent, who contacts me from the city, expects it to sell quickly. Despite having lived there for over ten years, I felt surprisingly un-sentimental leaving for the last time. In the end, it was just a flat, a series of now empty rooms, ready for new owners to start their lives there.

Maybe it's just my imagination, but it feels to me as though my acceptance of the role at the school has led to a new burst of optimism on the island. Jack managed to find a buyer for our parents' old house; a young family, friends of Emma and Duncan's who had been considering moving to the island for a while but had been hesitating while the role of headteacher was still unfilled. They have three small children, substantially increasing the numbers at the school. Jack and I are splitting the proceeds of the sale of the house evenly between us. The will left everything to Jack but he insisted. There are other changes in the air on the island too: Alice's sisters are visiting next week and attending a yoga retreat she's running, re-furbishments are in the pipeline for the community hall, there is a rumour (founded) of an upcoming art exhibition featuring work by 'local artists' (me and Mallachy), and Alice shared word from Christopher Brown that Jean's chemotherapy has started and the doctors are confident that it will be successful.

'I love this colour so much,' comes Alice's voice from the other side of the room. 'I'm tempted to repaint our entire house.'

Alice dips her brush admiringly into the duck-egg blue paint that I chose for this living room. I smile as I watch her, this woman who has quickly become a new but loyal friend. We've started a morning ritual of swimming together in the sea and it's something I've promised to keep up even after I've moved out from Hilly Farm. I still go on my runs too, using them as a way to rediscover the island where I grew up. I try to take the time to really *see* the things around me, pausing to examine wildflowers or listen to the call of the songbirds in the trees. I've bought several nature books and a pair of binoculars. Somehow this relearning of the old island makes it feel as though it's a new place entirely. Not the unhappy place of my childhood but somewhere full of possibility, of beauty, somewhere where I feel as though I could belong.

'Right, one shelf done, two to go.'

Mallachy's voice makes my head turn in his direction. He balances on the ladder, his sleeves rolled up to reveal the muscles on his forearms that I've become accustomed to tracing with my fingertips when we are alone together. His face is slightly flushed from the work and a ray of sun comes suddenly in from one of the windows, picking out the red and grey flecks in his beard and making his eyes shine. Watching him, a warmth spreads from my fingers to my toes. We've made no promises to one another. We both agree we should tread carefully, especially because of Ella and because we now live on the same small island. But I can't help but feel a sense of excitement just looking at him. Later, once the work on the cottage is done for the day, I'll cycle over to his house (on my own new bike this time). He will have a glass of wine waiting for me and if I'm lucky he will cook that morning's catch, the sound of fish sizzling in a pan greeting me as I arrive. We will spend time in his studio, drawing side by side and sometimes talking but sometimes just sitting in comfortable silence. At some point in the evening I will drop my paintbrush and instead reach for his hand, guiding him towards the bedroom. And with the view of the sea at our side we will find one another, our heartbeats in sync, our voices whispering in each other's ears. And I will feel a happiness I haven't felt in years, a sweet, tremulous joy that feels at times like fear but often like hope.

Mallachy looks up and catches my eye. He smiles broadly,

one eyebrow raised, a smile that tells me he is thinking about the same thing. I feel colour rushing to my cheeks but I don't look away. Instead I smile back.

Despite this unexpected happiness I've found with Mallachy, it wasn't him that made me come back. I hope things work out between us, but in the end, it was the thought of the friends I'd made here and of the family that Ella and I have gone so long without that made the decision for me. The feeling of being a part of something again after so many years living on the edges of life. I don't want to live the way Ella and I used to anymore, shutting ourselves off and existing inside walls. I want to open up our lives and let in laughter and the sweet, salty kiss of the sea air.

I turn towards my daughter and niece, who have now abandoned their play fight and are back to painting the wall in careful strokes, and reach for my own paintbrush on the ground.

'Right. What do you think, girls, do you reckon we can get this room finished today?'

The girls nod enthusiastically then return to their work with looks of concentration on their faces. I dip my brush in paint and then trace a long, smooth line of blue along the wall. And not just any wall. *My* wall. In what will soon be my cottage. Well, ours. Me and Ella, together in our cottage on the clifftop. I breathe in the smell of the paint and the ever-present scent of the sea that drifts in through the open front door. Around me, my family and Mallachy do their bit to help out. My stomach gives a small rumble and I wonder happily when Sarah and the others will arrive with tea and cake. I paint another stroke, watching the blue overtaking more of the room, feeling as though with each stroke I am reclaiming this space as my own. And although the cottage is far from finished, although there is still so much I don't know about what my future will look like, and although I will always wear the scars of everything that has led me to this point, finally, finally I am home.

ACKNOWLEDGEMENTS

A huge thank you to everyone at Orion for working so hard to bring this book into being, particularly during a really tough year. I feel so lucky to have such a wonderful team on my side and feel so grateful to every single person involved in the process of turning my ideas into a 'real book'. Thank you to my editor, Harriet Bourton, for pushing me to make this book the best it could be and to the rest of the dream team, in particular Virginia Woolstencroft, Britt Sankey, Cait Davies and Olivia Barber.

As ever, thank you to my agent Robert Caskie for your continued support and encouragement of me and my books.

To everyone who has read, borrowed, recommended, reviewed or generally supported my previous two books: thank you so much for enabling me to continue doing what I love the most in the world. I really do have the best job in the world and it's all of you who make it possible. To the librarians, book sellers and bloggers who do so much to champion books and reading – you all inspire me so much and your work is very much appreciated.

Thank you to everyone on the beautiful Isle of Eigg who talked to me about island life and helped give me inspiration for Kip and this story.

I feel very lucky to have such a brilliant network of friends and family who help me through the ups and downs of writing and life. This book wouldn't have been possible without your love, friendship and support, so thank you all. A particular thank you to my wonderful friend Alice for letting me use your name for one of the characters in this book. Because everyone needs an Alice in their lives.

A final big thank you to my husband, Bruno. Perhaps even more than previous books this feels like our book. Thank you for asking me to marry you on a tiny Scottish island – saying yes was the best thing I ever did. This book is about home and family: I feel so lucky to be building ours together.

CREDITS

Libby Page and Orion Fiction would like to thank everyone at Orion who worked on the publication of *The Island Home* in the UK.

Editorial
Harriet Bourton
Olivia Barber

Copy editor
Sally Partington

Proof reader
Linda Joyce

Audio
Paul Stark
Amber Bates

Contracts
Anne Goddard
Paul Bulos
Jake Alderson

Design
Debbie Holmes
Joanna Ridley
Nick May

Marketing
Cait Davies
Brittany Sankey